Lift Up Mine Eyes

A Novel

John Shivers
John Shivers

CRM BOOKS
Publishing Hope for Today's Society

Copyright © 2010 by John Shivers. All rights reserved.

Cover artwork by Christine Pace. All rights reserved.

For Information:
CRM BOOKS, P.O. Box 935, Indian Trail, NC 28079

Visit our Web site at www.ciridmus.com

No part of this book may be reproduced or utilized in any form
or by any means, electronic or mechanical,
including photocopying, recording,
or by any information storage or retrieval system, or transmitted,
without prior written permission from the publisher,
except by a reviewer who may quote brief passages in a review.

This book is a work of fiction.
Names, characters, places, and incidents either
are the product of the author's imagination or are used fictitiously.
Any resemblance to actual events, locales, or persons, living or dead,
is coincidental and beyond the intent
of either the author or publisher.

Printed in the United States of America

10-digit ISBN: 1-933341-35-1
13-digit ISBN: 978-1-933341-35-4

LCCN: 2010931525

To the many victims of domestic violence,
and to my loyal readers, who have made
Margaret Haywood a part of their families
and their lives...
who have agonized in their own hearts
over her circumstances.

"Inasmuch as ye have done it unto one
of the least of these my brethren,
ye have done it unto me."

Author's Notes

It hardly seems possible that it's time to hug Margaret Haywood, her family and friends, goodbye. Margaret and her story have been a very real part of my life for several years. It is with bittersweet emotion that I close the door to her new home behind me on my way out. I leave the Haywood Family to continue their recovery from the abuse that has been such a part of their lives for so long, confident they *can* become whole again. They've lived in a fishbowl long enough; it's time they had some privacy to heal. After all, they will forever be "recovering survivors."

With the publication of *Hear My Cry*, Margaret made her first appearance. She was bruised and confused, and totally in denial, as she fumbled to "fix" the demon called domestic violence that had captured her household.

In *Paths of Judgment* we found the recovering Margaret attempting to strike out on her own; escaping forever the violence she saw affecting each of her children – Brian, Sallie and Jason. For every step she took toward freedom, someone or something was there to cause her to misstep, to backslide.

Readers have demanded to know that Margaret survived both the brutality and the emotional injury inflicted by her abuser. More than that, they have clamored to know if she remains safe. *Lift Up Mine Eyes* does raise a few additional questions, but I trust it also answers those earlier questions. It will be up to the reader to discern the answers to these final queries.

Thanks to all those readers who have bonded with me, through Margaret. I am grateful for the many hundreds of new friends I've acquired. Thank you for sticking with Margaret, for refusing to assign her and other victims in this country to more abuse by ignoring this very real, very volatile scenario.

As always, there has been an army of supporters out there who have made a difference, who have made it possible for me to complete Margaret's story, even when I feared I couldn't. To Mr. and Mrs. Elmer Ritch and Catherine Ritch Guess, Tracy and "my family" at the *Laurel*, to Jan Timms once again for her proofing skills and encouragement, to my children, Sarah and Lindsay, and grandchildren, Grant and Lillie, friends Dale and Lynn and my brother and sister-in-law, Mike and Janet… I thank each of you and love all of you.

Last, but most especially, thanks to my wife, Elizabeth, who believes in me with a fierceness that lets me know I have to write these stories. I love you so much.

John Shivers

*I will lift up mine eyes unto the hills
from whence cometh my help.*

--PSALM 121:1 KJV

CHAPTER ONE

*M*argaret Haywood looked up from her work at the dining room table littered with cards, envelopes and well-marked, dog-eared lists. *Will I ever get these notes finished? I can't believe how many people responded.* Shoved to one side were a wilted yuletide centerpiece and a disorganized stack of opened Christmas greetings. *Rudolph the Red-Nose Reindeer* was playing softly in the background.

Got to retire those holiday CD's. Christmas was over two weeks ago. Not that the music did very much to make it joyous around here. I tried... for the children.

She wiped her forehead with the back of her hand, too weary to immediately act on her resolution. *I feel like I've been digging ditches. These last few weeks have been anything but "peace on earth, good will to men".*

The ringing telephone interrupted her mini-pity-party as she answered without remembering to check Caller ID. *Reporters are still calling occasionally*, she reminded herself, praying there was not one on the other end of the line.

"Margaret? Is anything wrong?"

P.C. Dunigan. Thank goodness!

"Wrong? Why do you ask?"

"You haven't called me in over a week. I was worried."

Margaret glanced around the tired, dingy dining room of the home she was renting from her parents, trying to find something positive. *All I see is that my entire life looks just like this whole house… in bad need of a total makeover.* "I just haven't been on top of my game," she told her friend, an attorney in Tennessee. "I thought divorcing Don was going to be difficult. That would have been a piece of cake compared to dealing with his death."

"It's been a rough go, hasn't it?"

Margaret fixed her eyes on a huge stain on the ceiling. *I feel soiled, just like that water mark.* "It's been hard on me, but it's been even worse for the kids." She ran her fingers through her hair. "Of course that's made it even harder on me, to see them repeatedly hurt and embarrassed."

She studied her nails that were in bad need of attention. *I've even been ignoring my salon appointments.*

"We both knew Don was going to meet his match one day."

"Agreed," she replied, unable to hide the bone-tired exhaustion that dogged her every move. "I'm still trying to believe he came to the hospital… with a gun, no less."

"I guess it never pays to say 'never', does it?"

"That's for certain. When he was arrested for shooting Jim, just because he was representing me in the divorce action, I thought that was as bad as it could get."

Details of that painful period were still fresh, as if they had just occurred. The middle-of-the-night call from the jail in Atlanta. "Come quickly," the deputy had stressed. Don had been badly beaten by an irate inmate.

In a matter of minutes Margaret—along with her children Brian and Sallie, and parents, Harold and Ruby Maxwell—were on the interstate highway heading south from Carter's Crossroads. *Poor Jason*, she'd thought, *I left him in the hospital simply because there wasn't time to get him released. Not that it would have made any difference.*

"Are the kids still being harassed by the media?"

"Not like they were. Not like it was that night at the ER. I'll never know how the TV stations got word of Don's death before we got there."

"Somebody at the jail probably called in an anonymous tip," P.C. suggested. "I'll guarantee you that's how they knew."

"Someone would do that?"

"Hate to burst your bubble, Pollyanna. That's probably exactly how it happened."

"They sure upset two already distraught children, I can tell you that." *All those lights and people jumping into their faces.*

"Besides the news media, how are the three Haywood children adjusting?"

How are my children? I'm their mother, but I don't know how to answer that question.

"I'm glad they have the routine of school to anchor them. They missed most of December, so it was a relief for me when classes resumed after the holidays."

"Do they talk about Don?"

They don't talk about anything with me if they can help it.

Margaret sighed; the air escaped her body, leaving her even more depleted—physically and emotionally. "You might as well know, P.C., I'm not my children's favorite mother right now."

"Meaning what... exactly?" Her question contained a sharp edge.

"It's difficult for me to talk about..."

"Well try, because you've been through enough without having to carry a load of undeserved guilt."

"They think if I hadn't started the divorce, Don wouldn't have shot Jim, he wouldn't have been in jail, and he would still be alive."

"They said that?"

Margaret hesitated, unwilling to assign guilt where none existed. "It's more what they haven't said than what they have," she answered finally. "They talk to me very little. It's like they've built a glass wall between them and me."

"That's ridiculous. How can those children possibly blame you?"

"They're hurting, P.C. Really hurting. I can understand; I'm hurting too."

"Of course you are, and the kids don't need to dump a load of unwarranted guilt on your back."

"They're not doing it deliberately. Don is never coming back and they're having trouble coming to grips. Just like I am. When I was going to divorce him, I was banishing him on my terms. But for him to be taken like he was... well... I feel like I was cheated."

"But you had nothing to do with that. Don was his own worst enemy; his arrogance convinced him he was omnipotent. When those type personalities fall, they always hit hard."

Because Margaret had been poking at a dead Christmas arrangement while she and P.C. talked, brown spruce needles were dropping all over the table top. *Just like the parts of my life.*

"In my heart, I know you're right on target. But my head is waging war on my heart. The fact that my children are withdrawing doesn't help."

"You want me to come down this weekend? I will, you know."

"You're always welcome," Margaret assured her friend. "But I don't know how much good you could do."

"Well somebody's going to have to do something."

"I agree. As unpopular as it's going to be in some circles, I'm convinced the first thing I have to do is to get us out of this house." She looked at the dirty, faded paint, the old carpet and the dated light fixtures. "It's bad enough that this whole house is even more depressed than I am, but with Mama and Daddy right through the back fence, I never will get my children back."

"Miss Ruby still giving you a hard time?"

Margaret's right hand found its way back to her furrowed brow, a place it had frequented many times over the past few weeks. "I strongly suspect Mama is feeding the children's belief that my actions led to Don's death."

"You know, I would say I'm surprised, but I'm not."

Shock evident in her voice, Margaret asked, "You aren't? Why?"

"It's a common trait in domestic violence. There's usually at least one family member who doesn't support the victim when she tries to save herself. In this case it's your mama."

"I always knew she was stubborn, but I've never seen Mama carry anything to the extent she has with this. You'd think after Don tried to kill a man, she'd see him for the monster he could be. But, no... Don's dead and it's all my fault."

"You know you don't believe that," P.C. affirmed.

"No, I don't," Margaret said sadly. "But my children do, and Mama's poisoning them against me. Which is why," she said with a sudden determination she didn't immediately recognize, "I've got to get us out of here."

"You mean out of that house? I knew you weren't all that keen about your dad buying it."

"I wasn't in favor of it, for all the reasons I'm seeing now. But at the same time, I thought it would be good for us to be in our own space for Christmas, instead of in with the folks." She examined the lines in the palm of her hand. "Now I'm not so sure it's been worth it."

"What will you do...go back to your house on Redbud Way?"

"No way," Margaret immediately answered. "That house will be listed with a real estate agent very soon. That's one thing the children and I agree about. None of us ever want to live there again."

"So where will you go?"

Should I broach the bold plan that's been emerging over the past week? I can trust her.

"You're the first soul I've shared this with," she cautioned her friend. "Please keep it under your hat until I tell you otherwise."

"Sounds almost clandestine. My curiosity's aroused, so tell all. My lips are sealed." Margaret could picture her friend making a turning key motion to her lips.

"I'm thinking seriously of leaving Carter's Crossroads. You know, make a totally fresh start. Somewhere that none of us have to live under the shadow of Don Haywood's legacy – even though all of it isn't negative."

I can't believe I've said those words aloud. It's the first time I've heard my thoughts verbalized.

"You would leave Carter's Crossroads? My gosh, Margaret, where would you go?"

Here goes nothing.

"I'm thinking about a small town somewhere, one where we're all strangers."

"OKAY, that takes care of you, but what about your children? What about them? Surely you don't think you'll get them out of Mount Zion School without a battle?"

"I don't think the kids are as enamored with Mount Zion as they were when Don was alive."

"You don't mean…?"

"I'm afraid so," Margaret replied, sensing the unspoken part of her friend's question. "It's like the school knows Don's money has stopped flowing. Suddenly my children are no longer special. Not that they ever should have…"

A knock at the front door interrupted Margaret. "There's someone at the door. Can I call you back?" she asked, already on her way to the door.

"Sure. Catch you later. Remember, I'll come if you need me."

"I know. Later."

Margaret squinted through the security peephole to find a neatly dressed woman standing on the other side. A closer glance disclosed that Annie Campbell, her friend and the director of Carter's Crossroads Battered Women's Shelter, was standing alongside.

"Be right with you," she called through the door, as she smoothed her hair and suddenly regretted she hadn't applied makeup that morning. She cast a quick, disapproving glance around the cluttered living room. *Time was I would have gotten up out of my casket to keep guests from seeing my house looking like this. All the more reason I've got to seize control and do something.*

She released the deadbolt and swung open the door. "Annie. It's so good to see you." *Suddenly a horrible thought struck her.* "We didn't have an appointment I've forgotten, did we?"

The short black woman stepped forward to take Margaret's hand. "Not to worry," she said, "you haven't forgotten a commitment. May we come in?"

"Oh... oh... of course, where are my manners?"

"Probably the same place mine are, since I didn't give you the courtesy of a warning call that I was on my way over," Annie replied, stepping aside for the other visitor to precede her.

"Please," Margaret offered, "make yourselves at home." *That's going to be a good one, since I can't even seem to accomplish that here.* She indicated two chairs across from the sofa, where she positioned herself as soon as the two guests had taken their seats.

"Margaret," Annie said, "I'd like to have you meet Barbara Kirkland. She's with the state domestic violence coalition, and she and I had an appointment this morning. Only when I heard what one of her needs was, I adjourned our meeting and dragged her here to meet you."

Me? "I'm afraid I don't understand."

"Trust me, you will." Annie turned to the other guest who,

Margaret realized, had been studying her intently. "Barbara, this is Margaret Haywood, the woman I was telling you about. She managed to pull off a marvelous holiday tour of homes for us, despite the worst of personal circumstances." She smiled affectionately at Margaret who tried not to feel like a freak in the circus sideshow. *Why am I the center of attention?*

"Margaret... May I call you Margaret?" Barbara inquired. When assured first names were acceptable, she continued. "First, please accept my condolences for all that you've been through, both before and after the death of your husband. I know none of this has been easy."

That's for sure.

"I also know," Barbara continued, "none of what happened was your fault. Regardless of what anyone else might say."

"I know that, only it's nice to hear someone else say it," Margaret confessed.

"Unfortunately, there are too many women, too many victims who blame themselves, and do an even more destructive number on themselves."

I can believe that.

"Margaret's been so strong through all of this," Annie Campbell interjected. "I've marveled at her strength."

"Please," Margaret protested. "Annie has always been my personal cheering section. But the truth is, I've been more the consistency of gelatin than steel. At first I didn't want to accept the truth. Once I did, there were so many times I wanted to call a halt when I saw what it was doing to my children."

"But you didn't," Barbara affirmed. "Which is why Annie thinks you would be perfect for a position we have in the state office."

Me? A job in the state office? But what?... How?

"You're absolutely perfect," Annie assured her. "When I told Barbara your background in fundraising for the school, and what you have triumphed over as a surviving violence victim, she couldn't wait to meet you."

"I'm afraid I don't understand. This all sounds terribly overwhelming."

"You'll have to forgive us," Barbara said. "In our excitement, I'm afraid we may have come on a little too strong." She reached across and took Margaret by the hand. "Why don't we begin again?"

Margaret smiled. "Why don't we?"

Over the next few minutes, the out-of-town visitor explained about her need for someone who was an articulate speaker, who could function as a public relations department of one, and also organize fundraising and awareness-raising events.

"Trust me," Annie explained, "this position has your name written all over it."

"Annie was so excited," Barbara continued, "that I allowed her to kidnap me and drag me over here." She smiled at Margaret. "I'm so glad I did, because I'm in total agreement."

Here I sit, in faded jeans and a sweatshirt, in a cosmetically-challenged house. My hair hasn't been combed today, I'm wearing no make-up, and she thinks I'm state-level material.

"Well, uh... uh... I don't know..."

"Don't give us an answer now," Annie advised. "Think about it a few days, and then you and Barbara get back together next week, after you've had time to process it. There's plenty of time to talk."

"I don't want to rush you, Margaret, but I did want to take the opportunity to meet you while I was in town. I hope you'll give this some serious consideration." Barbara fished in her purse and brought out a small white rectangle of cardstock. "Here's my card. Today is Thursday. Why don't you give me a call next Monday? I'll be glad to drive back up and visit further."

"You and I need to be going," Annie advised her colleague. "I'm certain Margaret has other things to do, just as we do."

After seeing her guests to the door, Margaret sat back down in her chair at the dining room table, deep in thought. After just a few minutes, she leaped to her feet and began to pace the house, unable to stay still.

Oh, Lord. I've prayed every night for guidance, for a direction. Could this be it? I feel so ill-equipped. How can I work effectively for other violence victims when I refused to see the demon that was in my own home until it was almost too late? Besides, this job would mean moving to Atlanta. Not a small town like I'd planned.

She was in the kitchen, fixing a toasted ham and cheese sandwich for a late lunch, when she heard what sounded like the front door opening. Startled, she dropped the cookie sheet she'd used to brown the sandwich. *Even after all these weeks, I still go weak when I hear an unexplained noise. Will I ever stop wondering if it's Don coming after me?*

She knew it couldn't be Don; nevertheless, she moved cautiously to the door of the dining room, where she could clearly see the front entrance. *Mama and Daddy and the kids all have a key, even Jason.* She consulted the clock on the dining room sideboard. *But it's too early for the kids, and Mama or Daddy would call out to let me know they were here.*

When she reached the door, it was shut, as if it had never been opened. *I know that's what I heard.* Closer inspection revealed the deadbolt wasn't engaged. *I threw the bolt home when I locked the door after Annie and Barbara left!*

Convinced someone had entered her house, she grabbed her phone and headed for the back door. Once in the yard, she called her parents' house, only a few hundred yards away.

"Daddy," she said without waiting, when she heard his voice. "Come quick. Please. I think someone's in my house."

"I'll be right there."

In a matter of seconds he was coming through the connecting gate he'd built in the shared backyard fence.

"What happened?"

"The only ones who have keys are you, Mama, me and the kids. They won't even be out of school for another hour yet."

"Your mama's at home, making a pot of soup." He gazed up at the house, his face a study in anger. "I don't want to take any chances. I'm calling the police."

After the way the police abused me when Don was pulling their strings, I'd hoped I was through with them for a long time.

"They're sending a car," he told her.

In just a matter of minutes, three or four at most, a black-and-white patrol car, with gold writing, pulled into the driveway. Margaret and her father hurried to meet them. She was chagrinned to see the two officers who'd responded to P.C.'s call at the Redbud Way house months before. *They didn't believed her then. Will they now? Now that Don isn't alive to poison their minds?*

"Yes, ma'am, Mrs. Haywood? Dispatch said you had a prowler?"

"I'm not certain." She went on to explain the sequence of events.

The older officer smiled, "It's probably nothing, we'll check it out and set your mind at ease."

How quickly, and easily, our attitudes change. Could you possibly be greasing the skids so I'll continue to bankroll projects like Don did? The minute she thought it, she regretted her rush to judgment. *That wasn't fair, but does the leopard change his spots?*

The two officers entered the house through the back door, their service revolvers at the ready. Margaret had drawn them a crude floor plan. She now stood with her heart in her throat, praying she wouldn't hear those guns discharged. *Please, Lord, let it be my imagination and nerves working overtime. Maybe I really didn't lock the deadbolt.*

She had convinced herself it was all in her mind, when the shorter of the two officers appeared at the back door. He motioned for Margaret and her father.

"You've got company, alright," he said, holding the screen door open so they could enter the kitchen. "But it's not what you thought. Come see."

He led them toward the bedroom end of the house, while Margaret fought to keep her curiosity and her emotions at bay. *What?*

Once outside Jason and Brian's bedroom, the officer halted and indicated that Margaret should enter first. She did, and as she was about to ask for specifics, her voice caught in her throat. The sight of her youngest son seated on the side of his bed, the other officer beside him, was a scene she wouldn't soon forget.

"Jason!" she exclaimed. "What are you doing home?"

"This is your son?"

"He is," she told the officer. "Only I don't know why he's here at least an hour ahead of the school van."

The officer touched her on the shoulder. "Since this is obviously a family issue, and not a case of an intruder breaking and entering, we'll be on our way. I think you can handle things."

Her father showed the officers to the back door, while Margaret searched for the proper way to approach the little blond-headed boy who wouldn't look at her. When her dad didn't return, Margaret knew he'd gone back home, hesitant to intrude. *Thank goodness it was him and not Mama.*

Before she could formulate an approach, the cordless phone she still held in her hand rang. *Mount Zion School.* "Hello."

"Margaret?"

The voice belonged to Catherine Poore, the receptionist. *I can remember a few weeks ago when I stopped being Margaret and became Mrs. Haywood. Looks like I'm back in good graces.*

"Yes, Catherine. You're calling about Jason, right?"

"Well, uh... uh, yes, I am. But how did you know?"

"Because he's right here with me."

"Did you know he was leaving school?"

"I did not. But I will deal with it and I'll talk to you all tomorrow. Thanks for letting me know so quickly." *They were probably afraid if they lost my child I'd pull my money. That was ugly, but it's going to take some time to forget how loudly Don's money talked there.*

"You know we should call the police," the receptionist informed her.

"They already know, because I called them," Margaret replied. "Just tell Headmaster Hunt that everything is under control. I'll see him tomorrow."

She sat down beside the forlorn little boy and cupped her hand under his chin. "Jason. I'm not angry, because I'm certain in your mind, you had a good reason for what you did. But just because I understand, doesn't mean it's acceptable. You and I have to talk."

She lifted his chin to where she could see into his troubled, teary blue eyes.

"I couldn't stay there, Mommie. I just couldn't."

"And why is that?" She hoped there was no threat in her voice.

"The other kids. They keep talking about Daddy, about how he tried to kill that man, and..." The child broke down in sobs and buried his face in his hands.

Margaret did the only thing she knew to do; she wrapped her arm around him and drew him close. *I'm just going to let him cry himself out. This is the first time he's shed any tears since we broke the news to him that his daddy was dead.*

Gradually, Jason's sobs began to subside. When she felt he'd regained control, she ventured gently, "Jason. You know you can talk to me about any problem you have. I won't be angry, I promise." *I hope I can keep that promise.*

The little boy looked at her, his face still red and puffy from crying, his eyes brimming with tears. "Mommie..." he began, then faltered.

"It's okay. Whatever's troubling you, just spit it out."

"What's sex?"

Sex! Where did that come from?

Margaret struggled internally with her response before finally saying, "Sex is something between a husband and wife that's very private to them. But why are you asking about sex?"

Jason was conflicted, every movement, every expression illustrating his discomfort. "Some older guys at school said Daddy was killed because he tried to have sex with one of the other prisoners."

His upturned face was illuminated with questions and concerns. "Is that what happened?"

I've got to walk this line very carefully. "Listen, Jason. We'll probably never know exactly what happened the night your daddy was beaten. I think, knowing your daddy's temper, he and the other prisoner got into a disagreement. What happened from there is anybody's guess. There was a physical fight and, unfortunately, Daddy got the worst of it."

"But why would those boys say Daddy tried to have sex if that's something a husband and his wife do? Daddy couldn't have done it anyway, because you're his wife."

There is no way I can explain what happened without giving this little boy more information that he's ready to process. What do I do?

"You know, Jason, it really doesn't matter what those boys said. They weren't there either and they don't know any more than we do." *Children can be so cruel.* "They're just talking because it makes them feel big."

"But it scared me, Mommie. I didn't know what this sex thing was, and I didn't understand what they were talking about when they asked me if I was a queer just like my daddy."

They didn't say that to this child!

"Do you know these boys' names?"

"No, ma'am. They're older boys. In the eighth grade, I think." The child looked expectantly into his mother's face. "I didn't understand the queer part, Mommie, so I couldn't answer them." There was no hesitation as he asked, "Am I a queer? That's why I came home, to ask you."

"Why didn't you just call me? I'd have come to school and brought you home."

"I didn't know what to do. I just knew I didn't want to stay there. So I came home to ask you."

He walked three miles to get away; to try and understand what these boys were saying.

"So why didn't you call out to me as you came in the front door? I heard the noise and thought someone had gotten in. That's why Grandee and I called the police."

Jason hung his head again. "Because by the time I got here, I was more afraid of being punished than I was of being a queer, so I came to my room," he mumbled, so softly Margaret had to strain to hear his words.

"Listen, son. You can't run away from school, ever again. If you have a problem, call me. But don't run away. Do we have a deal?"

She waited for what seemed like forever for his response, but in the end, Margaret was rewarded with a quiet "Deal."

"As for the boys calling you a queer, you're going to have to believe what I'm about to tell you."

He looked at her, expectation written all over his face.

"Queer is a term that isn't very nice and we don't use it. It's an insult."

Jason's eyes got larger.

"Take my word for it; you aren't a queer. Again, those boys were using words they don't even understand. I don't ever want to hear you use the word, either. When you're a little older, we'll talk about this again and I'll answer any questions you have. Deal?"

"Deal," he responded again, this time with the first sign of a smile she'd seen since the policeman escorted her into the bedroom. It felt like hours ago.

"Good. Now, how about an early after-school snack?"

"Yeah," he said. "Maybe some cookies?"

"Cookies? You got 'em."

The two were walking toward the kitchen when Jason offered, "You know, I'm tired of going to Mount Zion School. I'm even tired of living here in Carter's Crossroads."

"You are?" *I can't believe he's gotten so deep. A few months ago he would never have expressed his wishes so openly and independently.*

"Yeah, er... Yes, ma'am. I am. I wish we could all go somewhere where nobody knows us. And doesn't know what happened with Daddy."

Out of the mouths of babes!

CHAPTER TWO

*T*he next few days were a blur. *The last six weeks have been like being in a whirlwind. Why should now be any different?*

Margaret met with the headmaster at Mount Zion School the next day to explain Jason's actions. *There was a time when he couldn't be nice enough to me.* He sure let me know that confronting uncomfortable situations was a part of life. His only recommendation was for Jason to suck it up and learn to let those comments run off his back.

She said nothing to the children about Annie Campbell's visit, or the job offer. She did share the news with P.C., when the two spoke on Saturday.

"I know you can do the job. No question about it. The question is, 'Do you think you can do it?'"

Margaret reached for a strand of hair to twirl around her finger, a long-standing unconscious habit whenever she was confronted with a sticky situation. Only her hand found nothing. Then she remembered, for the thousandth time, she'd had her hair cut short. While she had wanted to change her hair for years, Don had refused. The transformation had come after she grew tired of seeing herself on the national news broadcasts. *Maybe it was a defense mechanism, but I needed some kind of make-over. And now I think I need even more.*

After church on Sunday, she'd invited her pastor, Samuel Bronson, and his wife Susan to the house for dessert and coffee. *Mama and Daddy are taking the kids to the mall shopping. This will be a good time for this conversation.*

The pastor and his wife arrived right on schedule. Margaret hugged them before leading them to the small family room at the back of the house. *After all they've done for me, I want to treat them like beloved family, not formal guests.*

"So how are things, Margaret, everything considered?" asked the young pastor, who'd ministered to her even before she was a member of his congregation. *My own pastor and church members kept their distance totally. It was like my children and I didn't even exist. But this angel of God was there for me every time I needed help. His church members went way above and beyond, providing food after Don was killed.*

"Things are better. I think. The pendulum swings back and forth, but I hope we're soon going to be able to drop off the news media radar. That will help tremendously."

"I don't imagine you're going to miss seeing your family on the six o'clock news," Susan observed.

"Not in the least. I would never have dreamed we would attract all the national exposure we've gotten."

"So what can we do to help?"

"You mean 'what else', don't you? I don't know what I would have done without either of you through all this."

"We grieve that you've had to endure what you have," the pastor said. "But we've only been following God's direction to minister to you in whatever ways you required."

"And I thank Him for you both every day."

"We give thanks for you, too," Susan replied. "Isn't God good?"

"I couldn't have made it through all this without Him. I still need to feel Him close to me."

"You can be certain He is."

"So, how can we help?" Susan asked again.

"The first Tuesday of next month, I'll have to stand on the courthouse steps and buy the house on Redbud Way. Haywood Tufters as well. Don left no will, so I'll have to buy everything he and I worked to build."

"That's rough," Susan said. "As astute a business head as Don had, you would think he would have provided for such a situation."

"I'd like to blame him," Margaret confessed. "But in truth, I never gave it a thought, either. Until he was dead."

"Will you be moving back into the house after you buy it?"

"No. That's not going to happen. In fact, just as soon as I get the deed in my hand, I'll be listing it with a real estate agent."

"But that's your beautiful home," Susan protested.

"From the outside? Yes. Inside is another matter, and it holds nothing but ugly memories for all of us."

"You mean the children are okay with selling the house?"

"It was a surprise to me, too. But they're the ones who told me they didn't want to live there again."

"Well," Samuel observed, "you obviously won't be homeless if you sell, because you've got this house as long as you want it. But why am I getting the idea there's more you haven't told us?"

He's perceptive.

"While this house might look like a Godsend, and I'm certainly not sorry that I had an alternative, there are many problems here. I'm not just talking about the cosmetics."

"Problems? Such as?" the pastor asked.

"The children have come to depend too much on my parents, going to them with questions and concerns they should be bringing to me." She spread her hands wide and separated her fingers, before continuing. "It's not that I'm jealous, but I'm getting vibes from the kids that they believe I caused Don's death." She realized how that sounded. "Indirectly, of course," she hastened to add.

"You're kidding, right?" asked Susan.

"Afraid not, Susan. The children barely speak to me these days, unless it's a case of have-to."

"You think your parents are a negative influence?"

"Mama still hasn't forgiven me for 'dragging Don's name through the mud', as she likes to put it. I have no doubt she's been talking to the children."

"But your dad..."

"Dad's solidly behind me," Margaret quickly interrupted. "But even that's a problem, because the children go to him for permission to do various things, and he gives it. He thinks it saves me from having to deal with it."

"I see what you mean," said Samuel with understanding.

"So what's the solution?" Susan asked. "Sounds to me like you have one in mind."

Margaret took a deep breath. *Okay... here goes.* "I'm thinking of leaving Carter's Crossroads. Selling out, pulling up stakes and starting over."

There was silence in the room as the pastor and his wife looked first at each other before, as if on cue, both turned their eyes on Margaret. "That's not a bad idea," he said. "Susan and I had already talked about it and wondered if you'd be willing to make such a break."

God, are You talking to me?

"You're serious?"

"Listen, Margaret. You know there are times in life when it makes better sense to start over rather than try to patch, repair or remodel what we have," Susan explained. "Yet we're all human. Most of us resist change, which is why a make-over usually seems more attractive than starting fresh."

I thought they'd be against it; that I'd have to sell them. If I didn't know better, I'd say they were trying to get rid of me.

"You think it's a good idea?"

The pastor rubbed his hand across his chin. "There are actually two questions here, you know. The first is, should you leave? The second is, where should you go?"

"Sad to say, Margaret, but you and your children have a lot of baggage here. Unfortunately, much of it is going to be hard to overcome. At least in the short term." Susan rose from her seat to pick up a framed photo of Don, which Margaret had displayed out of respect for the children.

"Despite all his negatives, which he showed almost exclusively to his family, Don had a high profile in Carter's Crossroads. He bought much of it, of course, but it existed nonetheless. As long as you have to confront that image, especially if you deviate from anything he did, you're going to want to hang your head."

"You don't deserve that," Susan said and slapped her hand on the table top beside her. "Neither do your children."

"Well," Margaret said, "it looks like we're on the same page. I think, for many reasons, it would be best for all of us if we relocated."

"Can we assume that you also have a destination in mind?"

"Atlanta." She took note of their expressions. "Before you say anything, I don't truly know how I feel about going there. It's another entire world away, I know."

She went on to share the possibility of employment with the state's domestic violence agency, noting her promise to talk further with its director in the next few days. "I had already been thinking about leaving before this offer ever materialized. I just didn't know where I would go."

"You could do the job, alright," Susan affirmed. "There's no doubt they would be lucky to get you."

"But are you sure the big city is the right environment for the kids at this juncture?" the pastor asked.

"That's what I'm asking myself. Trust me. I have agonized

over it."

"Do you have to have a job?" Susan asked. "Without butting into your business, I would have thought you'd have adequate financial resources."

"Once the house and Haywood Tufters sell, I'll be in pretty good shape, financially. But I'd like to be able to invest as much of that as possible, so that I can help the kids down the road, and not worry about my old age."

She took Don's photo from Susan and replaced it on the bookshelf. "Until then, I'm living on the cash accumulation in our checking account, along with some money I had squirreled away. Don's life insurance has paid off, but I've got that socked back for a rainy day. Who knows how long before either of the properties sell?"

"Sounds like you've crunched the numbers."

"I have. Repeatedly. Even if money weren't an object, I'm too accustomed to staying busy. I need something to do every day."

"You said the kids didn't want to go back to the old house. But did they also say they wanted to leave Carter's Crossroads?"

"Jason did, just a few days ago, after he ran away from school. Brian and Sallie haven't mentioned it. I don't imagine it's occurred to either of them that not going back to Redbud Way could also mean moving to another town."

"What about your parents?"

Margaret flashed an uncomfortable grin that morphed into a serious frown. "There," she said, "is one of the big rubs."

"You don't think they'll be in agreement?"

"I can guarantee you Mama won't like it. She'll be very vocal about it, too."

"I can just imagine," Susan agreed. "I've seen Miss Ruby in action."

"Daddy, on the other hand," Margaret continued, "won't be overjoyed, but at the end of the day, he'll support whatever I do."

"So what have you decided?"

"We're definitely going. And the sooner the better. Just as soon as I can get all the legalities behind me, I'm ready to call the movers."

"We must pray for Brian, Sallie and Jason. This is going to be yet another upheaval for them," Samuel observed. "The latest upheaval in six short months of turmoil."

"Don't think I haven't worried about that. I have. But my head and my heart tell me we'll all be better off to recover away from the spotlight, in a place where everyone doesn't know all the dirt."

Although given the amount of national media coverage we've had to endure, the TODAY show and the evening newscasts, I'm not certain there's anywhere in this world where people wouldn't recognize us.

"I'm going to talk to them tonight, which is one of the reasons I asked the two of you over this afternoon. I'm asking everyone I know to pray with me about this."

"Then let's go to God right now and lay your burdens on Him," Susan suggested. *"Dear Lord, You've been here for Margaret since long before she acknowledged Your help. You know better than even those of us closest to her the degree of agony, grief and pain she's endured. Now faced with helping her children recover from all they've been through, we realize that recovery may involve separating them from the only hometown they've ever known. Give her the wisdom and strength to evaluate her options. Be with her children as they learn of her plans and as they attempt to make such a drastic change. Remind all four of them, Lord, that You are always there for us, even and most especially in our darkest hour. We acknowledge, Lord, that instead of our lives being a series of peaks and valleys, that life is like twin rail tracks. One side is the good that is always there, and for which we should be grateful. The other side is the adversity that should, if we're truly Your children, lead us to cling closer to You. We thank you now for protecting the Haywood family through these many traumatic situations and acknowledge their dependence on You. Thank you, Lord, for being there for us when we're least deserving. In Jesus' name we pray. Amen."*

"Thank you," Margaret managed between the emotions, which threatened to erupt and follow the tears already marring her makeup.

The trio visited a few more minutes before Brother Samuel and Susan departed.

Through all of this, the pastor of my own church hasn't called but once, and that was only to ask why I didn't have him preach Don's service. "Funerals are for the survivors, not the deceased," she'd managed to tell him. *I did what I thought best for my children...and me. I'm not even a member of Brother Samuel's church, yet he's never failed to minister to me when I needed him.*

Later that evening, the three younger Haywoods returned from their shopping expedition. Laughing and joking among themselves, they piled in the door both cold and hungry, loaded down with bags and purchases.

Could it possibly be that life is getting back to normal? I miss our fireplace. Today would be the perfect day to sprawl out in front of a roaring fire and enjoy hot chocolate and pastries. But the inspector said this fireplace needed work before it was safe to use. Doesn't mean we can't have hot chocolate and pastry, however.

"Go stow your loot," she told the children. "I'll make us some hot chocolate."

"Hey, Mommie," Jason piped up, "you'll never guess what Sallie wanted to buy but Grandee wouldn't let her."

"Jason! You shut up right now..." the little girl with the pigtails screamed. "Just shut up!" She flounced off down the hall.

"Sallie... Sallie! Come back here right now."

Margaret could tell she'd been heard, but the girl only hesitated briefly before stomping away.

"Sallie. I know you heard me. Get back here. NOW!"

With poor graces, the child took yet another step away before finally turning, hesitantly, to walk back to her mother. "What?"

Margaret bit her tongue. "I beg your pardon, young lady?"

"What do you want?"

With difficulty, Margaret reined in the retort that was already half way out of her mouth. "Sallie. You don't talk that way to Jason, or to anyone for that matter. Furthermore, you're not going to answer me with 'What?'. You know why I called you back, so cut the innocence act. I'm not buying it."

Sallie drew herself up in a pout and screwed up her face. "You don't love me," she screamed. "My daddy's dead and all you want to do is fuss at me."

"Now listen here, Sallie…"

"Grammy says we're three orphans," Jason interrupted to inform his mother. "People need to treat us gently."

Mama, I don't need you constantly undermining me. I'm going to have to have a talk with Daddy, and one of the things I'm going to tell him is that we're leaving Carter's Crossroads.

Margaret fought again to control her emotions, which were now making her want to scream. "Listen you three…" She saw that Sallie was walking off again. "Sallie. This includes you, so come back."

The unhappy little girl's body language illustrated her degree of frustration, but she did as directed.

"Tell you what… let's go in the den where we can be comfortable. This may take a while."

The sister and brothers exchanged glances that Margaret clearly interpreted as, "What does SHE want now?" The children marched silently into the adjacent room where they took seats on the couch and the ottoman.

They're all looking at me like I'm an alien or something.

Margaret settled herself in the chair she'd claimed as hers when they took over the house shortly before Christmas. *Lord, please help me handle this without losing control.* She looked at her three children. It was only from Jason that she sensed even a glimmer of love and support. *This is not going to be easy.*

"Look, kids. There are some things we're going to have to get out on the table to talk about. Looks like now is as good a time as any."

"If you're going to talk about Daddy, I'm leaving," Sallie announced. "Grammy says its all your fault that Daddy's dead and disgraced."

Margaret felt the bile rise up in her throat. It was all she could manage to say, "Sit down, Sallie." Recognizing rebellion ready to emerge from her only daughter, she declared, "That's an order."

Jason, she noted, looked down as his lower lip began to tremble. *Are those tears in his eyes? Oh, son, I don't mean to hurt you.* In the meantime, Sallie had resumed her seat, but her face was covered in anger splotches. *For once I can't read Brian. His face looks like a plaster cast.*

Margaret took a deep breath. *Please help me, Lord.* "We've all been through a lot in the past six months. I'm sincere when I say I wish there was something I could have done to make things different. But there wasn't."

"Grammy says..." Sallie interrupted.

"Sweetie, I'd appreciate it if you'd let me talk first, without interrupting. Then each of you will have a turn as well." *I'd love to tell her I don't care what Grammy said or thinks, but she'd carry it straight back, so nothing gained there. I will have a conversation with Dad!*

The angry splotches on Sallie's cheeks became more pronounced as she clamped her mouth shut.

"Regardless of what anyone thinks, I did not want things to turn out like they did. Unfortunately, your Dad made some bad decisions that cost him dearly. I did not want him dead... it was all I could bear to start the divorce proceedings... but he's dead because of his actions. Not mine!"

"But Mom, if only..."

"Brian. I asked to say my piece without interruption, and I'm not finished."

"FINE!"

He clasped his arms across his chest and wrapped them around himself.

"Regardless of what you or anyone else says, or who you blame, nothing is going to change the facts. Your dad is dead. We have to go on with our lives, so that's what I want to talk about tonight."

"You're not going to make us go back to Redbud Way?" Brian broke his silence.

"I don't want to go back there, Mama. Please, not there!" Sallie's face lost its darkness as the color drained away.

What a contradiction. They want to blame me for Don's death, yet they don't want to go back to our house, because they remember the trauma that happened there.

"No, Sallie, we're going to sell that house and start over. That's another..."

"Oh!" Sallie crooned, "I know the *perfect* house, Mommie. It's just the yummiest place and I could even have a horse."

Horse? This child has never had the slightest interest in horses. But I'm not opening that can of worms right now.

She took another steadying breath. "Actually, you guys, I wasn't thinking of buying another house in Carter's Crossroads. That's what..."

"We're not going to keep on living here in this dump, are we?" Sallie's face was scrunched up like she'd bitten into a rotten apple. "I'm so embarrassed to have my friends come over."

She's on a roll.

"This place is almost as bad as public housing."

"Sallie...I have never been so disappointed in you as I am right now. You have absolutely turned into a little snob and I won't have it."

"She's right, Mom," Brian injected. "Have you looked at this place?"

"I most certainly have. It's old and worn, but it's a decent house in a decent neighborhood and we should all be thankful to have it." She stared off into space, praying for calm. "After all, we aren't going to be living here forever, you know. This is just temporary."

"Grammy says we're rich. We can live anywhere we want to."

Thank you, Sallie.

"Except she says people are going to talk about how you killed Daddy and then took his money and went wild." Sallie's chest was puffed out, showing she had obviously hit her stride.

Great propaganda snow job, Mama.

"She says she doesn't know how she's going to show her face down at the beauty shop. It's all she can do now to hold up her head, what with the shame you've brought on us."

"Are you finished, Sallie?" Margaret couldn't keep the razor edge out of her voice.

"Yes, ma'am. I guess?" The girl's body language screamed that she didn't understand what she'd done that was obviously so wrong.

"Grammy has her own opinions, to which she is welcome," Margaret managed through clinched teeth. "Unfortunately, she doesn't have all the information. I will have a conversation with her tomorrow."

She looked directly at the little girl. "From now on, Sallie, please spare me what Grammy thinks. Do I make myself clear?"

"Well, yeah, but..."

"Enough, Sallie. E-NOUGH!"

The lower lip pooched out again.

Sallie is going to be my drama queen, always able to rise to any occasion. Get used to it, Margaret!

"Now, this is what I wanted to talk with all three of you about." She paused to look at each of the three children, sure that once the words left her mouth, they could never be reclaimed. *Do I really want to do this? Do I have any choice, Lord?*

"How would you all feel about... feel about moving somewhere else?"

"You mean away from Carter's Crossroads?" Brian's question

was both immediate and explosive. The expressions that crossed his face represented a kaleidoscope of emotions.

"That's about the size of it. What do you think?" Her eyes anxiously sought those of each of her children, desperate for a clue as to how they were processing her bombshell.

"I'm against it." Brian's voice was flat and expressionless, the undertones of rage waving like yellow caution flags.

"NO! I won't," Sallie declared. "You can't make me. I'll... I'll... I'll go live with Grammy and Grandee. That's what I'll do and you can't stop me." Her face contorted as she screamed, "My Daddy is dead and you caused it. You can't make me move."

Although Margaret wanted to also scream and fly into a million pieces, she somehow managed to contain her anger and keep her composure.

"Sallie. You will never talk to me in that manner again, and you most certainly won't tell me what I can and cannot make you do. Do you read me, young lady?"

The silence that answered was deafening, but still, she trudged ahead. *I have to. I have to.*

"Brian," she said, directing her attention to her eldest who sat motionless, his body saying nothing, yet, at the same time, everything. "Brian, listen to me, son. There..."

"Don't call me son!" he uttered through clinched teeth. "I was Dad's son, but I'm not so sure I'm your son."

Lord, I think my heart is going to break. Please hold me and help me. I can't do this without You.

She reached across to place her hand lightly on the boy's shoulder. *He's absolutely rigid.* "Brian," she said softly, amazed at how calm her voice was, "why would you doubt you're my son?"

Silence.

"Brian, I really need to know," she pleaded.

Silence still.

"All of us are hurting in our own unique ways. That's why I'm trying to get us out of here, so we can truly begin to heal. Please, Brian... talk to me." *What else can I say? Or do?* "I promise... I'll listen to everything you say. I won't get angry." *Lord, You've got to help me keep that promise.*

Slowly the teenager turned his head. As Margaret looked him full in the face, her insides went icy cold. *There is pure venom in his eyes.*

Finally... he spoke. "I question if you're truly the mother of any of us."

What? Difficult as it was, she clamped her lips shut and waited. *Thank You, Lord.*

"Mothers...are...supposed...to...PROTECT...their...children." The words were bitten off without emotion. "We've...all been...humiliated...more than you...will ever understand." Tears began to puddle in his eyes. "Do you have any idea...what it's been like...at school every day? Never... mind... church... or... in... town," he sobbed. By now the boy's body was jerking. Tears streamed down his face as he dropped his head and hugged himself.

Do I hug him or do I let him comfort himself? Tossing caution to the wind, Margaret leaned across to place her hands on his arms, which crossed his body sentry style. "You're exactly right, Brian. I am your mother and it was my responsibility to protect all of you. I failed miserably." She put one hand out and gently lifted his chin until she could look him in the face. "But contrary to your opinion, my failure didn't just start after Dad got killed. It began many years ago."

"I think Mommie is a good mommie," Jason uttered softly as he scooted across the floor to lay his head in Margaret's lap, where she still sat in front of Brian.

I don't deserve your praise. You're one I think I've failed the most.

"What do you mean, Mom? I'm talking about how could you let us be treated like circus freaks? In the newspapers, on the TV news? The kids still call us names and talk about us." For the first time, his voice showed emotion. "How could you let that happen?"

She surveyed the room, pausing twice as long when she came to Sallie, who sat on the floor, leaning up against the couch while twisting one of her pigtails around her finger. *That's what she always does when she's conflicted. Just like me.*

"Okay. Are you guys ready to listen to me for a few minutes? Are you willing to work with me to try and help make things better?"

"Does it mean we have to move from here? From Carter's Crossroads, I mean?"

"That's one possibility, Sallie."

"But Mom..."

"Please, Brian, hear me out. All of you... please... just listen."

Margaret quickly fortified herself with an unspoken prayer, hoping the children didn't interpret the silence as a stall tactic.

"It's like this, you three. No one should have to endure what you have. I know you think I mean since your Dad's death. But it goes much farther back. I should never have allowed the hostility in our home to escalate to the level it did. Because I refused to acknowledge what I saw – basically a demon loose in our house – and allowed your Dad to abuse us and get away with it, I did indeed fail each of you miserably."

None of the three said a word. *They're just looking at me. Do I look like a deer in the headlights?*

"I hope you can forgive me." She tried not to plead, but her heart ached so badly; she had to see some sign that her children didn't truly hate her.

"But Daddy loved us," Sallie insisted.

"Yes, sweetie, he did. He loved each of you, but in his own way. I've shared with you how his daddy—and his mother, too—treated him. Unfortunately, in order to love someone else completely, you have to love yourself first. Your dad couldn't manage to love himself, a fact that left him angry and confused. Sadly, he took that anger out on those he loved most. The three of you...and me."

"So why, then, do you think you were a failure?"

"It won't make sense unless you think about it. But then, very little dealing with domestic violence makes sense." She paused to search the faces that sat across from her. *Looks like I've got their interest. Now if I can just hold it.*

"If I'd been able to understand your Dad's psychological problem a long time ago, I might have saved all of us a lot of pain and grief. But I didn't. When he would get violent, instead of making it clear to him that such behavior was unacceptable, I didn't respond at all." *I hope I'm not getting too deep for them.* "Every time an abuser is allowed to display his anger, without being called on it, it actually empowers him to do it again. Only next time, he has to top what he did before."

"That's really crazy."

"Remember, Brian. I said it wouldn't make sense until you thought about it. So you see, I failed all of us way back, when there was still a chance something could have been done."

Margaret looked at her children again, wishing she could see inside their minds. *And their hearts*, she told herself.

"I accept that I failed miserably when I could have done something. I don't accept that I'm either responsible for your dad's disgrace and embarrassment, or his death. HE brought those consequences upon himself, as a result of those actions he chose."

She could see the children beginning to squirm uncomfortably. *Is it from guilt or are they tuning me out?*

"As for the news media and all the comments from people in town, if there had been any way to stop that gossip, it would have been done. You've been subjected to ridicule you didn't deserve. This is merely another example of how domestic violence negatively affects innocent people. Short of barricading ourselves in the house and refusing to come out, I don't know how we could have avoided all that exposure."

"But Mom, the kids at school…" he faltered, "kids we thought were our friends have said things we didn't dare come home and repeat to you."

"Could it be those people were really your friends, or were they just friends of your dad's money?"

"Huh?"

"Think about it. If your dad took you to Atlanta to a Braves' game, weren't you always allowed to invite several friends to go along?"

"Yeah…uh, I mean, yes ma'am."

"Dad always dropped a chunk of change on those outings, didn't he?" Margaret could see the wheels turning in her son's head.

"Yeah. We always had the best seats and made as many trips to the concession stand as we wanted." His face lit up. "Hey, Jason, remember that time he rented a Hummer limousine for us to ride down in?"

"Yeah, that was cool. I enjoyed that, even though I fell asleep before the game was over and Dad had to carry me."

This is the first time I've seen his face glow in weeks. He still hasn't totally recovered from that beating Don gave him. I'm glad he has other pleasant memories of his dad. Thanks to the counseling we're taking.

"So you're saying these people weren't really our friends, that they just used us?"

"I don't think they did it intentionally. But the attraction of money is strong, especially to someone who doesn't have the financial resources we had. If those people weren't true friends… someone who cared for you regardless of your circumstances… then when the money is gone, so is the friendship."

How well I should know. I can count on one hand the people who reached out to me in those first few days after Don's death. They weren't the ones I would have thought a year ago, would be right there with me. Only two members of our Sunday School class even made an effort. It was obvious even that little expression was a very uncomfortable effort.

"The teachers at school are different, too." Brian's expression changed as revelation spoke. "Mom? Are we poor now? Or what?"

"We're not poor. Far from it. But right now, our resources are limited somewhat." Margaret spent the next few minutes explaining how legally she would get control of the house and the business and the investments. She described what would be involved in selling their home on Redbud Way and Haywood Tufters.

"Will we be rich then?"

Margaret hesitated. "I don't want to use the word *rich*. I would rather say we'll be comfortable, for that money will have to be invested to grow. That way we can have a monthly income, you three can all go to college and get launched in careers, and, I won't be penniless when I reach retirement age. Remember, we still have to buy another house."

"So we're not going to stay in this house?"

She smiled at her eldest. "No, son, we aren't. This house has been a Godsend, but it's not where we need to be for the long haul."

"Grammy says we have to live here because you need her to look after us," Sallie piped up.

Thank you again, Mama. Undermine me to my children one more time.

"And do you agree with that, Sallie?"

"Uh... not really," she said finally. "I don't like this house. But Grammy says she's afraid of what you may do with all Daddy's money, and that it's best we stay here so she can know we have a roof over our heads."

"Sounds like Grammy has lots of ideas."

"Oh, she does," Sallie chirped, "she says she knows just how everything needs to work out, that you need help being our mother."

That talk tomorrow is going to be as rich as Mama thinks I am.

"We'll always need and love Grammy, but I'm your mother. I think there are better ways to do things."

"What do you mean?"

"I'm very appreciative, Brian, that Grandee and Grammy

bought this house. As I said, it's been a Godsend in these weeks when none of us wanted to go back to Redbud Way. But this has just been temporary. I knew that in the beginning."

"This house is creepy... it's so old and shabby."

"None of those reasons are why I didn't plan to stay here, Sallie. You need to stop and think about what has happened to us."

She could see the lower lip pooching out again, but she charged ahead. "We had a beautiful home on Redbud Way. But look at all the pain and unhappiness that was hidden inside that beautiful box. I agree, this house is dated cosmetically, but just because you live in a pretty house on the right street, and drive the right kind of automobiles, doesn't mean you'll be happy."

"So where are we going? You told Sallie we might not buy another house here in Carter's Crossroads."

"I've been praying and looking around, looking for a place we could go, where we could all make a fresh start. A town where we aren't recognized on sight, and where your Dad's money hasn't made such a deep and false impression."

"It would be nice to go to a school where you didn't have to worry every time someone opens his mouth if you're going to be teased about what your dad did."

"Those were my thoughts, exactly, Brian."

"How about you two?" she asked the younger children. "Would you be willing to move away? To start over in a new place, so that we can all truly recover from what has happened?"

"I'll go anywhere, Mommie, as long as I'm with you. I don't like going to school at Mount Zion any more."

"I don't like it, either," Sallie interjected. "But Grammy's not going to like the idea."

"Don't worry about Grammy. I'll deal with that."

"So tell, us, Mom. Where do you have in mind?"

"I do have one location I'm considering very seriously. And

the offer just last week of a job there makes it even more attractive."

"You'd go to work?" Sallie asked in a childish whine. "What about us?"

"Remember, kids. I told you, we aren't going to be able to live as lavishly as we once did. Yes, I'm going to have to go to work."

"Uh... Mom," questioned Brian, "I'm not trying to be smart, but what kind of work can you do? Have you ever worked?"

He's on top of things.

"It's true I haven't worked for pay since you came along, Brian. Before that I was working with your Dad, when we first opened Haywood Tufters. *Don always conveniently forgot those long hours I worked, for NO pay, those first two years. Without me working for free, he never would have gotten the business launched. But he never gave me credit for any of OUR success.*

"It's a valid question, son, and it's one I also asked myself. Just last week, God blessed me with the opportunity to get a job that I feel very qualified to take. It's something I've been doing most of my adult life."

"Oh, my gosh! Cooking is all you've ever done," Sallie squealed. "Please tell me you're not going to be asking people if they want fries with their burger. I couldn't hold my head up if my Mom was working in a fast food place." The little girl's expression assumed grotesque proportions.

"Sallie Haywood! Even if I were asking people if they wanted fries, there's no reason for you to be ashamed."

"But Mom..." she wailed. "Only retards do work like that."

"I don't care for your snobbish attitude, Sallie. We'll talk about it later." She made a mental note to pull her daughter aside for a private conversation. *The sooner the better, too!*

Margaret told about the visitors she'd had the previous week and the offer to work with the state domestic violence organization.

"So that's why you said it was something you'd been doing all your life," Brian said. "That's pretty cool, Mom."

"It would mean we'd move to Atlanta."

"Can we buy a house in Buckhead or Dunwoody?"

"What do you know about Buckhead and Dunwoody, Sallie? Why would you want to live there?"

"Because that's where everybody who is anybody lives."

"We're not anybody. We're just plain us. And no, I can tell you right now that we won't be calling either of those places home."

I can see we're in for another pouting session. I really do have to give this child an attitude adjustment!

"Where would we go to school?"

Jason's been so quiet, I'd almost forgotten him. But that's a good question. I hadn't even thought about schools.

"That's something to think about, son. A lot of that decision would depend on where we lived, I'm sure."

"Anywhere is fine just as long as it isn't Mount Zion School. I wish we could move tomorrow," he finished, sadness evident in his voice. "Just don't make me go to Mount Zion."

It sickens me that my children have come to feel this way about the school that's been the center of their entire lives.

"So where would we live, Mom?"

Margaret settled herself in a more comfortable position on the floor, pulling her left leg up under her. "Here's what I was thinking…." She explained that selling both the house and the business might take some time.

"If we come to terms on this job, they'll want me to start pretty quickly, I'm sure. So it looks like it would make better sense to find a large apartment that we liked. At least three bedrooms, in which case you and Jason would have to share."

"That's okay," Jason answered. "I always feel safe when Brian is with me."

I saw that look Brian gave his little brother. He was so fearful Don had killed Jason that horrible night. I'm glad Jason feels protected by Brian.

- 37 -

"It won't be in public housing, will it?"

My poor little prima donna. "No, Sallie. It won't be in public housing. But that doesn't mean that public housing is bad or dirty."

The little girl gave a shudder of horror, but said nothing.

"How long would we live in the apartment, Mom?" Brian asked, appearing to be computing in his mind.

"I'll have to sign a year's lease, I'm sure. But that would give us time to sell what we have here, and to begin to look around for something to buy, without having to be in a rush."

"Sounds like a plan."

"It sounds like you're in favor of my plan?" The nod of Brian's head gave Margaret the necessary courage to look at her other children. "How about you two? Are you with us?"

She was about to share more of her plans with the children, when her cell phone rang.

Jim Deaton!

"Hello. Jim?"

"Yes, Margaret. It's me. Caller ID must have given me away."

"It did."

How he can want to talk to me after all the pain I cost him, I'll never understand.

"Can you hold for a second, Jim?"

She turned to the children. "We'll talk about this more tomorrow after I have a conversation with the lady in Atlanta. Right now I need to talk to Mr. Deaton."

Brian nudged his little brother and motioned for Sallie to follow. "Come on, you guys. We'll go to our room where we can talk about this some more."

"Why can't we go to my room?" Sallie whined.

"Fine," Brain agreed, "we'll go to your room."

My Brian is growing into such a man so quickly. I don't want to overload him. But right now I've got to talk to Jim.

"It's so good to hear your voice," she told her attorney. "You actually sound so strong."

The last time I saw him, he was hooked up to tubes and machines, so weak he couldn't even sit up.

"Just got home from rehab this morning," he confessed. "Man, was it ever good to see the lake again."

Margaret knew the lawyer she retained for her divorce had a condo in Atlanta and a cabin at Lake Oconee, about ninety minutes east of Atlanta.

"Why didn't you go back to the condo?"

It looks like the lake house would be too remote to be safe.

"Steps. I'm not good going up and down yet. But it'll happen."

It wouldn't have to happen if my denial hadn't ensnared you in Don's possessive wrath.

"I'd forgotten about your condo being a townhouse. I guess that would make it difficult."

"Yeah, I can handle two or three steps without a problem. It's an entire flight of those little boogers that does me in, but I'll get there."

"Jim, I'm so sorry about all that's happened. I don't think I'll ever forgive myself for what Don did to you."

"How about what he did to you? And the children?"

"But you didn't deserve to be injured."

"Neither did you. Or Sallie. Or Jason."

"I agree. But…"

"No buts," he interrupted. "No buts and definitely no 'if only's', either. What happened, happened. Nothing can change that."

"This has cost you financially and physically and, I dare say, emotionally as well."

"It hasn't cost you the same way?"

"Of course. But I'm different."

"Why? Because you were his wife, therefore the designated

victim, complete with all the pain and anger?"

"Yes. Well... no. Oh, you know what I mean."

"You mean that your husband shot me because I was trying to help you. Therefore you'll go through the rest of your life carrying a load of guilt over what happened to me?"

"You make too lightly of all this, Jim."

"And you make way too big a fuss. But let's don't argue. Hear?"

"Deal," she agreed. "It is such a relief to hear your voice, to know that you've been released from the hospital... to hear you sounding so strong."

"I'm doing okay, Margaret. I'm not there. Yet. But this is only a temporary thing. I will regain full use of my leg and all of this will become an unpleasant but distant memory."

How he can be so positive when Don's rage shattered his left leg bone in four different places? The doctors speculated he was aiming for Jim's crotch and was so enraged that his aim was affected. How like Don to extract revenge in such a personal way!

"I hope you will, Jim. I've prayed for you every day. But will you still be able to hike and play tennis?" She had seen the wall of tennis trophies in his office, and knew from previous conversations how much he enjoyed hiking.

"That remains to be seen. Right now I'll settle for being able to climb a flight of stairs to my bedroom or down to my seat in the stadium when Georgia tromps the stew out of Tech! Then we'll see about the other. Later."

Lord, please don't let Don's actions cripple this innocent man for the rest of his life. He's too young to be handicapped.

"When will you go back to work?"

"Been back at the salt mine for two weeks now."

"Two weeks? But I thought you said you just got out of the hospital..."

"I just got out this morning," he interrupted. "My secretary has been bringing work to the hospital for the past two weeks so I've been putting in three or four hours most days."

"I'm impressed."

"Hey, thanks to cell phones and the internet, you can do a lot from a hospital room that wouldn't have been possible a few years ago."

"When will you actually start going back to the office?" *That's going to be quite a drive from the lake to the office each day.*

"I'm planning to go back this coming Friday. There are still a few things you can't do long distance. That's one of the reasons I called you."

"I'm one of the things you can't do long distance?"

He laughed. "I hadn't thought about it quite like that, but in a matter of speaking, yes."

Now he's lost me.

"I've got business in Atlanta on Friday," he continued. "Got to be in court. I'm going to stay over in town Friday night, get a hotel room, then drive back to the lake on Saturday morning."

"You're able to drive?"

"It was my left leg, so my right one is fine to work the gas and brake. I'd drive back out Friday night, but I know I'll be tired after a full day of work. I don't want to push things too far."

"How does this all involve me?"

"Would you like to drive into Atlanta Friday afternoon, in time for an early dinner? We'd time it so you could get back to Carter's Crossroads by eleven, anyway."

"You want me to have dinner with you?"

"Unless you'd rather not."

"No. I mean, of course not. I'd love to see you again."

"Good. I'd like to see you again, too." He hesitated. "I've got something I want to talk with you about."

"Can't you give me a hint?"

"I could," he answered with a laugh, "but I'm not. Just call it incentive for you to show up."

"You know I'll come. Tell me what you've got on your mind."

"Nope. Everything in its own good time."

"Jim...!"

"Friday night, Margaret. I'll see you at the office just before five o'clock. Okay?"

"Okay, Jim. But I'm about to burst with curiosity."

"Don't burst. It would ruin a good evening out."

"I'll be there, Jim."

"See you then, Margaret. It's not that big a deal," he added. "We'll talk about it when I see you."

CHAPTER THREE

*O*nce Margaret got the kids off to school the next morning, she sat down to make a "to-do" list for the week. *Got to arrange babysitters for the kids Friday night. That's after the two most important things I've got to do today – talk with Barbara Kirkland and with Mama and Daddy.*

She knew her parents wouldn't be happy to hear her news, so she decided to make the call to Atlanta first. Then she'd tackle the unpleasant chore she knew awaited her.

If I talk to the folks first, I'll be in such a blue funk, I won't be able to talk with Barbara.

"Margaret, I was just thinking about you."

"Morning, Barbara. You had a good weekend, I trust."

"I did. And how about yourself?"

"Yes…" she said and hesitated. "Yes, it was a good weekend. Not without its wrinkles – I'm mean with three kids, there are bound to be rough moments."

Her new friend in Atlanta laughed. "Hey, if they're kids, there are going to be problems. You can go to the bank with that."

There was silence, as if neither quite knew what to say.

"So really, how are you, Margaret?" The jovial banter was gone, replaced by a more serious, yet totally friendly tone; much like two old friends who had shared much commiseration.

"It's rough some days, I won't deny it. And the kids are a part of that difficulty. They've had to endure so much ridicule from people they thought were their friends. We won't even talk about what the news media did to them."

"I know they've been turned upside down. While kids are sometimes more resilient than we slightly older folks, they often wound more easily as well."

"No argument there."

"But who I'm really concerned about is you. Margaret Haywood. You've been through quite a bit of hell as well. You can't be the mother your children need, until you can be the person Margaret needs. So what can we do to help you?"

"Quite frankly, give me a job so I can get all of us out of Carter's Crossroads."

"You would leave there?"

"Well, yes. Is there some reason I shouldn't?"

"It depends on why you're making the move. If it's solely to take a job with us, that's not necessary. What with technology, you can do ninety percent from home. I'd guess you might need to be in Atlanta two or three times a month." She hesitated. "In fact, you can't work here because we don't have desk space for you." She laughed, but Margaret thought it sounded a little apologetic and uncomfortable.

"I guess I just assumed I'd be working in the office. Not that it matters," Margaret hastened to add. *I don't want her to think I'm insulted or anything.*

"We're just maxed out on space," Barbara explained, "and right now the budget won't let us rent anything larger. That's why, when Annie told me about you, I thought it would be a win-win for both of us. We could get a highly-skilled employee and you could get a paying job without having to relocate."

She called me highly-skilled. That's intimidating!

"Ordinarily, it would be a perfect situation. But in this case, I was already seriously considering a move somewhere before Annie and you ever knocked on my door."

"Oh...?"

Margaret, who felt totally comfortable sharing the problems in her household with a woman she'd only met once, proceeded to explain all the dynamics and elements that were dogging her family.

If Annie trusts her, I do too.

"So, as much as part of me doesn't want to move, if we stay here, I don't feel my children can ever recover from all that's hit them in the past six months. Everyone not only knows our names, but all the skeletons in our closets, plus some that don't rightly belong to us."

There was silence again. Margaret wondered whether she'd said the wrong thing.

Finally Barbara spoke. "Have you talked with Annie about this?"

"I was going to take her to lunch this week for that very purpose. But, no, I haven't. Why do you ask?"

"We counsel women to use whatever means is necessary in order to escape an abusive relationship. Unfortunately, we sometimes don't take our assistance far enough. The same mindset and traits that lead a woman into her first abusive relationship can cause her to escape that one, only to find herself in a second identical situation."

"I don't think I understand. I'm not dating and don't plan to for a long time." She laughed, but there was no humor evident. "If ever."

"In your case, I'm not speaking of a dating relationship as much as I am your need to run to something."

Where is she going with this?

"I truly believe that your recovery and your children's ability to bounce back will depend on your mindset about leaving Carter's Crossroads. Will you move to Atlanta to get away from there, or because Atlanta offers something better? Remember, you do have a support system in place there. Here in Atlanta…"

"Neighbors often don't even know who lives in the next house or the next apartment," she interjected.

"That's about the size of it."

"Believe me when I say, a part of me is terrified at the thought of moving. I've lived in Carter's Crossroads my entire life. And I'm very thankful for that support system you talked about. But…"

Am I running away instead of running to?

"But I think, at least for a while, my children need an opportunity to go to school without fearing what may confront them every day. I deserve a chance to shop and buy groceries without understanding that I make some people uncomfortable." She thought for a moment. "Sort of like putting a seriously ill person in isolation to give them a fighting chance."

"Good," Barbara congratulated her. "Sounds like you're looking at it the right way. If this was to be an escape, you stood the chance of getting here and being abused again by the anonymity of the big city. Had that happened, everyone would still be miserable."

"I know," Margaret confessed, "we must put ourselves out there in an attempt to make new friends. They won't come to us. But neither will we be branded wherever we go."

"Are you saying goodbye to Carter's Crossroads forever?"

"I'll give you the same answer I gave myself: 'I don't know.' I've learned the hard way not to say never."

"Don't rush it," her new friend advised. "I think a year from now you'll have a lot clearer picture. You might return there, you might stay in Atlanta. Then there's always the chance that you'll end up in some other place you least expect."

Margaret laughed. "Not much chance of that. I'm not the

most adventuresome creature."

"I think you've got much more steel in your spine that you give yourself credit for. Which is why I was so excited about you coming to work with us."

"I'm excited to think about the possibilities. So what's the next step?"

"There's no question in my mind that I want you, but there are a number of things we need to talk about. Hmmmm." Margaret could hear pages rippling. "How about if I drive up there after lunch Friday and we sit down for an hour or so?"

"I've got a better idea," Margaret offered. "I'm supposed to meet a... a friend in Atlanta for dinner Friday evening. What if I drive in early and we meet on your end?"

"Well, sure, if you're coming to town anyway."

"We made the plans last night, so I'm definitely coming. Just tell me what time. I probably need to leave your office by four o'clock, four-fifteen at the latest."

"That'll work beautifully. Why don't you plan to be here at two o'clock? You can meet the rest of the staff and tour our spacious office. Then we can sit and visit."

After getting directions to the office, Margaret bade her new friend goodbye and ended the call. She tucked the note with the driving instructions in the front flap of her planner portfolio. *That's about five or six miles from Jim's office. I should be able to make it by five o'clock. No problem.*

The knowledge of her next chore weighed heavily. She sat for several minutes, pondering how best to proceed. *I don't know if I'm scared or what.* After several minutes she punched her parents' number on the cell phone.

"Hello?"

I figured Mama would get it. Now I'll have to undergo the third degree about why I want to talk to Daddy.

"Hey Mama, how are things this Monday morning?"

"Trying to get the wash done and dinner fixed. You want to come eat? I made chicken and dressing."

Mama grew up when Monday was wash day. She still clings to that habit, even though she's got automatic appliances that can do it any day or night.

"I may have to go run some errands, so I'm not sure about lunch. But thanks for asking."

"Well, we'll have enough, I suspect, so just come on over if you want to."

She suspects she'll have enough. She still cooks like she's feeding a restaurant crowd. There'll be enough.

"Mama, is Daddy where you can hand him the phone? I've got a question for him."

"He's in the other room, but you can ask me. I know most things he does."

I don't want to talk to you, Mama. Not yet. Not until I can talk with Daddy first.

"What do you know about car values?"

"Not much," she admitted, although Margaret noticed she did hesitate a moment before responding. "You're not fixing to waste some of Don's money buying yourself a new car, are you?" A loud sigh of annoyance preceded her next statement. "Folks in this town are talking bad enough now, honey. You don't need to be seen driving some new car around less than two months after your husband was killed."

Mama, the Lord loves you and I do, too. But you could try the patience of a saint.

"No, Mama, I'm not buying a new car. I want to ask Daddy about the one I have. Is he where he can talk?"

"Very well," Ruby Maxwell conceded with poor graces, "let me take him the phone."

In a matter of seconds Margaret heard, "Hey, sugar. Your mama says you got car problems."

That's not what I said but that's what Mama heard. You can't win with her.

"Not exactly a car problem, but a car question." She hesitated, knowing how she phrased the next question was critical. "Daddy, could you step over here a minute? ALONE? Just tell Mama you're coming to see about my problem... that she should stay with her dinner."

Dead silence. Just when Margaret was about to despair that she'd blown it big time, he said, "Let me suggest this. Why don't I walk over and see what you're talking about? Mama's finishing up our dinner and you can walk back with me and eat. She's cooked way too much, just like she always does."

"Margaret can't come eat. She's got errands to run. I already asked her," she heard her mother's voice announce.

Good old Mama. Set the record straight.

"I'll be there in just a minute."

True to his word, Margaret soon saw her father open the gate connecting the two yards and come up her back steps.

"I assume you really don't have a problem with your car?"

"I am thinking about selling it, and I wanted to pick your brain. Either now or later this week. But Mama jumped to conclusions when I told her I wanted to ask you a question about my car, and decided I had mechanical problems." She looked him directly in the face and continued, "But I do have a serious problem. I'm glad you saw how Mama drew her own conclusions and communicated them, with no concern about whether she was correct."

"Oh?"

"Come on in and have a seat."

The two made their way into the family room, where Margaret indicated the most comfortable chair. She seated herself on the end of the sofa nearest her father, with one leg pulled up under her.

"What's Mama done now?"

"Then you're aware there's a problem?"

"I know she's been really pumping the children for information about your activities and what you say."

"She's also been pumping them with her own version of how everything is." She got up and began to pace the room. "Mama is questioning what kind of a mother I am, and telling the children how I should conduct my life. Just like she did with you a few minutes ago."

It's the gospel according to Mama.

Harold Maxwell hung his head, but said nothing.

Margaret reached across and took his hand. "Daddy, I'd give everything I've got, except the children, if I didn't have to have this conversation with you. Unfortunately I've got no choice."

He looked at her. His facial expression hinted that he had something he wanted to say, but his mouth didn't move, so Margaret continued. She explained the problems the children were having, about Jason running away; how those that they thought were friends had suddenly dropped them.

"Those people aren't friends," her father said suddenly. "They're parasites who were hanging on to Don's generosity."

"That's what I told them. But between the other students in school, and people in this town who are determined to point fingers and wag their tongues, they've had a very difficult time. All the media exposure hasn't helped, but Mama has probably done as much damage as anyone."

Her face assumed a hardness she could feel, as she wished it didn't have to be that way. *I'm not angry with this dear, sweet man. Lord, please help me be upfront without hurting him more than is absolutely necessary.*

"You and I both know Mama is going to do whatever she wants to do. Nothing we can say or do is going to make a difference." She rose again from the sofa and moved to Don's framed photo on a nearby table. She picked it up and looked at it. "When I was about to divorce Don, it was a step I took reluctantly, with a lot of pain in my heart. In the ways he was loveable, he was so very loveable." She replaced the photo. "But in those ways he was cruel and destructive, those ways overshadowed all his good points."

"I know, honey. I know you did what you had to do."

"Then why can't Mama see that? Why does she have to undermine me every time she gets the chance?"

"Your mama is a sweet woman and I love her dearly, but when she makes up her mind on something, I've never been able to dissuade her."

He got up and put his arm around Margaret, pulling her close. "It's not that she doesn't love you, you know? She does. But she's just opinionated and strong-willed. She's gonna do what she wants."

He kissed her on the forehead. "Come on, let's go eat."

"Not yet, Dad. There's something else I have to tell you. I think you'd better sit back down."

With a wary look on his face and a pained expression that cut right to the quick of Margaret's soul, he reclaimed his seat. His expression was one of concern.

"The kids and I are leaving Carter's Crossroads."

At the look of horror on his face, Margaret hurried to finish her announcement before she lost her nerve.

"This is the only way we're all going to be able to heal and recover from everything that's happened. I hope you're going to support me."

"You're doing this because of your mama." He brought his arm up and slammed the palm of his hand down on his knee. "I told her she was going to run you off if she didn't put a muzzle on that mouth."

The grief on his face broke Margaret's heart once again. *God, I'd do anything to keep from hurting this sweet man.*

"Now she's done it. I hope she's satisfied!"

Margaret had only seen her father angry a few times in her life and she took no pleasure in the pain she saw in his face.

"It's not just Mama. You have to believe me." She took him by the hand and led him into the dining room, where papers were still scattered across the large oval table. "It's all of this, Dad. All of the reminders of how dysfunctional our family was, before and after we became media sensations."

She thumbed through a stack of newspaper clippings and retrieved an article written by a national news reporter. "Look at this tripe. Read it, and look at all the inaccuracies." She waved the piece of newsprint under his nose. "Read it and see how many locals took advantage of our misfortune to buy their fifteen minutes of fame. This is what my children and I have to contend with every time we walk out this door."

"I know it's been rough. And, in truth, I told myself the other week that you might be better off if you got out of here for a while." He hugged her tightly to him again. "It breaks my heart that I can't protect all of you, but I can't. So wherever it is you've decided to go, you'll do it with my blessing." He grinned at her. "You need help, anything at all, you call me. I may be old, but I still need to be needed."

I love you so much.

Margaret choked back tears as she hugged the man who had never failed to stand by her. "I'd trust you with my life. And don't worry, I'll always need you."

She could tell he was trying to control his own emotions, so she turned away and busied herself picking up the Sunday papers.

"Do you know where you're going?"

"Atlanta." She dumped the papers in the recycle box next to the fireplace.

"Atlanta? Isn't that a little drastic?" He shuffled his feet. "You've never lived in a big city."

"I'd be less than honest if I didn't say I was a little nervous. But I've prayed for peace that this is the right step. Last week I got my assurance." She explained about the job offer and how it had come to her.

"I'll meet with the agency on Friday of this week." She smiled at him weakly. "Unless they change their mind, I'm going to take the job. I need a fresh start, too. I need to be busy and challenged."

"You'll do good."

"Thank you. Your support means so much."

"Come on, let's go eat. Otherwise your mama's going to be over here to see what's keeping us."

As they walked across the back yard, Margaret tried to grasp all that had happened in such a short period of time. She rubbed her left arm, the arm Don had shattered the previous fall, and was rewarded with twinges that still struck when she least expected. *The doctor is amazed that I was able to regain so much use of my arm. He didn't understand that anything less than a complete recovery wasn't an option.*

"When do you want to tell your mama?"

"Let's wait 'til I get back from Atlanta. I want to be certain this is the direction I'm going before we say anything."

"That's probably a good idea."

Over chicken and dressing, mashed potatoes and black-eyed peas, Margaret and her father listened to a complete litany of Ruby's opinions, most of which centered on the things she believed Margaret was doing wrong.

Have I always been deaf to Mama's manipulations, or is she getting this way as she gets older? Either way, I don't like it.

"You're a widow now, you know. You can't go out spending a lot of money or looking like you're happy."

"But Mama..."

"Now you listen to me, Margaret. I'm down at the beauty shop every week and I hear what folks are thinking. More importantly, I hear what they're saying."

Bridle my mouth, Lord.

"Just what are they saying? I'd love to know."

As if she didn't pick up on the sarcasm in her daughter's voice, Ruby Maxwell continued. "They say it's bad enough you dragged poor Don's name through the mud before he was killed." She halted and looked first at Margaret, then her husband. "And that's what I think caused him to snap like he did. But they're calling you the…"

"So you're saying I caused him to go crazy and come gunning for Jim Deaton? He was trying to kill me, Mama. I'm the one he was after."

"Now Ruby, all you're…"

"You listen to me, Harold Maxwell. I've always been a submissive wife to you, but Margaret didn't know her place. Because of it, Don's dead and she's a widow. I guess you and me… well, we're going to have to help her finish raising those precious fatherless children."

Margaret leapt to her feet, sending the gold-and-red striped napkin in her lap tumbling to the floor. Her face matched the darker shades in the fabric. "No, Mama, you listen to me. Listen good."

"Remember who you're talking to," Miss Ruby challenged. "You don't know any more about being an obedient daughter than you knew how to be a submissive…"

"RUBY! Enough. Now!" The entire time he was calling down his wife, the elderly man was rising from his chair.

Margaret saw a look pass between the two of them that made her blood run cold. *I've never seen them like this.*

He put his arm around Margaret's shoulder, pulling her close to him. "I'm sorry, Margaret. Why don't you go on back to your house? I'll be over in a few minutes but I'd like to have a talk with your mother first."

As he spoke, he escorted her to the back door, opened it, then planted a loving kiss on top of her head. "Don't worry about Ruby," he consoled her. "You've got the courage to do what's right. Don't even think about changing a thing or hanging your head in shame."

"Daddy, I love you so much," she whispered, even as she knew the tears were about to spill over. *Daddy gets uncomfortable around crying females.*

As she walked back across the yard where she had played as a child, Margaret's eyes found the tree with the remains of the tree house her father had built so many years before. *Mama almost had a fit when I said I wanted a tree house. Said little girls had playhouses on the ground and tree houses were for boys.* She gave an inaudible chuckle. *Thank goodness, Daddy paid her no mind. He built it anyway.*

Back inside her own house, she collapsed on the den sofa totally spent. *If it was this bad just listening to Mama's cock-eyed ideas of what all I've done wrong, telling her I'm moving to Atlanta is going to be one pretty mess.*

Picking up the morning paper, which she'd tossed on the coffee table earlier, she scanned the front page headlines. *I used to grab the paper without even thinking twice, until I found myself in the headlines. It's just not the same any more.* She decided to check, instead, for her favorites on the comic pages until she was interrupted by tapping on the back door.

Daddy. It's really his house, but he respects it like it belongs to me. I love that man so much.

Margaret found an old man with a troubled face on the other side of the door.

"I'm so sorry, Margaret. Your mother has gone too far this time. I'm afraid, to add insult to injury, I told her so."

"Come on in," she encouraged, "Let's go where we can be comfortable." She led him through to the den. "So what did Mama say when you 'told her so'?"

Her father wiped his hand across his face in a gesture of frustration. "Just about like you can imagine."

"That's Mama. I love her, but I'm coming to see that I don't like her very much."

"Sadly, that's understandable, shug'. She's undermined your

position from the get-go." Tears appeared in his eyes. "As much as it breaks my heart, this is why I think it's probably best that you leave." His eyes grew wide with horror. "At least for a while. I'd hate to think you'd never come back here to live."

The two continued to talk about all that would need to happen in order to relocate.

"Now don't you worry one minute about this house," her father assured her. "I can easily sell it and get my money back, or I can rent it. I'm just glad I had it here for you to use. Certainly none of us envisioned how all this would play out."

That's a major understatement.

After her dad left, still looking as bereft as when he'd arrived, Margaret busied herself planning a grocery list and grabbing a pair of slacks to drop off at the cleaners.

Got to get these errands run. Want to have a good meal on the table for the kids tonight.

⚜

"So when are we moving to Atlanta?"

The family was at the table, enjoying Margaret's homemade chicken pot pies that were one of the children's favorites on nippy winter nights.

It wasn't cold when I was making my grocery list. That front they said was coming through in the middle of the night must have arrived early, because these hot pies really hit the spot.

"It'll be a few weeks yet. I'm supposed to meet with the rest of the staff in Atlanta this coming Friday afternoon."

There's animation in Brian's voice. Even Sallie doesn't look as sulky as usual. But poor Jason, he really looks like an orphaned child. I don't know what to do to reach him.

"You sound like you're excited about this move."

Brian played his fork around with the food on his plate. "I don't know if excited is the right word." He paused as he appeared to hunt for what he wanted to say. "Maybe intrigued is the better term?"

"That's an intriguing answer as well." She smiled and looked to her other two children. "How about you guys? You don't have to be intrigued as well. Excited is okay, too."

"I just want it over with," Sallie volunteered.

"Me, too..." Jason chimed in.

I've got to have another private talk with Jason, too. I've never even had one with Sallie.

"So why the anxiousness?" Margaret tried to ask calmly.

"It's all those kids at school," answered Sallie. "They just can't stop talking about Daddy and how you had him arrested." The color drained from the little girl's face.

"It's because they have nothing else to talk about," Margaret offered. "Sooner or later something else will take the spotlight off you."

"They're also repeating what they've heard their parents say," Brian volunteered. "I hate to say it, Mom, but the adults in this town are worse than their kids."

Don't I know it! How many times in the grocery store this afternoon did I feel people were looking at me and pointing their fingers? I don't know if I've gotten paranoid or what, but even if I am imagining things, it doesn't mean they aren't after me.

"I know, son. Believe me, I've felt some of those same arrows." Her face brightened. "Which is why I think this move will be good for all of us."

After informing the children they would be staying with Pastor Samuel and his wife Friday evening, while she met with her new boss in Atlanta and had dinner with Jim Deaton, she shooed them away from the table. "Finish your homework and get ready for bed."

"Are you going out on a date, Mommie? With a man?"

"A date! I should say not. Sallie. You know Mr. Deaton was my attorney. We have some unfinished business to wrap up, so he asked me to join him for dinner."

"Sounds like a date to me."

"Not you, too, Brian? Besides, Jim, er... Mr. Deaton is several years younger than me."

"I've heard that older women like to date younger men." He flashed her that wicked grin that had once been his mainstay trademark. *Older? How long has it been since Brian felt free enough to grin like that?*

"Well I don't," she declared. "I'm not interested in dating anyone, older or younger. You three get on those books. NOW!"

The children scattered, leaving Margaret alone in the dining room. *A date? They sure didn't indicate they'd be upset if I were to date again.*

❦

The week passed in a blur. Margaret busied herself dealing with the details of Don's estate. She prepared to bid on all the assets they had worked their entire marriage to acquire. *I can't believe I have to suffer this indignity as well. Makes it look like Don didn't care enough for his family to provide even the basics.*

Her dad checked on her during the week. Margaret didn't venture through the gate to her parents' home, nor did her mother call.

Daddy said for me not to look back, nor feel ashamed. That's easier said than done.

She also did a lot of online research into domestic violence, in particular regarding the Georgia organization. When she was shown into Barbara Kirkland's office that Friday afternoon, Margaret felt good about the situation.

I actually feel prepared. Now if only I can ace this test.

The agency head had been on the phone when Margaret arrived, but soon came out of her office to personally welcome the new employee. The two hugged.

"Come in my office and let's visit for a few minutes. Two of my staff are out at the moment. When they return, I'll introduce you to everyone."

Once in the small but tastefully decorated office, Margaret was amused to see a collection of cartoons depicting an crotchety old lady, the creation of a major greeting card company, lining one wall.

"She's my idol, you know."

"Mine, too," Barbara agreed. "She represents all that's crazy about this work we do, as well as some of the crazy notions we have to combat in domestic violence work."

"I get the gist of what you're saying, but you've lost me on the 'crazy notions'."

Barbara Kirkland grinned. "As vital as the work we do is," she explained, "there are so many myths out there that we have to combat." She pointed at the wall of frames. "Some of them make this loony old lady look downright tame."

"Such as?"

"Well..." There was a twinkle in her eye. "You know you weren't really abused because you don't fit the profile."

Margaret felt her left arm tingle. *Was it psychosomatic?* "But I was very much abused. He shattered this arm in several places."

"Oh you were a victim, all right. But you're also attractive, educated and intelligent, drive a luxury automobile and did live in what some would refer to as a mansion. Society cannot see you as a victim. 'Rich' people don't have abuse in their homes."

"I'm far from rich, Barbara."

"Yes, but you don't live in a tumbled down house in the wrong part of town, and look out on life with a slack-jawed expression. In the eyes of society, that makes you immune from domestic violence."

"I wish that were true."

"Let me tell you another popular misconception, and this one exists inside the ranks."

"I don't follow."

Her employer's face was sad. "Simply because someone is male doesn't automatically make him the enemy."

"You mean all men? Anyone who is male is automatically a woman's enemy?"

"That's about the size of things. I encounter it constantly in meetings with my colleagues and shelter leaders. Believe it or not, Margaret, there are actually a couple of state organizations in this country that have male directors."

"I never dreamed that."

"True. But all too often when men want to be our partners, want to believe in our mission and help advance domestic violence awareness and prevention, we slam the door in their faces simply because of their gender."

"That seems so short-sighted. All men aren't vicious and cruel." *Jim Deaton isn't.* "Why the taxi driver who carried me to the hospital the night Don assaulted me was male. He wouldn't take a fare for driving my children to safety before he took me to the ER, and he stayed with me until Annie got there."

"He is one of the friends of our cause who is unfairly tarred, simply because he happens to be of the "wrong" gender." The director slammed her hand down on the arm of the chair where she sat across from Margaret. "This is one of the reasons I was so excited when Annie told me about you. I think our state organization needs a breath of fresh air and vision, in the form of someone who has been a victim instead of an advocate."

She really thinks I can do this job.

"That someone, Margaret, is YOU!"

After a few more minutes of conversation—during which the two discussed salary, working arrangements, and explored the job description Barbara had created—Margaret accepted the position.

She promised to be on the job a week from the following Monday, even though she would still be living in Carter's Crossroads.

"I envision you driving to Atlanta about once a week so we can all put our heads together. Other than that, you should be able to handle all your duties from home."

I can't believe this is really happening. Who would ever have dreamed all that volunteer work I did because of Don's money would land me a paying job? That, and Don's abuse of me. What a bittersweet proposition.

"Welcome aboard, Margaret Haywood. Come meet your co-workers who are ever so excited to get to know you."

The next ninety minutes were spent with the newest employee being introduced to the other seven women who worked in the office, as she attempted to match names with faces and duties.

Will I ever get it straight who is who and who does what? This is going to be one disadvantage of working from home. I won't be seeing them everyday.

As if reading her mind, the receptionist Cathy, whose last name immediately left Margaret's mind, handed her a notebook with a number of pages already inside. "Here's a cheat sheet for you," she explained. "This is a staff directory with job descriptions, phone extensions and e-mail addresses. If there's something you need that I haven't covered, don't hesitate to ask."

Margaret opened the book to discover that in addition to the information promised, each staff member's name was accompanied by a photo. "Oh," she cried, "thank you. This should make everything so much easier."

"You're more than welcome," Cathy assured her. "We're just so thrilled to have someone like you working with us. Barbara hasn't stopped talking about you since she came back from Carter's Crossroads."

What all has Barbara been saying? What promises has she made that I can't fulfill?

"Don't believe everything you hear," she assured the staff

members clustered around her. "My feet are very cracked clay and my pedestal is badly eroded."

"Then you'll fit in beautifully," one of the other staffers volunteered. "We don't tolerate angels or saints easily."

"Fools, either," another chimed in.

I'm going to enjoy working with this crew.

A few minutes past four o'clock, Margaret reluctantly bade her new co-workers farewell, promising to be in touch, as she nagivated the red Lexus toward the Atlanta suburb where Jim Deaton's law office was located.

In some ways I'm going to miss this car, but it represents a part of the past I need to put away. So the Lexus goes.

Although the Friday afternoon traffic was heavy, Margaret managed to reach Jim's office nearly ten minutes before their appointed time. She quickly parked and entered the brick, two-story office building that reminded her of the historic structures in Colonial Williamsburg. After a quick elevator ride to the second floor, she presented herself to the receptionist.

"Oh, yes, Mrs. Haywood. Mr. Deaton's expecting you. Let me tell him you're here."

She picked up the phone, punched a button, and in a matter of seconds was speaking.

"He'll be right out."

Almost before she finished speaking, the door to Jim's office opened as the young attorney hobbled out to greet her.

"Margaret. It's so good to see you again. Especially since I'm not flat on my back this time."

Oh, Jim. What did Don do to you? You're so thin and pale. Your face looks like you've lost weight.

Instead of the thoughts racing through her mind, she said, "Jim. I'm so glad to see you up walking... er..."

"It's not exactly walking yet, my friend. But it will be. Just wait. In the meantime, I hope you didn't plan on dancing tonight."

Dancing? With Jim? Or anyone?

"It never crossed my mind. I was just so anxious to see you, to be sure you were alright."

"Am I?"

"Are you what?"

"Alright. Am I alright?"

"Well, you're... you're..."

He laughed. "Yeah, that's kind of how I was, too. The first time I saw myself in the mirror, I mean."

"Well, you... you don't look... you don't look bad or anything."

"But I don't look like I did. Do I?"

"No, it grieves me to say, you don't." Margaret blushed when she heard her words. "I don't mean you look bad. Or anything... You just look... different, sort of."

"It's okay, I promise you. You didn't look none too good either when you had that wire frame brace on your arm, you know."

"Daddy called it a tomato cage."

Jim pursed his lips and Margaret could see the wheels turning in his head. "Hadn't thought about it like that. Your dad's right. That's exactly what the contraption looked like."

"Felt like it, too," Margaret agreed with a laugh. "Was I ever glad to take it off."

He offered a smile faintly tinged with a bit of grief. "This too shall pass, in time," he said, indicating his cane and the black plastic brace he still wore on his leg. "I simply need more mending."

Time heals a lot of wounds, but I have to wonder if there's any way he can ever be whole again. Oh, Don... you're dead and gone, but the legacy of your anger is still extracting a toll from innocent people.

"Have a seat." Jim pointed to a comfortable wingback chair in the alcove across from his secretary's desk. "Give me about ten minutes to tie up a couple of loose ends. Then we'll be ready to boogie."

"Take your time. I'll be here when you're finished."

※

As she drove the darkened interstate north from Atlanta that night, Margaret's head was spinning.

If I thought my new work experience this afternoon was a load, talking with Jim tonight and learning he's also planning to change careers was even more of a blow. Not that I think he's making a mistake; it's just that I guess I thought he'd always be there if I ever needed him.

It was after ten o'clock before she finally parted company with her attorney. She had called the pastor's home immediately to assure everyone she was on her way.

"Don't worry about it," Susan assured her. "We're watching movies and eating popcorn. If you get here in time, there might be something left for you."

Margaret laughed as the connection ended. *I felt so funny asking Pastor Samuel to babysit my children, but I didn't want them going to Grammy and Grandee. Given how our friends have been acting, I didn't want to take a chance there either.*

Traffic was light on the multi-laned highway. Once she shed the congestion of the metro area, the road was wide open. *It's a good thing I don't have to concentrate heavily on my driving; there's too much going on inside my head.*

Jim had taken her to a new restaurant specializing in southern cuisine with a continental flair. She had chosen the French pot roast cooked with red wine, accompanied by duchess gold potatoes and steamed vegetables, while her host ordered braised pork loin lingonberry with Granny Smith apples in brandy sauce, served in a puff pastry. For dessert they enjoyed key lime pound cake, which gave Margaret a perfect recall of the five magical days she'd spent with Don in Key West shortly after Brian was born. *He said it was a second* honeymoon to celebrate the world's most perfect baby.

"The food was absolutely divine," she informed Jim as she downed the last bite of her cake. "However did you find this place?"

He grinned. "I'd like to say I scoured the city, dispatched all my minions to find the perfect place, but in truth, a client brought me here a few months ago. I've been wanting to come back, but this isn't a place where you come to dine alone."

"My compliments to your client."

"Yeah... it's a shame he's already paid his bill. Now I can't issue a credit to his account." He chuckled.

That laugh of his is wicked. But it feels good to laugh. I'm not sure I could that easily if I knew there was a chance I might never walk normally again.

While they had waited for their food, Jim confided the doctors' fears he might always walk with a limp, severe enough that both tennis and golf would be out of the question.

"So, I may have to make some physical adjustments in my routines and leisure time. But I'm not throwing in the towel until I've given it everything I've got," he assured her. "And if I do walk with a limp, then I walk with a limp."

"I feel so responsible..."

"None of that," he ordered. "We've been over all this. What happened is between Don and me." He displayed the wicked grin again. "Quite frankly, I know I got the better end of the deal."

Margaret knew better than to try to plead her case. Instead, she said, "I've got some news to share with you."

"Is it good news?"

She hesitated. "I think it is. I'm going to work for the Georgia Division of Domestic Violence as a public relations/fund raising employee."

Jim drew back in his chair, his eyes growing large. "Margaret! That's great. I didn't know you were looking for a job."

"I wasn't. It came to me."

She explained about Annie and Barbara's visit to make the offer. "I met with the director earlier this afternoon and I start a week from Monday." *I feel almost giddy.*

Jim rubbed his chin. "They're getting a winner," he crowed. "But are you sure you want to drive into Atlanta everyday?"

"That's the beauty of the job. I may have to be in the office one day a week. The rest of the time I'll be working from home."

"Sounds like a win-win, because you'll be great at the job."

"There's something else."

The expression on his face was one gigantic question mark.

"I'm also moving to Atlanta."

"Are you sure about this? This place is a far cry from Carter's Crossroads."

"That's what I hope." She explained the problems the children were having in school and on the street. Neither did she spare the part about her mother's interference.

"I'm sorry, Margaret. That's one the negatives of a small town."

"Don't I know it?"

"I'm glad you're moving into town then. Sounds like you need a totally clean slate."

"That's an understatement."

"Even if things were fine back at home, that commute into town each day is a killer. Trust me, I know."

"You don't live that far away. Do you?" *I know you've got the lake house down on Oconee, but where do you live here in town?*

"My condo's only ten minutes from the office, but when I go to the lake, I'd almost rather take a beating than fight the traffic into the office. Thank goodness that's about to come to a screeching halt."

"It is?"

Another grin. "That's why I asked you out tonight. I wanted to tell you about my new job. However I think you got the jump on me."

"New job? But you're a lawyer. You've already got a job."

"Let me see if I can explain..." Jim related how the days in bed following Don's attempt to murder him had caused him to totally re-examine his life. "God and I had a lot of time to talk. For a change, I let Him do most of the talking. I did a lot of listening."

He explained how he had gone into law because his father was a judge who killed his mother and got off with a light prison sentence. "I wanted vengeance for my mom, but there was no way I could extract even an ounce of blood from my old man. The only way I could figure to get it was by taking on other scumbags like him, seeing that they literally didn't get away with murder."

"What's wrong with that? Sounds most honorable to me."

"There's nothing wrong with my motives. What was wrong is that I was doing it with hate in my heart for the abuser, instead of love for the victim."

Gosh, Jim's a lot deeper than I ever realized. I would never have made that distinction.

"While I lay there in that bed, wondering if I would ever walk again, two major light bulbs flashed." He looked at her with what she could only interpret as wonder in his eyes. "The first was that walking with a limp would be wonderful. Every time I took a step, I'd be reminded of my own mortality."

Margaret had tears in her eyes, but managed to ask, "And the other epiphany?"

"That you can build better things from a basis of love than you can ever hope to build from a platform of hate. I've been going at it backwards. No wonder I didn't feel fulfilled."

"Oh, Jim. It sounds like you did do a lot of soul-searching. I never dreamed you felt the way you did. You were such... I mean, you ARE such a good attorney."

"But I think I'll be a better victim's rights legal advocate to the National Coalition for Domestic Violence, don't you think?"

"The National Coalition? You're putting me on."

He held up his hand scout-fashion. "On my honor, I'm going to work for them. One of the best things about the whole deal is I'll be working primarily from home, just like you. Which means I can live at the lake."

"Jim! That's great. Congratulations."

I knew he really wanted to move back to the lake.

"So when does all this take place?"

Jim motioned to the server for a refill on their coffee, then went on to tell Margaret all about the job. "It will take a couple of months to wind up my law practice. I don't want to leave anyone in a lurch, so I'll transfer my clients to other attorneys."

"That's why I liked you. You're so dependable. So tell me, how did all this come about? After all, you've been hospitalized until just a few days ago."

His face shown so brightly, Margaret thought it must be illuminated by celestial light.

"That's the main reason I wanted to tell you my news in person. If it weren't for you, I wouldn't have gotten the opportunity." He dropped his head, only briefly. When he raised his eyes again, Margaret saw they had tears in them.

If it weren't for me? I didn't do anything!

"Jim! What's wrong?"

"That's just it, Margaret. There's nothing wrong. In fact, everything's right."

"You've lost me."

"God is so good. He can turn the ugliest situation into an object of beauty. Only He can make something good, something positive out of all the trauma you and I have endured."

"Jim..."

"Just listen, Margaret. About a week after Don shot me, on one of the first days that I can even remember at all, I had a visitor. By this time, Don had already been killed and all our names were being bandied about on national TV."

"How well I remember. I couldn't believe small town people from Carter's Crossroads could be that interesting to people in Maine and California. I would give anything if it had never happened."

"But if it hadn't happened, don't you see, I would never have had this opportunity?"

Margaret leaned across the table, took Jim's hands and squeezed. "Would you please get to the point and tell me how Don getting killed, and you getting shot, got you a new career?"

There was that laugh again. "I'm sorry. I'm still just so blown away by all that's happened. I couldn't wait to tell you."

"Doesn't appear as if you're having too hard a job holding back right now."

"I'm sorry. Here's the scoop. Someone connected with the National Coalition happened to be watching the *TODAY Show* when our segment aired. If you remember, you gave them a few comments on the whole ordeal."

"Yes, I did. That was before I learned the hard way that the more I said, the more I had to say. I finally wised up and shut up."

"Well, I'm thankful you hadn't locked your lips at that point, because between what you said, and what the reporter said, these folks at the Coalition were intrigued by me. They did some background digging, found out about Mom and the old man, and how my practice has specialized in domestic violence related cases."

I know where this is going. Oh, God. Thank you for giving both of us something positive out of this nightmare.

He paused for a sip of coffee. "Three different times, people from Washington flew to Atlanta to talk with me. The last time they came, they made me an offer I couldn't refuse. They were even willing to wait until I finished my rehab and recovery, giving me time to close down the practice."

Margaret was near tears herself. "Oh, Jim. I don't want to say all this was worth the pain and suffering... the grief and embarrassment. But it is comforting to realize how God can create so much good."

As she neared the interstate exit that would take her to pick up her children, she knew she had a lot to share with them over breakfast the next morning. *Including the fact that I might have found a rental home in Atlanta we could all enjoy. I can't believe Jim offered to lease me his condo. He said if I didn't take it, someone else would. He's determined to move to the lake full-time. I'll never forget his words.*

"God has sent me a renter I can depend on, so I can go to the lake without worrying about my property. See, He even took care of all our housing needs."

"But Jim, I don't know how long I'll be living there. I'm going to be looking for a place to buy."

"When you find it, buy it. Until then, rent my condo for as long as you need it. When you need to move, no problem."

Talk about an easy-going landlord. In truth, Lord, I was dreading having to go through the rental process. I guess I've been a homeowner too long.

CHAPTER FOUR

*M*argaret woke to see that the clock read eight-fifty-five. *Oh my gosh. I've overslept.* Then, as she was struggling to roll out of bed, she realized the house was totally quiet.

There's no TV noise. No sounds coming from the kitchen. Even the kids are playing lazy this morning. I might as well join 'em.

She fell back into bed, where she floated between drowsy and semi-awake until finally, when the clock read nine-forty-nine, she made herself get up.

If this is what the morning after a Friday night date is going to be like, I'd better not get back out there. I'm too old to be a social butterfly.

In the kitchen, rifling through cabinets and the refrigerator while trying to decide what to cook for breakfast, inspiration hit her. *We're going to Atlanta for brunch. Then I'll drive the children by to see Jim's condo since he gave me a key last night. He won't be there. He was going to spend the night at a hotel because of the stairs.*

She hurried to wake the kids, all three of whom moaned and complained. "Get up," she encouraged them. "Hit the showers. We're driving in to Atlanta for late brunch. Then I've got a surprise for you."

"What is it, Mom?"

"Un-uh, Brian. It's a secret."

"You wouldn't be trying to bribe us, would you, Mom?"

"Maybe not. Maybe. I'm not talking." She waved her hands. "Now go on, get ready. I'm hungry and it's a long way to Atlanta."

∽

"Mommie, this place is beautiful."

"It is pretty, isn't it, Sallie?"

The four Haywood's had indulged in a delightful brunch at the hotel's restaurant. Then, without forewarning, Margaret drove them to the address Jim had given her the previous evening.

I've never been here, nor am I familiar with this part of Atlanta. But I like what I see. It's only fifteen minutes or so to the office whenever I have to go.

She drove as cautiously as Saturday morning traffic would allow, looking at each street sign until finally, she spotted the chic boutique with the distinctive lime green and turquoise exterior. *Jim said that was my landmark.*

"Just past that neon building, on the right, is Prado Way. Turn right. Go two blocks and turn left. After one block more, turn left again. My condo is number 721. Light tan stucco with burgundy shutters and a leaded glass front door."

Margaret executed the turns as directed. Within a matter of minutes, she was sitting in front of a three-story condo with a coastal accent to its exterior.

"Why are we here, Mommie?"

"I'll bet I know," Brian boasted. "Is this by any chance where we're going to live?"

Margaret turned so she could face all three of her children. "This condo belongs to Jim Deaton, only he's had to move to his lake house because of the stairs. He's offered to rent it to us for as long as we need it."

"Oh, Mommie. I wouldn't be embarrassed to live here."

I still haven't had a talk with that child. Her materialism bothers me.

"This is a nice complex, but it doesn't matter how it looks, Sallie. The important thing is that we're all together."

Sallie said nothing but Margaret could see the little rebuke had caused a big case of hurt feelings.

"Come on. I've got the key. Shall we go in?"

Margaret stood on the second level of the two-story foyer. She was thrilled to see this was a corner unit with some pretty woodland views. *This place is gorgeous. You'd never know a man lived here alone. I wonder if he used a decorator or if design is another of his many talents?*

"Hey, Mom, come up here."

Margaret looked above her, toward the sound of the voice, to find all three children hanging over the balcony railing.

"You gotta see this place up here."

I really wanted to finish seeing this floor first. But I need them to be excited.

She took the curving staircase to the top floor landing where the children began to all speak at once.

"There's a room for Brian and a room for me," Jason volunteered. "I don't know if I want to be away from Brian."

"Neither one of you had better have picked my room. I get the one with the window seat."

"Now Sallie..."

"Mom. Get a load of the master bedroom. You're gonna love it."

Just as Brian had predicted, Margaret did fall in love with the master suite.

Even the colors are my favorites. My furniture and bedding from the house will work wonderfully in here.

Then she allowed the children to show her the rooms they'd selected for themselves.

Thank goodness neither of the boys had dibs on Sallie's choice. That's one bit of confusion we didn't need. I can't believe this place has four bedrooms. I'll have to ask Jim if he was planning a large family.

When it came to the rooms for Jason and Brian, which conveniently had a Jack-and-Jill bath arrangement, it seemed that Jason most wanted the room that Brian had selected.

"Hey, it's okay," the older boy said, tousling his little brother's hair. "I don't mind taking the other room. This one is yours, sport."

Margaret felt a sob choke in her throat as she marveled at the mature gentleness with which he handled the issue. *Thank you, God, for giving Brian the heart to understand his little brother. I'll have to do something for him later.*

She did offer her eldest a nod of her heard, which he acknowledged with understanding.

"Hey, Jason. Look." Brian was showing his brother the bathroom. "Even though we'll be in separate rooms, we won't really be apart. All we have to do is leave both bathroom doors open. It'll be like we're together in one big room."

Afraid she would embarrass herself, not to mention her children, Margaret beat a hasty retreat to the master suite.

I don't deserve a son as compassionate as Brian. Thank you, Lord.

By the time the children trouped back through what would be her bedroom, Margaret had gotten hold of her emotions. She was ready to share how their furniture would work in the new house.

"This place won't hold everything we've got on Redbud Way."

"That's why we'll have to pick and choose some things. What won't work here, we'll put in storage."

"How soon are we moving, Mommie?"

"It'll be a couple of months yet."

All three faces fell.

"That long? You're supposed to start your new job in a week."

"Jim's got to have time to get moved out. Plus I've got legal matters to deal with in Carter's Crossroads."

She was making her way back down the stairs as she talked. "We've got to have time to get packed before moving. As for my job, since I'm going to be working mostly from home—regardless of where home is—that's not a problem."

Margaret checked to be certain they'd turned out all the lights and the security panel was armed, as Jim had instructed. Then she ushered the children outside before pulling the door shut behind them.

Home sweet home. Or at least it soon will be.

"How would you like to take in a movie before we head back? Maybe that new Matthew McConaughey picture... I can't think of the title?"

There was much discussion among the three, before Sallie announced, "That'll be good, Mom. Can we go out to eat when it's over?"

"We ate brunch out. Isn't twice in one day a bit extravagant?"

"It'll probably be time for supper when the movie's over."

"Point taken, Brian." Margaret thought for a second. "Supper in town it is, but with two conditions."

"What are conditions, Mommie?"

"She means if we stay in Atlanta to eat, we have to give up something else, sport."

Very intuitive, Brian.

"First, we don't tank up on high-priced goodies at the theatre, because then we won't be hungry enough to eat out. Second, we don't go anywhere expensive. It may just be burgers or pizza."

The children agreed as Margaret headed to a theater that had been one of their favorites in happier times. She was thankful it was playing the movie they wanted.

There's no time like the present to begin teaching the fact that we can't blow money the way we once did. There's nothing wrong with conditions.

"It's good to see you and the children out and about," Annie commented on Sunday. "Especially in church."

"Not nearly as good as it is to know that in a matter of weeks, we'll be in a new place," replied Margaret. "A place where we can really begin to heal. My three children have been through an absolute nightmare."

"Barbara called me after your meeting on Friday. She is absolutely on top of the world."

"I'm pretty excited myself. But hey… you get all the credit. You're the one who told her about me."

Annie hugged her. "But you sold yourself. You had a lot to sell. Believe me, Margaret, this is a terrific solution for everyone."

The two exited the sanctuary, speaking to Pastor Samuel at the front door, where Margaret thanked him again for babysitting.

Annie then pulled her friend away from the crowd in the church yard. "How is everyone with the prospect of moving?"

"The children are excited, especially with Jim Deaton's condo. I've still got to resolve the school issue. I can't decide between public school, which would be so much less expensive, and private school."

"I'd say find out what public schools are in the district. There are some very good public schools in Atlanta. Check them out. Then, if you aren't satisfied, look at the other option."

"Sounds like a solution. Now if you could just resolve the issue of how my mama is going to react when she finds out, I'd have no other worries."

"You haven't told your folks?"

"I told Daddy. But since we both knew how Mama would react, we agreed to wait until after I met with Barbara to tell her. We figured it best to wait until everything was official before we dropped that bombshell."

"Probably wasn't a bad idea. You really think Miss Ruby's gonna give you grief?"

"Nothing else I've done in the past seven months has met with her approval. You tell me."

Annie nodded her head. "You're probably right. So when are you going to tell her?"

"I'd like to wait until tomorrow morning, when the kids are in school, so that Daddy and I can sit down with her. I simply want get it over. She refused to take "no" for an answer to her invitation to lunch today, so this Haywood Four, as Jason has begun to describe us, are on our way there now. I'm not particularly comfortable with that prospect. But, now that we've gotten roped into it, I just pray all this won't get spilled in the middle of dessert."

Her prayers were answered... sort of. It didn't get spilled in the middle of dessert. It happened much sooner than that, in the middle of the roast beef and potato pancakes. They never got to dessert.

"So what did you children do yesterday?" Grammy asked as everyone dug into their food. "I came over several times, but no one seemed to be home."

"We went out to brunch, went to a movie and ate pizza for supper. Oh, we also looked at our new condo." Jason's face glowed with pride at what he considered an accomplishment.

"Jason, who never opens his mouth," Margaret relayed to P.C. later that same evening, "was suddenly a fount of information. Sallie? I'd expect that out of her. Not Jason."

"Condo!" Ruby Maxwell, her eyes shooting daggers, looked at her daughter. "Can't keep from spending Don's hard-earned money, can you? You've bought a condo when you've got a perfectly beautiful home! Not to mention we bought you a house as well!"

"No, Grammy. You don't understand," Sallie piped up. "The condo is in Atlanta. Where we're moving."

Margaret had never seen a person rise up in their chair as if by levitation, but that's exactly what it appeared her mother was doing.

"You're moving to Atlanta? I've never heard such nonsense."

"Ruby, we don't need to interrupt this delicious meal. Margaret and I will talk to you about this after we finish and the children have gone home."

The older woman fixed her husband with an icy stare. "You and Margaret will talk to me. Does this mean you've known about this and didn't tell me?"

Margaret could see her father's hesitation.

"She did tell me there was a possibility this might happen. The last time we talked, nothing was definite."

"Old man, have you gone as crazy as your daughter?"

"Ruby Maxwell, you will not speak to me in that tone of voice and you certainly won't refer to your daughter as crazy."

"What would you call it? The whole town is talking about how she made a complete fool out of Don. She backed that poor man into a corner and then set him up to be killed."

"Now wait just a minute, Mama..."

"I'm not talking to you. Yet." Mrs. Maxwell shook a finger in Margaret's face. "Right now I'm trying to straighten out an old fool." She turned back to her husband. "Now Harold, you listen to me..."

"No, both of you listen to me." Margaret rose clumsily from her seat, pushing the chair back under the table. "I know it's a sin to waste food, Mama, but I've had all of this I can stomach. Come on, kids. We're leaving."

She wrapped her arm around Brian's shoulders as she motioned for the two younger children to precede him.

"But I'm still hungry," Sallie wailed. "We don't have anything at home to eat."

"You leave that child here to finish her dinner. That's what kind of mother you've become. You'd let your children go hungry."

"I'll gladly take you somewhere to eat, Sallie, but we aren't staying here. This isn't open for discussion." She gave her daughter a shove. "Go!"

Walking out of her parents' house, leaving her daddy to face Miss Ruby's wrath alone, was one of the hardest things Margaret had ever done. Yet she knew the alternative would be to say something she'd later regret.

No one said anything until they were through the gate into their own back yard.

"Grammy was really coming down on Grandee."

"Yes, she was, Brian. Unfortunately I'm afraid he's taken a lot of grief on our behalf over the last few months."

"I don't like it when Grammy gets mad," Jason said quietly. "It scares me and makes me not want to love her."

Her son's words cut straight to the quick, causing yet another blow to Margaret's heart, which was already breaking. "It's not that Grammy doesn't love you... all of you," she explained, as she knelt down in front of the little boy. "She does love you very much, and she worries about you. Which is why she's so hard to live with right now."

"She says none of this should have happened," volunteered Sallie.

"Yes, honey. I know. But let's don't talk about it anymore now."

As if she hadn't heard a word her mother said, Sallie continued, "I heard her telling one of her friends on the phone the other day that she didn't know where you got your stubborn streak." She halted to catch her breath. "She said if you'd been a good wife, you would have been there for Daddy whenever he got angry. Then none of this would have happened."

"I know, Sallie. I know what she says. But in this case, whether she's my mama or not, she's wrong." She fixed her daughter with a hard stare. "So what do you want to eat? I know we're all hungry."

The children shifted from one foot to the other until, finally, Jason said, "I don't want anything."

"How about you, Sallie? You said you were still hungry."

"I don't think I want anything, either." she answered slowly, her voice totally lacking its usual bravado.

"Brian?"

"Nah... er, I mean, no ma'am, I'm not hungry either."

A most subdued group, they filed silently into the house where the children scattered to their rooms. Margaret retreated to her bedroom with the beginning of what she recognized as a killer headache.

How much of it is hunger and how much is stress? It doesn't matter. I'm not in the mood for anything to eat, nor do I know how to get rid of all this stress. I just hope things will be better once we move.

After promising herself to repeat the offer to take the children out to eat later, Margaret stretched across her bed. When drowsiness struck, she didn't resist.

I would have thought with a new job that I'm going to love and a beautiful place to call home, I'd be celebrating this afternoon. Instead, I'm taking to my bed with a headache. There's definitely something wrong with this picture.

When the noise began, Margaret thought she was dreaming. In her mind's eye, she kept reaching for one phone after another, only the ringing sound continued. Finally the incessant noise penetrated her consciousness. It was her cell phone, beside her on the bed, issuing the summons. As she reached for the offending appliance, she realized the sun was coming through the mini-blinds at an almost horizontal angle.

It must be pretty late. Have I slept all afternoon? "Hello?"

"Margaret? I was worried about you."

"Daddy. Where are you?"

"I'm riding around town. Anything to get away from your mother."

"I'm sorry I've gotten you into so much hot water. Daddy, I never dreamed Mama could be so obstinate."

"I'll have to admit, I've never seen her this bad in all the years we've been married."

She raised herself up on one elbow to where she could see the clock. Four-fifty-nine! *Good grief. It's almost supper time.*

"I only wish I could understand why she has taken such a personal crusade for Don against me. I mean, Don's own mother didn't take on even one-tenth the way Mama has. You remember how strangely she acted. Mama thought it was disgraceful, but I think the way she's acting is just as bad."

Margaret could still recall the exchange with Don's mother at the funeral. *I cannot call her my mother-in-law because I only saw the woman a total of three times in all these years. I couldn't believe she came to the funeral. Not that she showed any grief. She never even acted like the kids were her grandchildren – much less her only grandchildren.*

It was one of those watershed moments you always remember. The day, what the weather was like, who was standing where and what color clothes they were wearing. Even though Margaret didn't have a clue where Don's mother lived, and was uncertain whether his father was even still alive, P.C. had convinced her she needed to at least make an attempt to contact the woman.

I'd never been able to believe Mrs. Haywood didn't love her son. How can you not love someone you carried inside of you for almost a year, for whom you struggled to give life? If it was any of my three, I'd want to know.

P.C. had successfully reported to Margaret that Mrs. Haywood was coming to the service. At the funeral home beforehand, Margaret was approached by the funeral director, with an older woman in tow whom she didn't immediately recognize.

She had aged so much, and she'd changed her hair color. She looked like a little munchkin. If I hadn't been looking her straight in the face, and hadn't seen the resemblance to Don, I might never have recognized her. What really bowled me over was how she addressed me.

"It's Margaret, isn't it?" the little woman asked hesitantly. "I've never been totally sure what your name is."

"Yes, it's Margaret. I'm glad you could come. I just wish it weren't what it is."

Her mother-in-law's face assumed a stony expression. "I always knew Donnie would do something like this some day. He was headed to no good a long time ago."

"Still, you have to be hurting. I'm sorry I had to be the one to bring you here."

"Children are nothing but cause for heartache. That's why I'm glad I only had Donnie. Wouldn't have had him if I could have helped it."

I was in a state of shock. But that was nothing compared to what I felt when I introduced her to the children.

Brian had intercepted his mother's signal and corralled his sister and brother to bring them to where Margaret stood.

"Children, this is your dad's mother, your grandmother. Mrs. Haywood, this is Brian, Sallie and Jason." As she called their names, she touched each one on the shoulder. "These are your grandchildren you've never met."

The children stood with deer-in-the-headlight expressions on their faces unsure, Margaret could tell, how to respond. Before they could say anything, the elder Mrs. Haywood spoke.

"Three children are just three times the opportunity to have your heart broken. I pity you."

She walked away, never even speaking to the children, and took a seat on the back row of the chapel. Just as Mr. Haywood and she did at our wedding.

Try as she might, Margaret couldn't get Don's mother to sit with the family. In the end, she finally abandoned her quest to be polite. As soon as the minister pronounced the benediction and the casket was being loaded for the cemetery, Margaret saw her mother-in-law heading toward a gold Lincoln Town Car in the funeral home parking lot. The last anyone saw of the woman was her car cutting in front of the hearse, as she headed back to the small mountain town where P.C. said she now lived as a widow.

I guess she didn't even reach out to tell Don when his father died. Dead or not, she's still as much under his father's thumb and influence now as ever.

Her children had never asked why their grandmother treated them as though they were invisible. Margaret never volunteered any explanation.

"Let's face it, Margaret. Strange is one of the most polite ways I know to describe every encounter we've ever had with Don's parents. Even way back."

"I know, Dad. But I can't explain them any more than I can explain Mama. She's acting like a woman possessed."

"She'll get over it. Like she'll get over her objections to you taking that job and moving to Atlanta."

"You talked to her, huh?"

"I figured it had to happen sooner or later. What did I have to lose?"

"She didn't take it well."

"That's one way of putting it."

"Are you alright, Dad?"

"I'm alright. Heartbroken and disappointed, but I'm alright."

"Heartbroken and disappointed?"

"Hang on, let me pull over and stop. I'm getting too close to home and I don't want Ruby to see me drive by."

Poor Daddy. He's trying to protect me.

"She doesn't see why you need a job in the first place. Yet at the same time, she doesn't want to be held up to ridicule because you go through Don's money in less than a year and become homeless."

"You have got to be kidding."

"Afraid not, sugh. She's convinced you have no head for money and you're headed for ruin. Don made it and you're going to blow it, just to spite him."

She just gets more bizarre by the day.

"What about my job?"

"She feels you set out to destroy your marriage, to destroy Don simply because he had a few faults. Never mind the lavish lifestyle he provided for all of you."

"A few faults!"

"Just quoting your mama, honey. Not saying I agree."

"What else? You might as well tell me everything."

"She believes that organization you're going to work for trains women to destroy their marriages and hurt their children."

"I can't believe it. She can't be serious?"

"But she is," he said sadly. "I don't think there's anything you or I can do to change her mind."

"I just never…"

"Like I told you earlier, don't you let her get to you. Don't let her convince you that you're the one at fault. I know for myself all that happened. I loved Don like the son we never had, but I also recognized that he had his faults. I just didn't understand the full extent."

"That's because I didn't let you know. I was too ashamed."

"Look, I'd better be getting back to the house. I've got to try to get her calmed down. Just stay clear for a few days. I'll be talking to you."

"Will do, Dad."

I never thought I'd see the day I'd be hiding from Mama. Never mind, I think it's best this time.

❦

Hang the cost! I'm hungry and I want something to eat, even if we have to go out.

Margaret had wandered into the kitchen following the conversation with her father. While rambling in the cabinets and refrigerator in search of something to cook for the evening meal, Sallie showed up at the doorway.

"I'm hungry."

"Me, too, honey. Only I don't know what I want and for some reason I'm just not in the mood to cook."

"I know what I'd like."

"You do? What would that be?"

"I'm hungry for breakfast."

"That does sound good. I assume you're talking about bacon, eggs, grits, biscuits and gravy?"

"Maybe some cinnamon apples?"

"That works for me, only I don't have all the ingredients for that meal."

"Can we go out?"

"Sure. Why not? Where are the guys?"

"In their room, I guess. Want me to go get 'em?"

"Ask them to come help us decide about supper."

A few minutes later, they all piled into the red Lexus and headed out. Brian was driving.

He's been so mature about everything lately, I need to start giving him some freedom. I had thought I'd trade Don's SUV and this car in on whatever I buy. Maybe I should give the SUV to Brian instead. If he wants it.

Don's bronze Ford Explorer was only one of the items of property she would have to purchase from the estate.

I'll be so glad when all that's behind me.

They ended up at a restaurant in the next town that served breakfast all day long. Before they left, they had more than compensated for the loss of lunch. It was a lighthearted time around the table. No one mentioned the scene at noon until they were nearly ready to leave. Jason, who'd seemed to be in a world of his own, hadn't entered into the conversation free-for-all.

"Mommie?"

"Yes, Jason?"

The little boy began to sob so hard that his body shook. "I'm sorry I told Grammy about the condo in Atlanta. I didn't mean to make her mad."

Margaret was out of her seat and around the table faster than even she realized she could move. Once she'd embraced the child, she replied, "You didn't do anything wrong, Jason. I promise you, you didn't do anything to make Grammy angry. I'm sorry you had to hear all of that, but I am not mad at you. Not at all."

"Really, Mommie?"

"Really, truly. Scout's honor." She held up her hand.

The tremors in his small body lessened. She took her finger and raised his chin, noticing a small smile playing about the corners of his mouth.

"Come on. Smile for me. You know you want to."

༄

Margaret closed down the house and got ready for bed before she picked up her phone to call Tennessee. *I just want to have a nice, long conversation with P.C. I really need to vent and unload while picking her brain. This is going to be her lucky night!*

"Honestly, P.C., I've about had all I can take of people hurting my children."

"Do I hear the mama lioness roaring?"

"Not just roaring. I'm about to sink my fangs into a few people if things don't lighten up. Mama made a nervous wreck out of my children today. Naturally Jason blames himself."

"Children always think they're the reason things go bad."

"That's the way things were with Don. Back then, I stood by and let it happen. Mama isn't going to do another number on these kids."

She shared all the details about Jim's condo, her impressions of her soon-to-be coworkers, and how anxious she was to leave Carter's Crossroads behind.

"I never thought I'd see the day I'd even want to leave here, let alone be excited about the prospect. Now I'm more than ready to go somewhere we can all make a fresh start."

"So you're really going to sell the house on Redbud Way? You don't think you might want to hold on to it, in case you change your mind down the road?"

"Even if I did think I'd like to come back here to live, that house has too many bad memories. Besides, I'll inherit Mama and Daddy's house at some point..." She paused as the impact of what she'd just said hit her squarely in the face. "Not that I'm wishing them gone. However, perhaps I shouldn't count on their house after all. Mama would probably see a total stranger have it over me. Especially with the way she feels about me right now."

As she lay propped up on pillows and upholstered backrest for her nightly read, Margaret could see out the large, double windows of the master bedroom down the hill to her parents' home. Lights were still on in the den, but they were also on in the bedroom her parents occupied.

In all the weeks we've lived here, I never realized until now that I could actually look down and see their house. When you're in the other end of this house, the privacy fence blocks the view. Since lights are on in two different rooms at this time of night, they must be in different rooms as well.

"I tell you, P.C., I never in a million years dreamed I'd have to deal with this. It's like Mama is totally blind to every fault Don had. She's incapable of believing I can do anything right."

"I know it's rough," her friend commiserated, "but you can't let it get you down."

"Tell me about it."

The two talked for a few more minutes before P.C. asked, "About your house there, if you aren't planning to keep it, how hard do you think it will be to sell? The real estate market is more than a little depressed right now."

She isn't asking anything I haven't already asked myself.

"For sure it's not going to be the home everyone is looking for. That house was built on a large lot with a large family in mind. It'll have a pretty hefty price tag, but I'm willing to negotiate."

I'm not worried about the economy as much as I am everyone in this town knowing who lived there and what happened.

"You're right, it isn't your typical family home."

Margaret yawned in spite of her best intentions. "Hey, friend, that yawn wasn't because of you. It's just I'm getting weary all of a sudden. I think I'd better try to get some rest."

"That makes two of us. Call me tomorrow."

"Will do."

After she put down the phone, Margaret crawled off the bed to retrieve her Bible. *I don't know how I would have made it through these past few months without this Bible and God. Even when Jason was hanging between life and death after Don assaulted him, God kept me grounded and positive. I thought it was bad, Don shooting Jim, but being arrested was even worse. The hardest time, though, was driving to Atlanta when Don was killed.*

She opened the Bible to her favorite passage in Psalms. "I will lift up mine eyes unto the hills from whence cometh my help." *Oh, how true those words are. I've often wondered if the fact that your eyes are lifted upward means you don't see all the negatives that would trip you up, and you have to walk by faith?*

Reading until her soul felt as fed as she had been earlier in the evening, she engaged in a comfortable time of conversational prayer with the God she had come to depend on totally. It wasn't until Margaret put out the bedside lamp, and was in her comfortable, familiar sleeping position, that she again thought about her mother's actions.

Somehow I've got to reach her, to find out why she's reacting the way she is. You're gonna have to help me, Lord.

CHAPTER FIVE

*M*onday morning began with Margaret sensing an unsettled feeling that she had numerous tasks to accomplish before she officially reported to her home office.

I'm feeling very inadequate for this job. Am I making a mistake?

Once the kids had caught the van for school, she began looking at her temporary office—also known as the dining room—while pondering how she could craft herself a better work space.

I don't want to spend a lot of money on things I can't take to Jim's condo, but I need something more user friendly than an eating table and a straight chair. Plus I need some spreading out space.

The more she looked, the more she realized her office setup from the house on Redbud Way was the solution.

But I don't own that yet? Do I?

In a move more characteristic of her old self, Margaret grabbed the phone and dialed Joe Busbee. Joe had been Don's attorney before the two fell out over the way Don was jerking Margaret around. She had to wait several minutes before the receptionist would put her through to Joe's phone.

"Margaret. It's good to hear your voice." His voice dropped a couple of octaves. "Sorry they gave you the run-around at the front. The new receptionist still seems incapable of judging situations individually."

"Not to worry, Joe. I am an intruder this morning."

"You're never the intruder. I've given strict orders that whenever you call, you're not to be kept waiting."

"Oh come, Joe, I'm not that important." *Or infamous, I hope!*

"To what do I owe the pleasure this fine Monday morning?"

Margaret explained about the job, her need for a professional-caliber home office, and then posed her questions about her possessions in the other house.

"I don't want to buy what I already have, but do I already have it? Can I legally remove that furniture before I own it?"

Because Don had left no will, the estate had been thrown into the county probate court with another attorney being appointed administrator. Joe Busbee had applied, but the judge, who had a reputation for being difficult, stated his preference for someone fresh to the picture. Instead, he appointed Bobby Jackson, an attorney whose name Margaret recognized from the next town.

I'm not certain I totally trust this guy, which is why I'm talking to Joe.

"There shouldn't be any reason why you can't take furniture out, as long as you don't empty the entire house, and as long as it's your office furniture and equipment. You'd need to touch base with the administrator before you do anything."

"I don't like him, Joe. Call me crazy, but I don't trust him. I don't want to deal with him one on one."

"Want me to call him for you?"

"Would you? I expect to pay you. In fact, it occurs to me that I need an attorney in my corner through all of this. There's no one I'd rather have than you." She hesitated, fearful she'd said too much, putting him on a spot. "Unless you're uncomfortable because... well, you know, because..."

"Margaret, don't be embarrassed. If you want me to represent you, it would be my pleasure."

"You'll charge me the same as anyone else for the same work."

"I hear you. Let me put in a call to Mr. Jackson. I'll get back to you."

"Thanks, Joe. I owe you. Literally."

"Margaret… this is just a thought. There are a couple of nice, empty offices at Haywood Tufters. If you didn't want the hassle of setting up an office at home, you could always use one of those. You'd already have fax and copy machines at your fingertips."

There's no way!

"At the end of the day, the less I see of that business, the better I'll like it. There's just too much of Don there for my comfort."

"Hey, I understand perfectly. While we're talking, Margaret, I'm sorry you're leaving town, but I understand. It's probably for the best."

"Yeah, everyone around here is angry with me. It seems I did poor Don dirty."

"Oh, they're angry alright, but it's less about Don and more about which of them got interviewed, or at least pictured on national TV, and who didn't."

What? "You are joking. Right?"

"I've been known to do that on occasion, but this isn't one of those times. I'm serious. That's the big burr under their saddles."

"Well I never."

"Let me call Bobby. I'll get back to you shortly."

Margaret spent the day cleaning house, deciding where to place the office pieces from the other house while making lists of furniture they'd take to Atlanta, and which pieces they'd store.

I didn't bring anything other than clothing and personal items when we moved here. Daddy bought the place fully furnished. At that point I would have slept on the floor rather than move all that stuff.

Her father called mid-afternoon. "Your mama is still on a tear, hon. I'm sorry."

"I'm sorry, too. If you need to come over here, you know you're welcome."

"That really would set Ruby on her ear. Nope. The best way to handle this is stay close and wear her down."

※

"Bobby Jackson doesn't have a problem with you moving your office furniture, but he says he has to be there so he can certify everything for the court."

"That's crazy, Joe. I'm no crook. Besides, I shouldn't even have to be going through this nightmare. It's insane."

"I couldn't agree more, Margaret. That's why I didn't call until this morning. I knew what your reaction was going to be."

"I've got to have an office, but I refuse to buy something I already own. I guess I'll have to play by his rules."

"Shall I tell him it's a go? When do you want to get the stuff?"

Margaret thought for a moment. "I need it this week, so I can get things set up over the weekend. But I want you to go with me. I'm not going to be alone with that jerk."

"He's not really a jerk, you know. It's just he has a sworn responsibility to the court so he's covering his behind."

"Pardon me, Joe, if I'm overly-sensitive, but I've been put in this position by one man who felt he could run rough-shod over me. I'm a little leery of giving this man the same latitude."

"I understand, Margaret. Yet you've got to respect his legal position. He had nothing to do with Don's actions or, more precisely, his inactions."

"Whatever, it'll all be okay as long as you're there with me."

"That's a problem, my friend. If you need to get it this week, I can't be there. I'm leaving right after lunch today for Savannah to try a case. Won't be back until late Friday night. Might even be Saturday, if we run late."

"Joe," she wailed. "I can't do this without you."

"Sure you can. Bobby Jackson's a gentleman. How about if I caution him about his actions?"

"No, Joe. I need you."

"Not if you've got to get that stuff this week. Next week I'm available..."

"Joe!"

The silence between the two of them was uncomfortable.

"Hey, how about this? P.C.'s coming to town tomorrow. What if she went with you?"

P.C.'s coming down? She didn't tell me anything when we talked Sunday night. "Since when? I talked to her over the weekend." *What reason would she have for coming to town?*

"It wasn't decided until last night when we talked."

There's something he isn't telling me. I'll let it drop for right now. "Sure Joe. I'll be fine with P.C. I just don't want to be over there alone with Mr. Jackson."

"Why don't I see if he can meet you sometime Thursday after lunch? If I don't get back to you, my secretary will."

"That's great Joe. Thanks. Have a good trip to Savannah."

"It'll be all work and no pleasure, but it pays the bills."

"Okay, well... travel safe." She paused, debating her options. "Say Joe... do I need to clean off a bed for P.C.?"

"P.C.? Uh, no. She's staying at my house, while I'm in Savannah, to look after the dog and my plants. You know how I hate to board Rufus. He sulks for a week after he comes home."

Rufus was a big, overgrown golden lab who was so lazy, the energy it would take to sulk was more than he was willing to invest. *If using Rufus gives Joe an excuse for P.C. to come to town, who am I to point out that his dog is a comatose couch potato who doesn't care where he is?* "Yeah, those plants have to be watered just so."

Joe's blush was evident all the way through the phone. "Don't be tacky, Margaret," he said finally. "I'll talk to you over the weekend."

If I didn't know better, I'd say we have a romance on the blossom.

That night after the supper dishes were done and she had double-checked the kids' homework, Margaret put in a call to P.C.

"Hear you're coming down tomorrow."

"Well... uh... uh, yeah. Joe called and invited me to house-sit."

"So you're going to leave your law practice and come down here to walk Rufus and water a few plants?"

"Um, yeah, I guess. Besides, nothing much is happening in the office this week."

"P.C.? When are you and Joe going to realize we can all see what's happening? It's okay."

"You know... well... What exactly do you mean?"

"Oh come now, P.C. You don't even plead the fifth very well. Joe and you are smitten with each other and have been for several months. Everybody knows it. They're all fine with it." She pictured her friend's discomfort and grinned. "What we want to know is why Joe and you aren't comfortable simply saying, 'We're in love.'"

"Look, Margaret. I got burned really badly with my first husband. Divorcing him was my only option. I don't want to make a mistake the second time."

"But Joe..."

"Joe's a really sweet guy. He got hurt way back too. We've decided to take this really slow, one small step at a time."

How long have we known Joe Busbee? "I didn't know Joe had ever been married."

"Don't ever let on that I told you. He was very young. Too young, and he admits it. She was his high school sweetheart. You know, Joe grew up down below Atlanta."

That explains why I don't remember Joe from years ago.

"Anyway," P.C. continued, "Joe caught her cheating on him."

"Sadly, that happens more often than anyone realizes."

"Yeah, but she cut him a double blow. She was cheating with Joe's father."

"His father!"

"Low, isn't it? Joe's dad had the reputation for being a ladies man. He had cheated on his own wife for as long as Joe could remember. So when he found his father and his wife together in what we used to call a "compromising situation," that was the last straw."

"I can believe it."

Don did some dirty things to me, but even he didn't sink that low.

"That's when Joe packed his things and left for good. The plan had always been that he would finish law school and go back to his father's firm. Instead, he found Carter's Crossroads and set up shop."

That explains a lot. No one could ever understand why Joe wasn't married. He didn't date either. That situation must have really done a number on him.

"Joe's past is safe with me. Besides, I really think that Joe and you are safe with each other."

"You'd think, wouldn't you?"

Margaret changed the subject to explain how she needed her friend's help.

"I just do not want to be alone with that lawyer. It's not that I'm afraid he'll try anything, as much as I'm stung at having to ask permission to get things that belong to me. I'm being treated like a potential thief."

"Sure, I'll go with you. I also understand your anger. Or is it more hurt? You thought at the end of the day Don cared more for his family than he obviously did."

She's got that right. "Whatever, I can't change anything that's happened, but I do need my office furniture and equipment from the house. If you'll go help me, I'll be grateful."

"Hey, it doesn't take that long to care for Rufus and water the plants. I can go whenever you can make it work."

I'm not comfortable going back into the house at all. The sooner that place is sold, so I never have to darken the door again, the better I'll like it.

The two chatted a little longer before P.C. begged off, saying she had to get packed and loaded.

◈

"He said he'd meet us here at two-thirty." Margaret checked her watch for what seemed like the hundredth time since they'd pulled up in the driveway at Redbud Way. "It's almost two-forty-five now. We got here at twenty after. These guys have to get back to the plant so they can clock out on time."

Joe's secretary had called on Wednesday morning to notify her Mr. Jackson was available at any time on Thursday. Margaret had set the time.

"He asked if you were going to have movers there to load the items, or if it would be necessary to make a second trip back."

Gosh, I've been so worked up about having to be supervised getting my own stuff, I haven't even thought about the moving part.

"I'll have someone with us prepared to load right then."

"I'll let Mr. Jackson know."

I'm just not sure who I'll hire. Real movers will charge much more than the job is worth for such a small load. But I don't want to have to look at Mr. Jackson again. I don't want to have to go back into that house again.

That night, as she and P.C. were comparing notes over one of Margaret's home-cooked meals, she mentioned the need for strong backs. "I've got to get a truck, too. But that's the easy part."

"What about the guys at Don's plant who always moved your stuff in and out for parties? Could you get them?"

Why didn't I think of that? Those men I trust.

Even though it was evening, she immediately called Andy Davis—the banker acting as temporary plant manager under judicial order—to make her request.

"Sure thing, Margaret. We can spare those men tomorrow afternoon. What about a truck?"

"I'm going to one of the rental places."

"Save your money. We won't be using all the Haywood fleet tomorrow. Come by the plant when you're ready. They can follow you to the house."

"Thanks Andy. You're a lifesaver."

"Glad to help. You take care now."

Margaret dished up their delayed dessert, for which they adjourned to the den to enjoy as they relaxed. She explained how she planned to reconfigure the living room to accommodate the office arrangement.

"There might be times I'd have someone here. Naturally I don't want them to invade my privacy to get to my office."

"Smart thinking."

It was also smart thinking to use Haywood resources to help correct another Haywood mess.

"So where IS he?" Margaret demanded again, as she paced up and down the driveway. "I've got a key to the house... MY house... but I've got to wait outside because the administrator of the estate hasn't shown up."

P.C. pulled out her cell phone and Margaret noticed that she struck only one key.

"Who're you calling?"

"Joe's office. To see... Hello?"

She's got his office number on speed dial.

"He is. Great. Thank you," Margaret heard her friend say.

"Mr. Jackson is on his way over. He got..."

As she spoke, Margaret saw a long, black Mercedes turning into the drive.

The obviously new automobile glided to a stop next to where the two ladies, along with the moving men, stood in the driveway. A man alighted from the driver's side.

"Sorry I'm late," he said. "I had an unexpected delay. Shall we go in?" As he spoke, walking toward the house, his hand was fishing in his pocket for a key.

He didn't even exercise basic courtesy, greet me or anything. He may be the administrator, but this is still my house. It still will be, too, long after he's left the picture and bought himself another Mercedes.

Once inside, Margaret took no time to journey down memory lane. Instead, she led the group directly to her old office. "All of this is what I need," she explained to the attorney. "You're welcome to look through the drawers and even the files to see that everything in here pertains to me."

She couldn't decipher the look he gave her, but Margaret was relieved he responded in a manner totally unexpected.

"I'll take your word for it, Mrs. Haywood. Since we've already inventoried the entire house, it will be necessary for me to account for what's being removed."

"Meaning what?"

He better not tell me I have to pay for what I'm getting.

"We'll make a list of each item as it's taken out; then my secretary can update the inventory. To be certain we're all protected, I'll get my camera from the car and photograph each piece."

I don't like this feeling.

"Let me get my notebook and the camera. Then your men can get to work."

Thinking about it later, Margaret was amazed that in less than forty-five minutes everything was removed from the little room that had once been her sanctuary.

She never looked back as P.C. followed the truck down the driveway.

The sooner I separate myself from this house, the better things will be.

Back at the other house, the men moved the pieces Margaret indicated into the den and brought in her office, which was soon configured to her satisfaction. She also straightened the adjoining dining room, including trashing the long-dead centerpiece.

"I don't know why I couldn't manage to throw those flowers out. For the first time in a long time, I actually feel a small degree of normalcy."

"It's about time," P.C. agreed.

※

Monday morning was a time of conflicting emotions as she fed the children breakfast in preparation for getting them off to school. While she had spent much time during the previous weekend imagining what it would be like to be employed, actually working for wages, even her conversations with P.C. and Joe hadn't prepared her for this moment of reality.

I've got to call Barbara and report in. I'm not even sure what I'm supposed to do today.

In an effort to create the right psychological atmosphere, Margaret had resisted the urge to work in her pajamas, dressing instead as if she were going out to a job.

I didn't think I could get the right mind-set otherwise.

"Good morning, Margaret. Are you ready to get into harness?"

"Ready, Barbara. Except it occurred to me that I truly don't know what to do first. Or what to do. Period."

"Of course you don't. We haven't really had a chance to sit down and compare notes. The first item of agenda is to discover what we have on the calendar for the next few months."

"Perhaps I should drive down this morning. Or this afternoon? Whichever works best for your schedule?"

"I've got a better idea, if you're agreeable."

"Name it."

"I set aside all day today to work with you. But it occurs to me that there are really three of us in the agency that you need to hear from."

"If their schedules allow, I'll be glad to spend time with all of you today."

"I really think it would be better if the four of us could talk as a group. How about if we come to you?"

"I beg your pardon?"

Barbara chuckled. "This office is a zoo on a slow day. We've learned the hard way that we accomplish much more by jumping ship and seeking refuge elsewhere, so how about if we drive to Carter's Crossroads in about an hour?"

"Sure...if that's what you want to do," Margaret responded, looking frantically at the living room and dining room. The space that had seemed so perfect only minutes earlier suddenly looked sad and unkempt. *What will I feed them for lunch?*

"We'll be there shortly after eleven o'clock. That'll give you two hours to get your house cleaned. Oh, and by the way, don't sweat lunch. I'm buying."

This woman is a mind reader.

"Whatever you say, Barbara. You're the boss."

She spent the time before her co-workers arrived vacuuming and dusting again. By the time she answered the doorbell, Margaret felt good about herself and her house.

At least the part they're going to see. I even had time to hit the bathroom again after the kids getting ready for school in there.

The group settled down in the office sitting area. Barbara, with a multi-page calendar on her lap, began to share the organization's scheduled events and plans for the coming months.

"Your job, Margaret, is going to be two-fold at this point. First, you'll take over the details for these commitments. You'll also be in charge of scheduling upcoming events and seeing that all the preparation is handled."

"How far into the future do you work?"

The agency head flipped several pages. "Right now I'd say we have bookings at least six or seven months out. Let's see..." She fingered pages again. "Looks like the first one you'll have to worry about is mid-March. About two months away."

"I've been handling that one," the woman Margaret had come to know as Kirsten volunteered. "I'll be happy to hand over my files on that and bring you up to speed."

"That would be great. Thanks."

Looks like I'm going to be busy. Lord, I hope we all haven't made a mistake. I've never worked on anything of this magnitude before.

"The other area where you'll be working is finding funding for activities that we don't even know yet that we want to do."

The other co-worker, who wore a name tag identifying her as Evelyn, laughed as she said, "We're too close to the everyday work to be able to see what we want to do down the road. That's where you come in, sitting here in the calm of your home office. We want you to have the freedom to brainstorm. Create events, activities and, once we've agreed upon them, begin looking for ways to pay the bill."

Sounds a lot like Mount Zion School, except on a much larger scale.

After several more minutes of conversation, the group broke for lunch at a family-style buffet nearby. In a moment of inspiration, Margaret volunteered that she had a friend visiting from out-of-state whom she wanted the ladies to meet.

"Perhaps she can run over before you all leave to go back to Atlanta."

"Why not call and invite her to join us?" offered Barbara. "I was planning to see if Annie could turn loose."

Following the two calls, the group of four secured a table for six. Within a matter of minutes, the two invited guests had taken their seats. They group lingered around the table for quite some time after the server removed their plates.

Annie and P.C., who already knew each other well, were both supportive of Margaret and the job ahead of her.

"Believe me," Barbara affirmed, "it only took a few minutes after I first met Margaret to know she was the kind of player I wanted on my team."

"You all are embarrassing me, you know. I'd sure hate to disappoint anyone."

"You won't," Kirsten volunteered. "I agree with Barbara. It only takes a few minutes to know that Margaret has what it takes."

"Plus, she has one characteristic none of us have. She's a recovering victim. A survivor. She's been where we haven't, so she can identify with the victims we attempt to help."

"That's right," Evelyn agreed. "She's walked the walk and now she can talk the talk, with her head held high. She brings a totally new perspective to our staff and our mission."

When they finally departed the restaurant, Margaret climbed into the car to return to her house with a feeling she couldn't quite identify.

I don't feel smug, or cocky. But I'm not afraid either, Lord. It's like I feel complete, in an unfinished manner of speaking. Like I'm doing the right thing.

She knew her innermost thoughts didn't make total sense but she vowed not to share them with her new coworkers.

Back in her office, Margaret gathered her new team around her at the dining room table and began to absorb the contents of the day's crash course.

It was shortly after four o'clock when Barbara announced that her crew needed to head back to Atlanta. "I think this has been very productive," she told Margaret. "I'm even more convinced that you're exactly what we need in this job."

As she was gathering materials into her tote, Kirsten echoed Barbara's comments. "You're top notch, Margaret. You're going to take us to an entirely new level of visibility."

She watched until Barbara's car had backed down the drive and was out of sight. Before she left, the director had given Margaret the information she needed to create her own e-mail address within the agency's web site, and provided information on how Margaret's land-line phone would become an extension of the agency's main line.

After closing the door behind her, Margaret collapsed on the sofa and kicked off her shoes.

It's been too long since I dressed up to work. I need my jeans, sweatshirt and sneakers.

The week flew by as Margaret organized her days to get the kids off to school. A quick shower and comfortable clothes led her into the day's work which, as each day passed, she found more exciting, more challenging. A sandwich for lunch allowed her to work through and be ready to call it quits by the time the children arrived home from school. For the remainder of the day, she tried to be "mama", supervising homework, preparing a good supper and being available if the children had problems or squabbles.

This entire week has been one of the most tranquil I can remember since who knows when. The children seem more settled as well.

P.C. stayed through the weekend, with she and Joe insisting on taking the Haywoods out to eat Saturday night.

"You're leaving tomorrow?" Margaret asked as she stood with P.C. outside the restaurant while Joe went for the car.

"Joe and I will attend church and then have lunch together. Then I've got to hit the road. There are several developments at my office I need to deal with on Monday, so I've got to go home."

"When are you going to wise up and get admitted to the Georgia bar so you can practice here?"

"Interesting you should ask. I'm scheduled to sit for the exam the first week in February, as a matter of fact."

Margaret's face couldn't disguise her amazement.

"You're serious?"

"You bet I am."

"You're going to practice in Georgia?"

"I'm going to practice in Carter's Crossroads with the firm of Busbee and Dunigan."

"You aren't?"

"Yep. 'Fraid so."

"When were you going to tell me? I thought we were friends."

"We are friends, at least as far as I'm concerned. But you've had enough on your plate lately."

Margaret saw Joe's car headed their way and knew she didn't have much time. "So does this mean you and Joe are...?"

"It means," P.C. interrupted, "that Joe and I are forming a professional partnership. When we go home at night, it will be to two different locations."

"Sounds real romantic, not to mention businesslike."

"I told you, Margaret, we both want to take it slow. We're happy with the way this is all falling together. I hope you will be too."

"Of course... of course I will," she sputtered, as the Lincoln Navigator reached them and they piled in.

I've just been blindsided. How did I not see this coming?

The group returned to the Haywood's temporary home where the three adults visited until the hour was late. P.C. told Joe she had shared their news with Margaret. Joe gave her a look that told Margaret to keep any smart remarks to herself.

Man, Joe is touchy. But I'm not going to give them a hard time.

As the couple was leaving, P.C. paused on the front steps to pose a question. "When do you think you're going to be moving to Atlanta?"

Forgetting her vow not to tease her friends, Margaret quipped, "What? You don't want to move to town until I'm gone?"

"No, smarty. I want to rent this house from your parents."

P.C. living here in this house? Well... why not?

"You want to live here?" Somehow she was having problems getting that to compute.

"Well, sure. I assume your dad will want to rent it out when you're gone."

"Well, yes... I guess he'll rent it. Certainly he'd love to have you for a tenant." Margaret couldn't contain her own curiosity. "But why do you want to rent this house? You've got me curious."

P.C. traced her hand down the wood trim around the front door. "It didn't occur to me until we were sitting here tonight. My mother is coming to live with me. I'd figured on getting an apartment, but my little mama isn't going to be happy in an apartment setting. She'd rather have a house and, in truth, so would I."

Margaret's response was immediate. "You know how Daddy feels about you, so I'm sure he'd love to have you for a tenant." She hesitated. *Am I feeling guilty?* "I haven't talked with Mama at all since that day at lunch. Daddy has called me a few times on his cell phone when he was away from the house, where Mama couldn't overhear. But he hasn't even been over here and I haven't seen him, either."

Daddy's got to feel like he's being punished.

"You know what? It occurs to me that I need set that situation to rights, so I will be talking to him tomorrow. I'll mention that you're interested in the house."

After her guests had gone, Margaret made quick work of securing the house. She was soon in the bedroom, which had been her haven during those first few days following Don's funeral.

This room is certainly not the decorator's perfection I was used to on

Redbud Way, but neither is it the deadly war zone our old house represents. I will not grieve to see it go to someone else. Hopefully some family who can truly be happy there.*

She pulled her Bible off the bed side table and curled up in the overstuffed chair in the corner of the room.

Lord, I need some guidance tonight. I've got to mend this rift with Mama. For her sake, for my sake, and for Daddy who is the innocent bystander in this. He loves us both and it's unfair to make him choose. She flipped the Bible open, rifling the pages, searching. *Besides, I don't want to leave town with bad blood between Mama and me.*

After several minutes of flipping between passages, stopping to read a few lines of each, the third chapter of Colossians caught her eye. She read slowly. *"Children, obey your parents in all things: for this is well pleasing unto the Lord."*

Suddenly she was stricken by an attack of guilt. *Well, Lord, I don't guess You're very happy with the current state of things.*

Anxious for some absolution from her chafing conscience, Margaret continued to read. *"Fathers, provoke not your children to anger, lest they be discouraged."*

Discouraged surely describes how I feel right now. Mama, Daddy and I have always been so close. It hurts to be at odds with them. This scripture says "fathers." I wonder if it translates to mothers as well?

She read on, but kept returning to those two verses. *The twentieth and twenty-first verses. I think I will probably remember those two verses always.*

Closing her Bible, with her finger still marking the verses, Margaret bowed her head for one of her conversations with the God she knew had stood by her when no one else would.

Oh, Lord. I love You so much. Without You I couldn't have made it through all that has happened. I don't doubt that I need to take my children and leave Carter's Crossroads, at least for a while. Much like Mary and Joseph did with Your Son when they escaped from King Herod. Until we've had a chance to heal, and the town has had time to forget, I fear for all of us. Please help me understand Mama's attitude. Help me find a way to bring resolution to this conflict. In Your Son's name I pray. Amen.

CHAPTER SIX

*C*hurch was over, the lunch dishes had been washed and the kids were in their rooms doing homework. Margaret had spoken to P.C., who was on her way back to Tennessee. She shared her plan to sit down with both parents, together that same afternoon, in an effort to find resolution to the problems that threatened to split her family.

I might as well get this over, she decided as she left the kitchen.

"Mama?"

The call had been answered on the second ring.

I expected she would answer.

"I suppose you want to talk to your daddy. I'll get him."

"No... no, Mama. Actually, it's you I want to talk to. May I walk over?"

"Suit yourself. You always do what you want to do anyway. Why should this time be any different?"

Margaret bit back the retort poised on the tip of her tongue. *Help me, Lord. Give me the right words to say.* "I'll be right over."

When she entered her parents' kitchen, her mother was sitting at the table peeling potatoes. "What are you cooking?"

"Making a pot of beef stew."

"I knew something smelled good. Want some help peeling?"

"Suit yourself. You know where the knives are."
She sounds like she's got a copyright on that "suit yourself" phrase.
Margaret didn't respond, but reached into the drawer where the cutting knives had been for as long as she could remember. After selecting a paring knife, she grabbed a small dishpan, settled down across the table from her mother, picked up a potato and began to peel.
Here goes, Lord. Bridle my mouth and control my tongue. I have a feeling this is the last chance I'll get to make this right.
She was nearly finished with the first potato when she said, "You know, Mama, we need to resolve the problems we have between us. They're hurting everyone...including you and me."
"Only problem I've got is that no one thinks I know what I'm talking about. People go behind my..." Ruby halted in mid-sentence and dropped her head.
Margaret was certain she heard a soft sob. *Mama NEVER cries.* "Mama, listen to me. Please?"
The older woman neither looked at her daughter, nor responded. Instead, she began to peel another potato.
Margaret took the silence as permission and forged ahead, "I know you don't agree with everything I've done, Mama. You may never agree. But the one thing you haven't done is to give me a chance to present my side of the story."
Her mother said nothing, but ceased her peeling.
"There are two sides to every story."
Silence.
"I'm going to tell you my story. You need to know that I love you very much. I don't know where we all got off track, exactly, but we're going to try to get back on. We're going to do it today."
It felt as if her mother were staring right through her.
"I need to start at the beginning, Mama. Please listen to what I have to say and at least give me the benefit of the doubt."

Margaret explained how Don's behavior from early in their marriage had been controlling and verbally abusive.

"Mama, he called me names, language you wouldn't permit in this house. He decided whether I could cut my hair or even if I was sick enough to see the doctor. The more money he made, the more vindictive and controlling he became to those of us who lived with him every day."

"But he provided so well…"

"Materially, he did. I'll give you that. But in so many other ways, he abused us, Mama. He abused all of us."

"I never saw that side of him. He was always so warm, gracious and generous with us."

"Don't you see, all that was an act? A façade. That's what abusers do. They put up…"

"I wish you wouldn't use that word," Miss Ruby said, interrupting Margaret's explanation. "'Abuser' sounds so dirty, so common."

"Mama," Margaret explained patiently, "it is the correct term for what Don was."

"I just can't understand why he was so mixed up."

Mama simply cannot say the words.

"I have some theories and so do you, if you'll allow yourself to acknowledge the truth. But we can't change anything about the past. My children and I now have to heal in order to get on with our lives."

"People are talking all over town. It is so embarrassing to walk into a store, or even into church. People turn and look and then look away, while they whisper among themselves."

"Which is why I have to leave Carter's Crossroads. At least for a while. Plus I need a job that pays a salary. How much chance do you think I have of finding a job here? I doubt I could even get one in fast food."

"You caused Don so much public humiliation. He provided so

well for all of you. That beautiful house…the car…the ability to buy whatever you wanted."

"You call it providing, Mama. I see it now as bribery and still more of that façade. He made all of us reluctant to acknowledge the demon he brought into our house, because we did have such a lavish lifestyle. To the outside, the fact that we lived as we did made him look good to the community. He bribed this entire town as well by always funding some good cause."

"I never saw anything but the good in him."

"He wanted you to see that and…" Margaret made eye contact with her mother, "that's all you wanted to see."

Miss Ruby dropped her head again.

"What I did, I did because I had to protect my children from his physical abuse."

She saw her mother cringe.

I said that word again. Maybe she needs repetitive therapy where she hears the word abuse or abuser until it doesn't affect her any longer.

"I almost waited too late, Mama. Do you remember what he did to my arm? It was only a matter of time before he killed one of us. You see…" She lowered her voice in an attempt to remove any trace of accusation. "Don brought that humiliation on himself. Only he didn't want to accept the consequences of his actions. Everything was our fault."

Margaret could hear the ticking of the rooster clock across the room as it timed the response her mother finally offered.

"I wasn't there, so I have to believe what you say. I just know that when Don talked to me about all this, he said you were out of control and he didn't know what he was going to do with you."

"Don told you that?"

Her mother didn't answer but nodded her head instead.

"When?"

"We had many conversations. He came over here often, when

he'd take a break at the plant. I used to feed him lunch. He said he always considered me his mama, given, you know, how his parents were. I always thought of him as our son." She lifted up the corner of the apron she wore and dabbed at her eyes. "He seemed so troubled about your actions. I just assumed you had inherited the family curse."

"Now you've really lost me, Mama. The family curse? What are you talking about?"

"Both my own mother and her mother had mental problems. They kept my grandmother at home, because that's what families did in those days. But they locked her in her room, because she was dangerous. She'd grab butcher knives and run at people, threatening to kill them."

"Oh, how horrible. That sickens me."

"I was just about Brian's age when my own mother began to do crazy things. My daddy finally had to put her in a mental institution, where she stayed until she died. You were almost three when it happened."

"You always told me that Grammy O'Neal died when I was very young, but you never told me any of the circumstances."

"What would have been the use? What was done, was done."

"So Don convinced you that I was losing my mind."

"He sat right here in this kitchen, with tears running down his face, while telling me he was fearful you might harm the children. That's when I told him about Mama and Grandmama. It sounded like my worst nightmare had come true."

"You told all this to Don?"

"I was so afraid the bad gene had jumped me and got you. He needed to know."

Lord, I'm about to lose it.

"Mama, don't you see? You played right into his hands, and he used you. Used you big time."

"But he seemed so genuine."

"Don Haywood missed his calling when he didn't go into acting. Trust me, Mama, there wasn't a genuine bone in his body. He was running scared, because suddenly he wasn't in total control, and he was looking to you for reinforcement."

"The Don I know wouldn't do that."

"But the Don I know would. I promise you, Mama, that's exactly what he did."

The bowl of peeled potatoes, long forgotten by the older woman, rolled out of her lap into the floor, as she pressed her apron to her face. Margaret heard the sound of sobbing.

Deciding her mother needed time to cry, Margaret dropped to her knees as she collected the potatoes that had scattered across the kitchen. Once she had them gathered, she placed them in the sink and ran water into the bowl. She added the two potatoes she'd peeled to the others, then lifted the lid on the old Dutch oven her mother had always used for soups, to assure the stew mixture wasn't cooking dry.

"Look, Mama. Don't blame yourself, because I don't. You loved Don. Therefore you wanted to believe whatever he told you. Don Haywood was a con artist, Mama. It's just he had an upscale location from which to run his scams. Even in his mind he was a cut or two above the shell game artist at the carnival. But at the same time, that's exactly what he was."

"He played me for a fool!"

"You *and* a lot of other people. Believe me, Mama, a lot of those people who are talking about all of us feel duped as well. When Don showed his true colors, the community saw a side they didn't know. It bothered them."

"So what do I do?"

I've been asking myself that same question, Lord. I'm still not sure I have an answer. "For starters, have faith and confidence in me. I need your love and support now more than I've ever needed it."

By this point Ruby Maxwell was crying openly, making no move to hide her tears. "I don't want to lose you. Or the children. I love those three."

"And they love you." She hugged her mother. "We all love you, Mama. But this is one of those situations where I don't feel like I have a choice. We have to leave Carter's Crossroads."

"Why do you have to go to work? Don left you well fixed, with a house to live in. I know it needs sprucing up, but we can do all of that."

How can I make her understand this?

"I need to work, Mama, for money as well as my own peace of mind. I would never be happy sitting home all day. As for the money, I need to stretch Don's money as far as possible. That won't happen if I use it to live on."

"But why do you need all that money?"

Margaret could tell her mother was weakening her stance.

"I have three children to educate. I'd like to also be able to help them get established once they've finished college. I also have my own old age to provide for."

"We can help you. You're all we've got, so whatever we have goes to you anyway."

Margaret hugged the little woman again. "Thanks, Mama, but I want you and Daddy to enjoy your money while you can, for as long as you need it. Don't worry about saving it for me."

"But we love you. All of you."

"That doesn't have anything to do with it. Besides, Mama, you don't have enough money to quiet all the tongues that are wagging. Only time can do that. In the meantime, my children and I have to heal, recover and get on with our lives in the midst of all this confusion."

Miss Ruby reached out her hand and took hold of her daughter's arm. "If that's what you think is best, then you have our support." She halted as a sob overtook her. "Just please don't forget us. You're all we've got and you know your daddy isn't comfortable driving in Atlanta."

Margaret's heart was cut into pieces.

Don, you're dead but you're still causing heartbreak. If it weren't for all that has happened, I wouldn't be taking the children away from the only hometown they've ever known.

"Oh, Mama. You aren't losing us, nor do I want you and Daddy driving into Atlanta. You'll probably see us as often as you did before this nightmare started. We'll be in and out."

"I'm going to count on it."

"Besides, Mama, this job really excites me. I can use all the skills I developed doing volunteer work all these years as well as my knowledge of what it's like to be a victim. Perhaps, before it's too late, I can help some other woman who refuses to see the truth. Plus I'll get paid to do it."

The sound of footsteps could be heard coming up the basement stairs. In a matter of seconds, the daddy Margaret loved more than she would ever be able to tell him was standing in the middle of the kitchen, looking at the two women who both had tears in their eyes.

"What's going...?"

"It's okay, Daddy."

"Ruby, have you been...?"

"No, Daddy, she hasn't. Mama and I've been clearing the air. I think we understand each other a little better than we did."

The look of relief Margaret saw on her father's face made all the discomfort of confronting her mother worth the pain.

"You mean I don't have to choose which of you I love any longer?"

It was Ruby who spoke, interjecting her answer before her daughter could speak. "Margaret and I have done a bit of sharing this afternoon. I think we both understand things better." She dabbed her eyes again. "I'm still broken-hearted to think that Don was such a cruel man. I gave him credit for better. I'm still not happy that she's taking the children and moving to Atlanta, either, but I guess it's really for the best."

Margaret's mouth hung open and she sat, stunned, with the reality that she had won over her fiercest critic. *Thank You, Lord!*

"It really is better that she gets the children away from here, at least for a little while."

The three sat and talked for a few more minutes before Margaret announced she had to go.

"You all come back for stew tonight," her mother ordered as Margaret was about to leave. "I need to feed you every chance I get before you move."

"We'll be here. And don't worry, you'll get several more chances since we won't be going for another six or seven weeks." Then the light bulb came on. "Oh, Daddy, I almost forgot. P.C. Dunigan is interested in renting the house after we move."

"P.C. What does she want with a house here?" The question came not from her father, but from Ruby who was busy at the stove.

"She and her mother are moving here as soon as P.C. is admitted to the bar. She and Joe Busbee are going to be law partners."

"I wondered when she was going to wise up," Ruby replied.

Harold Maxwell scratched his head. "Sure. P.C.'s more than welcome to the house. I guess I hadn't even given a thought to what we'd do with it. But that's an awfully big house for just one person."

"Oh, she won't be here alone. Her mother is moving with her. That's why she wants a house instead of an apartment. Said she knew her mother would be more comfortable in a house."

"That'll give me a new backyard neighbor to eat my soup."

"Don't say that too loudly, Mama. P.C. loves your soup. Remember?"

"The house needs some sprucing up. I'd planned to do some remodeling before you moved in, but then you had to have it in a hurry."

"Good. I'll tell P.C. when she calls tonight that she's got a place to live."

Margaret found that she moved across the yard and up the hill to her own house with a much lighter heart. *It's amazing, God, what a good unburdening can do!*

Later, after the meal back at her parents' house, checking homework and getting the children to bed, Margaret found refuge by curling up on her own bed with her Bible.

I need some time with you, Lord. To share my blessings, such as my first paycheck, and to voice my concerns...because I've still got a mountain ahead of me.

On Saturday morning she had gone online to pay several bills. That's when she found her first paycheck had been electronically deposited the day before.

I knew yesterday was payday, and I knew I signed up for direct deposit, but it hadn't even occurred to me that it had happened. This is great!

She flipped open her Bible and began to read the parable of the talents, which she thought particularly applied at this moment. *You directed me to this passage, didn't You, Lord? That's Your message to me, that I need to make the most of this opportunity. Not just for battered women, but for me.* She finished her reading before spending a few minutes in prayer. Just as she settled into the bed and turned on the TV, her phone rang.

P.C.

"You made it home, I see."

"Ran into some heavy rain just inside Tennessee, but yes, I'm here. If you can call this home. I'm really looking forward to getting moved."

"That makes two of us. It's my pleasure to tell you Daddy was thrilled about you wanting the house." *Seems like there was something else I was supposed to tell her.* "Oh! He said he knew it needed some remodeling and sprucing up, but he's planning to do that."

"Thanks, friend. That is good news to know I don't have to house hunt."

"I agree. That is good news, but there's even better news than that." Margaret recounted the confrontation with her mother earlier that afternoon. P.C. was as thrilled as she that the problems had been resolved.

"Now all you have to worry about is the move to Atlanta."

CHAPTER SEVEN

"You guys are going to miss that bus if you don't get a move-on," Margaret Haywood cautioned her three children. "I've got to be on a conference phone call at nine o'clock, so I don't have time to drive you to school."

"Come on, Sallie. You, too, Jason," Brian encouraged his younger sister and brother. "Mom's right. Finish your breakfast so we can be on the curb when the bus pulls up."

Brian has become such an adult through all of this. But then he will be a senior in high school next year, so he almost is an adult.

After the three trooped out to catch their ride, Margaret made quick work of straightening the kitchen in the Atlanta condo where they had lived for almost a month."

There are still days I pinch myself when I think of all that went down those last few weeks in Carter's Crossroads. Those were some frantic days.

Margaret had stood on the courthouse steps where she bought everything she and Don had owned. Those purchases had included the home on Redbud Way, where they had lived for so many years with all its contents, both their vehicles and the biggest single item, Haywood Tufters.

It was over within a matter of minutes, but I was still terrified someone else would step up to bid against me. P.C. said it was very unlikely, but it could happen.

Once she had title to all the property, Margaret had immediately listed the house for sale, and traded her once-prized candy apple red Lexus in on a new Ford Expedition. Don's late model Ford SUV had been parked at her parents, waiting until Brian was a little older and more experienced behind the wheel.

I also put Haywood Tufters on the market.

Joe Busbee was handling those negotiations with the firm that had been interested several months earlier.

I'm leaving it in his hands. I've got plenty of other matters to occupy my time.

A few minutes before nine o'clock, she settled herself at her desk in the room she had converted into an office and pulled her notes together, ready for the call she expected. With a total of six persons on the conversation, Margaret did more listening than talking.

But that's OK, because they're giving me the information we need at the office. I'm glad Barbara and I are meeting for lunch today. All this is exciting, but I want to be certain I'm dealing with all the details. To have someone from the national level to come here to speak is big time. It's also thanks to Jim Deaton's intervention.

She and Jim had seen each other several times in the weeks before. When she mentioned to him her need for a major domestic violence authority for two days of speaking and workshops, her lawyer friend and landlord made a few phone calls.

She thought of him now, as she hurried around getting ready to leave, and still remembered how it felt to walk through the professionally-decorated home after all Jim's furniture had been removed; to wonder how her possessions would fit.

I knew if things didn't look right, I wouldn't ask Jim to redecorate just for us.

She had been relieved, however, to discover that her furniture and artwork fit wonderfully into the spacious three-story unit, creating a most welcoming backdrop for their everyday lives.

Everything fits as if it were made for this condo. That's been especially easy on all of us, since we've had so many adjustments.

Barbara had asked her to meet for lunch away from the office so they could talk uninterrupted. Margaret left early. She was still acclimating to the Atlanta traffic and had learned the hard way that a very short journey could take a very long time.

It all depends on what time I leave my house.

The two ladies arrived at the little neighborhood bistro at the same time and exchanged hugs in the parking lot. Once they were seated and had given their orders, Barbara inquired, "How did your call go this morning? Does it look like everything's a go?"

Margaret pulled her notes to be certain she didn't forget anything, and brought her boss up to date.

"Marvelous," Barbara crowed. "Margaret you've done us proud. This is going to be one of the best domestic violence awareness programs we've ever had."

It feels so good to hear her say that. I don't even feel like I've been working.

Their food was served and they began to eat in silence at first, then Barbara asked, "So how are your children adjusting? I've been anxious to know how they're settling in."

Margaret, whose mouth was filled with food, took advantage of the situation to formulate her answer.

In truth, I think they're doing OK. I wouldn't have said as much the first week.

"I think it was definitely the best course of action to put them in public school, even though they've always been in a private school." She laughed, but it sounded hollow. "Don saw it as prestigious to have his children in private school, not because there was anything wrong with the public school in Carter's Crossroads."

"Appearances, huh?"

"I've come to realize more and more each day that appearances were what Don was all about."

"Most abusers can be defined that way."

I hadn't really thought about it, but she's right.

"The kids are doing well. Thank you for asking." She took another sip of tea. "This is soooo good. The first week was a real adjustment, but after that, things really leveled out."

"I'm glad. I want you to be content in your job, but you're a mother first. If your children are unhappy, then you're unhappy and I'm out one of the best assets I've ever had."

It doesn't embarrass me to receive compliments, but all these folks must see something that I don't see, Lord.

"We're happy."

I'm not being totally honest, but I do think things are getting better. Sallie, especially, wasn't accustomed to being in classes with other races, and the class sizes are so much larger than they were at Mount Zion. It's been a learning curve for all of us.

"I'm not going to tell you there haven't been some problems; me included."

"Share with me, please."

Margaret hesitated as she searched for the words she needed. "A lot of little things, rather than one or two big things."

"Any of them deal-breakers?"

"Oh, no... no," she laughed. "Nothing like that. Just getting accustomed to new surroundings. Things at a different place in the kitchen. The traffic noise that we didn't hear round the clock before. Neighbors closer than we've ever had, and taking fifteen minutes to go two miles at the wrong time of day."

"Welcome to Atlanta," Barbara said with a laugh. "I guess we're all so used to the congestion, we don't give it a second thought."

"I'm sure in time, we'll become oblivious as well," Margaret assured her. "That's why they call it an 'adjustment'."

Following a few minutes more of comparing notes, the two women went their separate ways. Margaret made a grocery run before heading to the house.

I know this won't always be the case, but I've tried to be there everyday when they get home from school. That's the way it's always been, and I'd like to keep it like that for a while longer. At least until the children are better settled.

She heard the bus pull away from the curb. In a matter of seconds, the front door flew open.

"Mommie. We're home!"

Jason sounds happy.

Margaret hurriedly left her supper preparations in her rush to the foyer. She found her youngest with his blue eyes fairly glowing.

"I had a great day in school, Mommie."

Bringing up the rear, she saw Sallie and Brian climbing the flight of brick steps from the parking area to the covered front entry.

If the looks on their faces are any indication, they each had a good day as well.

"I'm glad you all are home. I missed you today."

"I'll stay home with you tomorrow," Sallie volunteered. "So you won't be lonesome."

"Hey," Brian protested as he gave his little sister a gentle poke. "That's my line. I'm supposed to say stuff like that."

The little girl beside him screwed her face up into a grotesque mask and crowned it all by sticking out her tongue at her brother.

"I can say it as much as you can."

Sallie's suddenly not a little girl any more. Since we moved here, she's stopped wearing her hair in pigtails, and she's really developing a personality. It's about time. What's more, she hasn't complained about missing her best friend, Audra, even once.

"Afraid, not," she told them, "you all have to go to school and

I have to work."

"Can't blame us for trying, can you?"

Margaret wanted to ruffle her eldest's hair, but knew he was too much of a man to appreciate it. Instead, she simply grinned at him.

"Can't blame me for saying no, either, can you Brian?"

"Touché." It was his turn to grin. "Anyway, school here is a piece of cake. We're all actually ahead of the other kids in our classes, so it's not such a hard haul. But it'll still be nice to be through with classes soon."

"When's your last day of school?"

"Seven weeks from day after tomorrow," Sallie volunteered. "I can't wait to spend my summer laying around the pool."

"Not me," Brian responded. "I want to try to find a summer job. I need to work."

He is really maturing. As soon as he becomes a little more familiar with Atlanta streets, and gets a little more experience with the traffic, I'm going to give him the SUV.

It had been, Margaret decided after she was in bed that night, a typical family evening. The kids had gotten their homework out of the way early and with the change to Daylight Savings Time, there was sunlight enough after supper for them to take a walk to the park just down the block.

People were relaxing as some watched their children play while others walked their dogs. Sallie asked if we could get a dog. I told her not now, not as long as we're living in rental property. But I think when we buy a house of our own, we're going to get a puppy.

※

The weeks flew by with such speed and tranquility that Margaret found her days less stressed than she'd known in years. Work proved to be both challenging and rewarding, while the absence of violence created a calm unlike anything she could remember. She tried to return to Carter's Crossroads a couple of times a week. While the children were in school, she checked on business and her parents. Then on Saturday or maybe Sunday, she and the children would spend an afternoon with Mr. Harold and Miss Ruby.

Usually she'd hook up with P.C., now settled into her parents' rental house with her own mother, who was enjoying having Ruby Maxwell as a friend. Margaret and P.C. would have lunch and compare notes. Her friend, who claimed she was truly enjoying her work for the first time since she finished law school, was thriving, Margaret noticed more than once.

When school was out for the summer, true to his promise, Brian found a job unloading trucks at a large discount store. True to her word, Margaret presented him with the keys to his dad's vehicle, causing her heart to swell at the pride she saw in her son's eyes.

"Now that you're working and earning some of your own money, I want you to know how proud I am of the man you're shaping up to be."

"Aw, Mom… don't get all mushy."

"OK, Brian. I'll try to refrain from getting 'mushy' as you say."

She did try. As she watched him bank his paycheck week after week, guarding his balance with a vengeance, she quietly took comfort that he had inherited Don's work ethic.

Evidently without his father's twisted outlook on life, she assured herself. *So often children parrot what they see. I guess all that family counseling we had after Don assaulted Jason has paid off. All three of my children seem more confident.*

Sallie and Jason, on the other hand, stayed closer to home, although Margaret did enroll them both in summer activities at a nearby YMCA. Then for two weeks, both of them went off to camp in the cool mountains in the northeast corner of the state.

It was totally different when just she and Brian were at home alone.

Is this what empty nest is like? I always figured when the time came, I'd have Don around to help me adjust. Now it's just me, and I'm already by myself much of the time, since Brian is making friends at work.

She recalled the number of evenings she'd already eaten supper alone.

Guess that's something I'm going to have to accept. Now that he has his own wheels, he's making a new life for himself. I've told him to invite his friends home, but so far he hasn't. I guess things are a lot different here than they were in Carter's Crossroads.

All in all, she thought, everything was pretty good. Except for one aspect: try as they might, none of them had been able to find a church where they felt they belonged.

So much for the right hand of fellowship that churches are supposed to offer. All the ones we've found have been suffering from a cold shoulder.

In the end, since they were going to Carter's Crossroads to visit the grandparents anyway, they went early and worshipped with the congregation that had ministered to their family in so many ways over the past few months.

Finding another church family, a real family, has been one of the most difficult aspects of this move. I'm constantly amazed at how some congregations can't see themselves the way newcomers see them.

～

Margaret's cell phone rang one afternoon while she was in the middle of a planning meeting with the staff. It was only the middle of July, but time was ticking away until the first week of October, and the series of domestic violence events she would coordinate.

Who would be calling me? I don't recognize the number.

"Sorry, guys," she said to her co-workers, "I thought I put my phone on vibrate." She silenced the little interruption and dropped it back into her purse.

It's probably a wrong number, since the number wasn't familiar. If it was for me, maybe they'll leave a message.

She continued with the meeting, which lasted until almost five o'clock.

"Ladies," she apologized, "I know this has been a full afternoon, but I'm comfortable we've covered every aspect of the events we'll stage in October. As you can see, we've got a full slate. Something for everyone."

"What I can see," Kirsten volunteered, "is that Margaret has been putting the miles under her while organizing all this. I've worked in this office for five years. During that time, we've never been as ambitious as we are this year."

Does she think I've gone overboard?

"Isn't it the truth," Evelyn agreed. "The programs for small children in the early grades are fantastic, Margaret. I can't get over how you've made family violence so easy to understand. Wherever did you find the concept?"

It was Barbara who answered. "Margaret didn't find the concept, ladies. She developed it. When other domestic violence organizations find out about Margaret's baby, I predict we're going to have to copyright it and sell rights to it."

"It was... such... such a no-brainer," Margaret insisted. "The younger we can get the message across to children, the sooner we can put ourselves out of business. I couldn't find a program structured in a way I felt was a positive, yet non-confrontational way to introduce the subject. So I developed one."

"'So I developed one,' she says. I suppose you also ran five miles, fixed breakfast, and knocked this phenomenal curriculum out between the biscuits and the strawberry jam!"

I know she isn't making fun of me, but I don't know exactly how to respond.

"Now Kirsten, let's give Margaret some well-deserved credit. She searched for weeks, previewing several early-age materials from different sources. When she couldn't find anything that satisfied her, she created the course she's just shown us."

"Oh, I'm not trying to insult Margaret. Far from it. We've looked for several years at taking the message into the schools, but all we did was complain about the quality of the curriculums out there. Then we discarded the whole idea. Margaret did what we wouldn't do; I take off my hat to her."

They compared notes, winding up the final details just as chimes from the church across the street marked the five o'clock hour.

"I've got to get out of here," Barbara announced. "I'm speaking to a group in northeast Georgia at seven-thirty so I'm going to cut it close."

"Go on," Evelyn said, "Kirsten and I will close up."

The group went their separate ways. It wasn't long before Margaret was behind the wheel of her Expedition, debating which way to go on a busy Thursday afternoon.

Do I go to the grocery now, and run later getting home, or do I go on home and take us out for pizza tonight? Better call and be certain Brian picked up the other kids. It sure is convenient having another licensed driver in the house.

As she fished the phone from her purse, it beeped to announce three waiting messages.

I totally forgot about that call. Now there have been two more. Better see who's been trying to reach me.

She punched the code to reach voice mail retrieval and, as she waited for the system to work through the steps, began to wonder about the number.

I'll bet it was P.C. Probably got herself a Georgia-based phone number.

When the message began, however, it wasn't P.C., but a man's voice that announced, "Mrs. Haywood. This is Detective Ronnie Duncan with the Fulton County Police Department. I need you to call me at your earliest convenience."

Why would a police officer be calling me? He's waited this long, he can wait another minute while I get hold of Brian.

She hit speed dial for Brian's cell number and was about to abandon the call, after seven rings, when the phone was answered. Instead of her son's voice, it was a male voice that quizzed, simply, "Hello?"

If I didn't know better, I'd say this man sounds just like the officer who left the message for me.

Trying not to panic, but with a cold fear beginning to gnaw in her stomach, Margaret said, "I'm trying to reach Brian Haywood. Have I dialed the correct number?"

I guess speed dial could mess up?

"This is Brian Haywood's cell phone. He isn't where he can speak right..."

"This is Margaret Haywood, his mother," she interrupted. "I don't know how you have my son's phone, but I demand an explanation. Now!"

"Mrs. Haywood, this is Detective Ronnie Duncan with the..."

"Yes, I know who you are," she interjected. "You left me a message and I was going to call you back, as soon as I checked in with Brian to be certain he'd gotten his brother and sister from day camp." She could feel beads of sweat popping out across her forehead. "Where is my son? Why do you have his phone?"

"I hate to have to tell you this, ma'am..."

Margaret felt her insides turn to ice.

He's been in a wreck. I knew it was too soon to let him drive down here.

"Your son has been arrested. How soon can you get here?"

"Arrested? But how... why... surely... surely there's been some mistake."

"I'm afraid not, Mrs. Haywood. It's your son, Brian. He is under arrest."

"For what?" she screamed, more like an exclamation than a question. "Whatever it is, he didn't do it. I know my son. He isn't a criminal."

"You know what, Mrs. Haywood, there's a large part of me that agrees with you. But sad as it is, your son is under arrest as an accessory to armed robbery."

"Armed robbery?"

With blackness swirling about her, Margaret knew she was hanging on to consciousness by only a thin thread. She pulled her SUV back into the parking space behind the office and turned off the motor.

"Please," she begged, "please tell me what's going on. None of this makes any sense."

"There was an armed hold-up of a liquor store earlier this afternoon. Thanks to an alert clerk who gave us a very accurate description, we caught the robbers less than two miles away from the scene."

"But what does this have to do with Brian? He would never hold up a business. I didn't raise him like that."

"This is no reflection on your parenting, Mrs. Haywood, but the fact remains, we arrested Brian behind the wheel of his vehicle, the one that is titled to you. The two robbers were passengers in the SUV at the time we pulled him over."

The blackness was attacking her from every side. "You're telling me he drove the get-away car?"

"Yes, ma'am, that's about the size of it. Brian even admitted that he drove the other two guys to the liquor store and waited outside for them."

Panic was rising inside her, threatening to choke off her air supply. She could sense desperation deep in her soul. "He didn't know what he was doing."

"Again, Mrs. Haywood, just between the two of us, I suspect that's exactly what happened. Unfortunately, the law doesn't allow for that little distinction. He did drive the vehicle that transported two robbery suspects away from the scene of a hold-up. Whether he knew what he was doing or not doesn't enter the picture." The detective's voice dropped a couple of octaves. "We had no choice but to arrest him along with the other two."

"Where is my son now?"

"He's being held here at the central jail, east of town. May I assume you'll be here soon?"

"You mean he's in a cell?"

The sordid memories of her own arrest at Don's hands and all the degradation she suffered flooded her mind. Oh, Lord. No. Not my baby.

"Yes ma'am. He's a suspect in an armed hold-up. He's just fortunate no one was killed. Otherwise he'd be an accessory to first degree murder as well."

Oh, Lord. What am I going to do? How could this have happened? He's been so mature lately, so helpful with Sallie and Jason.

Reality hit.

"Detective Duncan? My other two children. Were they with Brian?"

"No, ma'am. Why do you ask?"

"Because Brian was supposed to pick them up after day camp and take them home."

While she didn't think it possible, it felt as if her entire body were getting even colder.

My oldest child is in jail and I don't know where the other two are.

"Detective...?"

"Duncan," he supplied. "Detective Ronnie Duncan."

"I don't know where my two younger children are," she sobbed into the phone, finally unable to contain the hysteria that overwhelmed her. She looked at the clock on the dash. "Day camp closed over an hour ago. Everyone goes home." Her voice rose to a shrill scream. "I don't know what to do," she wailed.

"Mrs. Haywood...Mrs. Haywood! Get a grip. Let me help you."

"How... how can... you help?"

"Tell me where the children's day camp is. I'll dispatch a cruiser to see if they're still there."

Margaret gave him the address.

"You sit tight. Don't leave there. We should know something in a couple of minutes. A car was nearby and is already on its way."

"Thank... you," she sobbed.

Nothing that happened with Don hurt this badly. I think my heart is truly broken.

"Mrs. Haywood?"

"Did you find them? Are they there? I'm on my way." She couldn't stop her run-away mouth.

"No, ma'am. The car isn't there yet. I wanted to ask if there was any other address where they might have gone?"

"No. There's no other... well, not unless you count our home. But how would they have gotten there?" She gave the prospect some quick thought. "It's much too far for them to walk."

"Give me that address. I'll send a car in that direction as well."

After giving him the address of the condo, Margaret found that she was clutching the steering wheel in a death grip.

I'm afraid if I turn loose, I'll fly into a million pieces.

Still, she hung on to the wheel as if it were a lifeline and looked around the parking lot.

Does anyone see me? Can they tell by looking at me that my son helped hold up a liquor store? Oh, God, I'm so ashamed. I just know Brian didn't realize what was happening. But why did he have two people in his car who would do something like that?

She remembered the new friends he'd mentioned. *He never told me much about them, or what all they did when they were together. He never brought any of them around to the house, either. In Carter's Crossroads, we knew every friend he had, because they were in and out of our home and our lives.*

"Mrs. Haywood?"

The voice on the other end of the phone connection startled her so that it took a few seconds for her to remember the detective was trying to find Jason and Sallie.

I need to have my motherhood license revoked. I can't even keep in mind that two of my children are missing!

"Mrs. Haywood. Your children are safe on the front steps of your condo."

"They are?" She felt stupefied. "But how...?"

"One of the day camp workers drove them home, after they couldn't raise you on your cell phone, thinking perhaps there had been a problem."

Oh there's been a problem alright. If I hadn't been so wrapped up in my work, enjoying the accolades of my co-workers, I might have been on top of the problems my children were having today. I'm a total failure as a mother.

"Mrs. Haywood, what do you want to do about your children? I'm sure the day camp employee needs to get on home."

"What...? Oh... oh, yes. Of course." She consulted the clock again. "Can the two officers stay with them until I get there? I'm about ten minutes away."

"Yes, ma'am, that's what I was going to suggest."

"Thank you, Detective Duncan."

"Now, Mrs. Haywood. We still need you here at the jail about Brian. How soon can we expect you?"

I was so relieved about the other two I'd already forgotten about Brian. I really don't need children!

"I'll be there as quickly as I can. I have to find someone to care for the other two. We're new in town. No family and no close friends."

It wouldn't have been this way in Carter's Crossroads.

"I wouldn't advise bringing them with you."

"I wouldn't even if you did advise that." She was already pulling out of the office parking lot. "May I call you back as soon as I can get the other two situated?"

"Yes ma'am. That'll be fine." He paused. "And Mrs. Haywood...?"

"Yes sir?"

"Don't get a speeding ticket trying to get here."

"Yes sir."

In a matter of minutes she was pulling onto her street. She saw the Fulton County Police cruiser before she saw the officers or her children. When she finally did catch sight of Sallie and Jason, what she saw finished breaking her heart.

Both of them are ghost-white. I've never seen either of them look so frightened. Oh, God, what have I done to my children?

Margaret left the keys in the ignition with the motor running while she took off on foot. She quickly sprinted up the steps to where the two children sat, huddled together on the designer bench alongside the front door.

"Mommie!" Jason wailed. "We didn't know where you were and we didn't know what to do."

Margaret grabbed the little boy to her, clutching him as if he would evaporate if she loosened her grip.

He really had begun to come out of his shell and recover. Now...?

"What's wrong, Mommie? Why are these policemen here? Why didn't Brian pick us up?"

"I'm so sorry, you two." She knelt so that she could look at both of them on their level. "There were some problems so Brian couldn't get there."

"Is he hurt?"

"No, sweetie. He isn't injured or anything."

I hope he isn't hurt. Detective Duncan didn't mention anything about that. I didn't have sense enough to ask.

"Then where is he?"

I can't tell these children their brother is in jail. Their daddy went to jail and he died. They would both make the connection.

"I'm not exactly sure where Brian is. But I'm going to see him as soon as P.C. gets here to stay with you two."

"P.C.'s coming?"

Margaret had called her friend the minute she headed toward the condo. P.C. was as shocked as she, but she assured Margaret that she was already walking out the door. Margaret dismissed the officers, unlocked the house, and ushered the children inside.

"I'm hungry, Mommie."

Margaret looked absent-mindedly at her youngest son.

What is he saying? Of course... of course he's hungry.

"Sallie, can you and Jason find something in the 'fridge to snack on? I'm going to give P.C. money and ask her to take you to get supper."

While she waited for her friend, knowing only too well how long it would take to drive from Carter's Crossroads to Atlanta, Margaret made two calls. The first was to Barbara at home. After she got the answering machine, she remembered that her boss was headed to a speaking engagement in the northeast corner of the state. She left a message. "Barbara. It's Margaret. Please call me when you get this message. No matter how late. I have to talk to you."

Her second call was to Detective Duncan to assure him that she had someone on the way to stay with her other children; that she would be on down to the jail as quickly as she could.

"I'll see you when you get here. And Mrs. Haywood...? If you haven't already retained an attorney for Brian, you might want to see to that ASAP."

An attorney! Lord, how much dumber can I get? It never occurred to me that I needed to do that. Now here it is... She checked her watch. *After seven o'clock. Where am I going to find an attorney tonight? If I were back in Carter's Crossroads...*

"They're here," Sallie screamed. She had been watching out

the window.

Good...! THEY're here? Lord, did Joe come?

Sallie already had the front door open by the time Margaret got to the foyer where, to her relief, she saw both P.C. and Joe.

"We got here as fast as we could," P.C. assured her as the two embraced. "I called Joe as I left my house and told him to be waiting at the curb."

Margaret clutched her friend who returned the favor and, with great trepidation, slowly released her grip.

"Brian's going to need an attorney, you know."

"Why is Brian going to need an attorney, Mommie?"

Oops, I forgot little pitchers have big ears.

"He's in a little trouble, Sallie, but Joe and P.C. are here now. They're going to help him."

Joe reached across and kissed Margaret's cheek.

"I don't want to rush you, but the sooner we get there, the sooner I can make heads or tails of all this. We need to roll."

Margaret hugged both the children and gave each a kiss.

"I may not be back before your bedtime. If I'm not, you both are to go right on to bed. I'll be here when you get up in the morning."

"Don't worry about these two for a minute," P.C. assured her. "We're going out to eat, then we'll be back here watching TV until bedtime."

"Thank you, P.C. I don't know how..."

"Go. Go! We can talk later."

"P.C.'s right, Margaret." Joe took hold of her elbow. "We should've already been there. I'll drive."

As they pulled away from the condo, Margaret asked, "Are you going to be able to get Brian out of jail tonight?"

His answer was one she thought she'd remember always.

"I doubt it," he said at last, his eyes fixed on the congested street ahead. "I seriously doubt it."

CHAPTER EIGHT

*T*he sight of Brian in the orange jail jumpsuit, his wrists cuffed, was a sight Margaret knew would terrify her in the darkest hours of many nights to come. It was all she could manage not to fly into hysterics.

Oh, son, I have failed you so.

She and Joe were able to look at him through the glass, while the officer in charge worked to clear them to enter the holding area. When Brian first glimpsed them, Margaret saw, he dropped his head and, despite her fierce but silent pleas to the contrary, would not look their way again.

It hurts so bad. All I want is to hug him and wake him up from this nightmare.

"They'll let us in to see him in a minute, but I have to caution you… no touching."

"No touching? Joe… you mean I can't even hug my own child? He's not even an adult yet."

"That's neither here nor there. This is the big city. When they say no physical contact, that's exactly what they mean."

"Joe…" she pleaded. "How can one little hug hurt? I'm going

to ask Detective Duncan..."

"Sorry, Margaret." Her lawyer's face displayed the pain he was feeling. "Detective Duncan is the one who issued that order. If you touch Brian in any fashion, you will be escorted out." He cast her a pleading glance. "I really need you in there with me."

"If that's how it is, then I guess I have no choice." Her voice betrayed a note of bitterness and despair. "I'm not leaving my son."

After what seemed an eternity, they were both patted down. An officer relieved Margaret of her purse and cell phone, and barked an order to follow.

She's got about as much warmth and compassion as a polar iceberg.

As they approached the totally beaten looking teenager, she felt Joe's fingers cutting into her arm, which she interpreted as a reminder that she couldn't embrace her son. Margaret saw the boy sneak a glance beneath the eyelashes that had charmed females since he was born, then drop his eyes again. When she spoke to him, there was no return acknowledgement.

"Brian. Joe and I are here to try to help you, but we must have your cooperation."

"Too late," he mumbled.

Margaret felt the rumble of the muttered words as much as she heard them. "No, Brian, it's not too late, but we don't need to waste any more time."

"Just go on back home and leave me here. You obviously don't want me."

"Excuse me?"

"I've only been in here for five hours. First they can't get you to answer your phone, and then you take forever to get here. Now you won't even hug me; just go on back home. I'm sunk anyway."

Margaret's heart was torn in half. On the one half, it was breaking over her child's actions and total resignation. But the other half of her heart was spilling anger and daggers. From his defiance, she found the strength to exercise tough love, and did just that.

"Now you listen to me, mister. I turned my phone off because I was in a meeting, earning money to pay our bills. I couldn't drag your brother and sister down here, and you needed an attorney. I had to wait 'til Joe and P.C. could get here."

By this point her anger was giving way to hysterics, but she tried to hold things together. The best she could manage was to deliver her last declaration though the sobs that consumed her. "And...and as for...for hugging you, it's killing me right now that I can't. The police said..."

"Your mother can't hug you, Brian. I can't shake hands with you, either. Those are the orders we had to accept in order to see you any way but through a piece of glass. So get off your mother's case."

"Brian...Brian...Brian...!" Margaret waved her hands this way and that. "How could you do this? Helping rob a liquor store? If you hadn't been somewhere, doing what you had no business doing, we wouldn't be having this conversation." She felt the panic rising in her throat. "Have you lost your mind?"

As she asked the final question, Margaret watched the boy collapsing in upon himself. Before she could even grasp what was happening, the belligerent teen was in a heap on the dirty tile floor, crying hysterically.

"I'm so sorry, Mom. Honest I am. I didn't even know what those guys were doing until they got back in the car and told me to get out of there."

Just as I figured. Unfortunately, if Detective Duncan is right, that defense won't carry far with a judge.

Since they'd been ordered to keep hands off, both Margaret and Joe could do nothing but stand and watch the boy writhe in his own distress.

"Brian," she pleaded, "how did this happen? Why were you running around with people who would even stop at a liquor store?"

"Mom," he begged. "Help me. Please help me! I swear I didn't know what was going down."

"We believe you on that score, Brian. But we don't understand why those people were even in your vehicle. Were you giving someone a ride?"

Surely Brian's not naive enough to be giving rides to perfect strangers here in Atlanta. This isn't Carter's Crossroads.

As he spoke, the boy sat up while slowly collecting himself. He ran his manacled hands through his hair as best he could.

"You gotta believe me, Mom. I didn't have any idea what they were about to do."

Margaret knelt down beside him, ever mindful of Joe's hand on her shoulder and the message it conveyed.

"Look at me, Brian. Now!"

The boy raised his head and met her gaze.

"I do believe you. What I don't understand is why you were hauling people around who would do something like this."

He grimaced. "They were...they were my friends."

"Your...*friends?*"

"Yeah, my new friends from work. We unload trucks together."

Slowly an understanding began to form in her conflicted mind. "Brian. Look at me! Are these the new friends you never would bring by the house?"

He dropped his head. "Yes ma'am."

She thought for a second. "Just how old are these boys?"

For the longest he didn't answer. Finally he muttered. "I don't know. Twenty-two or twenty-three?"

Hardly boys, I'd say. "So when you aren't at work, you've been running around with grown men several years older than you are?"

"Yes ma'am," he mumbled.

"You know I never would have allowed this."

"Yes ma'am."

"This is why you never let me meet them." She was through asking questions. It was time for clear cut declarations. "Regardless of what penalty a court of law has for you, you're still going to have to deal with me at home."

"Yes ma'am, I know that."

"The wheels come back to me. Right now I don't know if you'll ever get them back."

"Yes ma'am."

Joe interrupted. "Margaret, enough about what you're going to do. All of it justified," he hurried to affirm, "but right now I need to ask Brian some specific questions so I know how to best proceed."

"Mr. Busbee," Brian whispered plaintively, "am I going to get to go home tonight?"

Joe was visibly struggling with his response.

He told me he doubted we could get him out tonight. We don't own property here in Fulton County and it's too late to get him before a judge tonight. If only we'd gotten here earlier. Maybe...

"I'm not going to lie to you, Brian. Chances are good you'll be spending the night. I can get you out on bail, but it's too late to get everything done tonight."

"Whatever."

"Brian, don't give up. This is bad, but we'll get through it."

Do I really believe we are? Lord, I've never felt so alone, not even the night that Don broke my arm.

"OK, Brian. I'm going to ask you some questions and I want honest answers. The whole truth, because if you lie to me even just a little bit, you're just digging the hole deeper."

"Just ask, Mr. Busbee. I'll tell you whatever you want to know."

Over the next ten minutes, Joe fired one question after another at the troubled teen and the answers were lobbed back over the net without hesitation or an attempt to withhold.

"Thank you, Brian. Thank you for being straight with me. Know how I can tell?"

"No sir."

"Two ways. You looked me straight in the eye, you never dropped your gaze. Second, you never hesitated, never appeared to try to form answers. Those two things make you come across as straightforward. Now, I need something from you."

"What can I do from in here?"

"I'm going to level with you, man to man, because you are closer to a man than a boy. I have no hope of getting you home to your bed tonight. You can tough it out for one night."

Margaret saw her son's face fall as he swallowed hard.

"Don't let this get to you. It's important you talk to the judge in the morning the same way you talked to me just now. Look the judge straight in the face. Respond with the manners your mother taught you. Be respectful, and don't fudge on the truth."

"Will that help, Joe?"

"I'd almost promise that it will. I haven't even met the other two men, but I can guarantee you they won't "show" as well as our boy right here. He really does hold his future in his own hands."

Margaret and Joe spent a few more minutes reassuring Brian, before they said good-night and watched as the guard escorted him out of the visiting area.

"Oh, Joe," Margaret sobbed. "I don't know how I can stand up under this."

"You may not know how, but God meets us where our needs are the greatest. You're going to have to lean on Him."

Lord, that's what I've been doing, and it still hurts worse than anything I've ever endured.

As they departed the jail, Detective Duncan intercepted them.

"I'm going to go check on the court schedule for tomorrow," Joe told her. "I'll meet you back here in a few minutes."

"Mrs. Haywood, thank you for honoring our orders that you not make physical contact with your son. I know it had to have been very difficult."

"You've never been a mother; you can't imagine how torn I was. Believe me, I'd willingly spend a night in jail right now if I could offer him just a few seconds of comfort."

"I hope you know that it isn't often I encounter a prisoner that I connect with emotionally, but your son is one of those select few."

"He didn't realize what was happening, Detective. Granted, he was hanging around with guys he shouldn't have, but I can guarantee you he would never willingly have gone along with a hold-up plan."

"Yes ma'am, I know."

"You do?"

"Yes ma'am. It's obvious your son has been raised right. Even when he was terrified under questioning, his answers were polite and respectful. He said 'yes sir' and 'no sir'."

"I told you Margaret," Joe said. He had walked up as she and the detective finished their conversation.

"But that still doesn't get him out of this awful place. I shudder to think about the type men he's going to be sharing space with."

Detective Duncan placed his hand on Margaret's arm.

"If I may be blunt, Mrs. Haywood?"

"Yes, please."

"As I said, it's obvious you've done a credible job with your boy. There's no denying he's made a couple of mistakes. I think spending a night here will instill in him a determination to never even get a parking ticket in the future."

"What you say makes sense. But I still worry about his safety and what he could be exposed to."

"I'm concerned as well. The YDC where he would normally be housed is full. I've asked the jailer to house him in a small holding cell we have within sight of the guard station. He'll be in the cell alone, where he'll be safe, and he'll be where he can see the guards."

"Oh, thank you, Detective Duncan," she exclaimed. "I could hug your neck."

"That might not be our wisest course of action right now, but I appreciate the sentiment nonetheless."

Margaret couldn't help herself. Tears that had threatened earlier finally made good and she was dabbing her cheeks with tissues from her purse.

"Contrary to popular belief, Mrs. Haywood, we aren't sadistic animals. Neither are we able to coddle or look the other way."

Joe interrupted, "He's going before a judge at ten tomorrow morning to be arraigned. We'll need to be here, so let's get home."

"You couldn't keep me away. I just wish I could speak to the judge."

"Well you can't," Joe advised. "You'd do more damage than good if you tried."

"But..."

"You can't speak, Mrs. Haywood, but I can. I will do everything I can to help Brian. The judge will rely heavily on my account."

"Why, Detective Duncan? Why would...?"

"Why would I help Brian? Because I believe in him. That young man sold me within minutes after he was brought in."

"Thank you. However this comes out, thank you."

The detective's face assumed a more severe expression. "But I don't like to be played for a fool. If I ever encounter Brian Haywood in an orange jump suit again, I will spare him no mercy."

Margaret knew he spoke the truth and didn't bother to plead for additional mercy.

After promising to be there by nine o'clock the next morning, she and Joe left to drive back to the condo.

"I need to look in Brian's closet when we get back to your house."

A cold fear struck Margaret. "Why? You're not looking for stolen money are you? Or liquor? Oh, Joe, not drugs?"

"No, no, nothing like that. Don't panic. I want to pick out clothes to take back to him in the morning. I don't want him to appear in court in the jump suit and flip-flops like the other two defendants."

"First impression?"

"You got it."

Once home, where P.C. assured Margaret the two younger Haywood's were already safely in bed, the three of them stood before a rack of expensive looking clothes. Margaret pulled out a particular sport coat she thought had always looked very smart on her eldest son.

I can see him in it now. This would make a good impression.

"Afraid not," Joe ruled. "Too pricy. Looks it, too. Chances are, if the judge has a teenage son, he or she will know exactly how much this cost. The last image we want to create is a spoiled young man from wealthy surrounds throwing himself on the mercy of the court."

"Joe's right," P.C. agreed. "Here..." She reached across Margaret and selected a simple navy blue blazer. Does he have a good looking pair of khaki's?"

"Yes," Joe said, "that's what I'm looking for."

Margaret went to the other end of the hanging clothes and picked up two different pair of casual tan slacks." She offered them to Joe. "Take your pick."

Joe held both pair up, looked at the fabric, before selecting the one in his right hand.

"Here. This pair looks just a little worn, but not shabby. Now, get me a white dress shirt and let's find a tie that blends. He'll need socks and a belt and shoes. Better get him clean shorts as well. It'll make him feel better to have on clean clothes from the skin out."

"I'm glad you have a feel for this. Obviously I'd have dressed him as inappropriately as possible." She tried to laugh and failed miserably. "I'd have probably gotten him a life sentence without parole."

"Look at it this way, Margaret." P.C. was putting all the clothing into a garment bag. "If he goes before that judge looking like a million dollars, it will scream 'money.' That will create exactly the opposite impression Joe wants. But if he goes in dressed with these clothes, the hint of money isn't nearly as strong as the assurance of respect for the judge and the court."

"This will help?"

"There's always one judge who has a heart of stone, but with any luck, we'll get a sympathetic jurist. We need to make Brian look as different from the other two as we can, without rubbing the court's nose in it. Our defense is that he didn't know what was going down. That will be so much easier for the judge to swallow if Brian looks like he isn't one of them."

Despite Margaret's protests, Joe and P.C. left shortly thereafter, with promises to be back by eight o'clock the next morning.

"Neither of you are going to get any rest."

"You worry about you and let us worry about us," P.C. ordered. "You need to look on top of your game tomorrow morning."

The two hadn't been gone but a few minutes when Margaret's cell phone rang.

"Who could...?" She saw the Caller ID. "Oh, it's Barbara. I'd totally forgotten about calling her."

"Margaret," her boss said without preamble. "I hesitated to call this late, but you sounded so distressed."

Margaret was too exhausted, emotionally and physically, to try and sugar-coat the facts, which she quickly shared.

"I am so sorry, Margaret. I know you are absolutely cut to the quick."

"If you could have seen him at the jail tonight, you wouldn't have to be his mother for it to break your heart."

"Listen. I'm going to say a prayer as soon as we hang up. For you and him. Don't you even worry about anything tomorrow except getting that boy back home."

"That's what I'm going to have to do," Margaret agreed. "I can't let this ruin his entire life."

After they ended the conversation, Margaret checked on the other two sleeping children. She then sought refuge in her shower, where she stood until the water ran cold and her tears ran dry. Once in her gown, she picked up her familiar, comforting Bible and with a heart full of grief, opened the book to search for the message her God had for her that night.

Oh, Lord. I need peace of heart and peace of mind to be able to sleep tonight and function in Brian's best interest tomorrow. You've promised us that You know our needs before we do. I'm clutching that covenant to my breast tonight. In Your Son's name, I pray for my son. Amen.

CHAPTER NINE

𝒥ason and Sallie were sleeping in. Margaret decided to let them stay where they were.

I promised them I'd be here when they awoke this morning, but I can break that vow. P.C. will see to them, and can even explain what has happened.

Margaret was ready before seven o'clock and paced the floor for the next fifty minutes, looking out the front window about thirty times. Finally, her vigil was rewarded, and she was amazed to see three doors open on Joe's Lincoln. The third passenger was Annie Campbell.

What's Annie doing here?

Her three friends were quickly ushered inside, where Annie grabbed Margaret and held her tenderly and lovingly, yet with amazing strength.

"My dear, I was so heartbroken when Barbara Kirkland called me last night to ask me to pray for all of you. Which you know I did."

If I hadn't been so fried, I'd have known Barbara would call Annie.

"Thank you, Annie. But praying is one thing. Being here is another." She gave her friend a long, hard look. "So why are you here?"

"She called my cell phone before Joe and I even got back to

Carter's Crossroads last night and insisted there had to be something else she could do. When I told her Jwe were coming back down this morning so I could stay with the children while you went to court..."

"I've come down to stay with Sallie and Jason so P.C. can go with you." She consulted her watch. "I also called Pastor Samuel. He and Susan should be rolling in any time."

"It won't take three of you to watch the children," Margaret offered.

"They're going to court with you," Annie said kindly. "Both of them are going to offer character testimony, if the judge agrees."

What did I ever do to deserve such wonderful friends?

"Can they do that?"

"It's possible," Joe advised. Ministers and other police officers can usually get an audience when ordinary mortals can't.

Like an ordinary mortal mother!

In a very few minutes the others had arrived and they were soon on their way to the jail in two vehicles, since the pastor and his wife would have to head back as soon as they offered their testimony.

When they arrived at the jail, Joe took the garment bag of clothes from Margaret.

"P.C. will help the three of you find the court room. I'm going to sign in, have a conference with Brian, and help him get ready." He nodded at Margaret. "Sorry, no ladies allowed where I'm going."

"Here," Margaret said hastily, digging in her large tote purse. "Here's his razor, shaving cream, toothpaste and toothbrush." *What else?* "Oh, and deodorant. I thought about all this while I was dressing this morning."

"That's what mothers are for," he said, as he hugged her, "but this stays with you. He has what he needs back there." He offered a consoling smile. "Relax. It's really not as black as it looks. We're going to get him through this."

I pray you know what you're talking about.

It was more than an hour before Brian's appointed time. *It is not a forgiving sixty minutes*, Margaret thought as she looked at the large clock on the faraway wall. *There's nothing to do but wait.*

Finally, when she believed she would absolutely go mad, she saw Joe enter from a doorway in the side wall. Behind him, walking confidently and escorted by a uniformed deputy, Brian looked worlds different from what she had seen the night before.

At least he's not wearing handcuffs! Hold him in Your hand, Lord. He needs You right now.

Even before Brian was seated, the same door opened again. Two other prisoners were led in. Both were in dirty, wrinkled jumpsuits and didn't look like they had even bathed or combed their hair that morning.

If those are the other two guys, I'd call them skanks if I saw them in the hallway, even if they hadn't gotten my son in trouble.

In her heart, Margaret knew Brian alone was responsible for his trouble.

But those guys didn't help the situation.

Unlike all the TV courtroom dramas she'd watched since childhood, very little was conducted the way those shows were scripted. Each defendant was called by name and stood. Brian, Margaret noticed, didn't hesitate to rise when his name was called. The judge read the charges against each of the three before calling Detective Duncan to the stand to testify about the events of the previous afternoon.

Consulting a notebook he pulled from inside his coat pocket, the policeman told of receiving a blanket radio transmission requesting the nearest unit to respond to a liquor store robbery at the corner of Piedmont and Grassdale. "My partner and I were returning from interviewing a witness in another case, and were only about two blocks away. I acknowledged and was on site in less than a minute. The clerk told me she'd been robbed, gave me a description of the get-away vehicle, and pointed out the direction the vehicle had gone."

He checked his notes again. "My partner and I initiated pursuit and within a mile and a half, spotted a vehicle matching that description. It was stopped in the parking lot of a medical office building. We were able to pull right alongside it."

He paused to survey the three defendants, stopping last on Brian. "Mr. Faulker and Mr. Jensen had seen us and were in the process of opening the door. They had partially exited the vehicle, but we were able to intercept them and place them under arrest. Then we..."

The judge, a stern looking black man of considerable girth interrupted the detective's testimony. "You say Mr. Faulker and Mr. Jensen were getting out of the suspect vehicle. What about Mr. Haywood?"

"He was in the driver's seat when we arrived on the scene. Even while we were detaining the other two, he did not move from his seat or attempt to abandon the vehicle."

"I see."

"I called for a cruiser and we quickly had the three on their way to booking."

The judge called each man's name and asked if he was represented by counsel. In the first two cases, public defenders identified themselves and asked for release on signature bond. When he called Brian's name, Joe identified himself as his attorney and asked for a cash bail of ten thousand dollars.

Margaret thought she heard a snicker from one of the public defenders.

Before ruling, the judge asked each of the first two defendants if they had anything to say in their own defense. In response, each man replied that he wasn't guilty. In each case, the answer was mumbled and the defendant remained seated, looking at the floor. Their two attorneys kept glancing at their watches, clearly concerned with other commitments.

How can they sit there and say that with a straight face, when the clerk identified them and they found the stolen money in Brian's SUV?

The judge consulted paperwork before him, and then announced both men would be remanded to custody, with bail granted only if a one hundred thousand dollar cash bond were posted.

"But your honor," one of the attorneys protested. "My client has no way to raise that kind of money."

"He should have thought about that before he held up that liquor store," the judge snapped. "I guess we'll be housing him for a while."

He is tough. Will he be equally hard on Brian? I can raise the bail money. I just wonder what other conditions he'll impose.

She didn't have long to wait. When the judge asked Brian if he had anything to say, Brian stood, and in a clear and confident voice, replied, "Your Honor, I was the driver of that car, but I didn't know what they were doing until they jumped back into my vehicle and yelled for me to get out of there. I was already out on the road before they told me they'd robbed the store. That's when I pulled over to try and decide what to do. I know what I did was wrong, but I place myself at your mercy. I'm willing to accept whatever you direct, even if it means I can't get out of jail."

Brian, you don't want to stay in that place!

"Your Honor, if I may have just a moment, I'd like to reiterate what my client has said," Joe added. "He is a sincere young man. I've known him almost since he was born. I can assure you he is not the kind of teenager who gets into trouble. By his own admission, he made a serious error in judgment when it comes to the caliber of people he's been hanging with. But these were co-workers of his; the three unload trucks of merchandise, so it's not like he went out looking for trouble."

"That's a very persuasive argument, counselor. But by your own admission, you've known him since infancy. One could say you're biased."

Joe grinned. "One could, your Honor. Which is exactly why I

brought along two character witnesses. One is a pastor and the other is a police officer in a north Georgia precinct."

"Bring them forward."

Pastor Samuel came forward, was quickly sworn, and didn't even sit while he testified to Brian's reliability, his rush to maturity, and the fact that, while he had made a serious mistake, he was also mature enough to accept responsibility for his actions. Susan followed him immediately, offering much the same testimony.

As they were returning to their seats, the judge quipped, "I'm always leery of anything an attorney might say. Been there, done that. But a minister and a police officer? Them I'd lean more to believe."

Is it possible he's about to show us some leniency?

"Are this young man's parents in the courtroom?"

Margaret stood, somewhat hesitantly, unsure of protocol. "I'm Margaret Haywood. I'm a widow."

The judge studied her at length.

"Tell me, Mrs. Haywood, what was your reaction when you learned your son had been arrested for robbing a liquor store?"

How do I answer him? I don't want to hurt Brian's case. I hope he doesn't connect Brian with Don!

Joe smiled at her. "It's okay, Mrs. Haywood."

"Well, your Honor. I'm a mother, so naturally my first reaction was that some sort of mistake had been made. But as soon as I got here and was briefed by Detective Duncan, I realized the mistake had been on Brian's part. And mine. My hands aren't totally clean."

"I'm afraid I don't understand."

"You see, my husband died recently, and Brian has been thrust into situations he shouldn't have had to confront. Not at such a young age, anyway. But I have to tell you, he's done an admirable job, and I've been so proud of him." She realized how that might have sounded. "I still am proud of him," she hastened to add. "I'm disappointed at the decision he made regarding who his friends would be, but I am so proud that he stood up like an adult and accepted blame for his acts. He has indicated to me that he's willing to pay whatever the price is and get it behind him. Nothing could ever make me stop loving him."

The judge said nothing, but continued to study the both of them. The black-robed official's eyes move from one to the other.

"One last question, Mrs. Haywood, if I may?"

"Yes, your Honor?"

"Are you prepared to accept whatever judgment this court hands down?"

"Yes, I am. I've already told Brian that I will stand with him, but he'll have to take his punishment."

"Did you tell him anything else?"

What is he getting at?

Joe smiled again, silently encouraging her.

"Well, your Honor. I told him if he thought he was in trouble with the court, he didn't have a clue what was waiting for him when he got home. Whenever that is."

"And what does await him, if I may inquire?"

Margaret didn't hesitate. "For starters, he loses the SUV. Indefinitely. He will have to quit the job he has, and I'll help him find another one that allows me more oversight into what he's doing and who he is doing it with. I'm prepared to pay whatever bail, fines, or court costs there are, but he will repay me, with interest. Last, he's grounded until I decide he's proven himself, or until he reaches forty. Whichever happens first."

Margaret noted that the judge's eyes were aglow.

Whatever does that mean?

"Mr. Haywood," he said, addressing Brian.

"Yes sir?" Brian rose to face the judge.

"Young man, I thought I was a pretty hard judge, but if I were in your shoes, I'd almost prefer jail over going home."

"Believe me, your Honor, I didn't sleep last night for thinking about that. My Mom's real cool, but she's also a stickler for what's right. I've hurt and disappointed her, so I imagine I'll pay dearly."

"Alright, I'm ready to reveal my decision. Is there anything else anyone would like to add?"

There was silence.

"Very well. I'm going to grant bail in the amount of five hundred dollars. There are, however, some conditions that go along with this bail." He took off his heavy horn-rimmed glasses and twirled them around on his finger. It goes without saying this young man will be present for trial when the time comes. Do you understand me, Brian?"

"Yes sir."

"You're released to the custody of your mother. Believe me young man, you don't know how fortunate you are that your mother loves you enough to hold your feet to the fire. You will surrender your license to her and not be behind the wheel of any vehicle unless she is in the car with you, and hands you that license temporarily, without coercion." He shook his finger at Brian. "If there is any revolt against her on your part, you will answer to me and it will be painful. Do we understand each other?"

"Yes sir. I understand completely."

"Just don't disappoint me. It would break my heart, although there are many in this building that don't believe I have a heart."

Oh, but you do have a heart. You certainly do. Margaret's own heart sang for joy at how it had all played out.

Thank You, Lord. Thank you!

The next few minutes were a giant melee. After Margaret and Joe conferred about the bail, she was finally able to embrace her son and indulge in her motherly instincts.

The pastor and his wife stopped on their way out of the courtroom to give Brian a hug.

"Thanks, you two. I didn't deserve the nice things you said about me. I know you helped to persuade the judge and I'm grateful."

"We're here for you, Brian. All you have to do is call on us," Susan assured him. "We're on our way back to Carter's Crossroads. We love you."

Finally Margaret got a chance to speak to her son.

"I'm so sorry, Mom," Brian whispered as she hugged him again. "I don't know how I'll ever make this up to you."

"You already have, son. You already have."

As he pulled away from her, his face was a gigantic question mark. "But I haven't done anything. I don't understand."

"Look, Brian. I'm not going to minimize the severity of all this. But I doubt there's anyone in this room, that judge included, who hasn't done something in the past that was stupid, maybe even life-threatening. I know I have. The important thing is we learned from our mistakes. You can, too, and come out better for the experience."

"Oh, I've learned a lot already, Mom. I really have."

"I believe what you say, because you stood up like an adult, like a man, and accepted responsibility. I've never been more proud of you than I was this morning."

"I promise you...."

Before he could finish what he was about to say, Detective Duncan slapped a hand on the young man's shoulder.

"Congratulations, Brian. I'm glad the judge saw fit to handle this in a way that we can all live with."

The young man grinned a sheepish smile. "Me too, sir, me too." He offered his hand to the detective. "Thank you for going to bat for me. You didn't have to do that."

"Oh, but I did. You see, Brian, we aren't all about administering punishment. We're about righting wrongs as well. You got involved in something that was wrong. True, your choice of companions wasn't top notch, but neither did the usual punishment fit the crime." He dropped his voice a couple of notches. "Just don't say I said that. Besides, it makes me angry that those guys used you."

"That they did, sir."

"But to your credit, as soon as you realized what had gone down, you didn't continue to flee. You pulled over and stopped, trying to decide how best to fix the problem when we drove up."

"I was really relieved to see you."

"I could tell. And I could also tell that you were a young man of character. It actually hurt to have to arrest you, because I knew you were several notches above those other two guys."

"I just hope the trial judge sees it this way when my case comes to court. I sure wouldn't want to have to go back to jail."

The officer put an arm around Brian's shoulders and drew him close. "Let me offer you a word of advice. You've never been in trouble before; just continue to be the good student and upstanding young man that we all know you are. I predict the judge will be hard-pressed to impose anything more severe than a year or two of probation."

"But he'll still have a criminal record," Margaret interjected. "I hate for this to haunt his college and job prospects in years to come."

Joe and P.C. walked up just in time to hear the end of Margaret's concerns, to which Joe added, "If Brian keeps his nose clean and serves out any probation he might receive, we can petition the court to expunge his record, which means he won't always be saddled with this one black mark."

Margaret looked expectantly at P.C. for a confirmation.

"Joe's right on target. Brian can still come out of this wiser and better, and without a criminal record." She tapped the boy on his arm. "There's a whole bunch of folks who're going to ride him hard to be certain he does just that."

"Believe me," Brian confessed to the small group clustered around him, "I know God gave me another chance. I don't intend to disappoint any of you, or myself and Him."

As they reached the parking lot, Joe reminded Margaret she had a vehicle that needed to be claimed. "Why don't we take you by the impound lot and drop you off, then we'll take Brian on back home?"

Margaret agreed. They were soon waiting while an officer brought the SUV to the entrance and handed Margaret the keys.

"I need to run by the office to pick up a packet of materials and I'll be right behind you," Margaret promised. "Brian can look after his brother and sister if you all need to leave before I get there."

She followed them for several blocks before hooking a left. When she got to the office, Barbara was just leaving the building, on her way to a meeting at the state capitol.

"Margaret," she called out when the two caught sight of each other. "I didn't expect to see you today. Is everything okay?"

The two hugged. "The judge imposed a very minimum bail, actually said he was impressed with Brian, and the boy is on his way back home right now with my attorney and his partner. I just ran by to pick up some material from Kirsten, then I'm headed home."

"Don't let me detain you, but I am glad things worked out this well." Barbara patted her employee on the shoulder. "We're all here if you need us, if you need a shoulder or an ear. Or both."

By the time Margaret arrived home, Brian had already explained to Jason and Sallie all that had happened, and the three friends from Carter's Crossroads were preparing to leave.

"You would have been so proud of him," Annie whispered, as she pulled Margaret aside. "I hadn't said anything to the children about all this, because I didn't know how much they already knew. They didn't ask and I didn't volunteer."

Poor Annie. She stuck her head in the lion's mouth without a flashlight.

"The minute he walked in the door, they were all over him wanting to know where he had been."

"What did he tell them?"

"The whole dirty story. He took responsibility for everything, admitting he had been running around with the wrong kind of friends. That he had done something very stupid and, as a result, he'd been arrested and had to spend the night in jail."

Annie hugged Margaret close.

"Then he told them if he had anything to say about it, neither of them would ever get into this kind of trouble, because he intended to see to it. He's a man, Margaret. He took total responsibility."

"That's what he did in court. He even thanked the judge for believing in him. I've never seen my son stand so tall." She choked back a sob as the vision of him in prison orange crumpled in a heap on the floor flooded her memory. "Even at one of the lowest moments in his life, he has never stood so tall."

"You know, my friend, just because he made a mistake doesn't mean he isn't an adult, and just because he's an adult, doesn't mean he can't still make a mistake."

That pretty well sums it up.

Joe and P.C. had been talking with the kids and came over to claim Annie.

"We've got to go. Believe it or not, things are happening in Carter's Crossroads, too. It may not be as fast-paced as Atlanta, but the calendar flips over there, too."

"I'll tell you for sure, Joe. I'm not convinced right now that this fast-paced life is all it's cracked up to be."

Joe hugged her, and P.C. said, "Atlanta has its faults, I'll give you that. But so does Carter's Crossroads and most every other town. You've been through an emotional wringer, Margaret. Give yourself time to process all that's happened before you start passing judgment."

"You're right. I know you are. If only I hadn't moved us here, Brian..."

"If chicken had teeth, they could eat steak," Joe interrupted. "Like P.C. says, give yourself time to recover from the trauma you've endured."

Annie hugged her again, as the three prepared to leave. "I'll tell you what, Margaret. I think Brian's in better shape right now than you are. If you need to talk, call me. Or we'll meet for lunch next time you're in town. Let me know."

Margaret watched as Joe's SUV pulled out of the cul-de-sac, then joined her children in the family room, where she found the two younger ones watching TV and Brian was sacked out on the couch, sawing logs.

"Don't bother Brian," Jason cautioned. "He had to spend the night in jail and he said he didn't get any sleep. He was scared."

He's going to be OK if he can say that all of this frightened him. At least he got to come home this morning. Those other two guys didn't. Lord, how did I abandon my responsibilities so easily?

But in her gut, Margaret knew the answer. Brian had assumed such a mature role following Don's death, she had allowed herself to forget that, in reality, he was still a child who needed her love and her guidance.

I dropped the ball and this is what happened.

"I won't disturb him," she assured Jason. "I'm sure he's exhausted."

"He said jail wasn't a very nice place," Sallie chimed in. "Said he didn't ever want us to have to go."

"I hope you don't, either."

"Why did Brian have to spend the night in jail?"

"Brian broke the law, son. When you break the law, there's always a penalty to pay. Don't ever forget that."

For once Sallie was unable to be flip or unconcerned, because Margaret saw her eyes fill with tears.

"I feel so sorry for Brian. I really do."

"But Brian said it's all going to be OK." Jason's expression was one of complete seriousness. "He said we were a family and nothing could ever separate us as long as we remember that."

Out of the mouths of babes!

CHAPTER TEN

Margaret could tell during the days that followed, that Brian was making an extra effort to reassure her that her faith in him wasn't misplaced.

Lord, I have to pin my hopes on You, who knows what it's like to see Your Son suffer, and on the positive things everyone has said about Brian's chances. I'm not going to be one of those parents who demand that their children not be inconvenienced; neither am I going to sit silently by and allow his entire life to be ruined.

In the first hours after the numbness wore off, Margaret found herself extremely angry with Don and blaming him for the chain event reactions that led to Brian's arrest.

But if I do that, I'm not being as mature as Brian. He could have blamed me, but he didn't. He took ownership of his deeds and I have to do the same.

The one thing that did occupy her thoughts day and night was whether she had made a mistake moving the family to Atlanta.

Should we have stayed in Carter's Crossroads, Lord, and stuck it out? Did I do wrong putting the children into public school when money is there to pay private school tuition? Have I been giving too much of myself to a job that I took primarily for me, at the expense of the three most important people in my life?

Should I have discouraged Brian from getting a job this summer? Was it wrong to give him his own wheels?

The questions were many and they intruded at all hours, while she went through the motions of doing her work, putting good meals on the table, and keeping up with the activities of all three of her children. Always in the background was a litany of concerns, a multitude of "what-ifs?", and the nagging feeling that she needed to revisit many of her decisions of the previous few months.

Grief counselors say you shouldn't make any major decisions for at least a year after a major loss, but I didn't have that luxury. If I'd taken my time before I loaded up, would things have turned out differently?

She bounced all of her concerns off Jim Deaton when they talked a few days later.

"I was so sorry to hear about all of Brian's troubles," her landlord offered. "P.C. called me as they were driving in to Atlanta that morning to go to court. I called her back that night to see how everything went."

"As bad as it is, I realize it could have been so much worse. I just give thanks every day that Brian was determined to take the blame."

"Brian's a good kid, Margaret. He's been through a lot."

"I agree, but that doesn't give him special dispensation to go hold up a liquor store."

"I'm not suggesting it should. I just know Brian Haywood, and he's an OK guy. Even OK guys make mistakes."

But this is my OK guy, Margaret reasoned with herself.

The two talked for a few more minutes. They were concluding the call when Jim Deaton asked, "So did you make good on having him quit his job?"

"He's working a two-week notice, but he is quitting. I told Brian it wasn't his employer's problem he broke the law, so he shouldn't make it the employer's problem by quitting without a notice," she answered, remembering how many times workers at Haywood Tufters would call in to say "I quit."

"Had the store heard about his problem?"

"Not until he told them the entire story. The other two guys who worked on the loading dock with him, his two cohorts in crime, are still locked up and neither has called."

"I assume they wouldn't be back if they got out of jail, so why does it matter where Brian works?"

I wrestled with that one.

"Brian asked that same question, but I told him I'd made statements on the record that he would quit this job. That was that."

"How'd he take it?"

"He's OK. He wasn't going to be able to continue working those hours anyway once school starts back. It's not that big a deal."

"Now you're home free?"

"Not really. Brian still has to stand trial as an accessory to armed robbery, driving the get-away car, and there was mention of harboring two fugitives since he was transporting them in his vehicle."

"Whew! That's pretty heavy."

"Especially at three o'clock in the morning; that's when I seem to find myself thinking about it most."

"What other steps are you taking?"

I've not shared this with any of the kids, or with Barbara or even P.C., so should I lay it on Jim?

"Believe it or not," she said finally, "I've been asking if I should move us back to Carter's Crossroads." She hesitated... "I never thought I'd see the day I'd take that step."

"You would do that?"

"That's just it, I don't know. But I have wondered if it's something I should do. Even if it means severing ties we've made here."

"Don't get too hasty, don't over-react."

"This is the first time I've mentioned it. But it is an option."

"Keep me posted," Jim encouraged. "You know if you decide to go back, you needn't worry about the condo. I can easily rent it."

I hadn't even thought about leaving Jim without a tenant. I hope he didn't think I was fishing around.

Later that same day, when Barbara Kirkland came by to visit with Margaret, the same topic ultimately landed on the table.

"You know, Margaret, when I offered you this job, it was with the idea you would work primarily from home in Carter's Crossroads."

She's right. I'd actually forgotten.

"I know, I was the one who wanted to get away from bad memories that people seemed determined we wouldn't forget."

"Are you saying you think you made a mistake?"

"That's just it," Margaret wailed in an uncharacteristic display of short temper, "I just don't know any more."

She buried her face in her hands and gave way to the tears that had threatened a coup for several days. Her friend and employer handed her several tissues from a nearby box.

I've reached the point where I can't make decisions any longer. At least none that I can feel good about.

"You know that you made this move because you felt it was best for your children. You made that decision based on the facts as you knew them. Now that you're here, additional facts have been revealed to you that may, or may not, change the way you look at things."

"So you're saying go back?"

The older woman reached over for Margaret's hand. "What I'm saying is you have to do what's best for you and your children."

"I thought that's what I was doing, but now I'm not so sure." She waved her hands about her head simulating a wind storm of confusion. "It's not just Brian's trouble. Sallie and Jason aren't making friends like they did and I can tell they're on the outside looking in. There are very few children in this entire complex. That's something I never thought to check."

"Then perhaps some changes need to be made. Maybe you do need to go back to Carter's Crossroads. Or perhaps you need to go ahead and buy a home in a neighborhood where they'll have roots and easily convenient playmates. The solution could be as simple as putting them into a private school. Let's not forget the option of calling a family meeting and agreeing to work harder to make the status quo work."

She's sure laid out a lot of possibilities I hadn't even thought about. I guess I really need to give this whole thing a lot more thought and prayer. She's speaking Your language, Lord.

"Thank you for understanding, and for your suggestions. I have to admit you hit on a couple of solutions that hadn't occurred to me. You really could be in full-time counseling, you know?"

Barbara hugged her as she prepared to leave. "I thank you for your kind words, but at the end of the day I'm just a domestic violence administrator who would do almost anything to keep from losing one of the best employees I've ever had." She grinned, then ducked her head. "I'm really a very selfish person, you know. Worse than a dog with a favorite bone."

Margaret spent the remainder of the day working in the condo washing clothes and dusting. In between she checked her computer for new e-mails and dealt with some details still unresolved for their full October schedule. Regardless of what she was doing, in the back of her mind were the many suggestions Barbara had offered.

Perhaps some changes need to be made. She sure did give me a lot of options. Only which of those possibilities is best?

Knowing that she would never get any peace otherwise, she finally laid down her dusting cloth and went to her bedroom, in search of her Bible. Once settled into the favorite chair that had come from the house on Redbud Way, she began to read and pray. Her initial intent had been to spend only a few minutes applying spiritual salve to her aching heart, but three hours later when her phone rang, she was astounded to discover she'd forgotten to claim her children from day camp.

"I'll be right there," she promised the counselor. "I am so sorry. The time simply got away from me."

Her face was the color of Christmas as she backed her Expedition out of the drive and hurried as fast as late afternoon traffic allowed to the YMCA, where Sallie and Jason waited outside.

"Hey, kids," she called as they began to board, "I'm so sorry."

"Is Brian in trouble again? He's not back to jail, is he?"

"No, Jason. Nothing like that. But why would you ask that?"

"I dunno. It's just the last time we didn't get picked up, that's what happened."

It's like he's waiting for the other shoe to drop.

"No, it's not that at all. To tell you the truth..." She laughed. "I was sitting reading my Bible and I simply lost track of the time."

"I don't think many people in Atlanta read Bibles, Mom."

Where did that come from? "Why do you say that?"

The little girl squared her shoulders and pulled herself up the way she normally did whenever she had a pearl of wisdom to unveil.

"When we talk with the other kids at day camp, a lot of them don't even go to church. A few of them say they've never even been inside a church, and they make fun of us because we do."

"That's right, Mommie. One of the boys in my group said only deadbeats and losers go to church."

I truly thought I was doing my children a favor to get them away from all the negatives in Carter's Crossroads, but it looks like I've simply exchanged one set for another. Are You trying to tell me something, Lord?

Since it was so near time for Brian to get off work, Margaret and the kids ducked into a nearby grocery store for bread and milk and a few other items she knew she needed, and killed enough time so they could drive straight to Brian's job and collect him.

"I bet Brian feels like a little kid being picked up by his

mommie," Sallie observed. "He was so proud having Daddy's Explorer."

I thought he was going to cry when I had it towed back to Carter's Crossroads. But he never fought me on it. Poor Daddy, when I had to call him to ask if we could park it at his house, I had to tell him what happened. He was heartbroken.

"I'm sure Brian's disappointed he can't come and go as he pleases. For that matter, I'd gotten accustomed to having a second driver so I didn't have to do everything myself."

About that time they caught sight of the eldest Haywood standing on the curb, looking about the parking lot.

"He's trying to see where we're parked," Sallie advised. "He kind of looks like a little lost kid."

"That's not very kind, Sallie. But this is a very practical demonstration of how wrong actions can hurt or inconvenience other innocent people."

"Hello, son. Hard day? You look beat."

As he closed the door and fastened his seatbelt, Brian favored her with one of his wry smiles. "We had two extra trucks today. School supplies getting ready for the tax free shopping blitz. I'm bushed. But it was nice to be busy. Takes my mind off things."

"Then why don't we head home and you can get a nice, hot shower and maybe that'll revive you?"

"That'd be great," he agreed.

"After supper can we go swimming, Brian?"

"Sure squirt, if that's what you want to do. You going too, Sallie?"

Margaret could see her daughter's quizzical expression reflected in the rearview mirror.

"I'd like to go swimming, but not in the condo pool. We're the only kids there and all those people look at us like we're trespassing or something."

"You hadn't mentioned this before, Sallie. Why do you think you're trespassing?"

Sallie's usually not shy about making her displeasure known.

"I dunno."

"Sallie's right, Mom. I don't think those guys around the pool every evening mind me too much, but they do look at Sallie and Jason like they're intruding on an adult event or something."

As I told Barbara earlier today, there are very few children in the entire complex. Most of the residents are like Jim Deaton; young, single and some young marrieds, but all of them professional people. Then a very disturbing thought struck her. *I'm probably one of the oldest residents in the entire complex.*

The prospect of being labeled "senior citizen" didn't rest well. "You kids go to the pool and enjoy yourself. Just don't get in the way."

"But Mom," Brian whispered sotto voice, "those folks sometimes use language and talk about things children shouldn't hear."

He's right on target.

After the supper dishes were washed, Margaret surprised even herself when she asked her children, "Would you mind if I went swimming with you? I haven't been in the water all summer."

She could tell they were surprised, but equally surprising was the warm reception her question received. Margaret quickly grabbed her swimsuit while making sure everyone had towels. They left by the back door to walk to the pool area about a quarter mile away. Upon arrival she noticed two things immediately.

The pool is fairly full, and they're looking at us like we're white trash come in from outside the complex.

Determined to beat them at their own game, Margaret immediately began to speak to those nearest to her, only to be answered with strained greetings of welcome.

Their welcome is for appearances only. It's obvious these people believe this pool is their special province and we're being tolerated.

They swam for about half an hour, dodging between people

who seemed determined to socialize, drinks in hand, while standing in the shallow end of the pool, much like livestock on a scorching summer day.

A couple of them look like cows, too! Immediately she regretted her rush to judgment, but she also knew what she saw and what she heard.

"Mom, I'm bushed and I'm ready to hit the bed. We can't even swim the length of the pool because people are standing in the way. If they want to swim, they need to swim or get out of the water."

Brian's right.

"Come on kids, let's get back before the mosquitoes get too vicious."

She gathered up her children and herded them from the pool area, but not without noticing the relieved looks directed her way.

"See what we mean, Mommie? They act like it's their pool and we shouldn't be there."

"Yes, Jason, I do see. All of you are exactly right."

I don't want to give my children the wrong impression here.

"You know," she said as she unlocked the kitchen door and held it for them to enter, "those people don't really think they own that pool. They've just fallen into the habit of using it without being bothered by outsiders."

"But we aren't outsiders, Mom. We live here," Sallie protested.

"No, we aren't outsiders. But we're not like them, either. Well, everyone needs a shower, then it'll be bedtime."

"They're kind of like a lot of the people at the church where we used to go," Brian said to his brother and sister as they all headed for their rooms.

Touché, son. Touché.

That evening, as she was taking an early nap, her phone rang.

Joe Busbee.

"Hello, Joe."

"Margaret. I hope I'm not calling too late."

"Never too late for you to call. How's P.C.?"

"She's fine. She's right here. I'll put her on as soon as you and I finish with the business I'm working on tonight."

It's after nine-thirty and P.C.'s still at his house? Wonder why he's calling?

"What's up, Joe. You're keeping late office hours, aren't you?"

"Have you got a minute to talk about Haywood Tufters?"

He's got something on his mind. He didn't even bite when I gigged him about working late.

"Sure. Talk. I'm all ears."

"It's like this, Margaret, Andy and I have been actively courting buyers, and there are plenty of them out there. Only everyone wants a bargain. We aren't comfortable disposing of a going, thriving business like Haywood Tufters like we were selling it at a yard sale."

"No... I don't endorse that option, either. After all, I'm selling it to raise money to ensure my children's futures and my old age."

At the risk of sounding greedy, I need as much as I can get.

"You're a long way from AARP status, you know." For the first time he showed a trace of his usual joviality.

"But I'm not getting any younger either. OK," she said, changing subjects, "you evidently have a suggestion or a proposal. Let's hear it."

"I do... I mean, we do have several ideas, but we'd rather sit down with you, in person, to explain our thoughts to try and arrive at a decision."

"That's not a problem. I'm more than willing to listen to anything you have to say. After all, it goes without saying that I have complete confidence in the both of you."

"Great."

"When would you like to meet? What's tomorrow? Friday," she answered her own question. "I can drive up there in the morning if you need me that quickly."

"You still planning to come up for church on Sunday?"

"You know it."

I can't believe how wonderful the thought of going back to Carter's Crossroads is.

"What if you came up tomorrow night and spent the weekend with your folks, so we could have as much time on Saturday as we need?"

"What are you cooking up, Joe? Why will we need all day Saturday?"

"I didn't say we're going to need all day, I just said it would give us as much time as we need. If you come up tomorrow, you've either got to make arrangements for the children, or you've got to watch the clock and get back at a certain time."

As much as it pains me to admit, he is right. But I still say he has something else up his sleeve.

"Hang on a second, Joe. Let me check with the children."

Margaret hurried to the upper floor, where she knew she'd find them sprawled out in front of the TV. They were, only Brian looked more asleep than awake.

"Kids. Hate to disturb you, but how would you feel if we went to Carter's Crossroads tomorrow night and spent the weekend with Grammy and Grandee?"

"Yeah," Jason volunteered without taking his eyes off the screen.

"Maybe I could play with Audra on Saturday?"

"That is an idea, Sallie."

"I'm OK with it," Brian agreed. "But why go for the weekend?"

"Joe Busbee and Mr. Davis need to talk with me about business matters. We just thought it might be easier to do it this way."

"Mom?" Brian asked hesitantly. "May I ask you something? And if the answer is, 'no', it's OK."

"Sure, son. Just ask it."

"Do you think I might be able to hook up with some of my old friends Saturday night, as long as you knew where we were, and I was home early?"

The judge said no coercion and he's certainly abiding.

"I'm not going to say 'yes' right now, but I'm not going to say "no' either. Joe's holding for an answer. Let me go back and tell him we're coming, and you and I will talk about this tomorrow. OK?"

"Sure, Mom." He grinned the toothy smirk that had melted her heart since he was just a toddler.

Margaret ruffled his hair. "Besides, you look like you need a good night's sleep. It's OK that you asked." She kissed him on top of his head. "I'll be back to tuck you two in as soon as I finish talking with Joe," she said to Sallie and Jason.

"Sorry to keep you waiting so long, Joe. The kids are all for it. We'll drive up tomorrow evening after Brian gets off work."

"Great. We'll talk Saturday morning. Good-bye... Uh, oh, wait. Here's P.C."

Margaret looked at her bedside clock. When she heard her friend's voice, she inquired, "It's ten-oh-nine, P.C. Do you know where your mother is?"

"As a matter of fact I do," her friend informed her. "She's sitting right here in the den with Joe and me. Any more questions, Miss Twenty Questions?"

Guess that told me!

"Nope," she quipped. "That's the correct answer. You just won the jackpot, just don't pass go and do not, under any circumstances, collect two hundred dollars."

Once they had finished poking fun at each other, Margaret asked her friend, "What's Joe got up his sleeve?"

"What do you mean?"

"Don't play innocent with me. Joe tells you everything, so why does he want me all day on Saturday?" She was suddenly very suspicious. "He's not setting me up for something, is he?"

"Look Margaret, I'm going to level with you. Joe believes you'd be doing yourself a real disservice if you give that business away. I agree. But they've come up with what I think is a fantastic solution. I can't wait for you to hear it for yourself."

"So what is that fantastic solution? You promised to level with me."

"And I did. I just can't tell you the specifics."

"Fine friend you are!"

"Look, you're making more out of this than it really is. Just wait until Saturday."

"I still say he's up to something."

"You might be right."

The two talked for several more minutes while P.C. brought her up to date on the remodeling Margaret's dad was doing on the house P.C. and her mother rented from him.

"You won't recognize it," her friend promised.

And neither will I be able to move back into that house, either. I would never force P.C. out. If we end up going back, I'll just have to find something else to rent.

Before getting into her gown, she went back upstairs to make sure the children were in bed. Then she came back to her bedroom, consulted the clock, and decided to wait until the next morning to call her parents.

It's getting a little late. I don't want to alarm them when nothing's wrong.

The next morning she ferried Jason and Sallie to day camp before dropping Brian off at his job. Then she drove to the domestic violence office, where she went behind closed doors with Barbara for a few minutes.

"Remember, I told you to do whatever you had to do for the best interest of you and your children. That hasn't changed. Just keep me posted."

Back at the house, she dialed her parent's number, the first phone number she ever memorized.

"Mama," she said with joy when she heard the sound of her mother's voice.

"It's not Brian? Nothing's wrong is it? I worry so much about all of you down there."

"Relax, Mama. Everything's fine. I just called to ask how you'd like to have four guests for the weekend."

"Four guests? Who...? What?"

"Us. Your daughter and grandchildren?"

"You're sure nothing's wrong?"

"Nothing's wrong. Joe needs me to meet with him tomorrow about the business, so I thought it might be nice to come tonight and stay 'til sometime Sunday afternoon."

"Oh, that would be wonderful! I can't wait to tell your daddy. He misses those children."

You do, too.

"Oh, your daddy. He's got to take me to the store. I don't have enough to feed all of us this weekend."

"Now, Mama. You know you're stretching the truth just a little. There's enough food stockpiled in your house to feed a small nation through a hard, cold winter."

"Maybe. But it's not what my grandchildren want to eat. Oh, it'll be so nice to have them to cook for again."

Mama's in heaven!

"Bye, Mama. We'll be there about seven o'clock."

The only response she got was the click of the line going dead.

Margaret busied herself finishing some work on the new round of grant proposals she was constructing and had promised by Monday, and e-mailed them to Barbara. Then she began to pull together clothes, giving each of them an additional outfit or two.

Just in case we should stay over 'til Monday? After all, we don't have to come back Sunday evening. Margaret couldn't believe she was actually comfortable thinking about going back home. *I called it "home."*

CHAPTER ELEVEN

The children were, Margaret realized, more animated on the trip north than she'd seen them in some time. The expression on her parents' faces, once they all settled down around the old oak round table in the kitchen, was a second reward money couldn't buy.

She allowed her parents to spoil them that evening with snacks and TV past their normal bedtimes. All of them, herself included, seemed to be the better for it.

This is good.

∽

"Run that by me one more time, Joe. This is definitely not what I expected to hear this morning. I just figured you guys had come up with some sort of creative financing solution that would get those guys to pay more and we'd all come out ahead."

"Look, Margaret, if you want to sell for what this business should bring, you're not going to be able to rush a deal. Which means you're going to have to hold on to Haywood Tufters a while longer."

"But I wanted out of the business. I was planning to buy a

house in Atlanta."

"You've got more than adequate assets to buy another house. You don't need to sell this profitable carpet company to make that happen."

"I didn't want to touch that pot of money, Joe. That's for my old age."

Joe laughed, not even trying to hide his amusement.

"Forgive me, Margaret, but you're not nearly long enough in the tooth to be worried about paying for assisted living."

"I don't want to overspend my capabilities."

Why is Andy scribbling so frantically?

"Consider it this way, Margaret. Even with optimistic interest rates, if you want to pay half a million dollars for a house in Atlanta, you'll lose less interest earnings on that money if you pull it out of the investments than you'll lose if you sell Don's business for less than it's worth, just to get it off your back. Plus, your house will be building equity that should be more than just the interest that half million would earn."

"So Joe, you're saying I can have my cake and eat it, too?"

"In a manner of speaking. I assume you're not interested in running the business day to day."

"No way. That's not me."

"But didn't you work with Don when he first opened almost twenty years ago?"

"I did. I also went to the house as soon as he could afford to replace me. In truth, I only got the job because I was willing to work for free so we could afford to eat at least once a week."

"Those were the days, I'm sure."

"You know what, Joe? Those were the days. If I could turn back the clock, I would."

"But you can't," Andy said patiently. "We have to decide what you're going to do."

"You see," Joe explained patiently, "neither of us wants to be in the carpet business either. We have day jobs."

Oh my gosh! In all my planning and moving, I never gave a thought to these two guys who were back here running my business, while I was off starting a new life.

"Guys, I'm sorry. I never really thought it through. I've been very thoughtless toward the both of you."

Of course they don't want to be in the carpet business.

"I guess I was naïve. I thought selling would be a slam dunk, then we'd all be about our business again."

"We can sell it that way, if you insist. There are buyers out there who will sign a contract on Monday. But you'll sell for far less than the business is worth. We don't want to see you walk away from that kind of money."

I don't want to jump over dimes to pick up nickels either.

"Soooo... if none of us want the job, who does? I assume from reading between the lines that you have a plant manager candidate to recommend?"

"At the risk of looking presumptuous," Joe explained, "we do. We felt like we could persuade you to see it our way, and we needed to make the most of this Saturday work session."

"Then lay it on me, although I have to tell you that I can just hear the Carter's Crossroads' grapevine now, when the merry widow hires a plant manager to run the business she inherited."

"We thought about that as well," the banker agreed. "But people may just have to talk. You've got too much riding here to throw it all away over a few wagging tongues."

"So how am I supposed to pay this person? Will that leave anything for me?"

Andy pulled a sheaf of papers from his portfolio. "The candidate we have in mind could easily command a salary of..." He consulted his papers and named the figure. "Based on what you've paid

Joe and me since we took over, it won't take that much more to hire this person. You've been getting a check every week so far. At the end of the day, you'll come out ahead. That's almost a given."

"Listen, Margaret. Haywood Tufters is sound. Don was a good business man. He wasn't carrying much debt, so when this current economic downturn put a damper on home construction, he was able to weather the storm without too much effort."

Don always did have a fantastic head for business. I'll give him that.

"When do I get to meet my new manager?"

Joe consulted his watch. "It's almost eleven now. I'd say your new employee could be here by two o'clock. Does that work for you?"

"It does, providing you let me buy lunch for us. Call your better halves and let's all go get a bite."

Over lunch the five of them visited and compared notes on community happenings. Before she knew it, Joe was calling time.

"We need to get back to the plant before the candidate gets there and finds the door locked."

Back in the conference room, Margaret tried to imagine what it would be like to see another man in Don's office.

It will be awkward, I imagine. At least in the beginning. But it would be kind of petty to tell the guy he can't have an office because that one is a shrine. I guess I could offer to let him redecorate if he wants.

She was lost in thought when she heard Joe who had stepped around the corner say, "Come right on in. Mrs. Haywood is waiting in the conference room."

Put on your nicest smile. This man had nothing to do with all that has happened, or the gossips in this town."

Then her jaw dropped and, despite her best efforts, her pretty smile went south.

"Margaret Haywood," Joe said, "I'd like to have you meet Amanda Butterworth."

She's a woman. Joe...?

Margaret recovered her composure as best she could.

"Mrs. Butterworth, I'm so glad... so glad to meet you."

"I'm glad to meet you as well." She looked at both the men. "These two didn't tell you I was female, did they?" She shot visible daggers at the guys.

"No. They didn't." Then in an effort to defend the men, she added. "But they didn't tell me you were a man, either."

"Listen, Margaret. I'll come clean. We didn't want to prejudice you either way."

"Joe, does P.C. know about Amanda?"

Joe hung his head.

"P.C. Dunigan is a long-time friend," Amanda explained. "She's the one who told Joe about me." She smiled. "She's told me a lot about you, too, Mrs. Haywood."

Just wait 'til I get my hands on P.C. She should have told ME!

"If you want to nail our hides to the wall, I'll get you the hammer and nails, if you'll just listen to what we have to tell you." Joe indicated that everyone should take a seat around the table.

"Amanda and her husband, Bruce, owned their own carpet company in Tennessee for years. When Bruce learned he was terminally ill, he convinced Amanda they should sell the business. He wanted her to be free to travel and enjoy life after he was gone."

"It was the biggest mistake we ever made," Amanda chimed in. "I've been absolutely miserable. I was in harness too long. Almost thirty-five years."

"When we began to rethink this whole deal, P.C. told me about Amanda and I called her. P.C. and I even drove to Tennessee and spent a weekend with Amanda, trying to make sure this could be a good fit."

I'm stunned. But this could work.

"Mrs. Haywood, I just want you to know that if you aren't comfortable hiring me, there's no hard feelings. But if you should see your way clear, I have a feeling we could work well together. I'll treat this business just like it was my own."

I like her.

"You know," she continued, "sometimes you don't realize what you've lost until it's too late. If God gives me a second chance with this job, I intend to make the most of it."

A second chance. Isn't that exactly what I'm talking about doing…coming back to Carter's Crossroads?

Margaret gazed across the table at the lady she estimated was in her mid to late fifties.

"Tell you what. I'm definitely interested. But I'm not going to make a decision right this minute."

"I don't blame you. I wouldn't either. You hardly know me."

I have confidence Joe wouldn't steer me wrong. But this is my decision. So here's what I propose…"

"Margaret, I'd…" Joe interrupted.

"As I said, here's what I propose," she plunged ahead, ignoring Joe. "You and I are going for a drive. I want to get to know you and I want you to get to know me. If I keep this business, I want the assurance I'm not going to have to step back in when I least expect it."

"Sounds like a winner to me, Mrs. Haywood," her manager candidate confessed.

"It's Margaret and Amanda or we don't even need to leave the building."

"Agreed."

"Bye, fellows. I'll call y'all some time this weekend and let you know my decision. You're not unemployed yet."

I'm pretty sure they're both out of a job, but let 'em sweat. I can tell they can't decide if I'm angry or not. Joe ought to know better.

The two women left the plant and got into Margaret's Expedition. For the next two hours, Margaret drove around Carter's Crossroads' upscale neighborhoods and through the public housing projects.

By the domestic violence shelter, the church where she had attended for years, and the small, modest, white masonry building where God now met her every Sunday morning.

They talked. About children and family. The carpet industry. Business and employee relations philosophies. The merits and demerits of a small town versus a larger city. They got to know each other.

"At this point, Amanda, I need your honest assessment. Are you still as interested in the job now as you were when you drove into town this morning? You won't offend me."

"I was excited about the possibilities. Now that I've seen your operation, the town, and I've met you, I really want the job if you'll have me."

"Before I give you my answer, I want to explore a couple of other topics that I think you might help me with."

"Certainly."

She's puzzled. It shows on her face.

"One of the reasons I've driven you all over town, is I want you to be happy here if you make this move."

"I believe I will be."

"Well... without casting doubt on your belief, I need to tell you that I felt the same way when I moved to Atlanta. But it has proven to be something less than the paradise I envisioned. My expectations weren't tempered with reality. I don't want you to make the same mistake I did."

As they had ridden, Margaret told her new friend all about Don, his abuse, his assault of her and the children, his attempted murder of Jim Deaton and, ultimately, his own death from a brutal beating.

"I'd say it was poetic, except that would be cruel," Amanda observed. "However did you stand up under all that?"

"If I'd been able to foretell the outcome, I probably wouldn't have made it. But between ignorance and God, mostly God, I got through. We all did."

Margaret's final stop brought the duo to the house on Redbud Way. Margaret drove up to the front steps before killing the engine.

"I have a favor to ask, but you're probably going to consider me either stupid or extremely silly."

"Maybe I won't. Why don't you tell me what you need?"

"I want to take you into this house, and I want your honest assessment. What feeling do you get from the house?"

"You believe that houses speak their own language, too?"

"I do."

They exited the car and entered through the front door into the massive two-story foyer. Margaret led the way, turning on lights, indicating direction and saying little.

"Margaret, this is a gorgeous house."

I wish you could have seen it before. I had to repair the damage with less quality in order to get buyers interested. So far we haven't had the first nibble.

Amanda continued to wander. She explored the second floor and rejoined Margaret in the family room.

"This was your home."

It wasn't a question.

"This is where you and Don lived and where he abused you, isn't it?"

"Am I that transparent?"

"I wouldn't call it transparent. But it's obvious that you have great emotions – good and bad – connected to this house."

"You're exactly right."

"You second-guessing yourself? I see it's on the market."

Margaret confided the nightmare of Brian's troubles in Atlanta, the fact the other children were unhappy and the truth she wasn't as enamored with the capital city as she'd thought she'd be.

"When you said earlier today that you didn't realize until it was too late what you'd lost when you sold your business, I couldn't help but think about this house."

"You don't want to jettison the home that has served you so well and then regret it later?"

"There's been a lot of love in this house. But there's been a lot of pain as well."

"But that's life, Margaret."

"It is, isn't it?"

I'd never thought about it like that. God, You've sent me a jewel here.

"I'm just afraid if I sell this house and come back here to live, I'll always regret it. But also I'm afraid of what it will be like to live here, day in and day out, seeing those things that constantly remind me of what was."

She's looking at me in a funny way.

"I'm going to go out on a limb here, and if I'm getting too personal, just tell me so."

"Okay?"

"I would venture that money isn't that big an issue. If you wanted to remodel this house so that it changed drastically from what it was when Don was alive and this place was an explosion waiting to happen, you could afford to do so."

I hadn't thought about that possibility.

"You see, Margaret, there's no shame in doing that. The same thing happens to us when we decide to ask God to walk with us though our daily lives. That act of opening our heart's door to Him causes our old self to be cast aside and we're made anew. He remodels us from the inside out."

She's exactly right. Oh, God, You do find some unusual ways to communicate with us.

"You're right. I could remodel. Don's insurance paid off the mortgage. For what I'm paying for rent in Atlanta, I could easily spend some money on this house."

I'm going to sit down with the children tonight. I'd not felt comfortable talking with them about coming back here to live, but now I am. God needed to introduce me to Amanda first.

Back in the car, Margaret headed to Haywood Tufters where Amanda had left her car. When they got there, her vehicle was the only one in the parking lot.

"Looks like the guys gave up on us and went home."

"Serves 'em right," Amanda agreed. "I couldn't believe they hadn't told you about me. You should have seen your face!" She cackled.

Margaret immediately found the sound of her laughter contagious. "You need to be here to see his face when I tell Joe I sent you packing back to the hills of Tennessee."

Amanda's face froze, then fell sharply. "I don't get the job?"

Margaret could feel the disappointment in her voice. She slapped the other woman on the hand. "Don't be silly. You had the job two hours ago. But that doesn't mean I have to let Mr. Joe Busbee down easy, now does it?"

The two locked eyes.

"Go for it, girl. He deserves it."

They talked for a few more minutes before Amanda said she would be ready to begin work a week from the following Monday. Margaret gave her the numbers where she could be reached, and the two hugged.

"Good-bye, Amanda," Margaret said to the disappearing rear end of her new employee's champagne colored BMW. "Welcome home to Carter's Crossroads."

Back at her parents, she deflected questions from everyone about where she had been all day and what had detained her.

I want to talk to the children before I say anything to Mama and Daddy. Mama claims she's changed, but I don't want to take any chances on this.

Once they had finished a Saturday night supper of fried catfish and hushpuppies and slaw and homemade lemon icebox pie, Margaret pulled her father aside.

"Daddy? I need a favor."

"Name it."

"Can you manufacture an excuse that Mama will buy to get her out of the house for about an hour?"

At the look of alarm that crossed his face, she quickly put her hand on his arm as she said, "I promise. Nothing's wrong. In fact, it could be just the opposite. But I need to talk to the kids first, before I say anything to anyone else."

"You're sure everything's okay?"

"Couldn't be better, I don't think."

He smiled. "Yeah, I think I can get her away for a little while." He disappeared into the other room and Margaret heard the sound of his voice.

Only I can't understand what he's saying.

Whatever it was must have worked, because it was only a matter of minutes before the two came through the house. Miss Ruby was taking off her apron and Harold Maxwell was grabbing his hat that he always wore outside.

The phone rang. Thinking she should ignore it, not knowing how long her parents would be gone, Margaret nevertheless looked at the Caller ID.

Joe!

"Why haven't you called me?" he demanded when she answered. "Surely you're not still out with Amanda?"

"No. I'm at my parents. Amanda's been gone for several hours."

"Well?"

"Well what?"

"What did you think of her? Do I need to call and make her the formal offer?"

"No. That won't be necessary."

"That won't be necessary? Margaret! Do you realize what you're saying?"

"Sure. I'm saying it won't be necessary for you to call Amanda and offer her the job."

"Don't tell me you're going to shoot this down? Is it because we didn't tell you she was a female?"

"I'll have to admit I wasn't very happy being blindsided that way."

"But you're cutting off your nose to spite your face. We won't easily find that perfect combination of talents again."

"Be that as it may, Joe, I sent Amanda packing earlier this afternoon. After riding around with her for a couple of hours and asking some really probing questions, I got a chance to see the real Amanda, and that decided it for me."

"The 'real' Amanda? I'm afraid I don't understand."

"You didn't see fit to bring me up to snuff before you sprung her on me, so I got pretty direct with her."

"Please tell me you didn't offend her?"

"I don't know, Joe. You'd have to ask Amanda about that. The last I saw of her, that pretty BMW was kicking up dust trails headed back to Tennessee."

"Margaret. I'm going to hang up now. I'm so angry I'm afraid I'll say something I'll regret tomorrow. So I think it best that I get off this call. I'll see if I can reach Amanda and try to do some damage control."

Margaret could feel the anger that was directed at her from across town.

"At the very least I need to apologize to her and tell her we'll send her a check on Monday for her time and travel expenses."

She didn't immediately respond, but finally asked, "Joe?"

"Yes, Margaret?"

"I know you're very angry with me right now, and I'm sorry. I think in time you'll come to see the merits of the decision I made today. But in the meantime, while you're talking to Amanda, would you tell her something for me?"

"I'm afraid you've already told her quite enough. I can't imagine there's anything else left to say."

"Maybe you don't think there is, but I can assure you she'll want to know that I've collected a number of pieces of information about rental apartments. I'll overnight them to her on Monday so she can begin to see what's out there."

There was dead silence on the other end of the line.

"Joe? Are you there?"

When she thought he had indeed hung up, she heard his voice asking, "I thought you said you'd made your decision and had sent her packing back to Tennessee?"

"You heard me correctly. I hired her and told her to hurry back to Tennessee and get ready to go to work."

"Margaret! This isn't funny. You led me to believe you'd turned her down."

"No Joe, you jumped to that conclusion yourself. I said no such thing. Just like you conveniently didn't tell me that Amanda wasn't a man."

"Margaret…"

"Gotch'a, Joe. Gotch'a good."

"I never knew you had such a devious streak."

"There's a lot of things you and a lot of other people never knew about me, but all of you are about to find out."

"I don't know whether to applaud or take cover."

"Oh, and Joe. Before you go patting yourself on the back, I need to tell you and P.C. that neither of you had anything to do with Amanda coming here today. God sent her to tell me what I needed to hear. It's what I've needed to hear for a long time."

"You lost me right after you deflated my ego, but I like that sound of fight and spunk I hear in your voice, so I'll say goodnight. We'll talk tomorrow before you go back to Atlanta."

"Goodnight, Joe. Tell P.C. I forgive her for her part in this 'pull the wool over Margaret's eyes' campaign." She chuckled. "You, I'm going to have to think about!"

Once off the phone she retreated to the basement playroom where she knew the kids were clustered around the TV. "Kids? May I talk to you for a minute? This is important."

"Is something wrong, Mom?"

"I don't think it's wrong, but I want to hear your thoughts on the matter."

Brian looked to his siblings for authority. "Sure, Mom. Whatever."

"Great!" She picked up the TV remote. "May I interrupt the distraction? This won't take long."

Margaret interpreted silence as approval and pressed the OFF button. She settled herself on the floor among them, being careful to put most of her weight on her right arm, aware her left arm still wasn't as strong as it needed to be. "I need to ask you some questions. There are no right or wrong answers. Only honest answers. Okay?"

The three children nodded, their faces clearly indicating the uncertainty they felt.

"How do you like living in Atlanta?"

Brian was the first to reply, practically jumping in before Margaret's words died out. "It was cool at first, but I don't like it now." His face mirrored the bad taste he evidently had for life in the big city. "It's not just because I got in trouble."

"I don't feel like I know anybody. I don't have any friends," Jason complained. "Even the kids I played with at day camp and at school last spring weren't my friends. I want to come back here and live with Grammy and Grandee."

"How about you, Sallie?"

The little girl fiddled with her hair and rolled her tongue around her mouth before finally saying, "It's OK I guess. We have a beautiful home, but it doesn't belong to us. But I don't have any friends either."

Margaret saw tears in her child's eyes.

"I didn't know what a good friend Audra was until we played together today. I don't have anybody like her in Atlanta."

"So, Mom? Are you going to suggest that we come back to Carter's Crossroads?"

"As a matter of fact, I am. To be honest with you, I've been disappointed in Atlanta just as each of you have."

She went on to explain about the meeting earlier in the day and the need to hold on to Haywood Tufters for a while longer. "It just looks like it might make better sense for us to live here. There's just one holdup and I don't know if it can be resolved."

"I know," Brian volunteered. "Your job. You love your work, Mom. I'd hate for you to give it up."

The two younger children nodded their heads in agreement.

I hate to make it look like this is his fault.

"No, Brian. I can live here and still keep my job. When Barbara first offered it to me, she didn't even know I was thinking about moving to Atlanta. She assumed I'd work from here and run into Atlanta to the office about once a week."

"Then what's the roadblock?" The boy had a truly puzzled look on his face.

"It's your probation status from the court. I don't know if the judge will let me take you out of Fulton County."

My heart is tearing out of my chest. He looks so stricken.

"I didn't think about that." He dropped his head. "Gosh, I'm sorry, Mom. Looks like I can't do anything right."

"Don't say that, Brian. Nothing could be farther from the truth. I'll have Joe go to work on that Monday and we'll just see. I have no problem going back before the judge and even posting a larger bond if he requires it."

"I'm sorry, Mom."

"Don't say it, Brian. We can't change the past, but neither are we giving up on the future."

"Will we live here with Grammy and Grandee like we did before?"

I can't read Sallie's mind. I'm not certain if she's in favor of living here or if she's afraid that's what will happen.

"That's the other thing I want to ask you."

Again, three sets of eyes were focused on her. But this time their faces wore smiles.

Somehow Joe has to work all this out about Brian.

"I don't think it's fair to Grammy and Grandee for us to pile in on them again. Especially as a permanent arrangement."

"I don't want to move back to that other house," Sallie moaned and pointed out the back of the basement, toward the rental house. "I don't like that house."

"No, we wouldn't go back there, either. After all, P.C. and her mother are living there now. We wouldn't want to make them move."

"Are you suggesting we'd buy a new house here in Carter's Crossroads?"

"Not exactly, Brian. Look, you three. I've got a proposal to make so I'd appreciate it if you'd let me explain everything before you give me your reactions."

She observed Brian's suspicion. "Our old house on Redbud Way is up for sale, but so far we've had no takers."

All three faces across from her fell.

"We didn't want it," she continued quickly, before they could object or she lost her nerve. "That house has bad memories, painful memories. There's nothing wrong with us feeling that way."

"Mom," Brian interrupted. "You said you'd never live there

again." Margaret noted a hint of criticism in his comment.

"I've also learned the hard way to never say, 'never.'" She braced herself and forged ahead. "Listen, you three. Even adults make mistakes. Sometimes you have to admit that you were wrong and take another path. That's what I'm suggesting the four of us should do in this situation."

"But Mom," Sallie insisted, "the house is all messed up. It's not like it was. And every time I see that place where Daddy threw Jason up against the wall, I'll always think about that night."

"That's what I'm trying to tell you. The house as it is, will always remind us of times we need to put behind us. But what if we could live there and not be constantly reminded? Remember, we had good times there as well as bad. It's just that we remember the bad most."

"How can we do what you suggest? You know, live there without being reminded of those times when Dad was so violent?"

"Some of this would normally be considered adult business, but we're all in this together. I would just ask that you not talk to Grammy and Grandee, or any of your friends, or even Joe and P.C. about what I'm going to tell you."

They're curious.

"When Daddy died, he had insurance that paid off the house. Where I'm having to pay rent to Jim Deaton for the condo in Atlanta, it wouldn't cost us anything to move back into our house."

"That would be an advantage."

"It would, Brian. Plus, if we're not paying rent, or another mortgage payment, there will be enough money to totally remodel our house. We could remove those old memories and give us a clean slate to make some new memories."

"Could I do my room any way I want?"

With Sallie "any way I want" could get dangerous. But we can split hairs later.

"Within reason, yes. Each of you could make changes to your rooms and we'd make the rest of the house look fresh and new as well."

"I like the idea, Mom. I really do." Brian's head dropped. "If the judge will let me live there."

"Don't throw in the towel yet, Brian."

"I'm all for it," Jason piped in. "Can we move tomorrow and not have to go back to Atlanta?"

Margaret ruffled her son's blond hair. "I'm afraid even I can't work miracles that quickly. Besides, if we're going to remodel the house, it's best to do all that work while the house is empty."

"Okay."

Oh, for the faith of a child.

"There's one other thing I haven't mentioned."

They looked at her expectantly.

"If we aren't paying a house payment, there would be money to pay tuition at Mount Zion if you all want to go back there to school."

Brian's head jerked upward and Margaret thought the expression on his face was one of sheer joy.

"You mean we really could go to private school again? Man! I didn't think I'd ever be excited about going back to Mount Zion. That would be great."

"How about you, Sallie? Jason? Talk to me."

Her daughter, she could see, was struggling with her answer. Finally she spoke softly.

"I'd like to go to school there, but I don't like how people were treating us before we moved to Atlanta."

"Me neither," Jason whispered. "They made fun of Daddy and us."

Margaret surveyed her children again before tackling the sticky issues they had raised.

Brian has become such a man through all of this. Even with his arrest, as horrible as it was and could still be, he's matured even more. Jason is still in his shell, but he was already there before Don assaulted him. He doesn't talk about those days. Sallie, my little drama queen, still has plenty of stage experience, but even she has begun to grow up.

"I can't promise the kids won't still try to push your buttons. But that's exactly what they're doing. If you'll react to their harassment, they'll continue to do it."

"You mean if we don't get angry or make a smart remark back, they'll stop?"

"You got it, Brian. I know how difficult it is to listen to some of the garbage this town as thrown at us, and not react, but that's the quickest way to cut them off. If it's no fun for them, they won't do it."

"I still want to go to Mount Zion," Jason said, showing more determination than Margaret had seen from him in several months. "I don't like Atlanta and I was wrong before when I said I didn't want to be there."

The three talked for a few minutes longer, breaking up only when they heard the Maxwell automobile pulling into the garage.

"Do me a favor, kids. Please don't say anything to Grammy and Grandee about us moving back until after I can talk to Joe about Brian's situation. I wouldn't want them to be disappointed if we can't make this work."

As the three nodded their heads in agreement, she looked at her watch. "If you're going to meet your buddies, you'd better be on your way, Brian."

He flashed her a grin she strongly suspected was meant to say "thank you."

"Be in by eleven," she reminded him. "Church tomorrow."

Now if I can just get Joe to tell me the judge can be persuaded. God, You've got to show me how to handle this.

CHAPTER TWELVE

It was after church and Sunday lunch was finished before Margaret got an opportunity to put in a private call to Joe Busbee.

"I'm glad you called," he said. "I was going to call you in just a few minutes, but this is fine."

"Put on your best lawyer hat, Joe. I've got a problem."

"This sounds serious. Are you alright?"

"In some ways I'm the best I've been in longer than I can remember. But there's one sticking point that may make everything very painful."

"Lay it on me."

Almost as if the words would not be contained any longer, Margaret launched into her dilemma.

"The children and I want to move back to Carter's Crossroads, Joe."

"Say what?"

"You heard me right. It's a unanimous decision. None of us are happy in Atlanta."

"Well, of course we'll be glad to have you back in town. I know your folks must be on top of the world."

"They don't know it. I haven't told them yet."

"But why? Oh... I know. P.C. and her mom are living in your house now."

"No, Joe. That has nothing to do with anything. I'm afraid the Fulton County judge won't let me bring Brian back here, since Carter's Crossroads would be outside jurisdiction. The kids and I talked this out last night. We aren't telling Mama and Daddy until we know it can actually happen."

"I didn't think about that. I guess I was in so much shock that you would even want to move back. You know, after all that's happened."

"So do you think we stand a chance with the judge? I don't want to go too far with this, because Brian's already beating himself up over the possibility that we may have to stay in Atlanta until after his trial."

"Tell you what," Joe proposed. "Tomorrow, first thing, I'll put in a call to Detective Duncan to explain the situation. He knows this judge fairly well. Maybe he can advise us how to best approach His Honor, with some idea of how successful he thinks we might be."

"Thank you, Joe. I'll be on pins and needles until we know something. Oh, and Joe. Tell the detective that I'm willing to post a substantial bail if that's what it takes to make this happen."

"Will do. That might be necessary."

"Whatever..."

"So tell me, Margaret, if P.C.'s living in your house, well... you know, your dad's house... where will you live?"

"Get ready for shock number two, Joe." She waited a minute, as if anticipating a drum roll that didn't materialize. "We're going back to Redbud Way. To our house."

"But I thought you said..."

"I did. I also decided that I might have been misdirected."

"Are you sure you can live with all those memories? What about the kids?"

"The kids are fine with it. As I told them, there are many good memories in that house, as well as the bad ones. We'll extensively redecorate and try to remove the most painful reminders of those bad memories."

"Well I never. What caused you to have this change of mind?"

"God did. Working through Amanda Butterworth."

"Amanda?"

"I told you last night that you didn't get the credit for bringing her here. God did that, because He sent her here with a message I needed to hear."

"I don't guess I'll ever totally understand all that's gone down in the past thirty-six hours, but it doesn't matter. Just so long as you're coming home."

Home! That sounds so wonderful.

"I'll call you tomorrow after I talk with the detective."

She felt the tears racing to the forefront and, before they could capture her voice, said, "Thank you, Joe. Thank you for everything."

§

They arrived back in Atlanta late Sunday evening. By the time they were unloaded and unpacked, it was bed time. Margaret was glad the kids weren't in school, knowing the following morning would have been unreal. None of them had been anxious to leave Carter's Crossroads and no one could seem to find the motivation to collect their belongings and load them in the car.

"Alright, you kids," Margaret ordered finally, "if you think by dragging around and not getting with the program you'll get to spend another night, think again."

"But Mommie, why can't we stay until tomorrow?"

"Two reasons, Sallie."

"Two?"

"Come tomorrow, you'll beg to stay yet another day, and Brian has to be at work at ten o'clock in the morning."

In truth I'd love to stay over, but I can't tell them that. Brian's job almost slipped my mind.

"My last day is this coming Wednesday. I can just call in tomorrow morning and tell them I won't be back."

"We've already had this conversation. You're going to work out your entire notice"

"It's only three days, Mom." He was evidently primed to plead his case. "It's not like this job was going to be my career."

"Listen, son. What's right is right; it doesn't matter about the job. You gave a two week notice and you still have three more days to work. Besides, who's to say that down the road, many years from now, you and your manager might not cross paths again? Only this time he's in a position to really help you or hurt you. What do you think will happen?"

Brian rolled his eyes. "I think I'm going to work tomorrow."

"I'm glad we see things the same way."

She reached across and gave him a hug.

He protested, but he didn't protest that much.

Assured the kids had put away their clothes and were ready for Monday, Margaret settled in bed with her Bible.

I feel really starved for Your word, Lord. I want to be optimistic about Brian's case, but I also know that the law can be very harsh and unforgiving. I know we were very fortunate that the judge was as lenient as he was in setting bail, but at the end of the day, Lord, Brian could still end up doing some jail time. That judge may rule he cannot leave Atlanta. If that happens, Brian is going to be devastated and I'm going to feel so guilty because I started all of this.

The next morning, following a hurried breakfast, Margaret dropped the two younger children at the Y day camp then deposited Brian at the front door of the store.

"Mom. Did you...? Will...?"

"I talked to Joe yesterday afternoon. He was going to start the ball rolling this morning; I'm sure he'll call me as soon as he knows anything." She patted her son's arm. "Now you know everything I do."

"Bye, Mom." His shoulders were bent and almost old, Margaret thought, as she watched him swallowed up by the big box discount store.

He needs to be working at Haywood Tufters. I need to call Joe and tell him. Maybe that could have a bearing.

When she called, however, Joe was with a client and his secretary promised to have him call. P.C. was in court, she said. Discouraged because she hadn't been able to speak with Joe, Margaret closed her phone. She had barely returned it to her purse when she heard it's distinctive ring.

"Joe," she said by way of a greeting. "I wasn't expecting you to return my call so quickly."

"I'm sorry, Margaret, I'm not Joe. But if you're expecting him to call you, I'll go and you can call me later today."

Barbara! It's Barbara Kirkland.

"I'm so sorry. Please forgive me."

She was relieved to hear her employer laugh.

"There's nothing to forgive. I gather this Joe person must be important."

"Joe Busbee from Carter's Crossroads. He's Brian's attorney."

"Then get off the phone. I'm sure you need to talk with him or you wouldn't have answered the phone as you did."

"I've got call waiting; he'll get through. I just needed to compare notes with him this morning."

"How is that situation developing?"

"Brian is all tied in knots, afraid he'll be sent to prison. I'm just as scared as he is, but I can't let him know it."

"Your friends have been praying, you know. Annie and I were talking about his troubles last week. She said if only that judge could know him like we do, there wouldn't be any question."

I wonder why Barbara's calling?

"We all appreciate the prayers. I don't know how people who haven't let God into their lives cope with things like this. I speak from experience, too."

"I hope things are soon going to level out for you. The last year has really been a roller coaster."

"For sure none of what has happened was in my game plan," Margaret agreed. "But I'm sure you didn't call just to talk about my life, although I sincerely appreciate your concern."

"You're right, I did have dual agendas, but I hope you understand that I'm always concerned about your welfare."

"I do. So now what's your other agenda?"

"There's a conference in early November I'd like you to attend. I know it comes right on the heels of National Domestic Violence Awareness Month, but I think it's important. I'll e-mail you the information as soon as we hang up."

Would that mean leaving the children overnight? What if it conflicts with Brian's trial? I don't want to give the impression I'm not a team player.

"It's a three-day event, dealing with special grants and other funding sources that like their money to go toward domestic violence causes. It'll be right in the middle of leaf season, so you'll see some of the most gorgeous color besides getting all that helpful information."

Now she has my curiosity aroused.

"Where is this conference? Maine or New Hampshire or some place like that?"

"Nope. Less than three hours away from Atlanta, in the northeast corner of the state. A little town called Persimmon."

"I know I've heard of the place, but I don't remember ever being there."

"Then you haven't been there, because you'd definitely remember it."

"I don't have a problem going. I'll need to get coverage for the kids, of course. And I'll need to find out when Brian has to be in court."

"Certainly if his trial should conflict with this conference, I'll just ask one of the others to go in your place. Brian comes first."

So many employers wouldn't be this understanding.

"Great. Send me the info and I'll go ahead and register. What kind of a town names itself Persimmon?"

Barbara's laugh gave Margaret another reason to like the woman. "Why don't you ask them while you're..."

Call waiting beeped.

"Barbara," Margaret interrupted, "it's Joe. Let me go."

"I'm praying that whatever you need from him, he'll be able to provide. Goodbye."

"Hello, Joe," she greeted him.

"Margaret, I got your message, but I was also about to call you. What's up? Phyllis said you sounded urgent."

"I may have been caught up in the moment," she confessed. Her accompanying laugh was, she thought, slightly self-conscious.

Memo to me: don't be so reactive.

"That's neither here nor there. What's troubling you?"

"Not troubling, exactly. I just wanted you to know if we can get the judge to allow me to move Brian back home, he can go to work at Haywood Tufters. Perhaps that might be something in his favor?"

"It won't hurt, but I've got something to share with you that could make everything a lot different. It wouldn't matter where Brian lived."

What is he talking about?

"I don't want you to take this as guaranteed, and..." he paused, "I don't think it's the thing to do to mention it to Brian at this point."

What?

"I just got off the phone with Detective Duncan. He shared some news that might have a positive effect on Brian's case."

"What, Joe? What? At this point I'll take anything."

"Now like I said, nothing's guaranteed. According to the detective, they've been working on the two guys Brian was driving that afternoon. One of them has indicated, verbally, that they thought Brian was a… well, I won't repeat the word the detective used. Let's just say they thought he was naïve and they decided to take advantage of him."

"That's what I've maintained all along," she cried.

"But us maintaining it and those two guys admitting it are worlds apart."

"So what does this mean? Level with me."

"If the two men will both agree that Brian was ignorant of their plans and was simply being used by them, it can make a world of difference for our case. Provided these guys each tell the same story and sign formal statements."

"Meaning Brian wouldn't have to go to trial?"

"We could petition the court to have the charges dropped. It would be up to the judge to either grant our request, or insist that the trial continue and that the evidence be brought out in court."

"Does it mean Brian would go free? With no record or black mark on his record?"

"Depends. If the charges are dismissed before going to trial, then yes, he would walk away free, with no record. But if the judge forces us to go to trial, then he will do one of two things."

This all gets so complicated. Can't anyone but me see that my child is innocent?

"He can dismiss the charges in court, in which case Brian will have a record and we'll have to ask that it be expunged. Or the judge will find him not guilty. Worse case scenario, he may find him guilty…"

"But Joe…" she interrupted, "Brian didn't…"

He cut her off. "Remember, Margaret. Whether we're comfortable with it or not, Brian *was* driving that vehicle. Ignorant or not, he was behind the wheel. He was an accessory. He admits it. Witnesses saw him."

"What does this mean?"

"Even if he's found guilty, I cannot believe any judge would sentence him to anything more than probation and maybe some community service. When the sentence is fulfilled, we'd ask the court to clear his record under the first offender status."

I think my heart is going to break. Doesn't anyone but me see the big picture here. It's soon going to be time to start applying for college. This will kill his chances if we can't get it cleared up quickly.

"So when does Detective Duncan think we'll know something? Has a trial date been set?"

"That's what I've been trying to tell you. The police believe Brian was duped and they're trying to help us. The first guy admitted as much yesterday evening. Today they'll interrogate the other guy again and try to get him to admit the same thing. But it won't happen until it happens."

"We're sitting on a ticking time bomb here, Joe. School is about to start and my children really want to go back to Mount Zion School. Brian needs to have this behind him. Isn't there something we can do?"

"Not giving you a short answer, Margaret, but the answer is 'no', unless you want to count prayer."

"Well I do want to count prayer. God has seen me through too much this past year to discount Him now."

"You know that P.C. and I are praying. Have been and will continue to be."

I know… I'm fortunate to have friends who believe as strongly in prayer as I do.

"I'll let you know something the moment I hear," he promised. "Got to go. A client is due here in five minutes and I've got to review his case notes."

"Thanks, Joe. I don't know what I'd do without you."

"Take care, Margaret. We'll make this work."

After she ended the call, Margaret sat in her home office totally oblivious to the pile of paperwork before her. She had planned a full day of working on program proposals and, while they were important, she knew she couldn't give them her best. Not when more urgent matters waved their angry red flags.

I'm going to call everyone I know. Even Mama and Daddy. This is their grandson and they love him.

Fortified by her new resolve, Margaret grabbed the phone and began to place calls. Annie Campbell and Pastor Samuel were the first two on her list. But she also called her friend, Alice Hanover whom she had helped to rescue from her own abusive situation, and Candi, the physical therapist who had meant so much during her recovery. Dr. Carr, the surgeon who had worked so valiantly late that night to save her arm, was only too glad to add his prayers to the cause.

After hesitating, but only momentarily, she put in calls to the headmaster at Mount Zion School and managed to locate the taxi driver who had rushed her children to safety the night she was injured. *For which he refused any pay.* She also called Sarah Lawrence, the next door neighbor on Redbud Way that she had always considered to be such a good friend.

I didn't hear a peep out of her this entire time, but if we're going back to Carter's Crossroads, there's not going to be any façade any longer. The money we have has no bearing on who we are nor does it make us more important than anyone else. I would stop and pray for any of these people. I want to believe they're equally concerned about us.

Indeed, even on those calls to people she hadn't had contact with in some time and once the initial awkwardness was breached, she found them all to be warm, more than sympathetic. Margaret related Brian's story so many times she began to feel like a tape recorder. The school's headmaster declared he'd be glad to welcome the Haywood trio back and that Brian's legal problems wouldn't have a bearing. Sarah, who began the conversation hesitantly, almost as if she feared Margaret was calling to chastise her for failing to be a friend, was in tears by the time the conversation ended.

Every one of them, down to the last person, was more than willing to pray for a positive outcome to Brian's plight. Several even insisted on having prayer with me before we ended our conversation. Sarah begged me to forgive her. She said she just couldn't face the fact that I was a stronger victim than her daughter had been.

The last call was to her parents. With the both of them on extension phones, she laid out the situation. "So you see, if these men will each confess that they took advantage of Brian, it may not get the charges dropped, but it will make things much better. We all need to pray, without ceasing, that their hearts will allow them to help a poor, unsuspecting teenage boy."

"Why honey, you know we'll do whatever we need to do to help Brian. And you."

"I know, Dad. You and Mama have been so good to us... this past year, especially."

"When do you think you'll know something?"

"The police are going to talk to the other man this morning... or at least some time today, Mama. So we could know something as soon as tonight. Then maybe it might never happen if this guy gets stubborn on them."

"I don't mean to sound critical, Margaret. But I really wish you'd never moved to Atlanta."

"Daddy, you can't be any more critical of me than I've already been. I feel like I should be the one going to jail, not Brian. Let's face it: I put him into a situation he wasn't prepared to handle."

"Now don't go blaming yourself. You did what you thought was best."

"That gives me little comfort, Mama. Practically none at all."

"Still," her father counseled, "you did what you thought was best at the time. That's all any of us can do."

"It sounds good when you say it, but it wasn't good enough. I unwittingly set my son up and he walked into the trap."

"I don't totally agree."

"What do you mean, Daddy?"

"Brian is a very intelligent young man. He had to know, deep down, that these guys weren't the same type people he was accustomed to associating with. You said yourself he never would bring his new friends home. So at the…"

"But…" she interrupted.

"Please, let me finish. At the very least he knew these men were not people you would approve. Did he know they were as dangerous as they have proven to be? I don't think so. But he knew they were different in a bad way."

"So what are you saying?"

"That Brian has learned a wonderful and valuable lesson out of this. We just have to pray that the cost of this learning opportunity isn't excessive."

"Which is why we have to pray," Ruby Maxwell volunteered. "Get off this phone, Margaret. I've got to call the prayer chain at our church and get them on this as well."

I can't believe that Mama, who once called us an embarrassment, is willing to ask her church to pray for Brian. God, You do work in mysterious ways.

"That would be great, Mama. Thank you. But before we hang up, there's one other thing I need to share with you."

"Not something about Sallie or Jason? They're not in trouble, too, are they?"

"Not to worry, Daddy. It's nothing like that. If we can make it work, we're moving back home. Soon."

"That's great, honey. But we've rented your house to P.C. and her mama. They signed a lease."

"When I say we're moving back home, I mean back into the house on Redbud Way."

"You would move back there? After all that's happened?"

"Do the children know?"

"The children and I discussed everything last Saturday night and they're all for the move. With one major condition."

"That would be?"

"We're going to completely remodel the house to reflect our new outlook on life. Since I won't have mortgage payments, I can afford to spend some money changing the house. For all of us."

"What do you mean, 'If we can make it work...'?"

"Brian's out on bail, Daddy. I can't move him out of Fulton County until or unless the judge gives me permission."

"I hadn't thought about that. It makes what's happening with these other two men doubly important."

"That's about the size of it."

"Well get off this phone," Miss Ruby ordered. "Harold and me got to have a few minutes of prayer, and I've got to get hold of the church."

"Keep us posted."

"I will Daddy. As soon as I know anything, you and Mama will, too."

"And Margaret..."

"Yes, Mama?"

"I'm gonna clean while I pray, and get your rooms ready. As soon as we get Brian free, you four are coming back here to our house to live while you get your house ready. You can't handle a major remodeling from sixty miles away."

"I love you, Mama. You, too, Daddy."

Oh, God. There is nothing more special than the love between a parent and a child. I'm just so sorry Don never experienced that and was never able to fully love our children or receive their love in return. They're all losers in that respect. Now, Father, Brian is about to lose even more than he already has. I agree with Daddy that in some small way, he knew he was keeping company with the wrong crowd. But he's stood up like a man and accepted responsibility for his actions. Father, if it be Your will, speak to the hearts of these two men who can lessen Brian's liability and give them the generosity to help out a young man whose life will be forever affected by a conviction and going to prison. In the name of Your Son who paid a tremendous price. Amen.

  Feeling she'd done all she could, Margaret tackled the mountain of paperwork on her desk. She still had a job to do.

CHAPTER THIRTEEN

Margaret Haywood and a gentleman wearing a hard hat stood in the family room of the Haywood home on Redbud Way in Carter's Crossroads. The room had been stripped of its sage green wall covering. In its place, bright, buttery walls provided a glow of sunlight, even though the day outside was grey and overcast.

This is what I want: the house and our lives to always be as open and upfront as a sunshiny day.

"Give me an idea of when you think you'll finish. I've got a landlord in Atlanta that needs to know when I'm going to vacate."

"We may not be totally finished with all the changes outside, because we've been concentrating on getting everything done in here. But I'd say in another eight to ten days, you can back your truck up to the door."

Once the green light to relocate Brian from Fulton came, Margaret wasted no time making the change. Since they wouldn't need the furniture and belongings they had in the condo, while they stayed with her parents, she decided to continue paying rent and leave everything in place. That would mean only one move.

"That would be great. My busiest month is October and I'd

like to get my children settled as quickly as possible."

"We'll shoot for eight days, but it may take a couple of days longer. That's the best I can do."

And when you honestly do the best you can do, that's all anyone can reasonably demand.

When she first heard about the possibility the two men Brian had unwittingly helped to rob the liquor store might actually clear him, she held her breath and prayed. But when day one became two, and then three, she found it difficult to keep up her hopes. Especially since Brian had no inkling any such rescue was in the offing.

When everything broke loose, a lot sure happened in a very short period of time.

One of the people she reached out for early on was Sarah, her long-time neighbor on Redbud Way. *After our earlier conversation, I want her in my life again.*

Margaret had insisted that Sarah meet her for lunch and the two were soon chatting while they waited for their food.

"So tell me," Sarah asked. "How did all this come about? What about Brian's arrest. I was just sick when I first heard."

"Well get comfortable," she instructed, "because this isn't a story that can be told in twenty-five words or less."

She began to explain all the factors that were playing for them and against them at the same time; how Joe Busbee's call, when it finally came, contained the best and the worst of news. The magistrate judge who had presided over Brian's preliminary hearing had agreed he could move back to Carter's Crossroads. At the same time, he had declined to drop the charges, even though both other men signed affidavits stating Brian hadn't known their intentions.

"How can he?" Margaret asked when Joe called. "How can he possibly want to see Brian go to trial? It doesn't make sense."

"He's the judge, Margaret. It doesn't matter what we think, it's what he thinks. I'd advise you to take what he's granted and get your family back here. We'll deal with the trial when the time comes."

That time is late October. Right in the middle of all my domestic violence workshops. But the others in the office will just have to handle it. My place is with my son, even if I have to quit my job.

"As soon as I knew we had judicial consent to return to the house on Redbud Way, I cancelled the real estate listing and within the same five minute span, called the contractor that handled a number of small remodeling tasks for us over the years."

She recounted the conversation and the demands she made on the builder: "I need this job done as quickly as possible. All the decisions have been made, and I can give you a detailed list of what I want done."

A demolition crew was on site the next day.

Margaret had elected to permanently vacate the original master suite and move instead into the adjacent guest bedroom, where she had felt so safe and comfortable in those days prior to Don's assault.

I just can't live in that bedroom, but I don't want to give up my master bathroom.

Fortunately the layout of the bath allowed for a new doorway to be cut in the wall the bath shared with the former guest room. Then the existing door into the old master bedroom was closed up, creating a new master suite and a new guest room.

Each one of the kids knew what they wanted to do in their rooms, and I let them make their own decisions. Even Sallie was able to show me exactly what she wanted, and it was all within reason.

Margaret's plans called for new paint colors throughout both floors of the sprawling mini-mansion as the real estate listing had called the home. On the ground level, she moved the formal dining room into the former family room. The family room then moved to the former living room and the living room took over the smaller space where the dining room had been.

Time didn't allow me to gut the kitchen, so I decided to paint the existing cabinets and change out the hardware and the countertops.

The plan was that the house wouldn't resemble any part of the home that had been such a painful nightmare for them all.

I most definitely intended to replace those cheap appliances Don bought for the kitchen after he had the house vandalized and tried to pin it on me.

As soon as she had work underway on the house, Margaret moved them all back to her parents. Everyone understood they would stay there, temporarily, until the remodel was finished and the house on Redbud Way was ready to receive its occupants.

Even Mama admits it will be best for the kids to be back at home. It's so nice to have her back in my corner.

As a part of her new philosophy about the town grapevine, Margaret made it a point not to retire from public view, or to shelter her presence. Whether it was going at mid-day to select paint colors, shopping for clothes for the children to wear when classes resumed at Mount Zion School, or calling and inviting friends to meet her for lunch, Margaret mounted and maintained a high profile status.

It was difficult at first. We've all been subjected to so much gossip and innuendo. Some of it true but most of it a blatant fabrication. Still, if I'm going to live here for the rest of my life, I don't intend to be like Boo Radley in To Kill a Mockingbird, *coming out only after dark when people can't see me.*

"You seem happier and more content than I've ever known you," Jim Deaton said when she called to formally give notice on the condo. "You don't know how good it is to hear the upbeat confidence in your voice."

"I almost hit rock bottom," she confided. "It got pretty rough."

"But you hung in and now you're out on top. What's next?"

Margaret shared the small triumphs in Brian's case.

"I was just so certain that judge would accept the word of those other two and dismiss the charges. I guess I let myself get too excited, because it was one more let-down when he didn't let my child go free."

"Don't sweat it too much, Margaret. I've got a feeling he's doing this just to drive home the point with Brian, and that he will be found innocent of all but maybe the most basic charges."

"It would have been so much easier to bear if this nightmare had been taken away. Now we still have to live with it, and, as you so aptly described it, 'sweat it'."

"Sometimes life isn't easy."

"You just said a mouth full, and I should know."

But I didn't have it as bad as Alice Hanover. At least we haven't been homeless. She would have been if I hadn't been able to help and even then it was a public housing apartment.

"You should also know that despite how rough it's been, you've been able to come out on top. It's quite the survival story."

It wouldn't have been a story at all if I had taken action when the abuse first began. But, no, I had to be in denial and pretend it wasn't happening; because domestic violence doesn't happen in homes like ours. In the end we almost didn't survive. Don most certainly didn't.

"I guess survival is the right term to use. If I'd known going in what I would be facing, I'd have turned and run away. But when you're in the middle, you either sink or swim. I couldn't go down."

"Now you're on top."

"I don't know if I'd call it 'on top'. Maybe 'pressing on the upward way,' like the line from the old hymn is a more apt description. But what about you, Jim? You paid an awfully high price for my refusal to face reality."

How Jim can stand to even talk to me when Don almost killed him because he was representing me; it's more than I can understand.

"Sometimes, Margaret, we all pay a hefty price when we deny what we truly know in our gut. You did, but in a sense, so did I."

"You've lost me."

"I've known for several years that I was unhappy practicing

everyday law. I knew I wanted something else, something more. But I was too stubborn to face facts and go looking. Those weeks in the hospital and rehab gave me a lot of time to come to grips with what was most important to me. Just look at me now, I'm the happiest I've ever been."

"But, Jim. You're going to walk with a limp for the rest of your life. You'll never be able to play tennis again."

"Sometimes, even when things head in a direction that's good for us, we pay a price for our weak faith. Walking with a limp is better than not walking at all. But I can still play tennis. I just need to be prepared to lose." He laughed and then was quiet for a few seconds. "Suddenly tennis isn't all that important in the grand scheme of things. In truth...I think I was probably using the game as an escape and a way to vent my frustrations because I was in a job where I wasn't fulfilled."

I wish I could be as positive, although I do believe we're doing the right thing to return home. But I thought we were doing the right thing by moving to Atlanta. So what do I know?

"Keep me posted, Margaret. You're under no deadline to get out as far as I'm concerned."

"But there are other deadlines that aren't as flexible and forgiving as you. Like all the domestic violence activities. The kids really need a normal routine again."

"You'll make it. Keep me posted."

There have been so many people who have helped me, who've been there to keep my chin up. Why just this morning when I stopped by Mount Zion School, one of the teachers I barely knew stopped to talk.

"Mrs. Haywood," she said, as the two met in the hallway. "I don't know if you remember me. I'm Cynthia Allison."

"Yes, Ms. Allison. I do remember you. Fifth grade... is that correct?"

"You have a good memory. I just wanted to tell you how good

it is to see you and your children back in town and back at Mount Zion School. I've prayed for you and I hope you don't mind, but I put you on our prayer chain at my church."

She barely knows me. I barely know her! But she was concerned enough to pray and ask others to join her?

"I really... appreciate... that," Margaret managed to stammer. *Why do I suddenly feel so uncomfortable?*

"You know, Mrs. Haywood," she dropped her voice to quietly confide, "Carter's Crossroads is famous for its gossip grapevine. I just wish our prayer chains could be as vocal for good as the gossips are destructive."

She's serious about this. "We do have an active gossip chain in town, don't we?"

"People would rather spread their fellow man's bad news than God's good news. I don't agree with that."

"Well I thank you for spreading my news among your church. I couldn't have made it through the past few months without prayer and God at my side."

"You've been through a lot, but you don't need to be ashamed. Despite what some of the people in this town believe, this is your hometown. You just hold your head up and go about your business. When people see they can't put you down, they'll leave you alone."

Isn't this basically what I told the kids about dealing with their classmates? Maybe I should have been preaching to myself as well.

"I think your children are adjusting well. I've been observing them and, while it was pretty rough the first few days, everyone seems to be settling in."

"I know the kids are glad to be back."

Even Jason is thrilled with his teacher and the fact that he now has a best friend. But the other two seem equally happy because I don't hear a lot of complaints. Maybe it took the move to Atlanta to show us all what we had and didn't recognize.

On her most recent visit into the office in Atlanta, her coworkers had been generous with their congratulations for the new life she was crafting out of what she had once considered a nightmare.

"Truly, Margaret, you are an inspiration to battered women everywhere. I venture to guess that when you speak to groups you're going to come off so genuine and authentic," Kirsten offered. "I wish I could be half as effective."

I've paid a high price for that authenticity, but I'm glad if my story will motivate and assure another victim out there, before her situation deteriorates as seriously as mine did.

"I'm very fortunate," she assured her coworkers. "Don't think I don't know it."

CHAPTER FOURTEEN

"The movers will be bringing all our furniture from Atlanta tomorrow," she announced at supper a few nights later. "I'll be going down as soon as I get you all off to school in the morning to supervise. Plus I've got to arrange for a cleaning service to get the condo ready to turn back to Jim."

"That's one nice young man," Ruby Maxwell volunteered. Jim had stopped in to visit Margaret as he was passing through the area, and Mrs. Maxwell had insisted he stay to eat with them that evening. "When he was here, he treated me like I was his mama."

Oh, Mama. How you have mellowed. Margaret found her thoughts rambling. *I don't know what I would have done without Jim. If only we weren't so far apart in age... WHAT am I saying? I don't care if we're both the same age. I'm not looking to get married again any time soon. If ever!*

"Jim misses his mother so badly, Mama. I'm glad he got a chance to enjoy a home cooked family meal with others at the table. He must get lonely always eating alone."

"So will we spend tomorrow night at our house?"

"Probably not, Brian. Maybe not even for two or three days."

"That's okay. We're fine here with Grammy and Grandee."

"Look you kids... I know you're anxious to get back into our house and to have your things around. But I don't want to camp out while we try to get everything unpacked and put away."

"You know you're all welcome as long as you need to stay."

I know we are, Daddy. I don't know how I would have made it without you and Mama. But I'm like the kids; I'm more than ready to be in MY house...it's going to be such a pretty house.

Margaret and P.C. had walked through the finished inside earlier that afternoon. While she still marveled at the difference the yellow paint made in the new dining room, she was also equally taken with the red and tan and hunter green in the new family room.

"That fabric in the Scotch plaid you chose for the windows in here just make this space," P.C. had offered. "It's so warm and inviting. There's definitely no hostility left in this house."

"Do you really think so?"

"I do. Even in the kitchen, where so much violence occurred, it's a totally different room. The cabinets with that coat of distressed sage paint don't even look the same. Throw in the new countertops and hardware... you got a brand-new kitchen for a fraction of the price."

"I thought so. I'm glad now there wasn't time to order new cabinets, because I'm sure I'd have done that." She grinned. "Saved myself a chunk of change."

"You know, if I get a house, I want you to do all the decorating." P.C. said. "I wouldn't think of calling anyone else."

"Is that a back-handed way of making an announcement?" P.C.'s blush clued Margaret she had struck a nerve. "You *are* making an announcement."

Her friend's ears turned an even deeper shade of port.

"P.C. Dunigan. You'd better talk to me right now. Don't you keep this a secret any longer."

"Okay, you win. Do you think I should change my name to Busbee or be a feminist radical and keep my maiden name? Or would

I look more prestigious if I were P.C. Dunigan-Busbee?"

"Oh, P.C. When? How long have you been sitting on this?" Margaret turned to her friend, her face a mask of provocation. "Why didn't you tell me immediately?"

P.C. laughed. "Relax, Margaret. It's only been three days since Joe proposed and I knew you were up to your ears getting this project finished." She blushed again. "Besides, I kind of wanted a few days to enjoy it just for me. I didn't think I'd ever remarry, and I'm still pinching myself."

Margaret said nothing but hugged her friend.

"I am so thrilled for both you and Joe. I've prayed for this to happen. I really believe the two of you were meant for each other."

They had made their way through the house and were sitting on the bottom step of the curving staircase leading to the second floor.

"Joe and I sort of agree with you." Her face reflected her joy, but then she visibly sobered. "After all I went through with my first husband, all that abuse and the whole judicial community turning a blind eye, I didn't know if I ever wanted to tie myself to another man."

"But Joe's not just another man. He's one of the finest people I know. Just like you," she added quickly.

"When you've been burnt, it's sometimes easier to pass up that fine man rather than take another chance."

Don't I know it? I'd be leery right now of any man who wanted so much as to take me out for a fast-food hamburger!

"You're not sorry you took the chance are you?" Margaret worried her friend was suffering premature cold feet.

"No, I'm at perfect peace that this is supposed to be. As is Joe. It's only because we took our time and worked our way through our hang-ups before we got to the place where we were ready to commit."

"So when's the wedding? I've got all kinds of ideas."

"Whoa. Slow down. Slow down. We haven't even set a date yet. He's taking me this weekend to pick out a diamond. After that, we'll be ready to announce the news."

"Like I said… when's the wedding?"

"Not until after the first of the year. Maybe February?"

"If you both know this is right, why are you waiting so long?" She poked her friend in the ribs. "You aren't getting any younger, you know!"

"Like you are?"

Margaret pretended offense. "Well you don't have to get tacky."

"Not tacky, but truthful. Seriously…" she turned to face Margaret. "Joe has a couple of big cases on the calendar between now and Christmas. I've still got some work to do in Tennessee, especially now that I know I'm going to be here permanently."

"So you both have jobs. Big deal. We can put together a beautiful wedding between now and Thanksgiving so you can celebrate the holidays together."

"You're rushing again, Margaret."

Oops. Guess I am.

"We've talked about it and this is how we want to do it. Also, we want to remodel Joe's house and add a private wing for Mama. We figure we'll spend the time between now and Valentine's planning our wedding and planning our construction project."

"But surely you don't want to begin married life in the middle of a construction zone. Believe me… there's not enough love out there to make that one palatable."

"Nope. We've got that all figured as well. My lease with your dad won't be up until August of next year. We're going…"

"Now you know Daddy's not going to hold you to some piece of paper. Especially when he finds out why you're vacating."

"That's neither here nor there, Margaret. We're going to get married. Joe will move in with Mama and me, while we re-do his house from one end to the other. When it's ready, we'll all three move into our new home."

"I have to admit, it sounds like a plan."

"Mama's all for it." Her face took on a look of absolute astonishment. "Would you believe, Joe asked Mama for permission before he even asked me?"

"He didn't?"

Although knowing Joe, that doesn't really surprise me.

"He did. Told her that the proposal was to the both of us, that he wouldn't marry me unless Mama agreed to live with us."

"Joe's a peach of a guy, alright."

The evening light was fading as Margaret closed the outside door. She and P.C. picked their way across the yard, around piles of building debris, to where she had parked.

"Next week they'll clean up all this mess and begin on the outside. Fortunately, it was past time to repaint the trim, so I don't feel too guilty about spending a little extra out here."

∽

"That's the last of it, ma'am." The voice belonged to a burly bear of a guy who had supervised the other three workmen loading furniture and boxes in Atlanta and then during the unloading in Carter's Crossroads.

He looks like a grizzly bear, but his temperament is more that of a loving puppy.

The men had worked steadily, taking items off the truck and into the house, placing everything in the rooms as Margaret dictated. It had taken all afternoon and the sun was starting to set when the foreman shoved a silver metal clipboard at her.

"If you'll walk through the house with me one last time, we'll be certain everything's here and in good condition. Then we'll get out of your hair."

It took more than half an hour to cover both floors and, in the end, Margaret signed her name with an excited flourish and handed the man a check.

"It's been a pleasure, Mrs. Haywood. You've got a beautiful home here; it just screams happiness. I hope you're going to enjoy it."

"Why, thank you. I strongly suspect we will."

"But if you ever decide you want to move again, give us a call."

"If I do, I'll certainly call you. But don't turn down any jobs waiting on that call. You might starve."

He laughed. "Can't blame a guy for trying."

"I don't. You fellows have been great to deal with. Thank you for taking such pains with all my furniture." Then she had a thought. "Maybe if I can't use you again, I can recommend you. I've got some close friends who're going to be moving out of a house in a few months so they can totally remodel. They're going to need movers."

"You tell 'em to call me, Mrs. Haywood. I'll take care of them," he promised.

Margaret's plan had been to take two or three days and get everything unpacked and put away.

"If I put in some long days, I can make it happen," she told her mother.

When the phone rang the next morning, however, it was a complete change of those plans.

I just had a feeling when I answered Barbara's call so early that it wasn't news I wanted to hear.

"It's Barbara, Margaret. I am sorry to be calling so early."

"Not to worry. I've been up getting the kids ready to leave for school. What's wrong?"

"You're a mind reader, my friend."

"Never mind the congratulations. You've got a problem."

"That I do, and I'm hoping you can help me out." She paused. "Please know I wouldn't ask this if I had any other options."

"It's OK. Just tell me what you need."

Margaret could picture her employer as she paced; could hear her labored breathing that meant she was in crisis mode.

"It's my mother-in-law. She was taken to the hospital in Nashville during the night, and it doesn't look good. I've got to go."

"Of course you do."

Poor Barbara. Her husband was an only child; when he was killed in that construction accident a few years back, Barbara got saddled with caring for her mother-in-law. The "old girl" as Barbara calls her.

"It would be so much easier if she would just let me move her to Atlanta."

Margaret heard what sounded like a grunt.

"I mean, I'd find her a place of her own; I don't want us living together any more than she does!"

"How long will you be gone and what do you need me to do?"

"I could be back tonight, although I doubt it. More than likely it's going to be several days. But with Evelyn out sick, it really stretches coverage for all we have going on."

Now I remember.

"You're talking about the three-day symposium you and Kirsten are doing in south Georgia tomorrow."

"Kirsten is the main facilitator; all I had planned to do was assist. But she can't do it without help."

Margaret didn't even stop to debate the issue.

"Tell Kirsten I'll be in the office by eleven this morning... at the latest. She can bring me up to speed, and we'll divide the duties. You head on out to Nashville and don't give this a second thought."

"You realize you're going to have to drive down tonight with Kirsten, so that both of you can be front and center tomorrow morning. The first session starts at nine o'clock."

Where is my brain? Of course I'll have to go down and stay. Which means I'll need to be packed to leave from Atlanta.

"Tell Kirsten I'll be there by noon. It'll take me a little longer to get my clothes packed."

"I'm sorry for the short notice. You know I wouldn't do this if I had a choice."

"Of course you wouldn't. But as good as everyone has been to cover for me these past few weeks, it's my turn to repay. Go see about Mrs. Kirkland and don't give it a second thought."

&

"I am whipped," she told her mother, as she collapsed on the sofa in the den and kicked off her shoes. "Three days of non-stop activities have done me in."

Margaret looked around the room and was immediately struck by the silence that echoed around her. "Where are the kids?"

"We let them go to the football game tonight. It seemed to be important for them to go and be with their friends from school."

"Sure. I'd even forgotten that it was Friday night and football season."

Shows how in-tune with things I am. I'm surprised I didn't forget where I was going when I left south Georgia right after lunch. She was quiet for a few moments. *This is the first football season in longer than I can remember that I'm not at the game, with my tailgate foods ready.* Then another thought hit her. *Don won't be calling the game tonight. I wonder who took his place?*

"That's great, Mama. I'm glad they felt free enough to want to go."

"Your daddy's gone to find a faucet for P.C.'s master bathroom. The old one sprung a leak this afternoon and can't be fixed."

Her mother prattled on about the headaches of owning rental property, how her stylist had done such a poor job on her hair that morning, and concluded by offering to serve up a plate of food.

"I kept it warm for you."

"Thank you, Mama. I'm more tired than I am hungry. I didn't stop once the whole time I was gone, and coming back through Atlanta at five o'clock on a Friday afternoon just about finished me off."

"You need to eat."

She's not going to let me skip supper, but I'm too wiped out to eat now.

"Tell you what? Why don't you serve a plate and cover it and put the rest of the leftovers in the fridge? I'm going to get a shower and lay down for a few minutes. Then when I get up, I'll microwave the plate and we'll all be happy."

Ruby Maxwell didn't look totally appeased, but she didn't argue.

"Then you go rest. You don't want to be midnight eating your supper. It's not good for digestion."

Margaret didn't even bother unloading her vehicle and was soon standing under the soothing jets of hot water. She toweled off, slipped on a gown, and lay down across the bed.

"Mommie? Mommie?"

Margaret heard the child's voice, but it took some effort to extricate herself from the clutches of blessed rest to respond. "Yes... Jason. I'm home. What do you need, honey?"

"I missed you."

Margaret pulled herself into a sitting position.

"I missed you, too," she responded, messing with his hair.

He's got to have a haircut. This coming week for sure. Maybe I can get Daddy to take him.

"Are you home to stay?"

"You mean for this weekend?"

"No, ma'am. Forever. I don't want you to go away again."

She brushed the side of his cheek. "Mommie does have some other meetings to attend in a few weeks, but I'm home for right now."

"Then can we move to our house tonight? I'm ready for my own room."

As she looked about her, Margaret realized it was dark outside. A glance at her bedside clock confirmed that darkness was appropriate.

Ten-thirty! I've slept almost five hours.

"I'm sorry, Jason. But it's too late tonight to try to go to our house. The beds aren't even made up and Mommie is really bushed."

"But I wanted to live at home tonight," he replied. "I can sleep in my sleeping bag. I don't mind."

"I don't have a sleeping bag. Besides, when we spend the first night in our new old house, we want our comfortable beds. Can't we wait until tomorrow?"

"I'd rather go tonight," he mumbled, "but I guess that will be okay."

Can I even get the house ready for us to stay there tomorrow night? Looks like I'm not going to have any choice.

"Let Mommie get a good night's rest, and we'll do everything we can to stay there tomorrow night."

"OK, Mommie. Can I tell Brian and Sallie?"

Why not? As tired as I am, I'm going to need all the motivation I can muster tomorrow to even make a dent in all that's over there.

"Jason? May I ask you a question?"

He looked at her with an air of optimistic openness. "Sure, Mommie."

"Why are you suddenly so anxious to move back to Redbud Way. Last week it didn't seem to matter to you when we got over there."

The little boy dropped his head. "'Cause."

"Now you know 'cause' isn't a reason."

"Well," he mumbled, scuffing the carpeting with the toe of his tennis shoe, "I've got to show somebody something."

"Who is 'somebody' and why do you have to show them... somebody... anything?"

"'Cause he bet me we aren't ever going to live in that house again. Said his mama said the house is cursed."

Dear Lord, the things children can manufacture!

"This is one of the boys in your class?"

"Yes, ma'am. When I told everyone we were moving back to our old house, one boy said his mama thinks our house has Daddy's ghost in it. He told me we won't ever move back there."

"I see."

Although I really don't.

"I told him I'd show him, that I wasn't afraid to stay there." He looked up at her with a desperate plea for approval. "I want to go back to school on Monday and tell everybody we've moved; that we aren't scared 'cause we're here to stay."

I guess we'll be moving tomorrow. I could never deliberately sabotage my son's position, just because his Mama is getting old and feeble and can't hold out. Gosh, I was looking forward to being lazy tomorrow.

"Well, if tomorrow's moving day, you better let me go grab a bite of supper Grammy is keeping warm for me. Then I've got to hit the sack, because I am pooped."

Jason began to skip from the room, then stopped and faced his mother. "Thank you, Mommie. You're the greatest!"

Don started that "You're the greatest," line and Brian picked it up when he was about Jason's age. Now it looked like it's filtered down to the youngest Haywood. This is one legacy Don left that I don't think will hurt us.

❧

"We're here," a voice called out the next morning.

P.C. She said she'd come help.

"I'm in the kitchen," she yelled toward the back door. "Come on in. But you'll have to look hard to find me. I'm up inside a cabinet and I'm not certain I can get out."

Even though the contractor's men had called themselves cleaning the site, Margaret didn't necessarily agree. The piles of sawdust inside the cabinets were one of the things that made her question how thorough they had been.

Clean enough for big, burly workmen, maybe. But not clean enough for me. Not by a long shot.

"You really are up in those cabinets, aren't you?"

"To be honest with you, P.C., I think I'm trapped. Once I realized this might be a problem, I was afraid to do a lot of moving until someone else got here. Somebody needs to be on standby with a power saw or at least a can opener, in case I get stuck."

'What are you doing in there anyway?"

"Wiping out sawdust. Those guys only half cleaned and I'm willing to bet they never looked inside the cabinets." She chuckled, "If sawdust was gold, none of us would have another financial worry."

"Well while you're negotiating the price of sawdust on the open market, I think Mama and I had better get to work. Where do you need us first?"

"Your mama came too?"

"She sure did. She and Joe are outside getting stuff out of the car. She's chomping at the bit."

"P.C.," Margaret hissed as she unfolded herself out of the cabinet onto the floor, "your mother's not physically able to do any of this work. What'd you bring her for?"

"'Cause she insisted and I'm an obedient daughter."

"Yeah?" The look on P.C.'s face was wicked at best, Margaret thought. *It clearly says: "Don't mess with me!"*

"Yeah!"

"Then put her to work. My children want to move in today."

Over the next hour Joe and P.C. began working to make beds and get the furniture in each room arranged as Margaret instructed. Mrs. Dunigan, whom Margaret decided was spryer than she wanted to admit, began to dust and plump pillows wherever she found one.

A few minutes after Sallie came to complain that her room didn't seem as large as it was before, Margaret's parents arrived.

"We brought lunch," Mrs. Maxwell announced. "Harold's unloading it now."

"Oh, Mama, thank you." She hugged her mother. "Leave it to you to be sure we all get fed."

"Working folks need to eat."

Margaret was again wedged up inside one of the cabinets trying to get all the errant sawdust, when she heard another familiar voice behind her.

"I came to help, so put me to work."

As she pulled out of her close confines, Margaret caught sight of her neighbor Sarah.

"Well, hello," she greeted her long-time friend.

"I'm here to help," the woman said again.

She still feels badly.

Margaret rose to her feet and put out her arms to invite a hug. "It's going to be so good living next door to you again."

"I don't know why you'd want to be neighbors with someone who won't stand with you when you need her." She huffed in disgust.

"You're standing with me now, aren't you?"

"But I wasn't there when you needed me most."

"But you're here now," Margaret insisted. "That's what counts. Come on, let me give you the grand tour. We've made a lot of changes."

A few minutes later, the two women stopped in the upstairs bedroom that would be Margaret's. P.C. and Joe were unpacking the room but stopped their work when Margaret introduced them.

"It's so good to meet you," P.C. said wiping her hands on her jeans before she offered her right hand to the guest. "I've heard Margaret speak of you. I know she's glad to get back to familiar territory."

"Oh, it's me who's so glad to see her back," Sarah exclaimed.

"She'll never know how many times I've looked over at this house and literally grieved over everything that's happened."

I didn't know that.

"Now I feel like we've all been given a second chance." She hugged Margaret closer to her. "I for one intend to make the most of this blessing." She looked at her neighbor. "Put me to work. That's why I'm here."

"Why don't you unpack Margaret's bathroom," P.C. suggested. "I was going to assign Joe that task, but something tells me he wouldn't even know how to begin." She looked to Margaret for confirmation.

"Gosh, Sarah, P.C.'s right. That would be a big help." She grinned. "I love Joe dearly, but I really don't want to look for all my cosmetics after he's organized them."

Joe colored, but nevertheless joined in the group laugh that followed Margaret's observation.

"Consider it done." Sarah headed into the adjoining bathroom.

Margaret left the upstairs crew and retreated to her kitchen, where she was deeply involved in organizing the work area as it had once been, when times were...

I won't say when times were happier, because in truth, they weren't. But I could always find solace when I cooked, and I want my kitchen back.

At noon her dad rounded up the workers while Margaret and her mother unpacked the two heavy hampers that had been hauled in earlier. Joe offered a word of thanks for all the blessings Margaret and her kids were enjoying. Before the group had even gotten started on the homemade fried chicken and vegetables, Annie Campbell and Pastor Samuel and his wife showed up dressed to work.

"Hey," Margaret called as she got up from her seat on the back patio where they had spread the food. "You're just in time for lunch. Grab a plate and dish up some of Mama's good cooking."

Before they finished the still-warm banana pudding, more members of the little church where Margaret and her children had been worshipping trooped into the yard.

I can't believe this.

"Why are all of you giving up your Saturday?"

"Because we want to," one of the ladies replied. "You need help, don't you?"

༄

After making one last pass through the house checking locks and lights, Margaret climbed the stairs to her new bedroom. The kids had gone up over an hour before, while she finished up the last of the kitchen unpacking.

Everything's in place in the kitchen, thanks to all the willing hands that accomplished so much in other parts of the house. As a result, except for a few more pictures to hang and some accessories still to unpack, we're settled in.

Margaret treated herself to a long, lazy soak in the giant jetted tub, until she feared she would fall asleep if she didn't move. Once out of tub and into her gown, the tired mover climbed into bed and reached for her Bible and a small book of daily devotionals one of the ladies in the Atlanta office had given her. She flipped to the page for that day, where she discovered a verse from St. Mark 5, verse 19. *"Go home to thy friends; and tell them how great things the Lord hath done for thee, and hath had compassion on thee."*

As she read the other verses, she saw that the passage actually dealt with the casting out of unclean spirits.

But in a way, that's what we've done here. The demon of violence no longer stalks this house and we've cast away the old and made everything new again. Oh, God, You are so good to us.

After she read a few more passages and had a few quiet moments of prayer, Margaret turned off the bedside lamp and snuggled down into the softness of the bed that had sheltered her before.

This is what I call being rich: a good, comfortable bed in a place safe from danger. It feels so good to be back...

CHAPTER FIFTEEN

At church the next morning, members crowded around Margaret. They congratulated her on the completion of the house renovation, sharing how thrilled they were about her return.

I never knew how many friends I had.

After lunch, while the children were out making the most of the rest of the weekend before school on Monday, Margaret placed a call to Joe Busbee. After exchanging greetings and pleasantries, Margaret came right to the point.

"Joe, I want you to level with me about what can happen when Brian goes to trial. Don't try to spare me; I want worse-case scenario."

"Aren't you borrowing trouble? At least just a little?"

"Look, Joe. Brian doesn't talk about it, but he's scared. Badly scared. Now that we've gotten settled in the house again, there's that much more he stands to lose if he has to serve time. Even if it is just a juvenile facility."

"I don't think he'll draw any time. Detective Duncan is staunchly in his corner, looking out for Brian."

"I know that. But I also know that if Brian does go to jail, I need to be quietly preparing him... him and me... for that possibility. Like I said, worst-case scenario."

"Okay. You asked for it. But I think you're creating problems where there aren't any."

"Nevertheless, I have an entire list of prayer partners who are planning to pray daily from tomorrow until the trial is over and we have a verdict and sentence. We want to know what, specifically, we should be praying for."

"When you put it that way, I can appreciate what you're doing so here's the very worst I believe can happen. But you also have to let me tell you best case, and what I think will happen."

"Deal."

Joe outlined the sentencing guidelines for juvenile offenders laid down by Georgia law. "Because he is a juvenile, if he is sentenced, it will be in a juvenile facility, not an adult prison. When he turns eighteen, he'll have to be released."

"So you're saying the most he would get would be," she paused for some quick mental math, "would be about nineteen months?"

"Exactly."

"Would that leave him with a record?"

"It would, but if he behaves himself for a period, we can have that expunged since he's under seventeen."

"What about the rest of his high school career?"

"It won't be Mount Zion, but he will have the opportunity to attend classes right there in jail and get a high school diploma."

But he won't get to go to any of the colleges he's selected.

"What else? Don't stop now."

She was busy scribbling on a legal pad as he talked.

"As for worse case scenario, that's about it. He may be fined as well as given jail time, but I doubt it."

"The money to pay the fine is no problem. Having to graduate high school in jail is another matter."

"But remember, I haven't told you the other side of the story."

"Let's hear it. I hope it's encouraging."

"I think it is." Joe proceeded to explain he felt the judge would come down hard on her son, in order to make a lasting impression. "Both Detective Duncan and the first judge were very impressed with Brian. They know what he's made of, and they want to make certain this sends him in the right direction. I think this other judge will totally put the fear of God in him during the proceedings, but when it comes time to pass sentence, here's what I think will happen."

As she thought about it in bed that night, formulating the words to ask her prayer partners to pray, she indulged in a good talk with the Lord. *Father, Joe believes the judge will give Brian a sentence that would last until his eighteenth birthday, but that he'll suspend the sentence, provided Brian gets into no other trouble, and that he reports to a probation officer every week. This would let him finish high school right here at home. He says the judge will probably order him to pay a fine of two or three thousand dollars, which he will have to borrow from me and repay with interest.*

She paused and grabbed a tissue for her eyes. *I'm not against him being punished, Father. In fact, I'm in favor of it. This boy has too much potential; he needs to learn a practical lesson. But I don't think anything will be gained by locking him up. So, Father, my prayer is that Brian will receive a suspended sentence, probation and a fine. But, as always, I submit to Your will, knowing that You know what is best for each of us. In Jesus' name. Amen.*

After reading several passages from her Bible, Margaret settled down, confident she could handle any outcome.

∽

"How about coming over for lunch today?" Margaret asked her friend Alice Hanover. "Do you have time? We need to talk."

"Well, sure. As long as I'm free in time to pick up the girls from school, my day is wide open."

"Great. See you at noon, here at my house."

MY house. That sounds so good. To say and to hear.

Earlier that morning, Margaret had acted on an impulse that had been with her for a couple of days, as she studied how to best accomplish all that she had committed for the month of October and still be there for Brian as well.

We have no way of knowing how long I'll be tied up with his trial, and possibly the aftermath. I love my job and I believe in what I'm doing, but Brian comes first. That's not up for discussion.

It had been a very busy morning. As soon as the children left for school, Margaret arrived at Haywood Tufters for her weekly meeting with the new plant manager. After friendly chitchat, she was encouraged by the financial reports she received.

"I cannot tell you what a blessing, and a relief it is, to know that Don's business... MY business... is humming along and I don't have to devote anything more than an hour on Monday morning."

"We're doing well," the manager informed her. "Fortunately you have a happy work force here. That translates into productivity."

"No thanks to you creating that climate. I'm sure the employees were a bit hesitant since they've never known anyone but Don."

Amanda laughed. "It didn't help that I was a female, either. But things are working out."

After they finished looking at the reports, including the new orders that had been received since the previous meeting, Margaret posed the question she knew she had to ask.

"If I'm out of line, tell me so. But in truth, while you're the plant manager, and I defer to you, I am the CEO. Is that correct?"

Ms. Butterworth agreed.

"As CEO, would it not be within reason I could employ an administrative assistant whose salary would be paid by the company?"

Again, she received the answer she wanted to hear.

"If we're in agreement, can the payroll stand the load of a 32-hour a week employee plus benefits and insurance? This person would work specifically for me, at my home and her home. I'll be honest with you, much of what she will do involves my domestic violence work."

The manager turned to her keyboard where her fingers began to tap across the keys. It was several minutes, during which time Margaret wondered if she had overstepped her authority.

Amanda began to make notes on a memo sheet. "At the end of the day, you are the boss. If you dictate that we hire this person, we'll do it. But as your plant manager, I would be less than diligent if I didn't advise you to use caution."

"Not to worry. I don't second-guess you and I don't pull rank. If it's not feasible to hire another employee, then say so. But... if we can hire her, can I use her in the ways that benefit me most?"

"Whatever duties you assign this employee are your call. Secretaries have been picking up their bosses's dry cleaning and buying birthday gifts for his family for years. Don't give that a second thought. As for the hit on the payroll, if your person... I assume you already have someone in mind... can work for this wage, we can accommodate it." She slid the piece of paper she'd been writing on across the desk.

Margaret studied it and smiled. *Even better than I had hoped.*

"Thanks, Amanda. You have no clue what a difference you've made this morning. In my life, and in the life of a woman whose abuser has almost ruined her financially."

She said much-the-same to Barbara Kirkland on the phone as she was pulling away from the carpet plant.

"I know a woman here in Carter's Crossroads. Annie knows her too, so as you might guess, she's a former battered wife."

Margaret explained her very real concerns about all the October domestic violence programs she had planned, her need to be with Brian without worrying, and about her friend, Alice.

"In some ways Alice is fortunate. Her husband is locked up and can't hurt her. She's in the process of getting a divorce. She isn't homeless, because she inherited her mother's house and a little money.

But she cannot afford health insurance for herself and the children."

"If she doesn't have insurance, she's hurting. Especially with children."

"She can get coverage for them through a private policy, but her income situation doesn't allow her to pay the high premiums."

"What are your thoughts?"

"Alice and I have worked together before. She's the one who actually pulled together last year's Tour of Homes. I was recovering from my injuries."

"Annie told me what a wonderful job she did."

"Which is why I want her working for me...for us. I know your budget can't accommodate another salary, so I've worked out a way to pay her instead and, with your blessing, I'm going to offer her a position as my administrative assistant at lunch today."

Alice would, Margaret explained, become an employee of Haywood Tufters, working exclusively for her, with salary and benefits paid by Haywood.

"But I'm going to utilize her primarily to help me with the work I do for you, and she'll do that work from my home and her home, since she has small children."

"I'm blown away," Barbara admitted. "That's some of the most ingenious thinking outside the box I've seen in quite a while. Which is probably why I hired you. Or at least that's what I'm going to tell people!"

I don't deserve praise. I just try to fix problems the best way I can.

"Then you're in agreement?"

"Hey, I'd be the last director to turn down a good pair of hands that came to me free. If you and Annie think this is the way to go, then let's do it. I have confidence in both of you."

"Thanks. I did talk to Annie about it over the weekend."

We were in the kitchen unpacking the pantry, when Annie told me about Alice's loss of insurance, how she was beginning to regret pressing charges against her husband. That's when this idea began forming and when I talked to Annie last night, she was all for it.

When Alice rang the bell just minutes before twelve, Margaret was just putting the finishing touches on the chicken salad sandwiches and fresh fruit she had prepared.

"Come in, come in. It's so good to see you."

Alice hugged her hostess. "It's good to see you. I've missed the good times we had 'way back when'." She looked around the foyer. "You know, I've driven by this house many times and always wondered what it looked like inside." She paused again as she took a second look. "But I never imagined anything as beautiful as this."

Surely Alice was in this house before. "You mean you've never been here? What about all the times we had the Sunday School classes?" Margaret asked, recalling her days as the unofficial church hostess.

"You forget," Alice chided, "those were the days when my abuser dictated where I went and where I didn't go. He would never let us take part in any of the social activities, as much as I wanted to."

"Don wasn't that restrictive, but still, it's such a pleasure to be able to go and do as I want, without giving it a second thought. I'm sure you feel the same way."

Alice's face froze, then as she relaxed her features, her eyes emitted a look of pain and loss.

"In some ways, it is very empowering. Unfortunately, I wasn't left very much money in the bank."

"Oh, Alice..."

"I hate to say it, Margaret. But it may bankrupt me to get rid of him." Her face became stormy looking. "It ought not be that way. Lately I've been thinking I made a big mistake."

"No, my friend, it shouldn't cost you. But I've got something to share. Hopefully this will convince you that you did what was best."

She led her guest into the breakfast room and in a matter of minutes, had lunch on the table and the two were sitting down to eat.

"Don't keep me in suspense," Alice begged. "What could you possibly have to tell me that would make a difference?"

While she had planned how she would deliver her news, in the end Margaret felt she should be quick and merciful.

"How would you like to go to work for me? As my administrative assistant?" She noted her friend's shocked eyes and pale face. "Not as a volunteer, but for pay? Including... insurance."

"But... how... how... why?"

Margaret quickly explained the details and watched as the expression in her friend's eyes changed from sorrow to one of sheer joy.

"I can't tell you..." Alice gasped. "You just have no idea what an answer to prayer this is."

"That prayer works both ways. But you better hear me out before you start thanking me. The money isn't that much and it may insult you, but it's the best we can do. It does provide insurance for you and you can pay a nominal sum for the girls' coverage."

"I could squeak by financially if it weren't for the high cost of insurance. I'd almost work for free, just to get the insurance."

"Don't sell yourself too cheaply. I wouldn't dream of not paying you."

"So what would I be doing? I don't know a lot about the carpet business."

Margaret laughed. "That makes two of us." She explained how Alice's work would be to help her; that she wouldn't even have an office at Haywood Tufters.

"You can plan that ninety-nine percent of your work will be domestic violence related. You see, October is National Domestic Violence Awareness Month, and I am covered up. Also, Brian's trial is the last week in October, and I have absolutely no idea how long I'll be tied up with it."

"It must be killing you. The thought of him going to jail, I mean."

"If only you knew, Alice. This has been like a nightmare that will not go away. I blame myself for turning him loose in Atlanta with very little supervision."

Alice patted her friend's arm. "Don't impale yourself on your sword just yet. Brian's an intelligent young man. From what you've already told me about his explanations, he knew he was hanging around with the wrong guys."

"Oh, he readily admits it. I'm just praying the punishment truly fits the crime."

The two had finished eating and, as they cleaned the kitchen together, Margaret brought Alice up to speed on the work she was doing, and how her friend's efforts would plug in and make a difference.

They adjourned to the den to finish talking business before Alice left in time to pick up her children from school, Margaret asked her, "What day this week or next would work for me to take you in to Atlanta to meet Barbara and the rest of the staff?"

"I don't have my calendar with me, but let me check after I get home. I'll call you."

Margaret hugged her. "That would be great. Can't wait for you to meet everyone, 'cause they're sure anxious to meet you!"

"Just wha… what have you told them?" Alice demanded, her voice rising a couple of octaves, a trait Margaret had seen before, whenever her friend was flustered.

"Nothing but the truth." She held up her hands, palms out, and apart over her head. "Don't shoot. I only told them the truth."

"I'll save my bullet until after I meet them. But don't get too comfortable or complacent."

After Alice left, Margaret busied herself hanging several more pieces of art.

Today and tomorrow are the last days I'm going to have for the next month or more to do anything in the house. It's almost like it's now or never.

As she drove nails and kept a simultaneous eye on the clock, she reflected on other matters that had to be dealt with as well, before she found herself launched out of a catapult into a full month of domestic violence activities around the state. She gave a silent prayer of thanks for friends who were willing to help.

You answer prayers so beautifully, Lord. All I had to do was voice aloud my concerns about what I would do with the kids all those days I'm going to have to be out of town. The phone rings and there's my answer. I really didn't want to have to separate them from this house, and I didn't want to burden Mama and Daddy.

The call had come late the evening before, from her favorite pastor.

"Margaret," he said in the voice she had come to appreciate while listening to his sermons, "Susan and I have something to suggest. God has literally laid it on our hearts that we should offer to move into your house and look after the children over these next few weeks, while you're gone. Would we be too forward to suggest this?"

"Too forward? Certainly not. Too generous might be a more accurate description. Are you sure you want to do this?"

"As sure as anything we've ever done. We're confident this is what God wants us to do."

"Pastor, I just prayed last night for a solution that would let the kids stay here and not have to drag them around for the next few weeks. You surely are an answer to prayer."

"So that's a 'yes'?"

"It's a yes on one condition. You and Susan have to come eat with us Tuesday night, so we can discuss the details on an adult level. You and the kids need to get on the same page."

"What time and we'll be there."

"Why don't we say seven o'clock and… and thank you, thank you again."

"What are friends for? See you then."

※

As Margaret sat in the Atlanta office, surrounded by her co-workers, she knew she was speaking to herself as well as the others.

"This is our chance for the big time, if you will. This agency is going to be more high profile during this month of October than has ever been the case. We need to take full advantage of the exposure and do our missionary work every chance we get."

It's big time for me, too. It's one thing to coordinate a fundraiser for Mount Zion School in your own hometown, or even the Tour of Homes for the shelter. I've never been so front and center, unless you count all the TV exposure and newspaper coverage we got when Don was wreaking havoc. All that publicity sent exactly the wrong message.

"Margaret is right," the agency director agreed. "We're going to be very much 'front and center', and much of the credit goes to her, for coordinating things so masterfully."

"While I appreciate all the nice words, it pains me to have to miss some of the activities at the end of the month. Right now I have no idea how much I'll be away."

"Margaret's son Brian will go to trial on the 22nd. Her first responsibility is to him. That isn't open for discussion."

"While I do agree with Barbara, it still bothers me that I can't see full fruition of what I've put together. And..." She dropped her head, "I feel like I'm running out on you guys."

"Now you don't need to feel that way," Evelyn protested. "You've done such a wonderful job of organization, we should be able to pick up the pieces with no problem."

"That's right," Kirsten agreed. "You have to be with Brian." She flashed Margaret a sympathetic smile. "It still breaks my heart that you all are going through this nightmare."

"But it's going to come out okay," Barbara interrupted. "We're all praying. We'll be here for you, so you can be there for Brian."

"Thanks, you guys." Margaret didn't trust herself to say more than that, because the tears of panic that had become her constant companion of late were threatening once again.

Lord, I know I'm supposed to turn everything over to You, and I try. But Brian is my son and I love him.

Changing the subject, she announced, "I have someone I want you to meet." She went to the door of the outer office and motioned for Alice to join them. With an arm around her friend, Margaret said, "This is one of the best friends I've ever had, and a darn good organizer, too. Alice Hanover." She introduced each of her co-workers and told Alice about their duties.

"Alice is going to be working as Margaret's administrative assistant in Carter's Crossroads, so we'll all be interacting with her frequently," Barbara explained.

Margaret watched as expressions of friendship changed to ones of suspicion. She instantly realized what was happening. *They're wondering how Barbara worked another salary into the budget and why the new kid on the block is getting an assistant when they don't have one.*

She quickly explained. "Alice has graciously agreed to work for me. I'm going to personally pay for what she does."

Faces relaxed, indicating Alice was going to be accepted. Conversation continued for over an hour, while each staff member reported on specific responsibilities for the month ahead, and asked questions.

I just wish I didn't have to pull away to deal with my own situation. But this time my priorities are in order. I know where I have to be.

∽

When October arrived, Margaret felt she was running a foot

race, always half a step behind. Between trips to various parts of the state coordinating all the programming she had planned, she was still unpacking her house and settling in. She was also trying to keep her son's rapidly failing spirits from bottoming out.

"Honestly, P.C.," she told her friend. "I just want this trial behind us, regardless of the outcome. The unknown is doing a number on Brian. He's so low right now I need a spatula to scrape him up."

"Do you want Joe to talk with him? Would that help?"

She ran her hands through her hair in frustration. "At this point I'm game for anything."

"I'll mention it when I get back to the office. He'll be glad to take him out somewhere... you know, man to man."

Margaret toyed with the miniature houses she'd unpacked from the latest box. Dusting and arranging them on shelves built specially for them, she added, "That's part of the problem. Brian feels he should be a man about this, but inside he's just a little boy wanting his mother to make everything okay." She sighed as a tear appeared at the edge of her right eye. "This is one thing Mama can't fix."

P.C. had brought a packet of papers for Haywood Tufters that needed Margaret's signature. The official business had only taken a few minutes. Then P.C. adjourned to the kitchen, at Margaret's suggestion, and cut them each a piece of icebox pie and a glass of Coke.

"This is soooo good," P.C. said through a mouthful of pie. "Where'd you buy it?"

"I'll have you know I made it," Margaret informed her guest. "Found the recipe in *Southern Living* magazine and just had to try it."

"You done good."

"So tell me, P.C., is there anything else we have to do to be ready for this trial? Is there anything else that we can do? It is literally hanging over this house like a funeral pall."

P.C. speared the last bite of pie. "Really and truly, Margaret. There's nothing else to be done. Just pray this superior court judge will be open-minded." She hesitated. "All of them aren't, you know."

She's thinking about Jim Deaton's dad and her own ex-husband.

"We're praying all right. I've reminded nearly forty e-mail buddies that the hardest part of this journey is still ahead."

I never dreamed a year ago that my life could take so many unexpected twists and turns. All because one man decided he had the right to control the lives of everyone around him.

CHAPTER SIXTEEN

*M*argaret, accompanied by her parents and P.C., took her seat in the front row of the Fulton County Superior Court courtroom. P.C. had steered them toward the defense side of the room, since Margaret had been determined to sit as close to Brian as possible.

"We're early," she announced to those trailing in her wake. "But I couldn't have sat still another minute. I have to feel like this nightmare is on its way to resolution."

Brian had ridden down with Joe, so the two might have some one-on-one time before the case was called, and Margaret knew that Annie Campbell and the pastor and his wife were coming as well. Even her next door neighbor, Sarah, had called to say she would be there.

"You don't have to drive all the way to Atlanta for this," Margaret had assured her. "Joe says the trial shouldn't take very long. Probably won't take over an hour or so, since there won't be a jury."

"It doesn't matter," her friend vowed. "I turned my back on you once and I won't make that mistake again. I will be there. For Brian, but for you as well. I'm a mother, too. My daughter, Rachel, was abused, remember? I know how it feels when your child is hurting."

"Bless you." *I'd forgotten about Rachel's situation.*

"Hey, we're here," a voice from behind announced. Margaret looked around to see the last four expected members of their cheering section taking their seats. Looking beyond them, she realized with shock that Barbara Kirkland was also walking into the courtroom. She saw her hesitate, look around. Once she spotted Margaret's group, her anxious face broke into a smile and she headed toward them.

"Thank goodness I found you." She slid in the seat Margaret indicated. "There are so many courtrooms in this complex, I wasn't sure I was at the right place."

"What are you doing here at all?" Margaret quizzed. "I happen to know you're speaking in south Georgia this afternoon. You couldn't possibly make it if you left right now."

"I'm not going."

"Not going? Why? You have to go."

"Because I felt like my place today was to be here with you." She patted Margaret's arm. "I've got a very capable substitute already on her way."

"A substitute?"

Barbara grinned. "Your assistant, Alice. She's going to speak in my place."

"But how? Why? I'm not sure Alice is ready for that kind of exposure."

"Evidently she is, because it was she who proposed the idea."

Alice is a lady of many talents. Obviously many more than I realized.

"I didn't know..."

"Alice didn't tell you. But she called me day before yesterday and suggested the swap. I was already feeling guilty because I couldn't be here. It was a perfect solution."

One more time Alice has spilled into the cracks and taken care of things. I don't know what I would have done without her.

Indeed, Alice had taken charge of Margaret's files and to-do list. Suddenly, almost without thought, things began to happen and

Margaret marveled at how much more productive she had suddenly become.

People came and went in the courtroom. Some were obviously attorneys and still others wore the unmistakable label of courthouse employee. But on none of their faces could Margaret sense any concern for what was about to happen to her child. Not a single one appeared to be burdened over what happened to people's lives once they passed before the judge in this room. She said as much to P.C.

"You have to understand lawyers. In truth, many of us can be a rather callous bunch. We dwell in a land of conflict of interest, especially those of us who represent clients accused of criminal acts. Such wouldn't be permitted anywhere but in the legal profession."

"Conflict of interest? I don't understand."

"Think about it for a minute. The attorney I work with on one case may be the attorney I oppose two cases from now." She laughed, although Margaret thought the sound was suspiciously devoid of mirth. "There's a reason an inside joke in law school refers to the practice of law as the world's second oldest profession, with a tendency to encroach on the oldest profession."

Margaret was horrified. "I always thought lawyers were upstanding and ethical." Her face displayed the emotions that were swirling, confusing her. "I mean you… and Joe…"

"At the risk of sounding egotistical, I like to think that Joe and I are ethical. And there are many others out there just like us. But far too many of my colleagues are looking out only for themselves. If they can prevail for their client, that's a bonus for them. But they get paid either way, and some don't care what alliances they have to form to make that happen."

This is making me sick at my stomach.

As she was about to say as much to her friend, a door near the front of the courtroom opened, and Joe and Brian, who was escorted by a uniformed deputy, entered.

"Oh... there they are."

In short order the enclosed area of the courtroom filled with people and in a matter of minutes, the judge entered from his chambers and court was underway. In the minute or so they had before they would be in contempt of court, Pastor Samuel waded amongst them, as he led them in prayer for Brian specifically, for Margaret, and for the outcome of the trial, according to God's will.

It was painful to hear her son publicly called a criminal; to hear the prosecutor's words that reduced the boy she knew to be a warm and generous and trusting person into a heartless crook. It tore at her heart.

Thank goodness there's not a jury. This woman is painting Brian as if he's been living a life of crime since he stopped using a pacifier. I just hope Joe's strategy works.

Several weeks earlier, Margaret had questioned the attorney about the process to come. "Why can't he just plead guilty and be sentenced? Why does he have to go through the shame of a public trial? Hasn't he been humiliated enough already?"

"We could do that," Joe agreed. "But I believe it's important to get Detective Duncan's input on the record. He's in Brian's corner, and he'll do everything he can to help him."

"But he testified in the other court when bail was set."

"And the judge, at his discretion, may or may not choose to read those transcripts. If the detective testifies before this judge, he's obligated to consider all that in rendering his verdict."

After the prosecutor concluded her opening remarks, which included asking the judge for the maximum sentence the law allowed, the ball was passed to Joe.

Maximum sentence is three to five years, even though Joe says they can't hold him past his eighteenth birthday. Still, that's too much.

Joe addressed the judge. "Your Honor. There is no dispute that Brian Haywood was behind the wheel of the vehicle... his personal vehicle... that served as the getaway car. Brian has admitted this from the beginning. The crux of this case depends on what Brian knew and, more importantly, when he knew it. We expect to show that he was duped, was used by the other parties to this robbery. Furthermore, we expect to show that when he became aware of what had transpired, he took steps to correct the problem. Thank you, Your Honor."

The first witness on the stand was a small, oriental woman, who identified herself as the clerk at the liquor store. She told in brief detail about the actual holdup and admitted that she had not seen Brian at all. She did see the vehicle the two holdup men entered as they fled the store with the money. She had given police that information, but hadn't been able to get a license number or a description of the driver.

When Joe took over the questioning, he asked, "If I understand your testimony, at no time was this young man..." He placed his hand on Brian's shoulder and continued, "ever in the store while the robbery was in progress?"

The clerk agreed. Joe thanked her for her testimony.

Detective Duncan took the stand next. Under the direction of the young woman who was representing the prosecutor's office, he related the events of that recent summer afternoon, when he was dispatched to a liquor store hold-up and the events that unfolded. When he finished, the prosecutor thanked him and indicated that Joe was free to cross-examine.

"Detective Duncan?"

"Yes, Mr. Busbee?"

"If I understand the testimony you've just given, Brian Haywood, the defendant, admitted to you that he was the driver of the vehicle in question. Is that correct?"

"It is."

"Can you recall at what point you first heard Brian make this admission?"

"I'd say it was within the first thirty seconds after we began questioning him."

"That quickly?"

"Yes, sir."

"And where was this initial questioning conducted? At headquarters?"

"We did question him further at headquarters, later that evening. But that first admission was made standing outside the vehicle in a parking lot just a few blocks from the liquor store."

"Did he initially deny being the driver and then change his story?"

"No, sir. He admitted it immediately."

"At any point did he ever attempt to flee? To escape? Was he ever uncooperative?"

"No sir. He stood there and talked to us. He didn't try to flee. His passengers were attempting to get out and get away as we drove up, but the defendant was still seated behind the wheel when we opened his door and ordered him out."

"Was there a moment, Detective, before police gained control of the situation, that Brian could have had a window of opportunity to drive away?"

"Certainly. Only he would have had to restart the engine first."

"Restart the engine? Let me see if I understand the picture you're painting here. You're saying you found the driver of a getaway vehicle still sitting behind the steering wheel, with the engine off, about four blocks from the scene of the holdup?"

"Yes sir. That's what I'm saying."

Joe stroked his chin. "Detective... can you give me a good-faith estimate of how much time elapsed between the holdup and the capture of this defendant?"

"I can tell you almost exactly." He pulled a notebook from his pocket, flipped through it and finally said. "Nine-one-one logged the call at three-forty-seven and the dispatch went out within thirty seconds. A vehicle matching the description given by the store clerk was spotted at three-fifty-three."

"Six minutes?"

"Six minutes."

"You and your men are to be commended for your excellent work in this case. I'd guess the only way you could have caught him any sooner would be if he had waited outside the liquor store."

The detective grinned and said, "He almost did that for us, Mr. Busbee. We would never have had him and the other defendants who will be tried later, if the getaway driver hadn't pulled over and stopped."

"Would you say he wasn't trying to escape?"

"Objection, Your Honor. It's obvious Counsel is trying to build a case and he's leading the witness to do so."

"Sustained," the judge barked at Joe. "I'm neither blind, deaf nor stupid. I pick up on inference, so don't insult my intelligence."

"I'm sorry, Your Honor." He faced the policeman again. "Thank you, Detective Duncan. That concludes my questions of this witness."

The prosecutor, after informing the judge she had no further questions, rested her case.

"Now it's Joe's turn. And Brian's," P.C. whispered.

Margaret's stomach tied into knots. Brian had told her the previous evening that he planned to testify in his own behalf.

"I'm scared, Mom. But Joe thinks it's the best way and I trust him."

Oh, Lord. Never mind how I'm feeling. Please surround Brian with Your love and protection. Calm his anxious heart and place in his mouth the words You would have him to give.

Brian, in a charcoal gray suit, white shirt and red and gray tie Joe had picked out a few days prior, took his seat in the witness stand. He appeared calm, but Margaret could see his arm moving. She knew he was kneading his kneecap with his left hand; she had been his mother long enough to interpret the sign.

He's terrified. I would be, too!

Joe began by asking the young man about the events that led up to the liquor store holdup.

"The guys... they told me where to drive."

"And why was that?"

"They didn't have a car, and they'd asked me to drive them several places to run errands."

"Neither of them has a car?"

"No sir. One of them doesn't have a driver's license since he got picked up for DUI and the..."

"Objection, Your Honor. Did the defendant personally relieve this man of his license?"

This woman is about to get on my nerves.

"Sustained! Can you rephrase your question, Counselor?"

"Brian, how did you know he didn't have a driver's license?"

"Because he told me. He told everybody at work. He thought it was funny."

"You're telling me if I questioned other workers at your job, they would tell me the same thing?"

"Yes, sir. He bragged about losing his license."

"And the other guy? Had he lost his license, also?"

"No, sir. He lost his car. Somebody came and repossessed it about a week before the robbery."

"Objection..."

"Just a moment, Ms. Forrester." The judge turned to Brian. "Mr. Haywood, was the car repossessed in your presence?"

"Yes, Your Honor. The man came in where we all worked and demanded the keys. There were several who saw him and heard what he had to say."

"Objection overruled. Proceed, Mr. Busbee."

"Was this the first time they had asked you to burn your gas hauling them around?"

Margaret saw that Brian looked confused.

He means was this the first day you had ever carried them anywhere. Think, Brian... Lord, Please help him.

Just when she thought her son would fumble, she saw the light of understanding shine bright.

"Oh, no sir. There were probably four or five other days when I 'burned my gas' taking them places."

"Several days then, huh, Brian?"

"Yes sir."

Margaret sat rooted in her seat, one eye on the courtroom clock that ticked off the minutes with maddening slowness. The other eye never left the young man sitting in the witness chair. It was almost as if maintaining a constant gaze could ensure that he would prevail.

I know Joe is building a solid defense. In the end, it should benefit Brian. But this slow, plodding pace of the testimony is almost more than my system can bear, Lord.

"What kinds of places would you take them, Brian? Do you remember?"

"Sure, let me think."

Margaret could see the wheels turning. She knew that Joe had deliberately not coached Brian on what to say, because he wanted his testimony to come across as natural and innocent as possible. He was banking on Brian's intelligence and savvy to bring it off.

Joe was adamantly against any coaching. He and I almost came to blows over that one. But I trust him. I just hope the judge does!

"Take your time, Brian. Just tell us what you remember."

"Yes sir, Mr. Busbee. Usually every afternoon after work, they'd both have places they wanted me to take them. On payday they wanted to go to the bank to draw out some money. A couple of times I took them to the post office, and I know I dropped them at a drugstore once."

"Did you usually take them home as well?"

"Usually."

"If you had to carry them home, how did they get to work each morning?"

"I don't know, sir." He hesitated and scrunched up his face. "I never thought about it."

"But you didn't pick them up for work as well?"

"No sir."

"Now Brian, were there any other businesses they stopped at while you were driving them around?"

The young man ducked his head. "They went to the liquor store every day. Said they needed something to wash the stench of work out of their mouths."

"This would have been the liquor store that was held up?"

"No, sir."

"No?" Joe feigned surprise. "You mean you went to a different liquor store?"

"No, sir. Different liquor stores, plural. They had me drive them to a different store every day."

"A different store every day. That's interesting. I would think that they might have had a favorite."

"Well, if they did," Brian volunteered, "they sure weren't loyal to it, because every afternoon we went to a different store."

"Did you ever go into any of the stores with them?"

"No, sir!" he responded quickly. "For one thing I don't have anything to do with stuff like that, and besides, I'm under age. I could have been arrested."

"Did the guys ever pay you for gasoline or offer to pay you?"

"You mean with money?"

"Yes, that's right. Did they ever reimburse you for gas?"

"No, sir."

"Did they pay you with anything else?"

Brian fidgeted in his chair.

"Please answer your counsel's question, Mr. Haywood."

The boy hung his head. "They offered to pay me...to pay me with liquor."

"Did you accept?"

He hung his head again, but sensing movement from the judge who sat to his left, he solemnly admitted, "Not after the first time."

"Why was that, Brian?"

"Because I didn't like the taste of it and knew I was too young to drink. Since I didn't want to get into trouble, I poured it out and dropped the bottle in a recycling bin." He looked at his mother. "I'm sorry, Mom."

"Mr. Busbee, please instruct your client not to speak unless spoken to, and definitely not to address remarks to anyone in the courtroom except officers of the court."

I don't know if I feel comfortable with this man. It's almost like he's trying to hard to prove a point. Especially since there isn't a jury present.

"My apologies, You Honor. I don't expect my client to make that mistake again."

Brian's face fell.

"So, Brian, let's recap here. Except for one small bottle of liquor, you've been unpaid transportation for these other two guys?"

"Yes, sir."

"And while you took them many places, you always stopped at a liquor store each day. Always a different liquor store."

"Yes, sir."

"So on the afternoon in question, when the men asked you to pull into the liquor store that was subsequently robbed, it was no different from any other afternoon. Is that right?"

"Yes, sir. It was just another liquor store."

"Now Brian, think carefully. When did you first realize that something was different? That something was wrong?"

The boy fidgeted.

"Well...always before they would take their time coming from the store to the car once they'd made their purchase. But on this day, they came running to the car, jumped in, and told me to get the..." He faltered. "I'm sorry Mr. Busbee, but I can't repeat what they said. There are ladies here and it was pretty raunchy."

"Then just paraphrase it, leaving out anything you think might not be suitable."

"They jumped in and told me to get the...to get out of there. I did, and then I asked them why."

"How did they respond?"

"They yelled at me that they'd held up the store and needed to get as far away as possible."

"What did you do?"

"I looked for the first place I could find to pull over and stop."

"Why?"

"Because I had to think. I knew what they'd done was wrong, but I didn't know how I should...what I should do." He floundered. "I didn't know how to go about getting them out or calling the police."

"So you did what?"

"Almost as soon as I pulled into that parking lot, a police car was pulling in behind me and that solved the problem."

"How did you feel?"

"I was glad to see the police. I thought if I told them what had happened, I'd be helping. I didn't expect to get in all this trouble myself."

"Thank you, Brian. If I may, I only have a few more questions." He looked intently at the young man. "Knowing what you know now, if you had it to do over, would you associate with these two men?"

"No sir." Brian asserted. "I realize now they were using me and taking advantage of me."

"Very well. Then knowing what you know now, would you still have stopped and cooperated with the police, or would you have kept going?"

"I'm not real happy about the possibility of going to jail, but I would still stop. It was the right thing to do."

Oh, Brian. I am so proud of you.

"No more questions, Your Honor."

Brian half rose as if expecting to leave the witness stand. "Just a minute young man. Ms. Forrester may have some questions for you." He nodded to the young dark-haired woman wearing what Margaret had decided was a perpetual sneer on her face.

The other attorney rose and approached the witness stand. Margaret braced herself.

This woman looks like bad news.

"Mr. Haywood," she began as she placed her fingertips under her chin tent style. "What kind of grades do you make in school?"

"Usually A's, but I have made a couple of high B's when I didn't study as hard as I should have."

"Would you say you're one of the smartest students in your class?"

Margaret could see an expression of concern forming on her son's face.

He doesn't understand where she's going with this and neither do I.

"No ma'am. I wouldn't necessarily say that."

"You wouldn't?"

"No, ma'am."

"But you do consistently make high grades? Can we agree on that?"

"Yes... yes ma'am."

"Then Mr. Haywood..." The attorney paused for dramatic effect. "If you are smart enough to make honor roll quality grades, do you really expect this court to believe that you were dumb enough to be duped by these two co-workers of yours?"

"Well... I... but I was." The boy was rattled.

"Let's get truthful here, Mr. Haywood. You grew up in a small town and when you met Mr. Faulker and Mr. Jensen, you were impressed by their worldly ways. You did their bidding and chauffeured them around because you really wanted to be just like them?"

"No. No! That's not it at all," Brian protested.

He is breaking out in a sweat. I can see the beads of perspiration. I've got to do something to save my child. He would never have gotten into this mess if I hadn't insisted on moving us to Atlanta.

On either side of Margaret, she felt support. P.C. had grabbed hold of one hand. Barbara had the other hand, and from behind, she could feel her pastor's hand on her shoulder. It was as if all three knew the tremendous pressure she was feeling to save her cub.

"Mr. Haywood? Didn't you yearn for some big city excitement and didn't these two gentlemen provide that for you? How else can you explain why two grown men would even be interested in hanging around with a kid?"

On the witness stand, Brian dropped his head. Margaret could sense he was close to tears.

"It wasn't that way at all," he pleaded. "Honest, it wasn't."

The attorney, who appeared crouched and posed for attack, finally said, "Let's investigate something else."

Brian looked up. The expression on his face clearly asked if the worst was over. "Yes ma'am?"

"Tell me, Mr. Haywood, is your father here in court today?"

What?

"No," Brian responded, "my father is dead."

"And how did he die?"

"Objection, Your Honor." Joe was on his feet and protesting. "I fail to see any relevance here."

"I'm inclined to agree, Ms. Forrester," the judge agreed,

speaking to the attorney.

"If you'll permit me one or two more questions, Your Honor, I think we will all see the connection."

What connection? How can Don's death have any correlation to Brian driving that getaway vehicle? This is insane.

"Very well, Ms. Forrester. Since there is no jury, I will allow you no more than two more questions."

The attorney stalked to the very edge of the witness box and propped herself against it. "Mr. Haywood. Is it not a fact that your father is dead because he first refused to recognize the authority of the local law enforcement in Carter's Crossroads where you live, then he later refused to submit to Atlanta police who subsequently..."

"Your Honor," Joe roared as he shot up from his chair, "this is a totally unacceptable line of questioning. Furthermore..."

"And isn't it true, Mr. Haywood, that you think you are as immune to the law as your father felt himself..." The prosecutor hurried to make her point before the judge could rule on the objection.

"Ms. Forrester! You will discontinue this immediately! I will not permit such a line of attack in my courtroom. Do I make myself clear?"

"Yes, Your Honor. I apologize."

Her face, with that "gotcha" smirk and body language, clearly scream her true emotions, making a lie of her words.

On the witness stand, Brian was struggling to maintain his composure.

Margaret could see his confidence had been severely shattered. *Joe. Oh, Joe, you've got to do something.*

The judge was ordering the court reporter to strike the last two questions and responses at the same time Joe, who evidently had read Margaret's mind, was asking for a fifteen-minute recess.

"So ordered," the jurist intoned. "Since it's so close to the noon hour we'll reconvene at one o'clock." He pounded his gavel and rose to leave the bench as Brian stepped out of the witness box.

How can any of us possibly eat anything with the axe of the unknown hanging over us? I so thought we'd be through with this by now. Margaret wanted to go to Brian, to comfort him, but willed herself to hold back. As Joe walked toward the boy, Brian suddenly detoured around the defense table and approached the prosecutor, who stood gathering her papers.

Mother's intuition told Margaret what was about to happen, but she was powerless in the few split seconds available to do anything but scream, "Noooo Brian! No!"

The young man, paying no attention to his mother's cries, put his face into the face of his accuser, and yelled, "You had no right to drag my father into this."

The entire courtroom froze, as one body. The next sound they heard was that of flesh hitting flesh. They watched as the young defendant slugged the prosecuting attorney.

As the lawyer in the red dress sagged to the floor, Brian returned to the defense table and reclaimed his seat. He was still sitting there, moments later, when two uniformed officers dragged him from the courtroom before his heartbroken mother could even reach him.

I didn't get to hug him. I didn't get to tell him that I love him.

Much of the melee that followed related to Margaret, who collapsed and had to be transported by ambulance to a nearby emergency room. The last thing she remembered was how much trouble her son was in.

I failed him.

CHAPTER SEVENTEEN

*F*or the first time since she had re-entered her newly-remodeled house in Carter's Crossroads, Margaret was unable to find any joy or any pleasure in the home she had created.

There's a gaping hole in our family and I don't know if we'll ever be able to mend it or overcome it.

P.C., who had come home with her to spend the night, had explained to Sallie and Jason all that had happened, and why Brian wouldn't be coming home.

I wish someone would explain it to me. That woman set out to destroy my child.

Margaret curled up on her bed in the fetal position, unable—or unwilling?—to accept all that had happened. *We were so close to going home with just a slap on the wrist. Even the prosecutor said so after it was all over.*

Before it was all over, however, Margaret had pled to at least speak with her son. She and Joe had met with him – hands off, just like before. The boy she found was anything but the confident, articulate young man who had presented himself so well on the witness stand.

Brian was kept and charged with more offenses than Margaret could even remember. Most of which would not have been nearly as serious if they hadn't violated the sanctity of the court and had it not been assault on an officer of the court. For those reasons, he was on his way to juvenile detention as they were escorted out.

"For the first few days, at least, I'll be the only visitor allowed," Joe had somberly informed her afterward.

"Why Joe? Why? I'm his mother."

"Look, Margaret. You might as well understand. Brian blew it big time in there today."

"But she goaded him into it. She deliberately baited him with that mess about Don. Even the judge thought she'd gone too far."

"She did go too far. It would have played beautifully to our advantage when it came time to pass sentence." He slapped his hand against the side of his head. "I guarantee Brian would have walked out of there with a few hours of community service or maybe just a few months probation. If only he could have held his temper. I never dreamed he could be that volatile."

"I've never seen it, either, Joe. At least not out of him. But I've seen it from his daddy on many occasions."

"I was thinking the same thing."

"So what do we do now?"

"There's nothing we can do. Except go home." The two were standing in a group outside the hospital following Margaret's release. He gestured for her to precede him across the street to the parking garage. "I'm going to let the dust settle today. Tomorrow I'm going to ask for a meeting with the judge."

"Do you think it will help?"

"We won't know until we try. Right now we're really low on options."

"There's always prayer."

"Then we better be praying, because I'm not a good enough lawyer by myself to convince that judge to forget everything that has happened."

P.C. tried to get Margaret to eat before they turned out the lights and went to bed, but the distraught mother refused food.

"I'm not on a hunger strike or anything, although I'd mount one if I thought it would make any difference. I'm just so sick to the pit of my stomach I can't even tolerate the thought of food. Maybe tomorrow."

"You can count on tomorrow," P.C. replied. "You have got to eat, so you might as well get ready for breakfast."

Both ladies were in their gowns and P.C. was curled on the foot of Margaret's bed rehashing the day's events.

"I simply cannot believe that even from beyond the grave, Don is still impacting his children's lives in a very destructive way. Brian's in jail for assault, contempt of court, assaulting an officer of the court and who knows what else. If the faces I saw on his brother and sister tonight are any indication, they're hurting as well."

"They expected Brian to come home. Pure and simple."

"There's nothing pure and simple about this entire saga."

"Listen, Margaret. There's something I need to say to you, and I want you to know that I love you. I love all of you like you were my blood kin."

"What is it? Has Joe told you something he hasn't told me? Are things really worse than I realize?"

"Oh, they're bad alright. But, no, this is nothing from Joe, although I believe he'd agree."

"Then tell me. Just spit it out."

"All this time you've been worried about Jason and Sallie, because of the physical abuse they received from Don. But you... none of us, have given much thought to Brian and how all this has impacted him."

"What do you mean?"

"Don never hit Brian, but as the oldest, he was naturally exposed to more of Don's melt-downs and physical tirades than either of the other two. You know, Margaret, emotional scars can be just as dangerous, just as deadly, as those scars on your arm."

"You're saying Brian is damaged emotionally from witnessing abuse, even though Don never inflicted any beatings on him?"

"That's exactly what I'm saying. What's worse, abuse, whether it's physical or emotional, begets abuse. I think what we saw today is a violent facet of Brian's personality that has developed because he was exposed to it for so long."

Once again, my refusal to see reality and deal with it years ago is still crippling my children. Don is gone and still he's doing harm.

"You know, P.C.... I've stood before groups of people over the past few months and explained to them everything you've just said to me. But I never applied it in my own life. How blind could I have been?"

"Now don't beat up on yourself. You know the plumber's..."

"Don't give me that plumber's leaky pipe analogy," she interrupted. "There's no reason I shouldn't have recognized the possibility that Brian was emotionally injured by all that has happened."

If only the judge could know the entire story. I wonder if Jim Deaton knows this man.

"P.C. I've got to talk to Joe. I don't care if I wake him, because I can't sleep unless I can talk with him about tomorrow."

Her friend didn't answer. Instead, she grabbed the cordless phone beside the bed and dialed a number. "Joe. Margaret needs to talk to you. NOW! Wake up."

Margaret took the phone. "Joe. I'm sorry to disturb you, because I know how hard you worked today. I'm sorry things turned out as they did, but somehow, we've got to make this judge understand... Brian is an emotional abuse victim who copied what he's seen."

"Believe it or not, that's the tactic I was going to use. Only I don't know how sympathetic this judge is to domestic abuse. I just hope I don't make things worse."

"Listen, Joe. I think the more people who crowd that judge's chambers, the better chance we have."

"You're not planning to mobilize all your prayer partners and descend on Atlanta by storm, I hope."

"I've already mobilized them to pray. But no, I don't plan to physically take them to see the judge. I do plan to take Jim Deaton and me."

"Now, Margaret, I don't..."

"It's not open for discussion, Joe. This is nothing against you; please don't hear it that way. But you've already admitted you have doubts about your ability to convince this man that leniency is in order. You need me. You need Jim, too, and I'm about to disturb his sleep as well."

"Look, Margaret. I don't have a problem with Jim. In fact, I'd welcome his input. But the judge might interpret it the wrong way if you show up as well."

"Like I said, Joe. It's not open for discussion. Now let's hang up so I can call Jim. It's getting late and we're all going to need our rest tonight."

"Fine. Call Jim. P.C.'s already invited me over for breakfast in the morning. We'll talk about it then."

"Good night, Joe. And Joe? Thank you. I mean that. What happened today was not your fault. It's mine. Which," she added with emphasis, "is why I have to help fix it."

The phone rang several times before a sleepy voice answered.

"Jim? It's Margaret. I am so sorry to wake you, but this is urgent."

She could feel him snap to attention.

"Not to worry, friend. Whatever is the problem?"

After Margaret finished recounting the day's events, there was dead silence. "Jim? Are you there? Did you go back to sleep?"

"I'm here," he said finally. "That was a lot to digest this late at night."

"It was a lot to digest at lunch, too. But we all had to swallow it."

"Gee, Margaret. Brian's a good kid, and I know Ms. Forrester. She hits below the belt regularly. Someday, some judge is going to call her on it. Unfortunately the judge has the authority. Brian didn't."

"I know that, Jim. But I can't undo what's been done."

Neither the abuse that Don inflicted nor the blows Brian struck today.

"So what can I do? Evidently there's something or you wouldn't have called."

Margaret didn't mince words. "I need you to go with Joe and me tomorrow to talk with the judge. A meeting in his chambers."

"Does Joe know you're calling me?"

"Just hung up from talking with him."

"What's his take?"

"He's fine with you going along. In fact, he said he'd welcome your help."

"But..."

"But what?"

"You were about to say something that started with the word 'but', and you hesitated."

"You're good. I'll have to give you that. The 'but' is that Joe doesn't want me to go along."

"I agree with Joe."

"Then I'll tell you like I told him. I'm going and that's not up for discussion."

"The judge may refuse to see you."

Can he do that?

"Doesn't matter. I'm going."

"Very well. When and where?'

"Sometime tomorrow. Morning, I hope. Joe's got to call for an appointment."

"Tell him to call my cell phone. I'll come on in to Atlanta early so I can be available."

"Thanks, Jim. I really appreciate it."

"You're welcome, Margaret. I just hope we can make a difference."

You're ever so right about that!

※

Margaret was seated at the breakfast bar, sipping coffee. The two younger children had left for school, and she and P.C. were waiting for Joe.

"Here's his car now." P.C. was looking out the window over the sink where she was washing dishes. "Joe's here."

The attorney entered through the family door. "Morning, Margaret. P.C." He crossed the kitchen to embrace his fiancée and the two exchanged a kiss.

It would be nice to be young and in love again. But it would be even nicer to be young, know what I know now, and be in love again. Oh well, there are some dreams that can never come true.

Joe crossed back over to the bar, pulled a newspaper from his coat pocket, and spread it out with the front page up. "Here. You might as well see this now, because I'm sure you'll see it once we get to Atlanta."

"Like Father, Like Son", the headline read. "Teen Whose Violent Father Died in Jail Fight Assaults D.A." There was a photograph of Brian being led out of the courthouse in handcuffs, as well as a smaller photo of Don and a short sidebar about how he died.

"I knew you would be upset. I know I..."

"This is wonderful!" Margaret crowed, interrupting what he was about to say.

The looks Joe and P.C. gave her clearly indicated they thought she'd finally snapped.

"Wonderful? Margaret... have you lost it?"

"No, Joe. Don't you see? What better basis to make our case to the judge than this front page article to demonstrate everything Brian has had to endure." She looked thoughtful. "For several years, really."

"You think this will make a difference?"

"I do."

"Then you're more optimistic than I am."

"Optimistic or not," P.C. said, "I'm convinced this breakfast I fixed is going to get cold. If you two are going to Atlanta, you need to get on the road."

"You're not going?"

I was sort of hoping P.C. would go along for moral support. Besides, women read men better than other men do. She's an attorney besides. I'd like her input with the judge.

"Nope. There's no telling how long this will take, and there's a little boy and girl who left here for school this morning very upset. Once the town sees this article, they're apt to come home more upset."

I'm so concerned with Brian's situation until I totally forgot about Sallie and Jason.

'You're right," Margaret conceded. "We need you here." She grabbed one last bite of her southwestern omelet. "Joe. You need to call Jim Deaton. Here's his number. I'll finish getting ready."

She slid a scrap of paper across the bar in his direction and left him attacking his own breakfast. Once upstairs, she quickly dressed. The last thing she did before leaving the room was to stuff an envelope of papers she'd assembled earlier that morning into her tote.

My son did something very wrong yesterday, but he is not going to pay excessively for his father's sins if I can help it!

On the ride into the city, Joe briefed her on his calls to the judge's secretary and to Jim. "We can have ten minutes at most with him as soon as he calls the lunch recess." That's not very long to change a man's mind. Especially this man."

"Is he that difficult?"

"He's very stubborn, Jim tells me. Once he forms an opinion, you could move a mountain with a teaspoon easier than you could get him to shift position."

"So let me guess. Yesterday he was on our side and now he's not?"

"That's about the size of it. But Jim and I are going to give it our best shot." He paused and Margaret wondered what was coming next. "I just hope Jim agrees with you. The front page newspaper coverage might be our one ace but it could also be the one thing that hurts us."

"I'm telling you. This is one time that all this misplaced newspaper coverage is good. This judge needs to understand the harassment this boy has endured and the embarrassment he suffered."

At the look her attorney gave her, she replied, "I know. What Brian did was so very wrong. I'm not excusing any of that. But I also know that he is still a boy, not a man, even though everyone calls him Mr. Haywood. He was pushed beyond the breaking point and he snapped."

Traffic into the city was getting heavier and Joe had to concentrate on negotiating around several damaged vehicles pulled to the side that were blocking one lane of the highway. "Another thing that Jim and I agree on is that this judge is not going to receive the evidence and suddenly all the charges will be dropped. There's going to be a price to pay, even if we negotiate leniency."

"I'm way ahead of you on that."

"You are?"

"Yes. I struggled with this most of the night, but just before daylight this morning, God and I worked it all out."

"Now, Margaret. I'm the last person who'd discount the power of prayer. But I am curious as to how you and God 'worked it all out', as you put it."

"We're not asking the judge to drop the charges. Any of them, because they're all appropriate."

"Then why are we going to see him? You've lost me."

"The charges have to stand. Besides, I don't see the lady Assistant D.A. agreeing to drop the charges."

"She could probably be persuaded, shall we say, that justice could best be served that way."

"Nope. She was assaulted. She egged it on, but Brian is the one at fault."

"So I assume you have the sentence all figured out."

"I do. To a point."

Joe was taking the Courtland Street exit ramp off I-75 and asked, "Then please tell me what we're asking for. We've got to meet Jim in a few minutes."

"We're asking that the charges all stand, but that punishment be administered with moderation. Brian is going to have to serve some time."

Perhaps if Don had been hauled down early on, he might not have progressed to the point of total self-destruction.

"You want him to serve time?"

"No, I don't, but I recognize that it has to happen. This is a cycle of abuse that we have to break. Now!"

"How much time?"

"I don't want to suggest a number. The judge will think we're being too pushy. But serving time is just part of what I want."

"What else is there? Are you talking about a fine?"

"Oh, I'm certain we'll be paying some money. I want the judge to order him to attend anger management classes and I want to offer to put my entire family into counseling. I can't go through this again with Jason, or even Sallie, down the road."

- 272 -

"Didn't Jason already go through counseling?"

"He did, but I can see now that we didn't address the deepest issues... the damage that witnessing abuse has caused."

"Hmmm." Joe was rubbing his chin. "The judge just might listen to us on those grounds. I'm going to be anxious to get Jim's take."

The pair circled the parking garage nearest the massive courthouse several times before, finally, a parking spot opened up. Joe shot his car into the space and he and Margaret gathered up their coats and various bags and departed the mass of waiting cars. True to his word, Jim was waiting in the main lobby. As he made his way toward them, Margaret saw that he wore a very dejected expression, and not just on his face.

"Margaret. Good to see you again." He hugged her. "I just wish your life could settle down and you could enjoy some good times." He stuck his hand around to Joe. "Morning again, Joe. Thanks for sticking by our friend here."

"Hey." Joe spread his hands out, palms up. "That my friend, is a given." He grinned. "Besides, now that Margaret and my fiancée are adopted sisters, I'm family."

I guess P.C. and I have filled the sister roll for each other. It was meant to be... it feels so natural.

"If you're so glad to see me again," she said to Jim, "why the long face?"

That's something Mama used to say to me when I was a child. Now here I am using it on a grown man.

"This," Jim said, "is the problem." He whipped out a copy of the daily newspaper. "It's got Brian and Don plastered across the front page."

"I know. Joe showed us back at home. Isn't it wonderful?"

"Wonder...?"

"Margaret thinks this is our ticket to pass 'Go' and collect a lighter sentence for Brian," Joe interrupted. "The more I think about it, the more I like the idea. But you know this judge, so let's talk." He glanced at his watch. "We've got less than a hour before we need to be in his courtroom, ready to meet with him in chambers."

The three retreated to an area with several chairs and few other people, while Joe brought Jim up to speed on his and Margaret's drive-time conversation.

Jim listened but said nothing, until Joe finished. "You're OK with Brian serving some time?"

"Neither of you has ever been a parent. I have and I am. I've stood and held my children while medical personnel administered treatment that was very painful, knowing that my child's screams of anguish were also the unspoken question of why wasn't I rescuing them. Why wasn't I protecting them?"

Sometimes being a parent isn't a joy.

"But I held them prisoner, if you will, because I knew that while it might be painful right then, that would pass and things would be better."

"Margaret believes ignoring this call for help from Brian will only make him more violent, more volatile, the older he gets."

"I would agree. I didn't know anything about all that happened yesterday until Margaret called me last night. The first thing that went through my mind was that abuse is a cycle; in far too many cases, abusers create a new generation of clones."

"Which is why, in addition to a sentence and any fines the judge thinks are appropriate, she wants Brian in anger management classes. When he's released, she's going to put the entire family back into counseling."

"Interesting."

"You think the judge will buy any of this? Or at least enough to keep Brian from growing old in jail?"

"I think he will, but there is something you need to know.

Margaret can't work in such a high profile position in domestic violence and give any impression that the punishment should be diluted because of her or because of Brian's young age and the fact that he is an abuse victim."

"I was there at four o'clock this morning," she assured Jim. "I agree completely."

The trio made their way to the courtroom, where they sat quietly near the front until the judge recessed for lunch. As he was departing the bench, the jurist said something to the bailiff who approached them. "Judge Arrowood asks that you meet him in his chambers. Follow me, please."

Aware that time was short, the three did as instructed and in less than a minute were in the dark-paneled office where the judge was removing his robe as they entered the door.

"Come in. Have a seat. As my secretary told you, I can only give you ten minutes, and I'm going to have to multi-task while I listen to you." He finished hanging up his robe and sat down at his desk, where he began to shuffle papers.

He's not really paying attention.

"Your Honor," Joe began. "We're not here today to try and negotiate any lesser charges for Brian Haywood. His mother believes all the charges should stand."

The judge looked up from his desk, his eyes widened. But he said nothing.

"Instead, we're asking you to work with us to design a punishment that will actually benefit Brian in the long run, while not mitigating the seriousness of his offenses."

Thank goodness Joe didn't call them crimes!

"If I may, Your Honor," Jim interrupted and introduced himself. "I'm here strictly as a friend of the family, but I'm also an attorney who has spent his entire career handling domestic violence cases. If I may, and with Mr. Busbee's permission, I'd like to explain what we'd like you to consider."

One of the main parts of the meeting that Margaret would remember long afterward was that the allotted ten minutes stretched to more than twenty, before the three left chambers. Jim, in very concise language, explained the position the three had formulated. He displayed the newspaper and pointed out how disruptive Brian's life had been for the past year, especially. Then he laid out their suggestions for punishment.

After he finished, the judge spent a couple of minutes reading the newspaper account, before he lifted his head and spoke. "I don't mind telling you that Ms. Forrester was out of line yesterday. I didn't even know any of this background, and still, I was ready to sanction her and send Brian back to Carter's Crossroads with six months probation."

I knew it. I knew it! If only Brian could have held his rage, we'd all be home now and life would be normal. But he couldn't keep his temper at bay because he's patterning what he's seen for most of his young life.

He leveled his gaze on Margaret, held up a warning finger, and said, "I'm very glad, Mrs. Haywood, that you didn't come in here this morning as an emotional, teary-eyed mother begging for mercy. I'd have shown you the door immediately."

"Your Honor. What Brian did was wrong. I cannot defend him, other than to say that he reacted in the way he has seen his father react many times. I can accept punishment for him, if that punishment is designed to break the cycle of abuse, not make him angrier."

"Just how long would you think he should have to serve?"

"The mother in me says overnight; that I should be able to take him home today. But the responsible parent and domestic violence worker says that you, Your Honor, would have a better grasp on that answer."

The judge grinned. "Gentlemen, I'd advise you both to watch your client carefully. She's sharp."

She's also desperate, but I hope that isn't showing.

"We've known her a lot longer than you have, Your Honor. She is sharp, but she's also a very good parent."

"Oh, that comes through loud and clear, Mr. Busbee. Which is one reason I'm willing to work with this case. I see many defendants come through my court that I know will return home and be held totally unaccountable. This is not one of those cases."

Thank you, Lord. Thank you!

"Tell you what, gentlemen... and Mrs. Haywood. I'm not totally unsympathetic to Brian's situation, but I am in total agreement with Mrs. Haywood. This young man has too much potential that would be wasted if we can't head him in the right direction."

"Oh, thank you, Your Honor." Despite her promise to the lawyers not to speak unless spoken to, the words escaped her lips before she could catch them.

"Let me have a conference with Ms. Forrester, and let me think about this for a day or so. I want to make some phone calls and talk to a few people."

"Do you think Ms. Forrester will be agreeable to what we're proposing? She's the victim."

The judge grinned again and Margaret decided his gruffness was a courtroom façade. "Ms. Forrester knows she went too far yesterday. She also knows she's going to have to come before me again some time in the future. I think she'll be... well, you get the idea."

Joe and Jim grinned at each other, and Margaret knew that look was from one attorney to another, who understood the danger in making a judge angry.

"Thank you, Your Honor," Margaret said as she stood and extended her hand. "I'm prepared to accept whatever punishment you think is right and fair. But I would ask one thing."

"The 'but.' There's always a 'but,' isn't there?"

"May we all three please see Brian today? I promise I won't

touch him if that isn't appropriate, but I think emotionally he needs to see us, to know what's going on."

"Mrs. Haywood, I don't often run into people like you, but you personify the term 'parent'. Yes, you may see him. I'll have my secretary call down to the YDC and clear the way. But there is one restriction I'll place on this visit."

I'd like to say "anything" but I'm almost afraid to.

"You may touch him, you may hug him. You can even take him a burger and fries if you'd like. And you may tell him that you've been to see me, to try and find out what's going to happen with his case." He stopped and leveled a gaze at the three of us. "You may not..." the judge waggled his finger, "you may not tell him any of the specifics of the sentence we've discussed or the possibility that circumstances may allow things to go easier than would otherwise be the case."

"In other words, you want him to sweat a little longer?"

"I told you gentlemen. She's sharp."

༄

As they stood in the secured visiting area, waiting for a guard to bring Brian to them, Margaret found some solace in the fact that she had been able to make the judge understand the situation. Getting to see her child was even more important at that moment.

"I'll have to hand it to you," Joe said, "you charmed His Honor."

"There was no charm to it, Joe. His Honor is all business. We recognized that trait in each other and that gave us a basis to go forward. Remember, he said himself it was because I didn't act like a typical, hysterical mother that he was willing to listen to what we had to say."

That, and God answers prayers. Mostly the latter.

The room was unadorned concrete block walls that had once

been painted a creamy off-white, but now wore scuff marks and grungy brown smudges. The effect, Margaret realized, was one of total disillusion and very little reason to see anything positively. The once industrial white blocks of tile on the floor showed a lot of wear, with patches of concrete peeping through in the heaviest traffic areas. The only windows were high on the wall, dingy, and served only to admit light.

There are beautiful woods surrounding this complex, but the young men housed here never get to see that view.

Her first sight of her son was heart-crushing. He wore a rumpled gold jumpsuit that was too large and puddled around his feet, which were shod in flip-flops.

The flip-flops don't even match!

His head, topped by a tousle of unkempt hair, was bowed, and she could see evidence of his youthful beard that hadn't seen a razor that morning. Without saying a word, Margaret moved to meet him where he was, physically and emotionally, and enveloped him in the hug she had been so long denied.

"Mom, I'm so..."

She could feel tears dampening her blouse, but she didn't care. "Hush, Brian. I know you're sorry. You don't have to say anything. Just hold on to me and we'll get through this."

Joe and Jim hung back at first, but as Margaret released the boy, both men moved up and extended their hands.

"I'm sorry, Joe. I blew it and I know it."

"You blew it big time, my friend." He reached across and pulled Brian to him. "But I blew it, too."

"You? How?"

"I should have realized how Ms. Forrester's over-the-top behavior was going to impact you. I should have been proactive."

"Not that how you answered her inappropriate behavior was any more acceptable," Jim warned. "But it's also understandable, given the circumstances."

"Circumstances?"

Mindful of the judge's conditions, Margaret grabbed the floor. "It's nothing to be ashamed of, Brian, but you are a child of abuse. You were abused by your dad in many ways, but the emotional abuse you suffered left an even bigger scar."

"I don't understand. What kind of emotional abuse?"

"Hear me carefully, Brian. I'm not trying to trash your dad. But for years you watched him hit us, talk to us like we had no rights of any kind. That is emotional abuse and it will mark you for life if you don't do something about it."

"But I knew as soon as I hit that woman that I shouldn't have."

"That's good. But we've got to get you to the place where you realize it's wrong before you strike that first blow."

"Ms. Forrester was out of line, Brian. There's no argument there. But so were you."

"I know, Mr. Busbee. I feel like I let you down."

"Don't you worry about me. I've got tough skin. Let's worry about you instead."

The boy hung his head again. "What's to worry about? They're going to lock me up in here and who knows when I'll ever come out." His entire body adopted a stance of dejection. "Let's face it. My life is over. Maybe I can get a G.E.D., but college is out. I'm ruined and I did it to myself."

"You're not ruined and you didn't do it to yourself alone. The way you were raised did not give you the coping skills you needed to let the prosecutor's barbs go over your head."

"But Mom. If I'm in here, I can't finish school and hope to get anything more than a G.E.D." He dropped his head again.

It's time for some more of that painful parenting.

"Look at me, Brian. I don't intend to talk to your hair."

Slowly the boy brought his head up until his mother could see the anguish in his eyes.

He doesn't want to look at me.

"That's better. Don't drop your head again, because you have no reason to do so. Now... let me ask you a question."

"Okay. I mean, yes ma'am."

"Do you want to stay in here until who knows when?"

"Gosh, no, Mom. This place is the pits. It stinks. In just one night I've learned there are some pretty rough guys here. I'm really afraid."

No more afraid than I am.

"Then here's what you have to do. First, you have to cooperate with anyone and everyone in authority. Keep your tongue and your hands to yourself. Whatever they say, you do it... willingly."

She paused to see how he was absorbing her words. Satisfied that he was hearing her, she continued. "Second, if they want you to talk with counselors or psychologists, do so. Tell them the truth, and hold up your head while you're doing it. And..." Again she hesitated. "You need to be talking really seriously to God for the peace of mind and peace of heart you need to survive in here."

"Do you... do you think I'm in danger?"

I don't want to scare him, but I want him on his toes.

"I think you're in more danger from yourself than from anyone else. You're not making some of the best decisions lately."

"I've been praying, Mom."

"I know that, son. But sometimes we have to make our prayers very specific. We have to tell God what we need. He wants to hear it from us."

"Well, I'll probably have plenty of time in here to pray. No one will tell me anything."

"Listen, Brian. You need to know that we... your Mom, Jim and I... met with the judge this morning to try and determine what your future looks like."

Margaret saw his eyes brighten and hated the disappointment she knew was about to follow.

"He listened to us very politely, and very patiently I might add. He could have refused even to see us. We didn't come away with answers today, other than he is exploring your case. He'll talk to us in a few days."

The dismay she expected was splashed all over his body.

"I won't get to go home with you today."

It wasn't a question and Margaret could feel the anguish in his voice.

"No, son, I'm afraid not. We were just lucky the judge agreed that we could visit with you."

"When can you come back? I need some toiletry items and I'd like a book or something to read."

"Tell you what," Jim volunteered. "Your Mom and Joe have to get back, but I'm here in town for the rest of the day. Let's get the guard and make a list of what you need, and can have, and I'll go pick it up."

"Jim. That's awfully nice of you."

"Not a problem, Margaret. I'm glad to do it."

He went in search of a guard while Joe and Margaret talked with Brian for a few more minutes. Then, before she was ready, it was time to go.

Even if it were this time tomorrow and I'd been here all that time, I still wouldn't be ready to leave. But I know I must.

She hugged Brian again, trying to capture and save the feel of his arms around her. He and Joe shook hands and, in an unexpected move, but one that Margaret took to heart, the boy reached out to the attorney for a hug as well.

He's crying for someone to love him.

The guard appeared to escort Brian back into security, while Joe and Margaret waited in the lobby. Jim joined them a few minutes later. Margaret had cash in her hand and thrust it at the attorney.

"Here, Jim," she said as she extended the bills. "If this isn't enough, let me know. And thank you."

"Sorry, Margaret. Your money isn't any good right now. I'm paying for this."

"But why, Jim? Why? You know I'm not strapped for cash or anything."

"Because this is something I want to do."

He could not be dissuaded and Margaret and Joe parted company to head north, while Jim went in search of toothpaste and shaving cream and a stack of magazines. Margaret was to learn later that the items he delivered to Brian that afternoon also included his favorite Burger King Whopper and a large order of fries.

There wasn't much conversation in Joe's car as they drew closer to Carter's Crossroads. Margaret was spent... emotionally and physically. Joe, she was sure, was mentally juggling all the work he had stacking up while he spent time dealing with her concerns.

"Thank you, Joe. For everything. I do expect to pay you well for all you've done."

"We'll cross that bridge later. Right now I want to be sure we get Brian headed in the right direction. I simply cannot believe I didn't tune in to how he would respond to Ms. Forrester's barbs. I could have prevented this if I had been on my toes."

"Now, Joe. We're not going to have any second-guessing. Like you said the other day, if chickens had teeth they could eat steak. I was sitting right there in the courtroom. I was also very angry with that little witch. I'm his mother, but I never saw Brian's reaction coming until it was too late."

Let's see you top that one!

"Still..."

"Still you did all you knew to do. Just like we all did. Unfortunately, our efforts weren't equal to the problem. You've put in quite a few hours and I expect to pay. If I don't have a bill in hand by tomorrow evening, I'm going to write you a check for what I feel like I owe and we can haggle it out later."

"You're a hard woman, my friend. Please don't give P.C. any lessons. OK?"

"If I'd been this hard way back when, we might not be having this conversation."

"Like you said about me, you did all you knew to do." He was quiet as he navigated the exit ramp off the interstate. "Let's just say both of us have learned some valuable, if not pricy, lessons."

"I guess you're right."

That night, as she put the younger Haywood's to bed, and explained to them in basic terms what was happening with their big brother, she was floored by a remark that Sallie, the self-absorbed drama queen, had to offer.

"I hope when Brian comes back home, he can be a happy person."

"A 'happy person'?" Whatever do you mean, Sallie?"

"Brian hasn't been happy in a long time. He says Daddy wouldn't have been so angry if he had been a better son. That maybe none of this would have happened."

Floored, Margaret finished tucking them in. She then retreated to her bedroom where she could be alone with her thoughts and her tears.

I'd say I've been a terrible mother if I couldn't see the load my son was carrying. But I'm not going to beat up on me.

She reached for her Bible and after reading for about half an hour, spent another few minutes in prayer, unloading all her burdens on the God she knew already understood her deepest needs and fears. Then she turned out the light and snuggled down in the bed to get comfortable with her newest determination.

Brian is going to be a happy person and I'm going to be a better mother.

CHAPTER EIGHTEEN

*T*he next few days were some of the most difficult Margaret thought she had ever faced. *At least when things were so bad when Don was killed, I knew what was happening. As it is, I don't know what the outcome of Brian's troubles will be.* Every time the phone rang, she jumped and grabbed, looking first at Caller ID, willing it to be Joe's number. Every time she was disappointed.

"It'll happen when it happens, friend," P.C. advised. "You forget, I was once married to a judge. I can't speak for all of them, but he ruled things at home the same way he did in the courtroom." Her face became serious. "It all depended on which side of the bed he got up on...what kind of mood he was in."

"You're kidding?"

"Afraid not. If anything, I'm not telling you enough; I just know I was mighty sorry for some of the defendants who came through his courtroom. They did not get a fair shake."

"Do you think Brian will get a fair shake?"

"I guess it depends on what constitutes a fair shake. My definition and yours might be worlds apart."

"I just don't want my son's life ruined by a couple of stupid mistakes that weren't all his doing." Tears began to tumble down her cheeks.

"If it's any consolation, Joe feels good about the judge. He's asked around. The guy is tough, especially if he thinks someone isn't being totally upfront. But if he believes in you, he isn't vindictive."

"That's my prayer. That's all I can ask."

The two had been comparing calendars, looking at possible wedding dates for P.C. and Joe, as Margaret sought to fulfill her responsibilities to the state office and care for her children.

Margaret's phone rang. She looked at the Caller ID to see it wasn't Joe, but Barbara.

"Hello, Barbara. I was planning to call you later today to play catch-up."

"Looks like I beat you to the punch."

"That's good, really. So what can I do for you this morning?"

"I need to drive up to Carter's Crossroads so we can have a conversation. Any chance I could do that today?"

Why does she want to come here? Am I about to be fired?

"Sure, Barbara, the day's wide open. Name your time."

"Say one o'clock, one-thirty at the latest?"

"That works. But let me ask you something. Is my job in jeopardy or something?"

"No, no, perish the thought," Barbara replied quickly. "I don't ever want to lose you, but something's come up I think we need to discuss. I'd like to do it today."

If I'm not being fired, why is she being so secretive? Has all the publicity about Brian caused problems for the agency?

"Well, sure. Come on. I'll be waiting."

"I'll leave shortly."

When she put down the phone, Margaret turned to P.C. and related the conversation. "She's got my curiosity aroused, that's for sure. But she said I wasn't being fired."

"Stop borrowing trouble, my friend. You've done a fantastic job for them. Barbara couldn't stop bragging on you when we were all in court. I mean, she told everybody who would listen."

Margaret rose from her favorite chair in the den and motioned for P.C. to follow. "I've got to cook. That's what I do when I'm troubled." She heaved a sigh. "Despite Barbara's assurances to the contrary, something's up."

"Then let's go cook."

Once in the kitchen, Margaret rifled through the pantry and the freezer before she finally decided to make a lemon meringue icebox pie. She pulled lemons from the refrigerator, putting them in hot water so they would relax and release their juice. At the same time, she put eggs out to reach room temperature before finding the ingredients for her pie crust.

"What can I do?" P.C. asked. "I assume you don't want me to leave."

"Most definitely I don't want you to go. I don't think I've ever been as nervous as I am right this minute."

"Face it, friend. You've been through the wringer for more than a year now. The element of surprise isn't as intriguing as it once might have been."

Margaret began to mix her graham cracker crumbs and sugar in bowl, at the same time she put a stick of margarine in the microwave to melt. "You've got that right. But the thing that gets me..." She removed the now liquid margarine and added it to the bowl of cracker crumbs, stirring furiously. *Perhaps more furiously than the recipe indicates.* "The thing that gets me is Barbara didn't sound angry or troubled. Yet it was urgent enough that she drive here this morning to talk to me."

"You know what I think?"

Judging that the crumb mixture was sufficiently blended, she poured the contents of the bowl into a pie pan and began to spread and pack. "If you can shed any light on all of this, certainly I want your thoughts."

"Well... I think you're going to have to get your panties out of a wad and just wait until Barbara arrives. If it's as urgent as she indicated, she won't waste too much time before she tells you."

"If I wanted logic, I'd ask for it." She placed the crust in the oven she had pre-heated earlier. "This has to bake for twelve to fourteen minutes. If you can't alleviate my fears, at least be sure I don't burn this crust."

Margaret cleaned up her mess and retreated to the other side of the breakfast bar where P.C. was sitting. "I suppose you're right. But it just sounds so mysterious. If it was all that important, why couldn't Barbara...?"

She was interrupted by the ring of P.C.'s cell phone, which her friend grabbed from her pocket and answered. "It's Joe," she mouthed.

"Yeah, I'm sitting right here. Why?... Uh huh, she called about twenty minutes ago. But why...uh huh. But can't you tell me why?... Okay." She laid down her phone and her face was a study in confusion. "You're right, Margaret. Something's going on and it looks like we're going to be the last to know."

"Why? What do you mean?"

"That was Joe..."

"I know that much," she interrupted. "Just the facts, ma'am. NOW!"

"Joe's on his way over." She waved her hand in an indication of dismissal. "I know," you're asking, "what's funny about that? He asked if you had talked to Barbara this morning and he knows she's on her way here."

"I'd like to strangle both of them. This feels like anything but Christmas morning around the tree."

"Naturally I'm thrilled there's a chance that Brian won't have to serve any more time, and can come back home where he belongs. I just don't know how he's going to feel about being made even more of a public spectacle and having to speak in front of groups of people."

It was Joe who volunteered, "I believe after the judge explains it to him, you'll find that Brian is a most willing participant."

"I'll have to admit, Margaret," Barbara explained, "when the judge called me to pitch his idea, I had some initial misgivings. But the more I thought about it, the more I saw what a marvelous idea it is. Brian can clear himself of the charges. He can cleanse himself through the act of talking. At the same time he's helping others, he'll also be getting things off his chest."

"Trust the judge on this. It's a great idea and a fantastic opportunity for Brian. As for having to speak to groups, he's always been a leader in his youth groups and church. Didn't he do debate at Mount Zion?"

"Yes, P.C., he won awards for debate, so I suppose he could handle the public speaking portion without a problem. I'm just not sure how he's going to feel baring his soul to strangers."

"That's why you'll be with him anywhere he speaks. In some cases you'll be a mother-son duo," Barbara clarified. "Brian will take a lot of his cues from you. If you're uptight, he's going to be uncertain as well."

"You know I've never backed up from telling our story." Margaret could feel her anger rising. *Or is it the mother lioness?* "Didn't I hold a press conference in Atlanta that was rebroadcast on the national news?"

"There's a difference, friend," P.C. said gently. "That was you. The children have always been in the background and you became very testy whenever their privacy was threatened."

"You're faulting me for that?" Her words were stiff and emotionless. *Lord, is she persecuting me?*

"Not faulting. Just observing. You were protecting your children. I, for one, happen to think that Brian needs this chance to tell the story... HIS story... so that once and for all, he can shed the undeserved stigma he has assigned himself."

"What's more," Barbara added, "since you're all going to be in family therapy and Brian's going to be taking anger management as well, he can also help to erase the shame that some people associate with counseling."

Lord, I said I'd do anything to get Brian out of jail with a clean record. That's all I want. Evidently this is how You propose to answer my prayer.

"OK," she said at last. "How do we proceed?"

It was Joe who answered. "I report to the judge that everyone is in agreement. Then he talks to Brian and lays it out. If Brian agrees, then he comes home on house arrest and with the agreement to perform 100 hours of community service speaking to various groups over the next year."

"If he does all this, completes his counseling and doesn't get into any more trouble, he walks free and his records for the holdup and the assault are expunged?"

"That's about how it shakes out," Joe agreed.

"Can I talk with him before he sees the judge? You know, to let him know that we support him doing this?"

"'Fraid not," Joe said. His voice was firm, but not unkind. "The judge wants to get Brian's feedback without any advance coaching. This time we're going to have to believe your son has the ability to fly solo and do the right thing."

This time we're going to have to pray harder than we've ever prayed. Brian feels so defeated, I fear he won't recognize this golden opportunity.

"How soon will all this go down?"

"I told Judge Arrowood I'd get back to him by mid-afternoon. He's prepared to go to the YDC later today and speak with Brian." He smiled. "We could know something before the day is out."

"He's going to go to Brian? Brian's not going to be shackled and brought to the courthouse to see the judge?"

"That's what he indicated."

This judge understands the situation even better than I first believed. Brian would have been a basket case by the time he got to see the judge. This way he doesn't have an opportunity to let his imagination run wild and build up anxiety.

Joe and P.C. left shortly afterward, with promises to let Margaret know as soon as there was any news. Joe had already used the Haywood phone to call the judge's secretary to say it was a go. She promised to pass the message along as soon as the judge called a recess.

Barbara remained behind, and Margaret was glad for the opportunity to talk with her employer without other ears overhearing.

"I'm sorry I alarmed you this morning," Barbara explained. "When the judge called me to float his idea, he told me Joe hadn't had a chance to talk with you. I couldn't say much more than what I did."

"No apologies necessary, I understand completely."

"I'm glad, because the last thing I'd want would be for you to think your job was in jeopardy."

Margaret shot her a look of understanding. "Believe me, after all the negative exposure you've gotten from me and my children, I couldn't blame you if you felt like you had to jettison a big liability."

"What you see as a liability, I see as a gigantic asset."

"You've lost me."

"Look Margaret, many employers, when one of their female employees is involved in a domestic violence situation that goes public, think they have to terminate her. That, as you know, plays right in to the abuser's hands and actually helps him overpower his victim."

I know where she's going with this.

"If I were to take that position in your case, our agency would be no better than those misguided employers. We'd be two-faced."

"I see what you mean. But I still don't understand how my family is a…" she searched her memory, "a 'gigantic asset', I think you put it."

"Because you endured the abuse and can stand up and talk about it without shame, is a true motivation to those silent, hidden victims out there who are struggling." Barbara went silent for a moment. "But it's Brian's story, if he can pull it off, that's going to be most powerful."

After her employer left, Margaret spent the remainder of the day dealing with household chores, trying to adopt a low-key philosophy over the chance that Brian might actually be released.

"Sallie and Jason will be in from school shortly, and I don't want to do anything to get their hopes up," she told her father who had called to get an update.

"I think you're wise there. Otherwise, how do they appear to be handling things?"

That's the question I keep asking myself, only I'm not sure I'm qualified to answer. Of late I've been seriously questioning all my parenting abilities.

"Sallie is very vocal, and her moods dictate how she deals with it. One minute she's very concerned if Brian's being treated well in jail, as she calls it. Ten minutes later she's hoping the news media doesn't splash us across the TV screen again."

"I'm a lot older than Sally, but my fears run the same spectrum. Enough already. So what about my man Jason?"

"You know how quiet and reserved Jason is. He always has been, and it's making it very difficult for me to read him. I won't deny it, I worry about Jason in some ways even more than I do about Brian."

"You've got three good kids. They've just been through more than any children should have to endure."

Margaret heard the sound of doors slamming and looked at the clock. "Gotta run, Daddy. Those two kids are home from school. I'll call you later tonight."

Those slamming doors didn't sound like the school's van. Hmmmm. Oh, well. What else could it have been?

In a matter of seconds, the two younger Haywoods tore through the family entrance and into the kitchen. Margaret took their presence as confirmation that it had been the school shuttle she heard.

"Mommie," Jason yelled, obviously intent on beating his sister when it came to delivering news they both obviously thought was of supreme importance. "Sallie and I got to talk about Brian at school today."

Her antenna went up. "You mean you were talking to your classmates about Brian?" *I guess I'm glad they aren't ashamed to admit their brother is in YDC. Sallie calls it jail. She thinks it sounds more dramatic; I think it sounds pathetic.*

"No," Sallie injected, obviously determined to have a speaking role even if she had to grab the floor. "To the television people."

Antenna rose another notch; red flags began to wave; Margaret could hear the sound of distant warning bells. "Sit down you two."

Both children climbed onto the stools at the breakfast bar and looked at her with expectation.

"Now, one at a time, tell me about the television people you spoke with." She looked from to the other. "Sallie, you first." From the look of disappointment on Jason's face, she tousled his hair. "You'll get your turn, I promise."

"Well," Sallie began, obviously relishing her role. "Jason and I were waiting to get on the bus, when these two women we hadn't seen before asked us if Brian Haywood was our brother."

"I told them he was my big brother," Jason exclaimed, unwilling to sit on the sidelines any longer.

"Then they asked if it was true he was in jail," Sallie added. Sensing that her younger brother was about to steal the limelight, she hurried to add, "I told them he was, but that he was sorry he hit that woman in court."

"You told them what?"

"That Brian was sorry. That's what you told us," she added defensively.

Margaret was doing a slow burn, yet she knew she had to hold it together if she stood any chance of getting to the bottom of their implausible story.

"Look you two." She softened her tone. "All you children have been told never to talk to strangers. Why did you talk to these people?" *More importantly, who were they?*

"Because they said you said it would be OK," Sallie answered. Her face betrayed the first hint that she realized things might not be exactly the way she thought. "They told us you wanted us to talk to them."

"Yeah," Jason piped up. "That's why we missed the bus so we could answer their questions and then they brought us home."

My children rode with total strangers? No wonder those doors didn't sound like the school van.

"I'm not angry with either of you; believe me. But I did not tell those people they could talk to you. I don't even have a clue who these ladies are. But I'm going to find out."

"They were from that dog TV station or something," Jason volunteered. The expression on his face was proof he felt he'd successfully identified the culprit.

*TV station...the dog? Dog? NBC is the peacock...CBS is the eyeball...*Margaret racked her brain, trying to make all the loose ends tie together, but with little success. There was no logical answer. Desperate, she grabbed the phone and dialed Susan Bronson to explain what little she knew in hopes her friend could make some sense of it. *Susan's a police officer. Surely...*

"Let me make a couple of phone calls and check this out. It doesn't matter what network it was, their method of doing business borders on illegal. I'll call you back."

"Did we do something wrong, Mommie?" Jason's voice was tiny as he cowered. "We thought that was what you wanted us to do."

Margaret wrapped her arms around the both of them, and pulled the children to her. *I don't know what I would do if anything happened to my other children.* "I understand what you did, and why. It wasn't wise, but I also understand that you thought you were making me happy."

This is one of the oldest scams a con artist will run on a child; convincing them they'll make their parents happy if they do what's been asked.

"So let's make a new rule. Today. Right now."

"Sure, Mommie. We don't want to make you angry."

"I'm angry, Jason. But it's not at you and Sallie. It's at those women. What they did was wrong." She slapped her hand on the counter. "Just plain wrong and what's more, they knew it was."

They thought they could take advantage of two gullible, vulnerable children and get away with it. I'm about to show them otherwise.

"From now on, if there is anyone I want you to talk with, I'll tell you myself. In fact, I'll probably be there with you."

She saw glimmer of recognition on both young faces.

"Those ladies tricked us, didn't they?"

Margaret hugged her youngest to her, "Yes, son, I'm afraid they did. But you're not to worry about it, because I'm going to straighten out everything."

When I get through with those TV people, they're going to wish they had never crossed the county line today.

"You two go change out of your school clothes and get started on your homework. I'll bring snacks to your room. Let's try to get everything taken care of before supper, in case we want to do something special this evening."

"Like what?" Jason's face was a gigantic question mark and his eyes were flashing.

"Maybe something, maybe nothing," she answered. "But if

you both haven't finished your homework, it won't matter, because we won't be able to do it."

As if that were motivation enough, both streaked for the staircase to the second floor. Margaret quickly put together cookies and two glasses of milk. As soon as she returned to the kitchen, she reached for the phone to call Joe Busbee. *I'm not going to turn my head on this one; I don't care if making a stink means we end up on every morning news show from here to outer Slobovia! So be it.*

Before she could dial the attorney's number, the phone rang. *Susan! That was quick.*

"It was FOX News," she announced when Margaret answered. "They were several places in town today."

Dog. Fox. I can see how Jason would have described them that way.

"Are they still in the area?"

"That's what we're checking now."

"Well whether they're here, or if we have to go to Atlanta... or wherever... and drag them back, I want their hides nailed to the wall."

"Have you called Mount Zion School?"

"Mount Zion? Why?"

"I doubt the school was a party to the deception, but they need to know what was happening on their campus."

She's right. I was so angry I hadn't thought that far.

"Hang up and I'll call them right now. And Susan... keep me posted. The news media has messed with my children one time too many."

The school was on speed-dial. In just a matter of seconds, Margaret was speaking with the receptionist who, since the Haywood's had returned, was once again her old, companionable self with Margaret.

"Hey, friend. How are things going?"

"Not good, Catherine. I desperately need to speak to Headmaster Hunt. It's urgent."

"Gosh, Margaret, he's in a faculty meeting right now. You know he doesn't like to be interrupted."

"Interrupt him. Security at the school has been breached, and he needs to know it. Now, please!"

For once the woman didn't hesitate or try to argue. "Hang on."

Margaret was counting the cabinet knobs in her kitchen for the second go-round, when she heard the headmaster come on the line.

"Margaret. What's this about security being breached?"

While he was busy trying to convince her that nothing was wrong, Margaret simply talked over him until, finally, he fell silent while she continued to relate what she knew.

"I'm not suggesting that Mount Zion School condoned or encouraged what happened. I'm not even suggesting that you knew what was happening. But you need to know that my children were approached on campus by these two television reporters, who should never have been there in the first place." She went on to explain that she'd learned they were from the Atlanta affiliate of FOX News.

"This is reprehensible, Margaret. No, we didn't approve their presence on campus; we didn't even know they were on the grounds."

"That's what I assumed. Well, you need to know that I intend to pursue this and press charges. I would hope that you would file charges of your own. Seems to me you've got more than enough grounds."

"I've just passed the receptionist a note to get hold of the police chief and our attorney."

Margaret could hear anger in his voice.

"You're not alone in this battle. Keep me posted and I'll do likewise."

The next forty-eight hours were a jumble of emotions and actions, all of which left Margaret in a state of confused euphoria.

After talking with the school's headmaster, but before she could dial Joe, the attorney called her with the word that Brian would be released to house arrest the following morning; that she and he would need to meet with the judge in chambers before bringing her son home.

Then Margaret shared with him the encounter Sallie and Jason had with FOX News, and Susan's discovery that the two women were still in town.

"They were filming a segment for part of this evening's news. Why do I think my children are going to be a part of that broadcast?"

"Probably because they are. Hang up and let me get hold of the police chief so he can move on this while they're still inside the county."

As Margaret watched the FOX News evening broadcast little more than ninety minutes later, she took little pleasure in seeing the local police walk up and arrest the reporter who was relating the story of the Haywood children, along with her camera-woman.

You knew you shouldn't have been messing with my kids. You may be under arrest, but that can't undo the damage you did!

Before the broadcast was over, Margaret had heard from Susan, who took part in the arrest, from Barbara who was calling to console over the FOX incident and celebrate Brian's pending release, from Alice Hanover, who wanted Margaret to know she was there in any way she was needed, and ditto from Sarah next door. Finally, her father called to ask, "Margaret? What else can happen? Why won't these press people leave you and your children alone?"

"I don't know, Daddy. I wish I did." She was busy putting the finishing touches on a dinner that should be a celebration. In truth, thrilled as she was about Brian's pending release, she just wanted to find a hole and crawl inside.

"It's criminal, that's what it is. I can't believe those two women thought they could use two little children to make brownie points with their bosses."

"It is criminal, Daddy. Joe says we're going to press every charge there is. By the time Mount Zion School joins us, I don't imagine those two will be able to get an assignment emptying the station's trashcans."

"Serves them right. But I am happy to hear that Brian's coming home. My heart hurts for that boy."

"Mine, too, Daddy. I can't tell you how badly I've hurt."

She checked the oven where a casserole was baking, and began paring vegetables to steam. "Listen, Daddy, Joe and P.C. are coming to eat, so he can bring me up to speed on everything. I need to finish my supper."

Later, when the five of them gathered around the table, it was Joe who led off the conversation.

"The judge was very impressed with Brian's attitude and willingness to cooperate with the community service program." He smiled what Margaret thought was one of the most beautiful smiles she'd ever seen. "Your son's coming home tomorrow morning, Margaret."

Those were beautiful words but not as beautiful as the sight of Brian the next day when she and Joe met with the judge to discuss the particulars of his release and home confinement.

"Mrs. Haywood," Judge Arrowood said, as he addressed them, "you need to understand that I am taking a chance on Brian, but I believe he's worth it. You've got a fine young man. I just hope he understands that if he blows this opportunity, the judicial system will deal with him in a very harsh manner."

"I do understand, sir," Brian replied. "Thank you for having confidence in me. I won't let you down."

"I want to thank you, too," Margaret told the judge.

"What we're about to do is basically an experiment. If it works, we'll be written up in glowing terms, commending us for being visionaries. If it fails, we'll be castigated and accused of trying to manipulate the system for the benefit of one person."

Margaret understood what he was saying and knew he was exactly right. *I have to make certain Brian clearly understands all the implications of his actions for the next few months.*

"I wouldn't even consider what we're about to do," the judge explained, "if our background reports on you and your family hadn't come back as clean as they did."

I hadn't thought about it, but I guess he did have background checks run. That's kind of scary. I'm surprised he even considered my request.

As if he had read her thoughts, the judge continued, "Believe me, Mrs. Haywood, when I discovered all that you and your family have endured over the past year, I'm amazed that Brian isn't more confused than he is. I do hope you still plan to enroll the entire family in counseling. It could be one of the best things you ever do for your children."

"I realize that, Your Honor, although it's something that has become more apparent to me over the past few weeks."

∽

Once back at home, in his familiar surroundings, Margaret could sense that Brian wasn't totally comfortable. *He's almost antsy...* She was at a loss to understand the source of this problem, and was certain only that something was troubling her son.

He doesn't seem willing to share or confide in me, and I'm hesitant to force the issue. Yet I'm legally responsible for his actions until his house arrest is finished and his probationary status expires. Lord, You need to speak to him.

Actually house arrest was a harsh sounding term for what Margaret felt was a most generous sentence. The judge had explained to Brian that he could be away from home any time of day or night, as long as Margaret or another responsible adult was with him. Even alone, he could still attend school and go to church. However his license was suspended and would remain so until the judge decided otherwise.

Usually house arrest restricts people to visits to the doctor or their attorney and even confined, they must wear an ankle monitor, so the authorities can track them.

After almost a week of watching Brian walk around on eggshells, Margaret reached the breaking point. She was in the kitchen working and could see him sprawled on the couch in the den watching TV. Earlier in the day, she had received details by e-mail on the conference in Persimmon that would occur in less than a week.

This will be Brian's first time speaking to a group. Barbara was able to get the program revamped to allow us to do a mother-son presentation. She said the organizers were thrilled at the possibility, although for some reason I'm not sharing their enthusiasm.

Using the newly-received information as an excuse, she approached Brian in the den and asked him to join her in the office. "We need to talk about what we're going to do in Persimmon next week."

Brian didn't protest, but clicked the remote to power down the TV. In the office he plopped down into one of the two club chairs across from her desk and twisted so that his legs were draped over one arm.

Margaret ignored his defeatist attitude and began to go over the plans for the conference. "We'll be there for a total of three days, Brian. You and I will have presentations at some point every day. We need to study the different groups and tailor our talk to each audience."

"Whatever."

Again, she chose not to respond, and continued reading to him from the e-mail on her computer. "How does that sound, Brian? Don't you think we can make this work?"

"I guess." The two words were uttered without emotion or any degree of investment.

What do I do? Ignore him or confront him?

She decided to give it one more try. "This is going to be a great chance for you to get your feet wet speaking to these groups. In fact, I'll bet that many of these people we'll speak to at this conference will end up booking you to come to their community to share your story."

"Whatever."

OK. This can't go on.

"Look, Brian. It's obvious you're in a blue funk." *He's scowling.* "I've tried to respect your privacy and allow you to work through it on your own, but obviously that approach isn't working."

The boy didn't respond, but continued to stare at something Margaret couldn't see.

"Brian. Son. I'm not angry at you, but I am concerned."

Still nothing.

Do I beg? Or do I plead? I'm afraid if I try to pull rank he really will withdraw and I'll never get him to open up. But we can't make those presentations if he's in this kind of mood. Oh, Lord. Please help me to know how to reach him.

Margaret did nothing, electing instead to sit very still, saying nothing. *I'm going to let the silence speak for me.* It seemed forever, although a cautious look at the clock on her desk showed it was only about two minutes before the troubled boy spoke again.

"When are you going to get mad at me?"

"When am I going to get mad at you?" she echoed. "Whatever do you mean? Why would I be angry?"

"Because you should. Everyone should."

"Brian, I don't want to appear dense, but I truly don't know what you're talking about."

He struggled to twist in the overstuffed chair and finally was able to stand. His stance was stoop-shouldered, at the same time that his face mirrored conflict. Margaret watched the image of the emotions that flashed across his young and troubled eyes. Then, when she least expected it, her son brought his hand down on the edge of her desk with a vengeance that sounded like gunfire.

KA-POW!

Margaret jumped, noting that even Brian himself reacted.

"What was that for?" she demanded, actually feeling the stirrings of anger within her for the first time.

"That's how I feel," he challenged her. "I've messed up my whole life and everybody keeps telling me they understand."

What is he telling me? The light bulb was beginning to glow ever so dimly. "You want to explain that, Mister?"

"What I did was unforgivable, but nobody will give me a break. They keep forgiving me and telling me they understand. Even that judge said he realized how that lawyer's attack made me feel."

"That's bad?" *Is this what I'm hearing him say?*

"Mom," he pleaded, "I was stupid to get messed up in that liquor store hold-up, but attacking that woman in court like I did was so far beyond stupid, it doesn't deserve to be forgiven."

The fact that Margaret was beginning to grasp what was bothering her son didn't mean she had an answer that would satisfy either of them. *Our family therapy doesn't begin until after the Persimmon Conference. Brian needs help now.*

She rose from her chair behind the desk and came around to take a seat on the edge of the other club chair. While his body language clearly indicated he was aware of her closeness, Brian's head remained hanging; it was evident he wasn't going to look her in the face.

"I agree, Brian... what you did was very serious and very stupid. But like I told you weeks ago there aren't any of us adults... me, P.C. or even Joe, who didn't do some things that were crazy or even dangerous when we were teenagers. It's what teenagers do. But we all overcame those moments when our brains were AWOL. We went on to make something out of ourselves. You can too."

"But you didn't go to jail. You didn't have your whole life story splashed across the front page of the newspaper."

"Granted, we didn't. You got a raw deal. The fact that your Dad..."

"But I didn't get a raw deal. I didn't even get what I deserved!" he screamed, as he jumped to his feet.

He doesn't think he got what he deserved? What is this, a form of mental self-mutilation?

Margaret reached for his hand, which he jerked away.

"How can you stand to touch me? I've humiliated all of us."

"Brian, you've got to listen to me and you've got to try and understand. Please? Sit down and let me try and explain."

He said nothing and, with obviously poor graces, reluctantly settled himself on the very edge of the other chair. *He looks like he's ready to fly away at the slightest provocation.*

"We can agree that you shouldn't have been a part of that hold-up and you certainly shouldn't have slugged the attorney. But neither of those faults is serious enough to bury your head and refuse to look the world in the face. In fact, you should..."

"But I can't look the world in the face," he interrupted. "I feel like the entire world is looking at me and talking about what a total failure I am."

"Total failure? Oh, son, believe me it's nothing like that. Two bad lapses in judgment don't equal the punishment you're inflicting on yourself."

He said nothing.

"Do you think the judge would have designed a sentence like you've gotten if he felt like you deserved to be punished for the rest of your life?"

Brian didn't respond.

"Look, son, I'm going to tell you something that even Grammy and Grandee don't know. When I was a couple of years younger than you, I broke into a school. Not out of any malicious intent; just simple curiosity. I had friends that went there and I thought it was a better school than the one I attended. So one evening, late, when I was riding my bike in the area, I saw a window that had been left partially open, I forced it up and crawled over the window sill."

Brian's head came up, but it was still far from meeting his mother's gaze.

"I bothered nothing; I just walked through the building, satisfying my need to know. Then I crawled back out, pulled the window down and left, looking over my shoulder all the way home. I suddenly realized what I'd done and the guilt was terrible."

"Nobody knew," Brian mumbled.

"I knew. On my way home I realized there would have been serious problems if I'd been caught. So, see, no one is perfect. I had to forgive myself and ask God to forgive me as well."

"But your imperfections didn't get broadcast for everyone to know. Like you said, even your parents still don't know."

"OK, Brian. Level with me here. What gives?"

Nothing.

"If I'm hearing you right, you're angry because people see potential in you, and understand that your actions were as much because you're an abuse victim as well as because you're young."

Still nothing.

"I don't understand, Brian. Did you like it that much in jail?" *I know I didn't the few hours I was there.* "You wanted to be punished more severely? WHY?"

Brian was the epitome, Margaret realized later, of a kettle of water on a hot eye: she could see the head of steam rising.

"Why..." he muttered finally, through clinched lips, "because if you truly loved me, for me, and not as one of Don Haywood's victims, you'd have thrown me in jail and never looked at me again."

His face, whose coloring began as a flushed red was fast becoming angry purple. "I am ME..." he screamed, "Brian Haywood. Not just the abused son of Don Haywood... not just one of three children 'affected' by domestic violence like the newspaper said." He halted to catch his breath. "I can never hold up my head in this town again. Everyone believes I got a special sentence for who I am."

I don't know what to say.

"He's dead but I can't get away from Don Haywood. If everyone truly loved me, they'd want to see me get the same punishment as anyone else. But that's not the way it works when you're a social justice experiment!"

"Brian, you're never going to get past this if you can't forgive yourself and your Dad,"

"Forgive Dad!" he screamed, the veins in his neck standing at attention. "You mean tell him it's OK that he messed me up."

"Please..." she begged. "You don't understand..."

"NO!" He screamed again. "YOU don't understand. I'll never forgive Dad and I won't forgive myself, either."

He left the room on a dead run, and Margaret was left sitting, in shock, uncertain of which way to go or what to do next.

Lord, that family counseling can't happen soon enough.

CHAPTER NINETEEN

*T*he ten days between the confrontation with Brian and the start of the Persimmon conference were tense ones in the Haywood household. Not because of any angry words or displays of temper, but because Brian was the most obliging young man Margaret had ever seen. Whatever she asked, he did without question or hesitation. When she initiated conversations, he picked up his end of the load and carried it to completion.

"There are days that I truly question if I dreamed the explosion in my office," she confided in P.C. a couple of days before she and Brian were scheduled to leave.

"But you know you didn't dream it."

"All I know for sure is that Brian is a very troubled young man and I fear he's truly building toward a blow that he doesn't have a clue how to handle. I just pray it doesn't happen at the conference."

"Joe said yesterday the sooner you get him into counseling, the better it will be."

"Yeah, if I can manage to hold him together that long." Her fingers plowed her blond locks as if a solution could be found there. "I didn't want him to do jail time, and I still don't... but I'm beginning to question the wisdom of this unique sentence."

"You hope it doesn't backfire."

"You've got that right, P.C. If it does, I don't even want to think about the fallout or the consequences." She fingered her hair again. "The one thing I do know is that it won't be pretty."

~

The drive through the autumn-hued mountains of Northeast Georgia should have been solace for Margaret's tired soul. *Any other time it would be.* Her heart was heavy, out of concern and fear, for the young man who sat to her right. *Will having to speak at this conference cause him to further unravel, or will it prove to be the beginning of the healing everyone else thinks will happen?*

Following their arrival at the lodge where the conference was headquartered, they were shown to the adjoining rooms Margaret had booked. She realized they had gotten a view worth much more than the per night rate she'd been quoted.

If only I had time and peace of mind to enjoy this beautiful piece of art.

They had driven up the afternoon before the conference began. Margaret hoped having a chance to arrive before the activities started would give both of them an opportunity to relax and settle in.

"Mom. Mom!" Brian's voice was calling from his room. "Come here. You've got to see this."

Is something wrong? He actually sounds more like his old self. "Coming." She put down the clothing she was stowing in the dresser drawer and hurried through the connecting door. "What's wrong?"

Brian was standing in the doorway to the balcony outside his room, looking at the massive view Margaret had already learned was Black Rock Mountain. He turned as his mother entered the room.

"Look, Mom. Get a load of this."

"Yes, it is beautiful." *Brian never looks at things like views. But at* least he's not looking at everything through pessimistic lens.

"I've never seen anything that looks like this. There's color everywhere."

"These mountains are hot destinations for tourists who share your opinion. I just never knew you to be so crazy for fall color. We're having a late autumn or much of this would already be gone."

"I can't explain it, but when I walked by the door, it was like the mountains just reached out and grabbed me."

"I've always felt the same way," she shared. "There's just something about the mountains in any season of the year that attract me. It's like I hear music."

Brian looked at her, the expression on his face one of total realization. "That's it!" he crowed. "Music. That's what I heard, only I didn't know how to describe it."

Margaret hugged her son to her and realized it was the first time in days that his stance wasn't rigid and unforgiving. "Sounds like you inherited my love for these hills," she observed. "All in all, not a bad thing to have."

Thank You, Lord. You're working on my son's heart. That's also music to this mother's soul.

"Say, Mom." Brian was pointing toward the far edge of the view. "What's that shiny thing right over there?"

"Where?"

"See? Look to the left of that big patch of red there on the mountainside. What is that? It almost looks out of place."

She saw something, but between shadows on the mountain and the brilliance of the afternoon sunlight, she couldn't make out the shiny object. "Probably something the National Forest Service put there. Who knows?"

Margaret returned to her room, where she turned her attention to the handout materials and other items she'd brought. *Got to get organized before I go to bed. Once this thing cranks up, there won't be time to get my act together.*

As the dinner hour approached, Margaret toyed with what she and Brian should do for their evening meal. Knowing they would be tied to the lodge for all their meals during the conference, she decided to make the evening special. She'd heard about an award-winning bed and breakfast nearby that also served dinner to the public by reservation on certain nights of the week.

I'll make sure we can get seats before I say anything to Brian. A quick call revealed that a table for two was possible at the eight o'clock seating. *This gives us two good hours before we need to leave. I'd best let Brian know the game plan.*

She knocked on her son's door. When he called for her to enter, Margaret found him sitting in a chair he'd dragged to the sliding glass doors. *It's like he's worshipping the view. I've never seen him like this.*

"You're really taken with the fall kaleidoscope as travel writers always describe this kind of scene."

"It's neat, Mom. The more you look, the more you see. Gosh. I wish we could move here."

"Move here! I hate to tell you, son, but we'd need more reason than a fall color show to pack up and move." She ruffled his hair and realized that he didn't pull away. "Besides, the color is only here for a few weeks each fall. What would we do for the rest of the year?"

He grinned, a little self-consciously, she thought. "I hadn't thought about that," he confessed. "I guess you're right."

"Besides," she reminded him, "sometimes we need to keep something as special and only use it on certain occasions. If we lived here year-round, we might actually come to appreciate the beauty less. As it is, those times when we visit, it'll mean more to us."

"So we can come back?"

I've got to make more of an effort to give my children a variety of life experiences. "Sure, we'll plan on making a get-away every once in a while. I need it, too."

She shared the dinner plans she had made, and he was agreeable. Brian was ready at the appointed time, and she followed the directions the B&B had given her, to a beautiful old rambling barn-like structure that, Brian was delighted to discover, also looked out on a different Black Rock view.

The meal was everything Margaret had been led to believe and then some. She and Brian enjoyed their food and, she realized, had the first real conversation the two had shared in many weeks.

Perhaps I need to make it a priority to spend one-on-one time with each of the children.

Following dessert, and a walk around the lighted grounds of the historic old inn, Margaret headed back to their own rooms a few miles away. "Tomorrow is going to be a busy day," she reminded her son. "Our first presentation is at ten-fifteen."

"I'm ready...but I wasn't sure until earlier this afternoon."

Thank You, Lord! Only what happened this afternoon? Margaret was at a loss to answer that question, and too grateful to question it.

When they were back at the lodge, Margaret went to check out the meeting room for the following morning while Brian went upstairs. She needed an idea of how many people the room would accommodate, as well as where she would arrange her visual displays. Once satisfied, she found the elevator and headed for the fourth floor.

Back in her room, she debated disturbing her son. *There's no sound, not even TV noise coming from his room.* In the end, she rapped quietly on the door. *If he doesn't answer, I won't bother him.*

"Come on in, Mom. I've been waiting for you." Inside, he sat in total darkness of the open doorway to the balcony. Without moving, he said through the blackness, "You've got to see this."

"Brian," she scolded, not meaning to sound so judgmental. "The leaves are beautiful, but you surely can't see them in the dark."

"It's not the leaves, Mom. It's something more beautiful."

More beautiful? She stepped to his side and stopped, astounded by what greeted her eyes. Where earlier, in the brightness of the afternoon, she had enjoyed the color show all she saw now was a huge, brightly-lighted cross burning through the night blackness."

"That's what we saw this afternoon and didn't know what it was," Brian informed her. "When I got back, I started to close the draperies and discovered... this." He pointed to the brilliant, almost blinding light invading even the tiniest crevice of Margaret's eyes.

"Ohhhh..." was all she could say.

"I called the desk to ask about it. Seems years ago there was a cross on the mountain, but politics caused it to be taken down because it was on public property."

"So how did it get back?"

"This isn't the same cross. A man who lived here died and left money and instructions that a new cross was to be erected on private property he had on the mountain. It's only been up a few months."

"It is beautiful, son. I can see why you were so dazzled."

"You know what else, Mom?"

"I don't, but I imagine you're about to tell me."

"When I looked at that cross tonight, I realized nothing I have done is so dark that I can't be forgiven. By God... and by myself. After I first forgive Dad."

Margaret drew a quick breath while trying not to show her surprise. *Or my joy,* she realized staring into his vulnerable face.

"Only now I understand that forgiving him doesn't mean what he did was right." He slapped his hand down on the chair arm. "It wasn't right. But I have to forgive him for me, not for him."

He was so intense Margaret was afraid to speak. *He's healing and I don't want to break the mood.*

"All I have to do is lift my eyes and look at that cross, even when things look the blackest. I know anything can be made whole again."

"Oh, Brian..."

"It's okay, Mom. I've been pretty messed up in my mind, but I'm not so confused any more. It's simple." He lifted his face and, in the reflected glow, tears were lurking around his eyes. "All I have to do is lift my head and look everyone in the face. I don't need to be ashamed."

Margaret said nothing as she hugged him, feeling his body melt into hers. *No Brian, you don't ever have to be ashamed.*

And neither do I.

About the Author

John Shivers began his writing career at age 14, stringing for his hometown newspaper. During those same formative teen years, he wrestled with a call to ministry, finally choosing to pursue a writing career instead. A freelance writer, editor and storyteller, John's byline has appeared in over 40 Christian and secular publications, winning him sixteen professional awards.

Hear My Cry, his first book, was published in 2005, and paths converged; his goal of becoming a published novelist was realized and with it, came the realization that writing could be a ministry. John explains that once his definition of ministry would have been defined and confined by structural and denominational walls. His writing allows him to minister to readers of all faiths and stations.

Broken Spirit and *Merry Heart* are the first two volumes in the Renew A Right Spirit trilogy and he is currently working on the third volume.

John, his wife, Elizabeth, and their Cocker Spaniel, "Miss Maddie," live on the family farm in Calhoun, Georgia where the wooded hills supply him with nourishment for his soul and his creativity.

www.johnshivers.com